TERROR IN TEHRAN

A THRILLER

TERROR
IN TEHRAN

A THRILLER

DON WILLIAMS

DBWilliams Publishing | Coral Gables, FL

Published by
DBWilliams Publishing | Coral Gables, FL

Publisher's Cataloging-in-Publication Data
Williams, Don.

Terror in Tehran : a thriller / Don Williams. – Coral Gables, FL : DBWilliams Pub., 2022.

p. ; cm.

ISBN13: 978-0-9601111-0-7

1. Tehran (Iran)--Fiction. I. Title.

PS3623.I556498 T47 2022
813.6--dc23

Project coordination by Jenkins Group, Inc. | www.jenkinsgroupinc.com

Interior design by Brooke Camfield

Printed in the United States of America
26   25   24   23   22   •   5   4   3   2   1

"Death solves all problems—
no man, no problem."
                                    —Anatoly Rybakov

CHAPTER 1

"Good afternoon. This is Captain Arvin Turani on the flight deck. We've leveled off at twelve thousand meters. Our flying time to Tehran is two hours, fifty-five minutes. Sit back, enjoy the flight, and thank you for flying Iran Air."

The tall, broad-shouldered passenger with dark, collar-length hair and Hollywood-issue looks didn't hear the captain. His AirPods were filled with Delbert McClinton singing "Shaky Ground."

He sat quietly in the first class cabin with his eyes closed and his legs outstretched as if he were asleep. But he wasn't. His scripted answers to the questions in passport control in Tehran were playing over and over in his head.

He was Thomas Davis, a thirty-one-year-old Canadian citizen with an apartment address in Mississauga, a suburb of Toronto. He was a salesman for Microscan Corporation traveling to Tehran to sell MRI body scanners. He had a reservation at the Shahr Hotel and a return ticket to Toronto in one week.

His bona fides would check out. They always did. His passport was replete with visa stamps, the most recent in London and Istanbul three days ago. Another masterful job by the cobblers back home.

Suddenly a violent jolt shook the Airbus 330. The fuselage creaked and groaned like a giant behemoth suffering a spasm.

Davis's eyes popped open.

"We're experiencing turbulence," Captain Turani announced. "All passengers and crew must remain seated."

1

The woman next to Davis reached across the center console and pinched his leg. On her ring finger she wore a marquise-cut diamond as big as any Davis had ever seen.

She was dressed in black—in a figure-flattering pantsuit, a silk blouse with a mandarin collar, and eloquent wedge sandals. A wisp of shiny black hair peeked from beneath a scarf covering her head.

The woman in black, he thought.

During boarding she'd had a haughty aloofness about her—snooty if anything. At first he'd thought she might be Princess Fathima of Saudi Arabia, the most beautiful woman in the Arab world. But the princess's husband was worth twenty-five billion. She would never fly commercially, and never to Iran. Not a chance.

Now the woman looked worried. Her jaw muscles were tight, and she was breathing through alternate nostrils. Her dark, almond-shaped eyes were focused like lasers on the galley.

When Davis followed her gaze, a column of bile rose in his throat.

Oh shit, he thought.

A male flight attendant lay motionless in the galley aisle. A man held a knife at his throat.

Just forward of the downed attendant, a second man held a camera in the face of a female attendant. The flash touched her nose, but instead of a camera smile she had a look of terror.

Davis's mind raced at warp speed. *The security hall.* He'd seen the two hijackers there.

They'd been in line in front of him. The knife wielder had cleared security first and stood waiting at the exit. The man holding the camera had been directly in front of Davis. Small and wiry with intense eyes and a boyish face, he was the spitting image of Mohamed Atta, one of the 9/11 terrorists. His only carry-on had been an odd-shaped aluminum case belted with an orange nylon strap.

As the photographer had approached the baggage scanner, a security agent stepped in front of him. The line had stopped. After a negative swab for explosives, the agent had opened the case. "Camera?" he'd asked. The photographer had nodded.

Davis had edged forward to look over the photographer's shoulder. Sight of the vintage box-shaped camera with its oversized flash lamp had jettisioned him back to his childhood, to one of his favorite TV programs, the *Adventures of Superman*, a 1950's classic. George Reeves. Seven o'clock black-and-white reruns, Monday through Friday, on a station in Rapid City. This was a camera exactly like Jimmy Olsen's.

When the agent had gestured to the photographer to close the case and move on, Davis had stepped back.

No camera inspection. Strategic mistake, he now thought.

A third attendant stood aghast in the galley, shaking like a leaf, her hand over her mouth.

Davis removed his AirPods.

"Call the pilot! Change course! To Galkayo," the photographer shrieked.

Davis understood every word.

He figured the camera had been fitted with a high-voltage capacitor wired to deliver a paralyzing shock through the flash. A jerry-rigged stun gun. *Zap.* It had taken out the male attendant on the galley floor.

The knife wielder's weapon had a ceramic blade with a high-tech polymer handle. It had escaped detection during security screening.

Clever bastards.

As Davis unclipped his seatbelt, the woman in black turned to him. Her eyes pleaded, "Please do something."

He touched her arm as if to say, "Not to worry. I'll take care of this."

CHAPTER 2

Davis lifted his six-two, 210-pound frame out of his seat, ran his fingers through his hair, and pushed up his sleeves. He clenched his fists, then slowly relaxed his fingers.

The first-class cabin was deathly silent except for the thrum of the jet engines. The stares of the passengers weighed heavily on him.

Time began to slow as he walked forward. It always did in the run-up to something like this. In his mind's eye he saw what was about to happen. It would be over quickly. Just a few seconds, if that. But then the Iranian authorities would focus on the Canadian salesman named Thomas Davis, immeasurably complicating his mission in Tehran. Lots of probing questions and careful inspection of his documents—just what he didn't want.

The photographer was a raging madman, his eyes wide, the veins on his forehead bulging like worms.

The attendant stood sideways in the aisle just aft of the cockpit door with her back pressed against the wall. Panicked, she was biting her lower lip with tears streaming down her cheeks.

The third attendant's face was ashen, her knees giving way.

The immediate threat was the knife wielder. But if Davis didn't deal with the photographer quickly, a high-voltage shock to the attendant's face would blind her.

The knife wielder faced forward, astride the downed attendant.

Davis turned sideways as he neared the knife wielder. "Excuse me," he said.

When the knife wielder looked up, Davis kicked him in the head with a side sweep. *Smack.* Boot on bone. Up close and under full power. Devastating. The kick snapped the knife wielder's neck, and he crashed into the aisle wall.

One down, one to go.

Momentum from the kick spun Davis. As he stumbled forward, he hit the photographer with a roundhouse right. His fist glanced off the man's head and knocked the camera away.

Quickly righting himself, Davis put all his weight behind a straight left. His fist was a blur, like it had been shot out of a cannon. The man never saw it coming. *Thump.* Blood and spittle spattered on the attendant and across the galley walls.

Before Davis fully extended his arm, the man was six inches off the galley floor, catapulting backward. He crashed into the cockpit door then crumpled to the floor.

When the camera smashed into the wall, the flash discharged. An acrid smell of burning plastic filled the galley.

The attendant let out a deep sigh, swallowed hard, and slumped to a sitting position with her hands covering her face.

The other attendant lay motionless on the floor in a tangle of arms and legs.

Davis's eyes shot through the first-class cabin to the coach section. He saw no movement and hoped that meant the hijackers were acting alone.

With a beaming smile, the woman in black sat forward and began to clap. The other passengers joined her, curious about the hunk who had just saved them.

The attendant who had fainted regained consciousness. She pushed up on her elbows and mumbled, "Is everything all right?"

"It is now," Davis replied.

She was badly shaken, barely able to stand. Davis decided to put her in his seat until she recovered. The woman in black could babysit her.

"You're going to sit in my seat," he said.

"Whatever you say."

He gathered her in his arms and carried her to the seat. As he buckled her in, the woman in black squeezed his hand. "Thank you," she whispered breathlessly.

"You're welcome. Keep an eye on her." Davis winked.

"I will," she said.

With relaxed jaw muscles and a smile, she was even more beautiful.

The male attendant had wiggled out from under the knife wielder and slumped into a jump seat.

"Are you okay?" Davis asked as he helped him buckle his seatbelt.

"I think so. My head hurts," he said pointing to the back of his head.

"Let me take a look."

There was a silver dollar-sized burn on the back of his head with singed hair and blanched scalp.

"You have a burn where the camera flash touched you."

"I don't remember anything."

"You should be okay."

The attendant who had come close to being blinded recovered quickly. She wiped her face and apron with a moist towel, blew her nose, and adjusted her scarf as if nothing had happened. Davis was impressed. Her name tag read Laila; she was the flight purser.

"You all right?" he asked.

"Yes. I am now, thanks to you. Been flying over twenty years. Never dreamed anything like this would ever happen."

"Sorry I sprayed you," Davis said, as he bent down to search the two unconscious hijackers.

"No problem. Good thing I had on this apron. Saved my uniform. The two of them rushed the galley. The guy with the camera zapped Mo in the back of the head. The other one jumped on him with a knife. I was next."

"The camera was converted to a stun gun to deliver a high-voltage shock. It knocked him out. He has a burn where the flash touched his head. Make sure he sees a doctor. When I saw the flash in your face, I was afraid you'd wind up blind."

"The guy with the camera was out of his mind," she said. "What were they after?"

"Money most likely. The plane alone is worth tens of millions." Davis finished searching them. "Nothing on them but boarding passes and cell phones. I need to secure them to seats."

"Use our jump seats," she said, handing him headset wires. "I'll start cleaning up this mess."

Davis bound the two men to the seats and secured seatbelts across their chests to hold them upright.

The photographer showed signs of awakening. His nose was broken and he had missing front teeth, but the bleeding had almost stopped. Davis hoped he would survive for questioning.

The knife wielder was unconscious with agonal breathing. Suddenly he lurched forward and vomited, a forceful green projectile that shot across the galley and sprayed the fuselage door. After a series of violent spasms, he gagged and stopped breathing.

Davis checked for a pulse.

"Dead."

Without looking Laila nodded, as if she already knew, and handed Davis a blanket to cover the body. She then busied herself scrubbing the walls, spreading blankets on the floor, and spraying air freshener, while Davis secured the camera in a locker.

After finishing, she checked on the two flight attendants and said, "They're both okay. I gave Mo some ice for his head. And the galley looks better. That green stuff really stinks. Would you like something to drink?"

Davis leaned against the wall, rubbing the knuckles on his left hand, wondering where he would sit. "A double bourbon on the rocks would be great. Just one ice cube," he said.

"Anything for you. We don't have the good American stuff, but I'll see what I can find. Here, take this for your hand," she said, handing him a bag of ice.

"Thanks. I guess I'll have to sit in one of the hijackers' seats in coach."

"I suppose. There's only one seat left up here. You gave away yours." A winsome smile crossed her face as she mixed Davis's drink. "Are you an American air marshall or a law enforcement officer?"

"No. A salesman from Canada."

"A salesman? That's hard to believe. You knew exactly what to do, like you've done it before. It all happened so fast. No one without special training could do what you just did."

Smart lady.

"Didn't feel like going to Somalia. I'll head back to coach now."

"Hang out here with me for a while. I feel better when you're around. You need to keep an eye on this one anyway," she said, gesturing to the photographer. "I have to talk with the captain. I should have done it right away, but I wanted to clean up the galley first. He'll want to speak with you, I'm sure. Here's your drink. I hope it's okay."

CHAPTER 3

It was Irish whiskey. Tullamore Dew. Two nips. One ice cube. Not bad.

But it didn't help.

Something was gnawing at Davis, something that had happened in the security hall in the Istanbul airport. It was locked in a subconscious compartment, just out of reach. He closed his eyes and replayed the security line in his head again.

The photographer was directly in front of him.

The security agent stepped in, swabbed the case, then opened it.

When the photographer was cleared, the agent closed the case. It was then.

Davis dug deeper. It had happened as Davis stepped back, just before he'd begun fussing with his laptop. He'd been worried about it clearing security.

Then it played—a tiny snippet.

The photographer turned, looked back—to someone behind Davis—and nodded.

It was a message. *"I've been cleared."*

That someone wasn't the knife wielder. He was already at the exit. That meant the hijackers had an accomplice on the plane.

While Davis mulled over his next move, Laila reported the attempted hijacking to the captain.

After a lengthy conversation, she handed Davis the cabin phone and said, "Captain Turani wants to speak with you."

Reluctantly, Davis took it. "Thomas Davis, here." He spoke in Farsi.

"This is Captain Turani on the flight deck. Laila just told me what happened. It's unbelievable. We've never had a hijacking on this airline. I heard something crash against the cockpit door. I thought it was one of the serving carts. But I understand one of the hijackers bounced off the door, when you hit him. I want to thank you for what you did, Mr. Davis."

"No thanks necessary. One of the hijackers is dead. The other is restrained and should survive. The cabin is secure."

For the moment, Davis thought.

"Laila told me. She said you dealt with them in a matter of seconds. One kick. One punch. Amazing."

Two punches.

"As long as things are under control, I'll continue on to Tehran. Easier for us to deal with the authorities there. We can talk more when we land."

That was precisely what Davis feared. The authorities would question him interminably about his background and why he was traveling to Tehran. They would be suspicious that he was a foreign agent and take a hard look at his bona fides. After all, how could a salesman dispatch two hijackers in a matter of seconds without special training?

"We're secure back here, Captain. But you and your co-pilot should stay in the cockpit, and have the attendants hold on cabin service."

"I agree. I'll contact the tower in Tehran, apprise them of our situation. You speak good Farsi, Mr. Davis."

"Thank you, Captain."

"Are you from the U.S.?"

"No, sir. Canada."

"That's good. We're not happy with the U.S. sanctions."

"Canada isn't happy with the U.S. either," Davis said.

"Did you grow up in the States? A few words have an American accent."

Davis fought off the urge to ask which ones. He had worked hard to rid himself of his accent.

"It's not easy sometimes to tell a Canadian from an upper Midwesterner," Davis said.

"You mean someone from Minnesota and Wisconsin?" the captain asked.

"Yes, sir. How did you know?"

"It's a long story. I spent time over there. What brings you to Tehran?"

"I sell medical equipment."

"I'm glad you were on board, Mr. Davis." The captain chuckled and echoed Davis's words. "I didn't feel like flying to Somalia today. If there's anything I can do, contact the flight deck."

"I will, Captain."

"And put Laila on. I'll tell her to hold cabin service."

Davis hoped Captain Turani had bought his story, but he was sure Laila hadn't.

CHAPTER 4

A knot began tightening around Davis's stomach. He had to identify the hijackers' accomplice. But how?

Without conveying why, he suggested to Laila that they look for carry-on bags that belonged to the hijackers. Since the flight was full, the empty seats in the coach section would belong to them.

They found the camera case and orange strap on a starboard aisle seat in row forty-two.

Davis remembered that the photographer had carried only the case. He opened it and found only makeshift foam inserts. The passenger in the next seat was a veiled woman holding hands with the man next to her.

The second empty seat was also a starboard aisle seat in row forty-four. They opened the overhead compartments four rows fore and aft of it. All bags had name tags and were identified by passengers.

When Davis pointed to a tattered valise with a broken handle, a man in the window seat in row forty growled, "Mine." He wore a black-and-white checked keffiyeh and a full-length thobe and nervously fingered Muslim prayer beads. A scruffy beard and dark glasses made it impossible to estimate his age, but wrinkled skin with a sprinkle of sunspots on his hands meant he was older than the hijackers.

Was he the senior member of the hijack team?

When they returned to the galley, Davis said, "I'm worried the hijackers have an accomplice on board."

"Why?" Laila asked.

"The photographer was in front of me in the security line. His camera case was opened. After he was cleared, he nodded to someone behind me."

"The man with the knife?"

"No. He was ahead of the photographer. Someone else. The man in the window seat in row forty, the one with the beard and prayer beads. He bothers me. What's his name?"

"He doesn't look Persian to me. Let me check." She scanned the passenger log and said, "Name's Malik Al-Ajlani."

Davis thought for a second. "How about the man in the bulkhead seat two rows in front of me?"

"Dietz Meyer," she said looking at him curiously.

Davis wondered why he'd asked. He knew who the man was. Meyer was the reason he was on the plane.

"Why do you ask?"

"Just curious. And the woman next to me?"

"The looker?"

"Yes."

A sheepish grin crossed Laila's face. "Well, she's listed here as Ziba Vijany. There's an asterisk next to her name. Anything else Mr.—?" She glanced at the passenger log again and said, "Mr. Davis. After everything that's happened, I don't even know your name. Sorry."

Davis smiled. "That's okay. Just call me Thomas. What does the asterisk mean?"

"It means she's important. Very important. She's supposed to get special treatment because she's rich, famous, or a high up Iranian government type."

"Which is it? Davis asked.

"I don't know." Laila winked. "You'll have to ask her, Thomas. She doesn't look government to me."

That she doesn't, Davis thought.

"At first I thought you were traveling with her. You two look like movie stars on their way to a shoot."

Davis laughed. "She is very attractive. Not too friendly though. She alerted me to what was going on."

"Good for her. I'd bet if you sit with her now, she'll be very friendly."

Davis changed the subject. "Can you get the captain for me?"

"A problem?" she asked.

Maybe a big problem.

"Just want to talk to him about Al-Ajlani."

Laila phoned the captian and handed the receiver to Davis.

"Everything okay back there, Mr. Davis?"

"Yes, sir, but a man in coach is acting suspiciously. I want to make sure he's not an accomplice of the hijackers. Name's Malik Al-Ajlani. Can you check his passport? And the hijackers, too."

"Laila gave me their names. I'll check."

The answer came back quickly. Laila handed Davis the phone.

"Mr. Davis, all three have Saudi passports. Just because Al-Ajlani has the same passport as the hijackers doesn't mean he's their accomplice. What are you going to do?"

"Talk to him. If he's working with them, I'll deal with him."

"How'll you find out?"

"Don't worry. I will."

"You sound very confident, Mr. Davis. Like someone with lots of experience doing this stuff. Let me know what happens."

"Will do, Captain. Thanks."

When Davis ended the call, Laila said, "Saudis hardly ever fly Iran Air. When they do it's always up front."

The knot tightened a little more around Davis's stomach. The old Arab in row forty *was* an accomplice of the hijackers. He just had to prove it.

"Who's the woman sitting next to Al-Ajlani?"

"I knew you'd ask. Name's Hami Rahbar."

"Instruct the attendants to stay in the aft galley. Block the aisles with service carts. Page passenger Rahbar to the fore galley. I'll visit with Mr. Al-Ajlani then."

While Laila paged the woman, Davis put a pair of headset wires in his pocket.

Hami Rahbar looked befuddled when she heard her name, then stood up and walked forward. Davis squeezed by her in the aisle and took her seat.

Al-Ajlani continued to finger the prayer beads, rocking back and forth and mumbling under his breath. He stank of cigarettes and body odor.

Davis squeezed the old Arab's hand.

"Mr. Al-Ajlani, who are you traveling with?"

Al-Ajlani remained trance-like, staring forward, continuing to rock. When Davis squeezed harder, the old Arab grimaced.

"Answer my question, or I'll break your fingers."

Al-Aljani's eyes suddenly widened. He shouted, "Allahu akbar!" and began to punch Davis.

Davis blocked the punches with one arm and wrapped the other around the old Arab's neck. He locked his forearm in place compressing both carotids. Seconds later Al-Ajlani slumped in his seat.

Before he awakened, Davis had searched him, tied his seatbelt in a knot, and secured his arms to the seat rests with the wires.

Laila appeared and reassured the wide-eyed passengers silently watching that the situation was under control. Then she instructed a male attendant in coach to sit with the disruptive passenger.

Davis went forward to the first-class galley with Al-Ajlani's valise and personal effects.

CHAPTER 5

Al-Ajlani's valise held nothing out of the ordinary for a Muslim man who was a heavy smoker and traveling light. His passport was in a side pocket along with the hijackers'. Al-Ajlani was sixty-two years old and well traveled.

He had arrived in Istanbul two days before the Tehran flight. Nine days in Somalia before that. And two trips to Mogadishu and three to Paris in the last six months. Davis wondered if the mastermind behind the hijacking was headquartered in France.

In the last three years Al-Ajlani had visited every Islamist hotbed imaginable: Damascus, Bagdad, Cairo, Casablanca, San'a, and Tripoli, as well as Paris and Marseille. He'd stayed only a few days in each place and had never been to the United States. At least his passport had no entry stamp.

Davis emptied Al-Ajlani's wallet and found the usual litter: a small amount of cash, a Saudi driver's license issued to Malik Al-Ajlani at an apartment address in Riyadh, two credit cards, one in the old Arab's name and another in a different name, and a Saudi NHS card.

A tattered photograph and a folded square of paper in a hidden pocket caught Davis's attention. In the photo a young woman sat alone on a stone bench with a flat-roofed, mud-brick building in the background. She had a long, thin face, a prominent dorsal nasal hump, and appeared to be forcing a smile for the camera. Not at all happy. Davis wondered who she was. Al-Ajlani's daughter? The folded square of paper had a handscrawled note in Arabic. Davis was a fluent speaker, but not a good reader.

Laila translated.

Remember—
Move separately in airport
Do not sit together
Execute hijacking according to plan
Reroute to Galkayo, refuel in Sana'a
Default plan over Tehran if hijack fails
Allah be with you

Davis chuckled. Al-Ajlani had forgotten to pass along the instructions to his two young accomplices. They had passed through airport security together.

Then his smile faded. Al-Ajlani *was* the mission leader. Whoever was masterminding the plot had given the old Arab instructions—a reminder just in case and, of course, a blessing.

CHAPTER 6

avis switched to coffee. No sweetener. No cream. Strong, bitter, and stoked with caffeine, it wasn't the best, but it would do.

While he sipped from a paper cup, the fifth line in the instructions replayed in his head.

Default plan over Tehran if hijack fails.

What was the default plan? Why execute it over Tehran?

Was the aircraft still in jeopardy of being hijacked or was something else planned? Something even more sinister?

With caffeine catalyzing the adrenalin surging through him, Davis's mind was in overdrive. He took a few breaths, reminding himself that the lives of the passengers and crew were in his hands.

The mastermind had crafted a default plan if the hijacking failed. It was meant to draw attention to the terrorists' jihad and to punish the crew and passengers.

What would be the most dramatic way?

What would hit the news services like a bolt of lightning?

A bad feeling took hold of Davis. In his mind's eye he saw something horrific, as clearly as if on the plane's monitors—Iran Air flight 1645 exploding over the Iranian capital. Three-hundred nine passengers and a crew of nine killed with a swath of unimaginable devastation on the ground. The hijackers martyred for the cause. The terrorist mastermind cheering. The world in shock.

Davis wondered about a bomb with a timer in the cargo hold. A replay of Lockerbie?

But this terrorist bombing was different.

Iran Air flight 1645 was supposed to be hijacked. The bomb was a default plan if the hijacking failed.

If the hijacking was successful and the aircraft rerouted, how would a bomb in the hold be defused?

If it wasn't defused, it would explode over the Red Sea. A flight delay in Istanbul meant a mid-air explosion even sooner.

Defusing the bomb from the cabin would require a Bluetooth-type system. Or maybe a satellite phone linked to the detonator. Both were highly sophisticated technologies, beyond the reach of Malik Al-Ajlani and his Saudi co-conspirators.

But Davis searched the camera case again anyway and tore the lining from the old Arab's valise. No electronic devices. No laptops or personal tablets either.

Davis had Laila call the flight deck again.

"Captain, this is Davis."

"Yes, Mr. Davis. Is everything okay back there?"

"I restrained Al-Ajlani. You checked his passport for me. He's an accomplice of the hijackers."

"How do you know?"

"He had a note in his wallet about the hijacking. Can you find out if one of them checked a bag in Istanbul?"

"Why?" Turani asked.

"Just to be safe."

"If you're worried about a bomb in a checked bag, I'll have to land immediately."

"I'd be surprised if they checked a bag. We should be able to continue to Tehran."

"What if one of them did?"

"We'll talk then," Davis said.

"You're making me nervous, Mr. Davis."

"Please check, Captain."

Fifteen minutes later Davis had his answer—no checked bags.

He shuddered.

If he was right about the default plan and there were no checked bags, a suicide bomber was on board.

CHAPTER 7

Davis walked through the plane studying the passengers like a flight attendant checking seat belts. He didn't know what a suicide bomber looked like minutes before the fatal act. And what if the bomber was a woman . . . a veiled woman?

More than half the women in the coach cabin wore veils. All appeared to be with a male companion, but one caught Davis's eye. She sat between two teenage boys. A well dressed older man sat next to one of the boys. The woman stared mindlessly while the boys played video games on laptops. The man was asleep. No one else in the coach cabin stood out.

The tension in the aircraft was palpable, with just about everyone except the very young on edge. Two babies cried, but the usual undercurrent of chatter was absent.

It was to be expected, Davis thought, *after the captain announced that there was an incident in the first-class galley.* "But everything is under control now and we're flying on to Tehran," Turani had added matter-of-factly.

Davis exchanged glances with the woman in black. She seemed surprisingly composed now, sitting quietly, no longer doing yoga relaxation breathing. But when their eyes met, she quickly looked away. He was used to having women stare—all over the world. Why was she different?

CHAPTER 8

Davis wondered about Al-Ajlani. Was he the bomber?

He was old-looking—well beyond his years—and decrepit. Not the bomber type.

It was someone else. Someone young. Someone programmed to mindlessly detonate a device.

A suicide bomber was like a guided missile, directed to a target at a specific location, where the explosion would inflict maximum harm. The bomber strolled into a crowded café, boarded a packed train, or sauntered into a bustling airport terminal. Then, *boom.*

Today there was a twist. The target was moving—an airplane. The location was fixed and critical—over Tehran. The bomber was already inside the target en route to the location. The bomber was instructed to wait until the target reached the location.

So how would the bomber know when the plane was over Tehran? Simply stare out the window until the suburbs came into view? Low-lying clouds might obscure the ground. What then? What if the bomber was sitting in the center section without a window view?

Something else was the cue. Something the bomber could count on to signal the time. Something in the announcement just before landing.

"We're in our final approach to Imam Khomeini International Airport," Turani would say.

Final approach. That was the cue.

Seconds later there would be a spectacular flash in the sky. Molten shards of metal, sofa-sized wing sections, and a confetti of body parts would rain down on the Iranian capital. The collateral injury on the ground would be horrific. Lockerbie all over again. Maybe worse.

"Terror in Tehran," the news services would caption it.

Davis ran through the passenger log again with Laila, looking for the same last name as one of the Saudis.

A warm surge ran through him when he saw the name of the woman in black. And Dietz Meyer's name was still there. But no one with the same last name as the terrorists.

Suddenly Davis's ears popped. The plane was descending.

He asked Laila to call the flight deck. He took the phone.

"Captain Turani, this is Davis again. There's a suicide bomber on board."

"What?" Turani cried.

"You heard me. There's a passenger with a bomb that'll explode during landing."

"How do you know, Mr. Davis?"

"The note. The one that talks about the hijacking. It has instructions to defer to a default plan over Tehran if the hijacking failed."

"Default plan. What does that mean?"

"A bomb. I'm certain. If the hijackers failed, they wanted to make a statement, to shock the world. What better way than to blow up an Iranian airliner over the capital city."

"Then why hijack us in the first place?"

"I haven't gotten into the hijackers' heads. I imagine to collect a ransom for the pasengers, the crew, and the plane."

"Usually bombs are in the cargo hold," Turani said.

"Remember, no checked bags. But if there was one with a bomb, there'd have to be a timer. They'd need a way to defuse it, if the hijacking was successful. Otherwise it would explode on the way to Somalia."

Silence for a few seconds. Then the captain said, "Oh boy. Maybe the suicide bomber checked a bag with a bomb. You don't know who it is."

"Like I said, they'd need a way to disarm it from the cabin. It would have to be a very sophisticated electronic device. These bad guys don't have anything like that."

"You're probably right," Turani agreed.

"My ears just popped. Are we descending?"

"Yes. We land in less than twenty minutes. There's an army of security agents at the airport. A hero's welcome awaits you, Mr. Davis."

The attention of the Iranian authorities was exactly what Davis didn't want.

"How long can you stay airborne?" Davis asked.

"Let's see. We have enough fuel for forty minutes. We run lean from Istanbul. Homemade jet is cheaper."

"Call the tower. Tell them there's a suicide bomber on board, but we don't know who it is. Then go into a holding pattern for as long as possible."

Turani sighed. "This is terrible. What else can I do?"

Damn it, just do as I tell you.

"There *is* something you can do. The bomber will detonate the explosive when you announce we're in our final approach."

"How do you know?"

"Trust me, Captain. I know. It is the only way. Don't make any announcements before landing."

"Mr. Davis, I'm putting my trust in you. I'm the captain of this aircraft and I'm ultimately responsible."

"I understand that, Captain. If I'm wrong, the only thing you haven't done is announce we're landing."

Turani said nothing for a few seconds. Davis heard him breathing.

"Are you still there, Captain?"

"Okay. I won't make an announcement."

"Good. Even so, if the bomber misses the cue, I'm sure the bomb will go off when the tires hit the runway. That'll be better than in the air," Davis added.

"It sounds like we're doomed no matter what. Let me radio the tower at Khomeini."

A minute later Turani was back.

"The tower assigned us a holding pattern. Hundred-fifty kilometers out."

Ninety miles, Davis thought.

"We can stay in it for fifteen minutes. Then we'll have to make our approach. They're scrambling military jets. A bomb threat is extremely serious, Mr. Davis."

"How much time will that give me?"

"For what?"

"To identify the bomber."

"Thirty minutes max. I can't run the tanks dry."

"If nothing happens during landing, stop the aircraft as far from the terminal as possible. Kill the engines. Then institute an emergency evacuation."

"I'll announce it," Turani said.

"No. I'll have Laila pass it to the cabin attendants. Don't make any more announcements under any circumstances."

"Mr. Davis, you talk like someone with authority and experience. You must have special training. Who are you? An American agent?"

Davis wasn't sure what to say. He paused, then replied, "Captain, I'm just a medical equipment salesman from Canada. I'm doing what I can to save your aircraft."

"If you say so my friend. I checked you out. You're on a Canadian passport. But you're fluent in Farsi with very little accent. And Arabic too. I'm told you look like a movie star. You have martial arts skills. Who are you?"

"We're wasting time, Captain.?"

"What's your plan?" Turani asked. "You don't have much time."

Davis sighed. "I'm working on it."

"I feel helpless up here. Anything you need, contact me. I'm looking forward to shaking your hand Mr. Davis . . . or whoever you are."

"I hope you have that chance, Captain."

Davis started the stopwatch on his chronograph and set the alarm for thirty minutes. He hoped he'd live to hear it beep.

Laila stood by listening.

CHAPTER 9

*T*hirty minutes.

Davis felt bad. He had misled Captain Turani. He had no idea how to identify the bomber. But Laila, an experienced flight attendant, might spot someone behaving suspiciously.

Davis was weary of looking for the *tell*, something that might identify the bomber. And he couldn't see the faces of the veiled women. Everyone looked alike. Everyone except his target Dietz Meyer and the woman in black.

Meyer was slouched in his bulkhead seat staring straight ahead, his arms crossed and his legs outstretched. His messenger bag was at his feet. He'd have to stow it overhead before landing. Luckily Davis had dealt with it during boarding.

The attendant in Davis's seat and the woman in black were chatting in low voices. Although he couldn't hear what they said, both had serious looks, like defense lawyers whose murder-one client faced an imminent guilty verdict.

"Let's walk through the plane. Look for someone acting suspiciously," Davis said.

"You mean the suicide bomber?"

"You listened to my conversation with Captain Turani."

She nodded and tried to smile. "What does a suicide bomber look like?"

"They're usually young, sometimes female, and often dressed in a long coat or carrying a backpack. But on an airplane, in a seat, I have no idea," he replied.

The veiled woman between the teenage boys had caught his attention on his last pass through the cabin. He wasn't sure why. She hadn't been acting suspiciously. Even though he couldn't see her face, he wondered if she might be the woman in the photograph. Conservative Muslim women were forbidden to show their faces in public. He couldn't unveil her without creating a major hullabaloo. And what if she wasn't the woman?

Davis and Laila held hands like newlyweds as they walked through the first-class cabin, Laila's head arcing back and forth, surveying the passengers. *The bomber isn't in first class,* Davis thought.

When they approached the woman in black, she looked up. She had adjusted her head scarf to cover more of her face and her eyelids drooped.

He wondered what was wrong. When he stopped, Laila tugged on his arm. "Come, Thomas. Time for that later."

A crazy thought shot through Davis's mind—*maybe she's the suicide bomber.*

He glanced at Laila. Although she was a strong lady, bearing up like a warrior in battle, the stress had begun to weigh on her. Her dark eyes had lost their sparkle and the dimples in her cheeks from her I'm-happy-to-be-alive smile were gone.

They walked down the starboard aisle in the coach cabin past Al-Ajlani. The male attendant was reading. The old Arab sat quietly with his eyes closed.

No doubt he's praying, Davis thought. *He knows the end is coming.*

As they neared the rear of the cabin, Davis noticed that the seat between the boys was empty.

He squeezed Laila's hand. She stopped.

"A veiled woman in the center section, third row from the back. She caught my eye. Her seat's empty now."

"The veiled ones never travel alone. The port loo is occupied. I'll bet she's in there."

"We have to see if she's the woman in the photograph."

"That won't be easy, but come," she said.

When they reached the galley, Laila pushed aside the serving cart. Three female attendants were belted in jump seats with beleaguered looks. One was filing her fingernails and the other two were talking. Leila had already apprised them of what had happened after takeoff.

After exchanging a few words with them, Leila knocked on the lavatory door.

"Hello in there. Are you all right?"

No response.

Laila put her ear to the door. "Sounds like she's retching."

She's the suicide bomber, Davis thought. *She's having second thoughts at the last minute and became ill. Either that or she's going to do the dirty deed locked in the lavatory, when the tires hit the runway.*

"Laila," one of the attendants said and raised three fingers.

Laila whispered to Davis, "This is the third time she's gone in there."

Laila knocked again, harder this time. The door rattled.

"This is Laila, the cabin purser. I must speak with you. Come out."

When there was no response, Laila raised her voice. "We can open the door."

The sliding bolt moved to the open position, but the door stayed closed.

Davis tensed, readying himself to seize the woman. He'd pull off her veil and identify her, then find the bomb and defuse it.

He glanced at his chronograph. Seventeen minutes and twenty-eight seconds left. Time was running out. Soon Turani would leave the holding pattern and begin approaching the airport.

Davis couldn't restrain himself any longer. As he pushed the folding door in, Laila blocked his arm.

"Let me handle this. I'll go in and talk to her. Step away so she doesn't see you," she said.

"Okay. Is there enough room in there?"

Laila looked down at her pear-shaped body. She grinned and said, "It's going to be tight," and gently pushed Davis aside.

He hesitated for an instant.

The girl's photo. Damn it.

He'd left it in the fore galley. He pushed the serving cart aside and sprinted toward the first-class cabin.

When Davis returned with the photograph, Laila was still in the lavatory. The door was locked.

Davis imagined there'd be a struggle if Laila tried to subdue the woman, but the only sound he heard was muffled voices.

After a few minutes, the sliding lock clicked, and Laila came out with an Iranian passport in her hand. Her face was etched with sadness.

"She's not the bomber," she said flatly.

Davis held up the photograph from Al-Ajlani's wallet.

Laila shook her head and handed him the passport.

While he studied it, she continued, "She's a young girl. She has a serious blood disease and travels to Paris every month for treatment. It makes her sick. Been vomiting. She removed her veil for me. She looks terrible, pale with sunken eyes and no hair. Look at her passport; she was a pretty girl."

Davis stared at the passport photograph.

Laila was right. The girl was pretty, and she wasn't the one in the photograph.

Shit, Davis thought. *What now?*

After Laila told the attendants to help the girl back to her seat, she took Davis's hand and they walked down the port aisle. They saw no one acting suspiciously.

When they got back to the galley Davis's ears popped. He checked the time—only ten minutes and four seconds left.

The knife wielder was slumped forward. The blanket had slipped off him. His jaw hung open with grotesque swelling around his eyes and mouth, and an odor filled the galley. Death had cankered the air with its vile stench. Davis draped the blanket back over the body and tucked the edges behind the jump seat.

The photographer's lips were moving and he stared mindlessly as if in a trance. Davis figured he was reciting his final prayers . . . like the old Arab.

After Laila sprayed the galley with air freshener again, she buckled herself into a jump seat across from the hijackers.

Davis stepped in front of the photographer and looked into his eyes. "There's a suicide bomber on the plane. Who is it?"

The photographer's lips stopped moving, and a smile spread across his face.

Davis shook him. "Who is it? Damn it, tell me."

The photographer's lips started moving again, but he said nothing.

Davis shook him again. Harder.

"Tell me."

The photographer's eyes fluttered, but he remained unfazed.

He knows, but I'm wasting my time.

Davis would have to sit in the photographer's seat. Hami Rahbar was in the knife wielder's. But before sitting he'd make one final pass through the aircraft.

He kneeled in front of Laila and saw tears in her eyes.

"When the tires hit the runway huddle against the cockpit door," he told her. "Cover yourself with blankets. It might help."

Trembling, Laila squeezed his hand.

"May Allah bless you Thomas for what you've done for us. You're a wonderful man."

As she spoke, the plane bounced again.

"You should sit Thomas. It's getting rough. We'll land soon."

Al-Ajlani's cell phone had slid off the counter and landed at Davis's feet.

CHAPTER 10

It was an old-fashioned flip-top model.

No doubt a burner.

A thought popped into Davis's head.

He picked up the phone and opened it. Punched the on button. For once today lady luck smiled down on him—no password required. The screen filled with the usual icons. He pressed the green phone symbol. A keypad flashed. The phone icons were below it. He pressed the clock icon and a list of recent calls appeared. He recognized the Arabic numbers.

The last call was at 2:11 p.m. The flight had started to board at 1:30 p.m.

"Laila, what time was boarding completed?"

She pointed to the galley wall above the counter.

"The passenger log is there. It'll be recorded."

Davis retrieved the log and handed it to her.

The plane bounced again. Davis steadied himself against the galley wall.

"The doors closed at 2:07 p.m.," she said.

That meant Al-Ajlani had placed the call after he'd boarded. Was he calling the fourth member of the team? The suicide bomber?

Davis scrolled back in the recent calls list. At 1:11 p.m. the old Arab had called a different number. Davis checked the names on the hijacker's boarding passes. It was the photographer. But the name opposite the 2:11 p.m. call didn't match either hijacker's name.

Davis didn't trust himself reading Arabic, particularly names. Sometimes they were crazy nicknames. Laila would have to translate.

"I need your help," he told Laila.

He scrolled to the last call and pointed.

29

"What's that name?"

Her eyebrows wrinkled, and she mumbled under her breath.

"What'd you say?"

"Aibnat Al'akh Meera. That's what it says."

That's the suicide bomber's name, Davis thought. It's different from the names of the hijackers.

Davis handed her the passenger log.

"Quickly, find that name for me."

His ears popped, and he took a few deep breaths to calm himself. He checked the time. Just a few seconds more than three minutes until the alarm sounded.

He glanced out the galley window.

The plane was still in dense cloud cover, but soon the ground would appear.

Davis followed Laila's finger down the page.

The name has to be here, he thought.

There were five pages. She was still on the first.

"That's a strange last name," she said.

"What?"

"Meera is a woman's first name, not a last name. It means princess.

She seemed a little befuddled.

Davis squeezed her arm. "It's not a last name?"

"I suppose it could be, but Aibnat's not a first name. Aibnat Al'akh means niece."

The bomber is Al-Ajlani's niece, Davis thought. *Her first name is Meera. The princess.*

"Find the woman with the first name Meera. We don't have much time."

He looked at his chronograph. Two minutes and thirty-six seconds left. Just 156 seconds.

"Come on, come on," he muttered under his breath, then began to count backward in his head.

When he reached forty-seven Laila looked up. "There's no one named Meera."

Davis's heart sank.

It's over, he thought.

He looked out the window again.

The tops of buildings sped by and the wingtip of an Iranian military jet was in the distance. The airport runway was just ahead. The Airbus would touch down in a few seconds.

Shit.

Then Laila pointed to the third name on the second page. "Amira Shadid. Amira means princess, too."

Meera was Al-Ajlani's nickname for his niece. He'd called her on his cell phone after boarding.

"She's the bomber! Where's she sitting?"

"Seat 31C. Center section. Aisle. That way," Laila blurted, pointing to the starboard side of the aircraft.

As the words left her lips, Davis was gone.

When he passed row thirty in full stride, the plane bounced on the runway.

The tires screamed, and Davis was thrust forward.

CHAPTER 11

*P*op.

He hit the woman square in the jaw.

Her head bounced on the seat, and she was out cold. Instantly.

Davis pulled off her niqab. Her face was thin and gaunt, and there was a big bulge under her abaya. A pair of headphones sat in her lap, the old-fashioned type with a wire, the French manufacturer's name stamped on the earpieces.

As the aircraft's reverse thrusters roared and the plane slowed, the alarm on his chronograph sounded. He exhaled long and slow, as he turned it off.

Laila had followed on his heels and stood next to him.

Davis's heart was racing and he felt breathless. He looked at her and smiled. Her eyes were wide.

Then the gravity of the moment seized him.

The bomb.

He had to defuse it. And he had forgotten to tell Laila to evacuate the plane.

"Laila. Emergency evacuation. Now! Get everyone off. Into the terminal. As fast as you can. No one on the ground is to come aboard. Leave the hijackers behind."

"Aye, aye, Thomas," she said and ran forward.

But Captain Turani was one step ahead. As Laila rushed to the galley, he announced the emergency evacuation of the plane. It was brief.

"This is your captain. I am ordering emergency evacuation of the aircraft. The cabin attendants will direct you to the exits. Move as quickly as possible to the terminal. Leave all personal items on the plane."

Davis had been in an emergency evacuation on a military aircraft a time or two, but never on a commercial airliner. It was quite an event.

A noxious alarm sounded, the exits fore and aft flew open, and inflatable slides deployed. The passengers stepped into the aisles and filed to the exits, the attendants directing them like ushers at a wedding. There was no shouting, no confusion, and no pushing or shoving. An air of cautious relief had settled over everyone except Davis. Tendrils of fear were unfurling around his throat.

When the evacuation was complete, he heard Captain Turani shout from the fore exit, "Thank you, Mr. Davis. I'll shake your hand in the terminal."

Then Laila added, "Hugs and kisses. Thanks, Thomas."

Davis shouted back, "Get off. This isn't over."

It seemed like an eternity until he was alone with the woman. With the exits wide open, warm air laden with jet fumes wafted across Davis leaving a chemical taste in his mouth.

The empty coach cabin was enormous, seeming to expand each time he looked around. An eerie feeling began to tug at him, some form of agoraphobia.

Suddenly the evacuation alarm stopped, and the overhead lights went out. With only the emergency lights in the aisles on, the cabin was draped in eerie shadows and deathly silent.

Davis wasn't sure what to do next. He had to disarm the bomb. And he had to do it now.

Explosives weren't his thing. Nor were guns for that matter. He was a hands-on guy—literally—so he searched his memory for an early morning lecture almost ten years ago. It was at Fort Bragg. A crusty old FBI explosive expert from Huntsville named Carmichael chewed on a cigar while he talked. A full hour with him. Horrific photographs. How could Davis ever forget?

"C4's the favorite of the damn Islamic terrorists," Carmichael had begun.

He'd gone on to describe C4 as extremely powerful, yet stable, easily molded like putty around doors or air vents. It burned slowly when lighted with a match. Soldiers in Viet Nam had actually used it for cooking. "I was there," he'd growled proudly. But even a small amount was lethal when detonated by an electrical charge. Carmichael had held up a small package of Philadelphia Cream Cheese from the breakfast cart and said, "A block this size'll destroy an armored Humvee and everybody near it."

Davis figured the C4 was under the woman's abaya. Because she was made to look pregnant, the normal screening in the airport's security hall had been altered. That or a compatriot who worked in the airport, perhaps in food service, had smuggled the setup past security and rendezvoused with her at the gate.

The woman's right hand rested between the earpieces in her lap. The black wire that normally attached to an audio source disappeared into her abaya along the front zipper.

Davis gently touched the bulge on the woman's flank. He expected something soft and easily compressible. Maybe a feather pillow. Instead, the bulge had a firm quality like a woman's breast implant. Or a pregnant belly?

He knew what a breast implant felt like, but he had never pushed on a pregnant belly.

Was she really pregnant? Was it possible he had the wrong woman?

He turned her head toward him, and held up the photograph from Al-Ajlani's wallet. The suicide bomber *was* the woman, and even more haggard in the flesh. And her eyes were locked in a blank stare.

CHAPTER 12

Just the thought of targeting the wrong woman triggered a lightning round of second-guessing.

Had he made a mistake staying behind?

He'd be safe in the terminal now. In the confusion, he might be able to get his passport stamped and skulk away from the authorities. He had important business in Tehran with Dietz Meyer.

But he had to defuse the bomb. He couldn't let someone else do it. This was his mission. He didn't trust the Iranians anyway. They'd screw it up.

Finishing—the end game—meant everything to him. It was woven into his DNA. It was one of the special traits that made him who he was.

Okay. You're here. Stop second-guessing. Get on with it.

Davis examined the abaya. A zipper ran from the neck to the hem. He opened it down to the waist. Underneath was a light gray Silastic form, held in place by velcro straps. It might be used to make an otherwise slim actress look pregnant.

Davis's eyes traced a red wire disappearing behind the form.

"Black wire on the outside, red wire on the inside," he muttered under his breath.

He turned the edge of the abaya back and found the black wire on the outside connected to the red wire on the inside. A female connector on the red wire was fastened to the edge of the zipper. When the bomber poked the male connector on the black wire through the cloth into the female connector on the red wire, presto, the circuit was complete. The bomb was armed.

The headphones were the charge generator. They were battery powered with an on-off switch on the outside of one of the earpieces. When the headphones were turned on, a tiny light near the switch glowed red. The switch controlled the charge to the detonator. Turn it on, the red light glowed, and the C4 detonated. But he couldn't be sure. There might be a switch somewhere else, inside one of the earpieces, maybe motion activated.

Taking great care not to disturb the headphones, he removed the Silastic form. It was a tedious exercise.

Under the form there was a wide belt around the woman's waist with six zippered pockets. Each pocket held a block of C4, double the size of Carmichael's block of cream cheese. The detonator looked like a thick hypodermic needle inserted into one of the blocks. The red wire attached to it.

Davis estimated there was enough C4 to blow the Airbus to smithereens. Anyone on the ground near the plane was in harm's way.

He traced the wires from the headphones to the detonator again . . . just to be sure. Beyond the coupling there was nothing that could generate an electrical charge. The simplest way to disarm the bomb was to pull apart the red and black wires at the connector.

But the thought of the C4 exploding in his face was mind-numbing in an end-of-days way. He and the bomber would be vaporized. The magnificent French-built aircraft would be a runway IED—lethal projectiles launched in every direction. When the fuel tanks ignited, there would be a moving wall of fire. Fortunately, they were nearly empty.

Anyone near the plane was toast—literally.

Fretting about the people on the ground made him think of the woman in black. She was an extraordinary expression of Middle East genetics. He'd been all over the world, had Lebanese blood himself, but he'd never seen any woman quite like her.

And Laila. If he were to design a sister—he was an only child—it would be Laila, except she'd be five inches taller and thirty pounds lighter with a duchess nose.

The man behind the voice from the flight deck, Captain Turani, was a trusting soul with a cool head in the most stressful situation imaginable for an airline pilot. It would be an honor to shake his hand.

Davis surveyed the woman again. She was alive. Breathing normally. A strong pulse. But her eyes had that unmistakable empty stare. The lights were out. She wouldn't awaken for a while. Maybe never. He had time to see what was going on outside the aircraft. What were the damn Persians up to?

He walked portside and peered out the window. Turani had stopped the plane at the end of the runway several hundred yards from the terminal and cut the engines, exactly what Davis had told him to do.

Kudos to him.

Emergency vehicles—ambulances, fire trucks, and police vans—formed a protective wall in front of the terminal. Huddled behind them elbow to elbow was an army of men in swat gear. A melange of flashing red, blue, and yellow lights cast a purple hue across the runway. The sky was gray with low cloud cover. The last of the passengers were scooting into the terminal.

He walked back to the starboard side of the aircraft and looked out a window. Nothing but black macadam and tufts of brown grass as far as he could see.

When he returned, the bomber's eyelids were fluttering.

Maybe the lights will come on, he thought.

Suddenly he felt weird. Really weird, like nothing he'd ever felt before.

It was an other worldly sensation. He was floating out of his body. Some type of depersonalization. A horrible chemical taste filled his mouth.

He looked down at himself.

A soft voice inside of him muttered, "Do it."

CHAPTER 13

"**L**et's take a short break, Mr. Davis." The man gathered his cigarettes and lighter and left the room.

His name was Amir Golshiri. He was a balding, middle-aged Persian with shadows around dark, deep-set eyes. Smoker's creases furrowed his face. When he wasn't drawing on a cigarette, he had an annoying habit of darting his tongue out like a lizard. His dark blue suit was a half size too big and his skinny geek tie was loose at the collar. A flesh-colored wire from an earbud disappeared under his lapel.

Davis figured Golshiri was with Iran's Ministry of Intelligence—the Iranian secret police. They'd been at it for thirty minutes.

Golshiri was the second to interrogate Davis. The first was a nameless airport security agent who'd robotically asked the standard demographic questions. They'd met in a small room off the security hall, just a desk, two straight-backed chairs and two uniformed NAJA officers.

Davis had been fuzzy-headed at first, but after he was asked his name his edge returned. He had answered the questions according to the script and thought his delivery was perfect.

After that, he'd been taken to a processing center in the basement of the airport terminal. There he'd been photographed, fingerprinted, and had a buccal smear taken for DNA analysis, the worst things imaginable for a man like Davis.

Then the two NAJA officers had driven him to a five-story, unmarked concrete and steel edifice outside the airport. They'd passed through a pair of gates with armed guards in eloquent seaweed green uniforms and parked in an underground garage. After an elevator ride to the fifth floor, they'd followed a wide corridor to a windowless conference room with monitors on all four walls. No microphones or cameras were visible, but Davis knew they were there.

The guards had left Davis alone in the room. His cell phone and wallet sat on a long rectangular table with twelve high-backed chairs. They were the only things he had in his pockets during the memorable flight from Istanbul. The cell phone looked like an iPhone, but it was special. He couldn't risk losing it.

He'd checked his wallet and found his cash and other litter untouched. He'd put the wallet and phone in his pocket.

His carry-on bag was missing. The last time he remembered seeing it was when he'd slid it into the overhead compartment next to Dietz Meyer's messenger bag. His Canadian passport, laptop, and other personal items were in it. He had no checked luggage.

Like the cell phone, the laptop was special.

Davis had waited in the conference room, pondering his fate at the hands of the Persians. It was part of their strategy, to put him on edge and tighten the noose around his neck.

The Iranians were suspicious he was an American agent, considering what had happened on the airplane. They just had to prove it.

After what seemed like an eternity, Golshiri had appeared carrying an ashtray. He'd shaken Davis's hand and gestured for him to sit at one end of the table. He'd sat at the opposite end, lit a cigarette, and introduced himself by name only.

Golshiri had played nice guy to put Davis at ease, to get him comfortable talking. Davis had answered the questions, but volunteered nothing. He was trained not to fall into a trap by mindlessly chattering.

Goshiri had tried his best but hadn't gotten anywhere. He knew it and was frustrated. And so the questioning had ended and they'd taken a break.

Davis wondered what was next. Drugs? Torture? Or more of Golshiri? Anything was possible in Iran.

CHAPTER 14

After a few minutes Golshiri returned and took his place at the table. He tore open a fresh pack of cigarettes, lit one, and took a deep drag.

Even at a distance the secondary smoke burned Davis's eyes and throat, but complaining wasn't a good idea.

Golshiri looked at Davis and tried to smile, but it was clear his demeanor had changed.

"Why did you travel to Iran, Mr. Davis?" There was a new sharpness in his voice.

No more nice guy. Round two, here we go, Davis thought.

"With all due respect, sir, I've answered that question. I'm a salesman for a medical equipment company in Toronto. I'm here to sell body scanners."

"We've called our major hospitals. You have no appointments."

"I'll be cold-calling. That means showing up on the client's doorstep without an appointment. We think there is a good market for our products in Iran."

"And the name of your company?"

"I've told you."

"Tell me again."

"Microscan Corporation. You called our corporate offices and talked to my boss."

The man on the other end of the call wasn't his boss. In fact, Davis didn't even know who he was.

"Mr. Davis, you are a Canadian citizen?"

"Yes, sir, I am. Born there."

"You speak Farsi."

Davis said nothing.

"You didn't answer my question, Mr. Davis."

"That wasn't a question, sir; it was a statement."

Golshiri glared at Davis. "Where did you learn it?"

"When I was growing up, our housekeeper was Iranian. She taught me. And before you ask, my mother taught me Arabic. She was born in Lebanon."

Golshiri looked at Davis curiously as if to say, "Do you think I believe that?" But it was the truth, the first truthful answer out of Davis.

"Why are you carrying U.S. dollars?"

"My company was told that Iran is cash-only for foreign travelers. No credit cards. U.S. dollars are preferred. I converted my Canadian money at the airport in Toronto. I brought enough cash to pay for my hotel, meals, and ground transportation."

Golshiri nodded. He seemed satisfied with that answer.

"What happened in the first-class galley shortly after take-off?"

Davis summarized the events, but left out how he'd disarmed the hijackers.

"What was their condition after you restrained them?"

"The man with the camera was unconscious and bleeding from his nose and mouth. The man with the knife died shortly after I tied him in a jump seat."

"So the man with the camera was unconscious and the one with the knife died?"

"Yes, sir," Davis replied, wondering why Golshiri was focused on the physical state of the hijackers.

"Do you have martial arts training, Mr. Davis?"

"No, sir."

Golshiri's jaw muscles tightened. He didn't like that answer.

"You killed one man with a kick and knocked the other out with a punch, and you don't have martial arts training?"

Laila or the woman in black must have described what happened in the first-class galley, Davis thought.

"I said, I didn't."

Golshiri shook his head and moved on. "How did you know there was a third hijacker?"

Davis explained how he'd discovered Al-Ajlani was an accomplice.

"How did you restrain him?"

"I sat in the next seat. While questioning him, he became agitated. I tied him to the seat with audio wires."

"What was his condition after you tied him up?"

"He was fine. A male attendant sat with him."

"How did you discover there was a suicide bomber?"

Davis outlined the note he'd found in Al-Ajlani's wallet and how he'd concluded a default plan over Tehran meant a suicide bomber on the plane.

"How did you identify the bomber?"

Davis explained how he'd identified the woman from Al-Ajlani's cell phone and the passenger log with the help of a flight attendant.

"What did you do then?"

"I ran to her seat and knocked her out. I had no choice. I was sure she was about to detonate the bomb."

"Describe the woman."

Davis described her and how she'd been dressed.

"Mr. Davis, how do you know the names of Muslim women's clothing?

"From my mother."

Golshiri shook his head. "Okay. Describe the bomb."

Davis's detailed description aroused Golshiri's dander. He sat forward, stubbed out his cigarette, and lit another.

"How do you know so much about explosive devices?"

"I read military books. I've learned a lot about guns and explosives. I read that C4 is the terrorist's favorite. You asked me to describe the bomb. I did the best I could."

Golshiri sighed. "How did you figure out how to defuse it?"

"It was easy. Like I said, a red wire and a black wire were joined together under her abaya. The red wire led to the detonator, the black wire to the headphones."

"Mr. Davis, weren't you afraid the bomb would explode?"

"Sir, I was scared to death."

Golshiri glanced at his ashtray, flicked ashes, and took a deep drag. "What did you do after you pulled the wires apart?"

Davis hesitated. What had he done? He couldn't remember. Couldn't even remember pulling the wires apart.

"I'm sorry sir, but I don't remember."

Golshiri lunged forward in his seat and snarled, "You don't remember, Mr. Davis?"

Davis said nothing.

After a pause, Goshiri asked, "Well, what's the first thing you remember then?"

Davis felt warm. His stomach gurgled and a wave of nausea rose in his throat.

Where did the gap in his memory end? He knew where it started—just before he pulled the wires apart. He racheted his thoughts back to Goshiri shaking his hand, to the car ride with the guards, to the processing center, to the small room in the airport. He saw the nameless security agent typing and the guards standing at attention. A small desk was in front of him with an S-shaped scratch on the top and cigarette burns along the edges. The security agent asked, "What is your name?"

"What is your name," he blurted.

"What's my name?"

"I'm sorry, sir. The first thing I remember is a security agent in the airport asking me my name."

"You're joking, Mr. Davis. The first thing you remember is giving your name in the airport?"

"No, sir. The first thing I remember is being asked my name."

"You don't remember sliding down the escape shoot?"

"I slid down the escape shoot?"

"Yes, you did."

Davis shook his head.

"You don't remember walking across the tarmac to the terminal pulling your carry-on bag behind you?"

"No, sir. I don't."

"You don't remember the explosive belt draped over your shoulder?"

"The explosive belt . . . draped over my shoulder? You're kidding."

"I'm not kidding, Mr. Davis. You slid down the emergency escape shoot and walked across the tarmac with the belt over your shoulder, pulling your bag. We have it on video, in color. I can show you if you like. Then you were escorted to a private passport control office, then to a processing site, then here."

Davis was flabbergasted. What had happened to him?

"Truthfully, sir, the last thing I remember before I was asked my name was a bad taste in my mouth, like being in Los Angeles on a smoggy day."

"I thought you were Canadian, Mr. Davis."

"I am. But I've been to California on holiday. Everybody has. Haven't you?"

Golshiri's eyebrows arched. "No. Not yet."

Davis smiled. "You should visit. It's a lovely place. Except for the smog."

"What was the woman's condition when you left the plane?"

"I've already told you, I don't remember leaving the plane."

"What was her condition before you pulled the wires apart?"

"I don't remember pulling the wires apart."

"Then what was your last memory of her?"

"She was breathing. Her eyelids fluttered. She was waking up."

"So the last thing you remember about the woman was she was waking up."

"That's right."

Davis felt like a defendant being cross-examined by a hostile prosecutor.

"Have you interrogated her yet?" he asked, turning the tables and asking a question of his own.

Golshiri pushed back his chair and crossed his arms. His eyes bored into Davis and he said sotto voce, "Interrogated her? She's dead, Mr. Davis."

"Dead? She was alive the last time I saw her. What about the hijacker with the camera and the old Arab?"

"Dead. Both of them."

Silence fell between them, Golshiri waiting for a response and Davis in a state of shock.

Suddenly Golshiri's eyes shot upward, and he nodded.

Davis feared the worst.

Someone was probably speaking to Golshiri in his earbud, ordering him to have the American agent shackled and taken to jail . . . to Evin Prison, most likely, where he would be charged with spying and murder.

Goshiri's eyes focused on Davis. He had a strange look, something between a smile and a frown, as if he was unsure whether he was happy or sad.

"Mr. Davis, please excuse me again. Is there anything you'd like?"

"I have a few questions, if you don't mind."

"Forgive me. I'll answer them in a few minutes."

Goshiri gathered his cigarettes, lighter, and ashtray and left.

CHAPTER 15

Davis was worried.

Had he killed the woman, the old Arab, and the photographer after defusing the bomb?

The last thing he remembered was the horrible taste in his mouth and feeling strange. After that his memory was blank, until he was asked his name in the airport.

According to Golshiri, he'd slid down an emergency shoot and walked across the tarmac pulling his carry-on bag with the explosive belt draped over his shoulder.

That meant he had removed the belt from the woman after defusing the bomb and retrieved his carry-on bag from the overhead compartment in the first-class cabin. But he had no memory of doing either. And what else had he done before he left the plane?

Davis was in a world of hurt.

The Iranians had reason to detain him as a foreign agent and maybe even charge him with murder. There were no laws in Iran to protect foreigners from unjust incarceration. On a whim he could be held indefinitely, tortured, and executed. His only hope was that someone above Golshiri, someone very powerful in the theocratic hierarchy, felt Davis's heroics on the plane trumped everything.

The likelihood of him sleeping in his hotel room tonight was slim. It would be a cold, dark cell. He could only imagine what was in store after that.

※ ※ ※

The conference room door swung open, and Golshiri stepped to the side.

A tall man with an American flattop, a clean-shaven face, and an aquiline nose stood in the doorway. His rheumy, dark eyes were striking, seeming to swim in cunning and radiate the full measure of his power. He wore a tailored black suit, a crisp white shirt with gold cuff links, a black tie, and shiny tassel loafers.

With a gorgeous purposefulness he strode toward Davis.

The big guy. Golshiri's boss, Davis thought.

Golshiri stood by the doorway with a pensive look, holding Davis's carry-on bag.

"Mr. Davis," the man said extending his hand. "I'm General Cha Mogadan, director of the Ministry of Intelligence of the Republic of Iran."

Davis stood and they shook hands.

"It's a pleasure to meet you, Mr. Davis. I apologize for Colonel Golshiri's behavior. He was doing his job, trying his best. You are a hero in our country and soon all over the world. Please sit."

Davis was dumbfounded. Why the sudden change of heart? He slumped in his chair, and Mogadan sat down next to him.

"The colonel was polite, I must say." Davis nodded to Golshiri who sat in his place at the far end of the table. No cigarettes now.

"I'm glad to hear that," Mogadan said, glancing at Golshiri.

"I explained to him what happened on the airplane. The last thing I remember is a bad taste in my mouth. I don't remember disarming the bomb. Or leaving the airplane and walking across the tarmac. After that the first thing I remember is an agent asking me my name in the terminal."

Stop! You're rambling, Davis told himself. *Exactly what they want you to do.*

Mogadan's eyes bored into Davis. "The four Saudi terrorists are dead. They'll undergo autopsies at one of our military hospitals. Of course, the one with the knife died from a blow to the head during a struggle with you. He shouldn't have tried to hijack one of our aircraft."

"And the others?" Davis asked.

"The one with the camera died of aspiration."

"Aspiration?"

"Yes, of course. He aspirated blood into his throat from a broken nose, choked, and couldn't breathe."

"And the man in row . . . ?" Davis's mind was blank. He couldn't remember the old Arab's name or seat.

"You're referring to Malik Al-Ajlani in seat 40A. He was a heavy smoker, like someone I know." Mogadan glared at Golshiri. "It will be found that he died of a heart attack. And before you ask, Mr. Davis, the female had a serious heart problem from birth. Her autopsy will show she died of an irregular heart beat."

"The colonel was focused on their condition. He asked me a lot of questions. The implication, General, was that I did something to them."

"You mean like kill them?" Mogadan asked with a mischievous grin.

"Yes, sir," Davis replied.

"They're dead, Mr. Davis. It doesn't matter if it was at the hands of Allah or some other less divine force. But if you did kill them, you are extraordinarily skilled with your hands. Their deaths save us from awkward judicial proceedings and messy executions with unpleasant push back from the Saudis and the Western human rights pundits."

Davis decided not to pursue the deaths with Mogadan. There was nothing to be gained and everything to lose. The unpredictable Persians might change their minds. Charging a suspected American agent with murder would force Washington to intervene.

The Iranians had exonerated him. That was all that mattered.

But Thomas Davis, newly proclaimed national hero, would be the focus of the Iranian intelligence machine. As long as he was in Iran, they'd relentlessly investigate him until they uncovered his identity. His every move in Tehran would be monitored, immeasurably complicating his business with Dietz Meyer. Davis knew what they would do if they discovered who he was.

"For some reason the colonel asked questions about my identity. Do you think I'm someone else?" Davis asked in a mildly plaintive voice.

"It doesn't matter who you are . . . at this point, Mr. Davis. All that matters is that the passengers and crew of Iran Air flight 1645 are alive, and our magnificent Airbus is safe at Khomeini. You are a national hero. You will be treated as one, no matter who you are."

So Davis's heroics on the plane *had* trumped everything.

The general reached into his jacket and handed Davis an envelope.

"This letter states that you are a national hero and our esteemed guest. It gives you carte blanche to just about everything: hotels, restaurants, the theatre, whatever your heart desires . . . and perhaps a little more if you like." He winked at Davis. "It is certified by me. My contact information is with it, should you incur any problems or need anything. I have taken the liberty to upgrade your hotel to our very best. All charges will be covered. I have my personal car waiting to take you there. Your friend, Colonel Golshiri, will introduce you to our major hospitals if you like. I am sure you'll enjoy a booming business in Tehran."

"You are very kind General, but I can't accept this."

"I insist, Mr. Davis. Iran is a very authority-centric society. Things work in strange ways here. This letter will open many doors for you."

The general handed Davis another envelope and smiled. "And this . . . you will find most intriguing to say the least. You are a very lucky man. My country thanks you, Mr. Davis . . . or whoever you are. May Allah be with you."

CHAPTER 16

"**W**ell done, Mr. Thomas Davis. You're in," Clint Jarrett muttered under his breath, slouched in the back of General Mogadan's limousine. Thomas Davis was Jarrett's legend for the Tehran mission. Jarrett was on Iran Air flight 1645 from Istanbul to Tehran because he was tracking a man named Dietz Meyer, known in the underworld as Demus.

Jarrett's tag in the black ops world was Paladin after the character played by Richard Boone in the television series *Have Gun—Will Travel*. Boone portrayed a mercenary gunfighter who traveled through the Old West helping people in need. In the Middle East and the horn of Africa Jarrett was known as Jenni, the invincible shapeshifting demon in Muslim mythology.

Jarrett had grown up on the Capistran Ranch in the Blacks Hills of South Dakota, the only son of Caleb and Miriam Jarrett.

Jarrett's mother was a Lebanese national and a renowned Hollywood makeup technician. She'd met his father during the filming of an epic western on the Capistran Ranch. William Holden and Earnest Borgnine drank coffee in the ranch house kitchen the day Caleb proposed to her.

After Jarrett's birth an Iranian woman named Jana had moved to the ranch to nanny her best friend's newborn son. By age six the youngster was fluent in both Arabic and Farsi. In addition to Arabic, Jarrett's mother taught him her makeup skills.

Jarrett had attended an Ivy League college on a full ice hockey scholarship and earned All-American honors three years in a row. After college he'd enlisted in the Air Force. *Top Gun* was Jarrett's favorite movie and his dream was to fly combat jets. He was soloing over the plains of South Dakota in his father's Piper Super Cub before he had an automobile driver's license.

A strapping six-foot-two, Jarrett looked like a dark-haired, youthful Clint Eastwood. He was a deadly marksman and his Lakota friends had taught him to use a bow and to throw knives and tomahawks. And on top of that he was a black belt in jujitsu.

When the Pentagon learned they had a recruit who spoke Arabic and Farsi fluently, had firearm experience, and extraordinary hand-to-hand combat skills, they pulled him from pilot training.

After a year working with the Navy SEALS and Delta Force in various JSOC sites, Jarrett began assassinating targets in Europe, the Middle East, and the horn of Africa. When the target's location was identified, he flew in, took care of business, and vanished like a killer leopard. He always worked alone, and his hands were his weapons.

Jarrett left the military when his four-year tour was complete. He was tired of traveling alone all over the world and wanted to get back to the life he loved and cherished.

A year after he returned to South Dakota, his father died in an automobile accident. A prolonged drought had befallen the plains states, and when the cattle market crashed, Jarrett had to take out a mortgage to cover expenses. When the money ran out, he was in danger of losing the property to the bank. It had been in his family for three generations, but more importantly ranching was his life and the cowboy lifestyle was in his blood. Other than financial worries, Jarrett's life was beautifully uncomplicated with just his mother Miriam, their housekeeper Jana, his dog Woody, and the ranch livestock to worry about.

Then Dodge Sedgewick had called.

Sedgewick was Jarrett's best friend. They had been college roomates, fraternity brothers, and Sedgewick had been the hockey team's goal tender. After law school Sedgewick had joined the CIA and enjoyed a meteoric rise in the clandestine service. At Langley he was referred to as a "fast burner."

Jarrett had become increasingly distressed by the horrific acts of terrorism around the world, and the desire to do something to serve his country had begun to stir in him. With the prospect of losing the family ranch, restless to jump back into action, and with a personal issue haunting him, Jarrett had signed on as the president's assassin.

Three or four times a year, he left his idyllic life in the Black Hills to dispatch a high-value Oval Office target in some godforsaken hellhole. He enjoyed the challenge, he felt good about serving his country, he was paid very well, there was no tax on the money, and each time he came home there was one fewer of the bad guys out there. No one knew his identity except for the president and Sedgewick; his military record had been expunged from all databases. Even his mother didn't know that her beloved only child was an assassin in the service of the Oval Office.

Jarrett's last mission had been to assassinate a CIA analyst at Langley believed to be an Iranian spy. When Jarrett learned the analyst wasn't a spy, he became the target of a well-connected Washington deep-stater who was the real spy. Fearing that Jarrett knew his identity, the spy had taken out an assassination contract on him brokered by a mysterious man called Demus.

Jarrett dealt with a wave of assassins sent by Demus, and in the course of one violent encounter, he'd learned Demus's cell phone number. Ultimately, Jarrett had identified the spy and terminated him.

The Iranians had a longstanding suspicion there was an American spy in the Revolutionary Guard. The wily Demus convinced them that Jarrett had learned the spy's name from the CIA agent he was to assassinate. Demus viewed Paladin as a formidable competitor in the world of contract assassination and was incensed the American agent had killed one of his clients.

The Iranians agreed to pay Demus one million dollars for the spy's identity, a windfall for an assassination broker. Demus ordered his agents to find Jarrett, torture him until he gave up the spy's name, then kill him.

It was a perfect arrangement. The Iranians would get their spy, and Demus would rid himself of Paladin and fill his coffers with Persian money

Jarrett learned about the Iranian contract on him during an abduction by Demus's operatives. After he dispatched the abductors and escaped, he went black. He planned to track down Demus and kill him. But before Demus's last breath he would give Jarrett the name of his contact in the Revolutionary Guard handling the contract.

With Demus out of the way, Jarrett planned to pose as his partner and frame a mid-level agent in the Guard as the spy. He would pass the name to Demus's contact, and the Iranians would rescind the contract on him . . . he hoped.

Jarrett recognized that posing as Demus's partner and framing an agent in the Guard for spying was a formidable challenge for an assassin with no espionage experience, but he had the CIA's backing and the blessing of the president. If he didn't succeed, it meant WITSEC for life.

Finding Demus was the problem.

He was an enigma, clever and resourceful, with a daunting reputation in the black ops world. Although he brokered assassinations for governments—including the CIA—no one knew his identity. The cell phone number Jarrett had was a Turkish burner.

NSA was monitoring it 24/7.

Jarrett was waiting.

CHAPTER 17

Outside Edinburgh, Scotland, two weeks earlier

When Jarrett went black, he became Malcolm Sussfield, a ne'er-do-well trust-funder living outside of Edinburgh in a compound owned by a CIA shell company.

The property's centerpiece was a stone cottage—a Victorian-era jewel—at the end of a gravel lane on an eleven-hectare tract. It was deliciously comfortable with a picture-postcard view of Loch Leven and its historic castle. A small barn, a stone's throw from the cottage, had a security center with two guards in residence. Jarrett's live-in housekeeper, an elderly Scots woman named Mrs. Cameron, was a neat freak and made the best haggis in the county. There was a wonderful library with a potpourri of British and American titles, and Jarrett had honed his chess game against Stockfish 9. But he was bored and restless. He hadn't heard from Sedgewick in more than a week.

The call finally came out of the gray on a rainy overcast day.

"Jarrett, how are things?" Sedgewick asked on a secure satellite link.

"Scotland's great. Single malt's the best. But it rains all the time."

"I take it you switched from bourbon."

"Temporarily. I hope you have news."

"I do indeed. NSA got three hits yesterday on Demus's burner."

"In one day?"

"In one day."

"Finally," Jarrett muttered.

"The boys tell me it's turned on just once a day. He must check for messages. Amazing. Six weeks and nothing . . . until now. Guess no one's been looking for an assassin."

"Tell me about them." Jarrett couldn't hide his excitement.

"The first went to a travel agent. Demus asked for a flight to Tehran. Said, and I quote, 'June 2, the usual time.' Didn't mention an airline."

"That means he makes the flight regularly."

"The call was short. They couldn't fix his location but got the number he called. Aegean Travel in Istanbul."

"Demus never mentioned his name?" Jarrett asked.

"No. The agent must have recognized his voice. There was one other thing. He requested a car to the airport. When the agent asked, 'Crown? Pick up at the usual place?' Demus replied, 'Yes, of course.' That was it."

Jarrett groaned. "Then all we know is that he'll arrive at the airport in a Crown limo on June 2 and fly to Tehran. We don't know his name or what he looks like. And we don't know what airline or flight. Damn it!"

"Calm down, Jarrett. Believe it or not there are eleven flights a day from Istanbul to Tehran on nine different airlines."

"You're kidding. That many? To Tehran?"

"I was surprised, too. Demus flies on Iran Air flight 1645 at 2:35 p.m. on June 2."

"How do you know?" Jarrett asked.

"Well, we figured he'd fly first class on a major carrier. Iran Air or Turkish Airlines. Nothing but the best for your pal."

"He's not my pal."

"So we hacked their computers. Less than an hour after Demus called his agent, Aegean Travel booked a first-class seat on Iran Air to Tehran for Dietz Meyer."

"Who the hell is Dietz Meyer?"

"Demus. That's his name. Dietz Meyer. And the agent gave his passport number to the airline."

"Then you have his address," Jarrett said.

"It's a Turkish book. Issued three years ago to an apartment address. The building was torn down a year ago. I'll bet when he renews, he'll rent another apartment, use the address, and have the book sent there."

"He's clever."

"Very. We got into the Crown system thinking he might be picked up at his home. Low and behold, he'll be picked up at the Raffles on the morning of June 2."

"What's the Raffles?"

"One of the best hotels in Istanbul."

"Maybe he'll stay there the night before his flight."

"Nope. I had them get into the Raffles reservation files."

"That means he takes a taxi there or gets dropped off by someone in the morning."

"Exactly. Like you said, he's clever. That way Crown doesn't have his address on file."

"Damn it. I guess I'm going to Tehran."

"There's more. We've had a guy named Dietz Meyer on our radar for a long time."

"Really."

"Yes, really. If it's the same character, he's a bad dude. One of the worst. Dietz Meyer is the bastard son of Erich Meyer."

"Who's Erich Meyer?"

"You've forgotten all the classroom bullshit at the Farm," Sedgewick chided. "Erich Meyer was one of the top dogs in Stasi, the infamous East German secret police. He spent time in Russia. We think he had a son by a Russian woman. That would be Dietz. If he's the same guy, his tag in the underworld must be Demus. He's got nastiness in his DNA from his dad. Maybe his mom, too. You know firsthand how bad those Russian broads can be."

"One tried to kill me in Damascus."

Sedgewick laughed. "I can't imagine being in the sack with a gorgeous blonde with a great body and have her stick a knife in me while we did the horizontal mambo."

"The knife went in her. And we weren't dancing."

"Okay. Okay. Back to business. If our Dietz Meyer is your Demus, contract killing is just a side line. He's an arms dealer, dabbles in drugs, and maybe human trafficking. But he's smarter than most of those characters and elusive as hell. He disappeared from St. Petersburg three years ago, about the same time he got the Turkish passport. I guess he relocated to Istanbul, a little closer to the action in the Middle East.

Deep in thought, Jarrett only half-heard Sedgewick. If Demus was Dietz Meyer, he'd be a formidable adversary. And getting into Iran and dealing with him there would be challenging. And risky. Very risky.

"I need to know what kind of plane he'll be on."

"Hold on a second. Let me check the file."

Jarrett heard a keyboard clicking.

"It's an Airbus 330. Demus will be in seat 1G, bulkhead, center section along the port aisle. Before you ask, there are four seats across in first class. One at each window and two in the center with an aisle on each side."

"You must have a hotshot cybergeek working for you."

"I do indeed. Not a Yalie unfortunately. A Bulldog. Smart as a whip. He'll have my job before I know it."

"Do you have a photo of Meyer?"

"We do. Not worth a damn. Grainy. Taken at a distance. He's wearing a fedora and sunglasses with his collar up."

"Do you know how tall he is or if he has any distinguishing marks?"

"No," Sedgewick said.

"You mentioned three calls. What about the other two?"

"To Tehran. Thirty minutes apart. And short. Both after the travel agent call. He turned the phone off after each one. The first went to an unlisted number in Tehran. A landline, probably residential. We're trying to pinpoint an address, but it's not easy. He left a message."

"Voice on the answering machine. Male or female?"

"Let me check. Male. A default recording. Whoever is on the other end didn't want their voice on the recording."

"Lots of people don't. What'd he say?"

"He said, and I quote, 'See you June 2. Make a hotel reservation in the usual place.'"

"What language?"

"Why do you need to know?"

"Just curious. Arabic or Farsi?"

"It says the default greeting was in Farsi, but Demus talked in Arabic. With a heavy accent, I might add. These NSA nerds are pretty damn thorough."

"How about the third call?"

"A little more intriguing. Went to a blocked number. A man answered. Demus said that he would arrive on June 2 and would call to set up a meeting. The guy said, 'Important we meet as soon as possible,' and hung up."

"What does a blocked number in Tehran mean?" Jarrett asked.

"I'm told it's encrypted. Not blocked as we know it. NSA thinks it's a government landline."

"Not a blocked cell?"

"Couldn't be. Iranian cell service isn't compatible with Turkish service. Demus used his burner. Unless he called a sat phone."

"What language? And don't ask why."

"That's odd." Sedgewick paused. "Says here Demus spoke in Russian. The guy who answered spoke in Russian too. Nothing about accents. I guess that means they're both fluent speakers."

Jarrett's mind began racing to put together the language puzzle, to figure out what it meant . . . if anything.

After a few seconds he said, "With a Russian mother Demus's first language was Russian. He also must speak Arabic with an accent. Doesn't speak Farsi. The first call to Tehran went to someone who speaks both Farsi and Arabic. I imagine lots of folks in Iran do. The second was to someone who speaks Russian, maybe his contact in the Guard. They spoke in Russian because Demus doesn't speak Farsi. Don't imagine a lot of people speak Russian in Iran."

"Some do for sure. The Russians and Persians are tight now."

"I'll bet Demus spoke to the travel agent in Arabic."

"Says here he did."

"So Demus is Dietz Meyer, who you've been tracking."

"We think so," Dodge replied. "But there maybe another one. Meyer's a fairly common name. A photo would help. Our tech guys can compare it to the one we have. Come up with a match probability. I'll bet they're the same. Our Dietz Meyer is your Demus."

"I've got to be on that flight to Tehran, in the first-class cabin, directly behind him."

"Why?"

"Because he'll have a briefcase like every business man. He'll put it in the overhead compartment. He has to, because he's in a bulkhead seat. When I put up my bag, I'll tag his with one of your little tracking devices. I can follow him in Tehran with the tracking program on my phone or laptop."

"Whew. That may take some doing. He's on Iran Air. If he were flying on a U.S. carry, it'd be a helluva lot easier."

"Put your new Bulldog hacker on it. And I'll need a new legend. Not the Scottish one."

"You'll have to tell them in the airport in Tehran why you're entering the country. It better be good. The Iranians are suspicious bastards. And with the sanctions cranked down and the assassination of Soleimani they don't like Americans. Not one bit. Maybe a traveling hookah salesman from Cairo?" Sedgewick laughed.

Jarrett paused a few seconds to think. "I'd better be Canadian. Born there. Lived there all my life. Maybe a medical equipment salesman from Toronto. I'm making calls on hospitals in Tehran. I sell those special MRI body scanners. My name should be easy to remember, even easier to forget."

"Like Clint Jarrett."

"Don't be funny. Like Thomas Davis with the usual bona fides."

"Got it. Thomas Davis. A medical equipment salesman from Toronto. How long will you be there?"

"One week. I hope no more. But you never know."

"If Demus turns out to be Dietz Meyer, there'll be a lot of happy campers around here when you take him out."

"I'll have to visit with him first, find out who he deals with in the Guard. After that, the real trick'll be getting the Iranians off my back. I'll need your help."

"You know you've got it. Anything your heart desires. We're here for you."

"I'll fly from Edinburgh to London as Sussfield. Have the Davis passport stamped as if I flew from Toronto. Make it look like Davis travels a lot for business. Okay?"

"Fuck you, Jarrett. You think this is my first rodeo with you? I know exactly what to do."

"I know. I'm sorry. You know me. Just being anal and thinking out loud."

"You've probably got the whole gig planned in your head already. Any sexy disguises for this one?"

"No. But when I get to Tehran, I'll need an alternate legend just in case. It should be Lebanese or Turkish, not Iranian."

"That'll be easy. You can look like a towelhead when you need to, and you speak their language fluently . . . "

Jarrett interrupted, "And I can act like one when I need to."

"And you are one, if you want to know the truth."

"I've heard that too many times."

"It's one of the reasons you're so effective in the Middle East. But this time you're heading into the lion's den, the Islamic Republic of Iran. A theocracy with malignant disdain for Westerners, particularly Americans. And you're going up against a bad dude. Be careful, my friend. Keep in touch. Your phone works anywhere and has the best encryption there is."

Jarrett suddenly felt a chill running through him.

Would Demus finally prevail, or would Jarrett spend the rest of his life in Evin prison?

He ended the call without another word and Googled Erich Meyer on his laptop.

The elder Meyer had died in 1996 in Berlin at age ninety-four. He was a lifelong, second-generation communist. Jarrett wondered how he'd lived so long simmering in that fetid ideologic stew.

The official picture of Meyer as deputy minister of state security of the German Democratic Republic showed an intense man with a scowl and malevolent eyes. There were no distinguishing features other than hard angles to his face and a high forehead with a receding hairline.

With no mention of a son named Dietz, Jarrett figured Demus's mother had been his father's mistress. Meyer had lived in Russia for a period of time when he was in his fifties. If Dietz was born then, he was about sixty now. How much he resembled his father was another question.

Jarrett's missions always involved highly detailed intelligence. The target's physical description was critical. For most contract assassins, killing the wrong person was all in a day's work. For Jarrett it was the worst error imaginable.

But the Tehran mission was different.

He knew exactly where Demus would be on June 2—on Iran Air flight 1645 to Tehran. He even knew Demus's seat assignment. But he didn't know what Demus looked like. If Demus's seat assignment changed at the last minute, Jarrett could target the wrong person.

The name Crown popped into his head. He envisioned a company logo on the side of a long black limo.

He called Sedgewick.

"Add a good camera with a telephoto lens to my kit. Not a teeny, weeny spy camera either, something a tourist into photography would carry. Have the kit with the camera delivered here as soon as possible. I'll fly to London with it, then connect to Istanbul the same day. I need two days there, then on to Tehran."

"What the hell are you up to in Istanbul?"

"I'll take a photograph of Demus before he gets on the plane and send it to you. If his seat changes, I'll know."

"If you don't hear from me, Demus is in 1G. But if his seat assignment changes at check-in or the gate we won't know. Not enough time to eavesdrop and get back to you," Sedgewick said.

"Got it. If I know what he looks like it won't matter. And don't forget the little tracker."

"I won't. The tech guys put together a clever way to get it through security. You'll like it. Good luck."

"Thanks."

The critical piece of intel was the Crown limo to the airport.

Jarrett's plan was set.

CHAPTER 18

Jarrett's Arabic was crisp, but his Farsi wasn't as good, so he spent his mornings listening to tapes at the University of Edinburgh library and working on his accent.

The documents for Jarrett's legend—Thomas Davis—arrived via courier. Included was a passport stamped with the date he was to arrive in London from Toronto and a robust travel history. There was a Canadian driver's license, credit cards, an ATM card from a Toronto bank, a national health insurance card, business cards for Microscan Corporation with an 800 number, four thousand American dollars in cash, a camera with a zoom lens, and the tracker. A call to the 800 number went to Langley where Davis's "boss" would answer. There was also a Microscan website for the internet curious.

Jarrett's secure satellite phone worked through a special network at Langley. The phone looked exactly like an iPhone but had two operating systems. The first opened with a password like any iPhone. It had standard cell service with text messaging and e-mail, and a number of common apps. The techs at Langley would switch his service from a UK to a Canadian carrier.

The second system was accessed by opening the Extras app on the first system, tapping the calculator icon, and adding the numerical date—day and month—together. Two icons flashed on the screen, one for the program that interfaced with the tracking device Jarrett would put on Demus's briefcase and the second for the satellite phone equipped with a new reflective technology with ultra-encryption developed at NSA. It was impossible to ping the call or eavesdrop on a conversation. His laptop had two operating systems in the same configuration as the phone.

Jarrett was in awe of the little tracker. It was the size of a dime but thinner and had a solar battery and one sticky side. The appearance of the tiny disc under x-ray—a jumble of wires and dots—would raise the curiosity of airport security. But the techies at Langley had found a spot for it on the underside of his laptop. When scanned, the tracker circuitry appeared as an integral part of the computer.

Demus's movements would be displayed on a map of Tehran on Jarrett's phone or laptop. When Demus met with his contact in the Revolutionary Guard, Jarrett would know. The only caveat was that Demus had to carry his briefcase to the meeting. Jarrett hoped to get a photograph of the contact and identify him through the CIA's visual recognition software. That would forego a nasty interrogation of Demus. Either way the Russian was a dead man.

* * *

Jarrett flew from Edinburgh to London on British Airways with his bona fides for the Davis legend, his airline tickets, and hotel confirmations in Istanbul and Tehran in his carry-on bag. The tracker was taped to the underside of his laptop. In the Heathrow terminal he passed his Sussfield documents to a CIA contact. He hoped he'd never have to use them again.

He checked in with British Airways in Heathrow for his flight to Istanbul using the Davis passport. The flight took two hours and forty-five minutes. The ride was smooth, and the plane arrived on time. The arrival gate was in the international terminal. Two days later his flight to Tehran would leave from there. He cleared passport control and customs without difficulty.

After a recent terrorist bombing in the Istanbul airport, security was tight, or at least it appeared that way. Armed guards in military fatigues with automatic rifles were everywhere. People were stopped and searched at random, particularly young men with long coats and backpacks.

He passed the Iran Air check-in counter and walked out of the terminal at the departure level. The Crown limousine would stop at curbside here. Luckily, a five-level, open-air garage was directly opposite the terminal.

He crossed the roadway and took an elevator to the second floor. An excellent vantage point to surveil the international terminal entrance was adjacent to the elevators.

He returned to the terminal, hopped a shuttle to the car rental center, and rented a VW Jetta.

He drove the rental into the airport and parked it in the garage near the elevators. Then he took a taxi to the Hotel Amira and registered with the Davis identification. A careful check of his room revealed no bugs.

Two blocks from the hotel he found a camera shop and bought a tripod, a spare memory card, and an anti-glare lens cover. He had played with the camera in Scotland and found it took sharp long-distance photographs. On the way back to the hotel he bought a small cooler and a six-pack of bottled water.

After a delicious dinner of *kuzu tandir* with rice and yogurt, a bowl of *gullac* for dessert, and two glasses of Barbare Elegance syrah in the hotel restaurant, he slept like a baby.

* * *

Late the next morning Jarrett taxied to the airport with the camera, tripod, and the cooler filled with bottled water on ice. The driver dropped him in front of the international terminal and he rode an elevator to the second level of the garage. He set up the camera on the tripod, focused it on the terminal entrance, and sat down on the cooler.

A few minutes later a security guard appeared. He was an older man dressed in a blue uniform with a cap embroidered with SECURITY and a tarnished brass badge pinned to his shirt. His face was stamped with years of cigarettes and alcohol.

Jarrett volunteered that he was a struggling paparazzo commissioned to photograph a famous Italian singer who would arrive from Rome. The man graciously accepted twenty lira and a cold bottle of water. When he disappeared, Jarrett put the camera, tripod, and cooler in the Jetta's trunk and took a taxi back to the hotel.

CHAPTER 19

At 11:00 a.m. the next morning Jarrett checked in at Iran Air. The agent was a bubbly young woman in uniform with a black scarf barely framing her face. He told her he was on flight 1645 and presented his Davis passport. When he said he had no bags to check, she looked at him curiously.

As she handed him a boarding pass, she said there was no priority line for first-class passengers in the security hall. She added that he could wait in the airline lounge until boarding. It was quiet and comfortable with complimentary coffee and pastries along with newspapers and magazines.

Jarrett thanked her and glanced at the boarding pass. He was in seat 3G. If Demus took his assigned seat, Jarrett was two rows behind him. Sedgewick had come through again.

As Jarrett hustled toward the terminal entrance, he heard the agent's voice. "Mr. Davis."

He stopped and turned.

"Security is that way," she said pointing in the opposite direction.

"Oh, I was just going out to smoke. Thank you."

Jarrett crossed the roadway and rode an elevator to the second floor. He put his carry-on bag in the Jetta trunk and retrieved the camera, tripod, and cooler. It was a bright day with no cloud cover. He fastened the anti-glare cover to the lens and secured the camera to the tripod.

He figured Demus would arrive two hours before the flight. It was 11:25 a.m. He sat on the cooler and waited in the shadows.

The security guard appeared again. After they exchanged pleasantries, Jarrett remarked that the celebrity hadn't shown yesterday, but today was the day. The guard accepted twenty lira and a bottle of water but complained that it wasn't cold. He slinked off with a wry smile on his face.

Jarrett had found an elaborate Crown Limousine website on the internet. The vehicles pictured had a gold emperor's crown on the front doors. Jarrett's fear was that Demus would exit the vehicle without turning. That meant his clothing, likely his shirt, would be the only way to identify him. And Jarrett wouldn't have a facial for Sedgewick.

Demus's arrival unfolded quickly.

Jarrett was ready.

A Mercedes sedan with dark tints and a gold emperor's crown on the front doors pulled to the curb. When Jarrett focused the camera, the entire vehicle was in the field.

After the car's hazard lights flashed, the driver stepped out and opened the trunk. He removed a large suitcase and gestured to a nearby porter. Jarrett wondered what he would do if Demus didn't have a briefcase.

The driver opened the rear curbside door, and Demus stepped from the car. He was broad shouldered and half a head taller than the driver. He turned to survey the surroundings, the natural instinct of a paranoid bad guy worried about a sniper.

When Demus's eyes panned across the garage, Jarrett recorded three shots on the memory card. *Click. Click. Click.* With the noonday sun in his face, he congratulated himself for using an anti-glare lens cover.

Demus put on a straw fedora with a black band, slipped on a pair of dark glasses and strode imperiously into the terminal. The porter followed with the suitcase. Jarrett snapped a fourth frame and retreated to the backseat of the Jetta.

On the frontal shots Demus looked nothing like his infamous father, more like an aging, pretty-boy Russian mobster. He had thick, straw-colored hair that looked artificially colored, bushy eyebrows, and large, deep-set gray eyes. The skin on his face was stretched tight with prominent folds tenting the edges of his nose. His lips were full.

Too full for a man.

Jarrett figured Demus had undergone cosmetic surgery—a lot of it. Probably a face lift, a nose job, and work on his lips. He wondered why. To look younger or to change his appearance for some devious reason? *Maybe both.*

On the fourth photograph, Demus's backside was considerably wider at the middle. A white silk shirt hung over baggy black slacks.

As Jarrett studied the backside shot, he breathed a sigh of relief. A leather messenger bag was slung over Demus's shoulder.

He removed the memory card from the camera, put it in his wallet, and replaced it with the new one. He would e-mail the pictures to Sedgewick from Tehran. The new card had touristy photographs of Istanbul he had taken yesterday.

Jarrett quickly sanitized the car and wiped down the tripod, cooler, and car keys. He put the keys in the ignition, the tripod and cooler in the trunk, retrieved his carry-on bag, and stowed the camera in it. He took an elevator to the departure level, walked through the terminal to the security hall, and took a position in a long queue.

The man in front of Jarrett caught his attention.

He was swarthy looking and was nervously fidgeting with an aluminum case.

In the U.S. he would have beeen swarmed by TSA agents.

A security agent stopped the man before the x-ray scanner. The case was swabbed for explosives and opened. Jarrett was surprised it held an old fashioned box-style camera with a large flash. The camera jogged Jarrett's memory back to one of his favorite television programs as a child—reruns of the 1950's *Superman* series.

When the camera owner cleared security, he nodded to someone in line behind Jarrett, then joined a man near the exit. They walked off together.

Jarrett removed his laptop from his carry-on and placed it in a plastic tray. The tracker was taped to its bottom. He put his carry-on and the tray with the laptop on the conveyor and walked through the passenger scanner. When the laptop disappeared in the scanner the conveyor stopped moving.

The agent monitoring the scanner was studying it. Jarrett focused on him. The agent's eyes stayed fixed on the screen and didn't move. Seconds later the conveyor began moving again.

Jarrett breathed a sigh of relief. *Clear.*

On the way to the gate he passed the airline lounge. Demus would be there.

Five minutes before boarding Demus appeared with the messenger bag.

During boarding there were two people between Jarrett and Demus. The attendant directed Demus to the port aisle and the two behind him to starboard. Jarrett showed his boarding pass to the attendant and she gestured for him to follow Demus.

Demus sat down, placed his bag at his feet, opened it, and took out a laptop.

Jarrett removed his laptop from his carry-on and put the bag in the compartment above Demus.

A woman with dark glasses was already in the seat next to him. She was very attractive. Stunning. *Was she Princess Fathima?* When he slid into his seat, she turned away ever so slightly, but enough to send a message. *Don't bother me.* After fussing with her head scarf and removing her glasses, she opened her handbag and took out a breath mint and a copy of *Elle*. She smelled of expensive French perfume and a hint of cigarettes. A shopping bag from Le Bon Marche was at her feet.

A flight attendant gave Demus a glass of champagne and reminded him to put his bag overhead before takeoff.

Jarrett and the woman accepted champagne as well. Once the plane left Turkish airspace, there'd be no alcohol served. He finished his in two gulps; she nursed hers.

When boarding was complete, Demus put his messenger bag in the overhead compartment above him.

Jarrett was poised and ready.

He removed the tracking device from the bottom of his laptop, peeled off the protective covering on the sticky surface, and stepped forward. After he slipped his laptop into his bag, he slid his hand under Demus's bag and pressed the tracker against the bottom. *Done.* He shut the compartment, sat down, and fastened his seatbelt. The woman next to him was intent on her champagne and magazine.

Jarrett put in AirPods and selected the iTunes app on his phone.

He closed his eyes and stretched out.

Delbert McClinton was up.

CHAPTER 20

Tehran, later that day

Mogadan's driver weaved in and out of traffic, cutting into the oncoming lane and running red lights with regularity. A red lamp on the dash flashed, and he used his horn like a New York hack. Jarrett felt important.

He had missed the meeting to pick up his secondary legend. It was essential if he had to go black in Tehran. Twice in the past he had used one, most recently in Washington after the spy's contract was taken out on him.

Today the meeting was to be at the train station in Rah Ahan Square, exactly three hours after his flight arrived. The contact would have waited thirty minutes. When Jarrett didn't show, the meeting was aborted.

Jarrett would have Sedgewick set up another meeting. He had other things to discuss with his friend as well, and he had to e-mail the photographs of Dietz Meyer.

His carry-on bag was on the seat next to him. The first thing he had done when he got in the car was remove his passport. Both his passport and visa had entry stamps. The letters from Mogadan were tucked in a side pocket.

He opened Mogadan's letter first. It was typed on official stationary in both Farsi and English and signed by the general. The English translation was choppy and filled with spelling errors, but it conveyed the gist of what the general had said. When Jarrett used it, the secret police would know exactly where he was.

Clever.

Jarrett figured the second envelope held a copy of Mogadan's letter, one he could use in lieu of the original.

He was wrong.

It was a handwritten note in beautiful calligraphic script. It read:

My Dear Mr. Davis,

How do I thank you for what you did today?
Please join me for dinner tonight.
The penthouse at Senator Palace in Zafaraniyeh.
9:00 p.m. Casual dress.
I look forward to seeing you.

Ziba Vijany—the woman next to you on flight 1645.

A dinner invitation from the aloof woman in black. Jarrett was surprised. Laila had said Ziba Vijany was important but she didn't know why. If the head of the secret police delivered a personal note from her she had to be *very* important . . . or she was one of his agents.

Jarrett glanced at his chronograph. It was 6:45 p.m.

Then he remembered he hadn't set it to Iran time. He turned the dial ahead to 8:15 p.m.

He chuckled to himself. His curiosity was eating away at him.

He had a lot to do before 9:00 p.m.

CHAPTER 21

Jarrett presented Mogadan's letter at the Espinas reception desk. They were anxiously awaiting his arrival. The manager appeared with a full entourage in tow, and after a glass of orange juice and an effusive welcome, Jarrett was escorted to his room. His passport stayed in his bag and he never signed anything. He felt important. Again.

His room was a corner suite on the eighth floor. It had a sitting area with a giant flat-screen television, a spacious bedroom with a king-sized bed, and a bath with a Jacuzzi tub and walk-in shower. There were decks off the living room and bedroom. The décor was traditional Persian—heavy, ornate wood furniture with Persian rugs scattered over marble floors. He didn't like it one bit—too many nooks and crannies in which to hide cameras and microphones. But the room smelled of orange blossoms and came with a complimentary bowl of fruit, two bottles of Evian water, and to his surprise, a bottle of Chateau Duhart Milon 2016 on a small dining table.

A quick once-over revealed no bugs, but he wished he had a CIA electronic sniffer.

The woman in black, Ziba Vijany, was front and center in his head. He googled her but found nothing. The Senator Palace's website showed a ten-story building that looked like an Austrian castle. One of the units was for sale. He followed a link to a real estate website, where the 350 m2 unit with four bedrooms and five baths was offered for the equivalent of 7.9 million U.S. dollars.

Ziba Vijany is either one very rich woman, or she had married well, he thought. *But why nothing on the internet?*

Next he e-mailed the photographs of Demus to Sedgewick. His laptop began to beep which meant it was being scanned, but the encryption program protected the transmission.

He took a quick shower and dressed. On his way out he hung the Do Not Disturb sign on the door and attached a tiny sliver of clear tape across the top of the doorjamb.

When he stepped off the elevator in the lobby, two men in dark suits were waiting. They smiled but said nothing and followed him out of the hotel as if they were his bodyguards.

Although Jarrett was now a national hero in Iran, he was on the secret police's watch list. Because he knew it and they knew it, there was no reason to be sneaky about following him.

It was a glorious evening with clear skies. The city was alive with young people crowding the sidewalks and bumper-to-bumper traffic on the boulevard fronting the hotel. Many of the cars were expensive European models—BMW, Audi, Mercedes, and Jaguar—with a baby-faced driver smoking and listening to music.

Were the U.S. sanctions really working? Jarrett couldn't help but wonder.

He paused to access the special operating system on his phone. He needed to contact Sedgewick. Mogadan knew he had a cell phone with Canadian service, and that he hadn't purchased an Iranian burner yet. Canadian cell service wasn't compatible with Iranian service. If the babysitters reported he used his cell phone while walking, a sharp agent at headquarters might connect the dots. The only way Davis could complete a call was with a satellite phone. Mogadan's suspicion that Davis was a foreign agent would rachet up a notch.

Jarrett hoped the Iranians wouldn't piece the phone puzzle together. By noon tomorrow he'd have a burner. He dialed Sedgewick's number and began walking.

"Jarrett, you're in Tehran walking up Keshavarz Boulevard. I've been following you. You went directly from the airport to the Ministry of Intelligence's headquarters then to the Hotel Espinas. You're supposed to be at the Shahr. We got a lot of noise over here about an attempted hijacking of your flight from Istanbul. What the hell have you been up to my friend?"

Jarrett detailed the incident on the airplane and the interrogation at the Ministry of Intelligence. Sedgewick told him that the photographs of Demus were already sent for comparison to their file photos.

71

Then Jarrett said, "What I don't understand is why Mogadan suddenly declared me a national hero with carte blanche in Tehran. I was treated like royalty at the hotel. I fully expected to be detained. But here I am, walking along with two babysitters following me. I suppose if I confronted them, they'd say they're my bodyguards."

"No need to be cute," Sedgewick said. "Leave them alone. Dump them when you need to."

"I have a feeling there's something else going on. Mogadan gave me two envelopes. One was his letter proclaiming me a national hero. The other was a handwritten note from the woman who sat next to me on the plane, the one I told you alerted me about the hijacking. It was a dinner invitation." Jarrett glanced at his watch. "I'm supposed to be at her place now."

"Are you going?"

"Of course I'm going. I'm curious as hell about her."

"Mogadan is a major player over there. He has a degree in political science from Columbia."

The eyes tell all, Jarrett thought.

"He told me he was head of the Ministry of Intelligence. I never suspected he had an Ivy League education," Jarrett went on. "I missed the meeting in the train station. You need to set up another. I have a sneaking suspicion I'll need the secondary legend and kit. Maybe throw in a 9-mil just in case."

"We got one for you. Extra ammo too. I'll e-mail new instructions as soon as I hook up with your contact. What does the woman from the plane look like?"

"Drop-dead gorgeous. But full of herself, like a lot of beautiful women. For some reason she didn't want to connect with me on the plane, even after I took out the hijackers. She lives in an expensive condo. The flight purser told me she's someone important, but didn't know why. She must be well-connected if the head of the Ministry of Intelligence delivered a personal note from her. Her name's Ziba Vijany." Jarrett spelled it. "At this point she's a bit of a mystery. See what you can dig up on her."

"You have a knack for attracting the beautiful, mysterious ones."

"My goal tonight is to find out who she is and how she knows Mogadan."

"That's all?"

"That's all."

"After what you did on the plane, Mogadan's suspicions about you must be off the charts. And let me tell you, he's one smart *hombre*. It might be a honey trap," Sedgewick said.

"Been there and done that. Several times."

Sedgewick laughed. "Oh, do I know. E-mail a pic of her if you can. Might help us identify her."

"You just want to see what she looks like."

"Of course." Sedgewick laughed.

"I'll be in touch."

"Be safe, my friend."

CHAPTER 22

When Jarrett ended the call and turned around to walk back to the hotel, the babysitters stopped dead in their tracks. As he passed them, they stepped to the curb and looked away.

Moments after he had the doorman order a taxi, a non-descript sedan appeared. The babysitters got in it, as Jarrett gave directions to the taxi driver. The car followed him.

After a ten-minute ride to the Austrian castle, the taxi was met by a thick-necked man in a dark suit with an earbud and a bulge under his arm. He inspected the vehicle inside and out with a flashlight, checked under it with a scanner, then opened the door for Jarrett and gestured to the building's entrance.

A doorman escorted Jarrett across a spacious lobby to a bank of elevators. A massive crystal chandelier cast spires of light on alabaster walls with giant seashell sconces. With polished aqua-blue marble floors and lights twinkling overhead, Jarrett imagined he was walking on water under the stars.

A clone of the man outside stopped Jarrett at the elevators and asked to see his identification. He studied the Canadian passport and frisked Jarrett.

When he nodded and stepped away, the doorman pushed the up button on an elevator.

It had no floor buttons inside, and Jarrett rode to the tenth floor wondering about the guards. Were they security for the building or for one of the tenants?

When the elevator opened, Jarrett stepped into a mirrored anteroom. A *rich man's mudroom,* he thought.

A woman stood across from him. She wore a black sleeveless blouse, flesh-hugging black slacks, and black skyscraper heels. Her arms were toned and her legs long and muscled like a swimmer's. A gold braided chain with a ruby inset into a scarab hung from her neck, and giant hoop earrings dangled from her ears.

Was this the woman next to him on the plane? She'd worn a diamond and a wedding band. This woman had no jewelry on either hand.

The eyes were the same, dark and almond-shaped, but now molten with blue eye shadow and mascara accents. Her long black hair sparkled in the mirrored light, flowing over her shoulder in a twist with a gold sash around it.

The word *byoodefel*—beautiful—flashed in Jarrett's head. It was one of the first words he'd learned in Farsi. Jana used it often to describe Jarrett's mother.

There was nothing mysterious about *this* woman. With her hands on her hips and her head tilted to the side she had a felicitous air of unpretentious confidence, as if she understood she was beautiful, but found no need to flaunt it.

She can't be Ziba Vijani, he thought.

"Sorry. I have the wrong apartment," he blurted.

"You don't remember me, Mr. Davis? I sat next to you on the plane. I'm Ziba," she said in perfect English and kissed him on the cheek.

"Without a scarf I didn't recognize you. You look different."

"Well, I hope you like what you see."

Was she kidding?

"I'm late. I apologize. It's been a hectic day."

She laughed. "To say the least. I'm surprised you were able to make it after all you went through. Come in. I've been waiting for you."

A woman dressed in a black chador with a white apron closed the door behind them.

"This is my friend Bita."

"Hello, Bita," Jarrett said extending his hand.

The woman cowered and scurried off without a word.

"Bita's shy around men, particularly Western men. Let's have a drink. A toast."

Jarrett couldn't take his eyes off Ziba.

She touched his arm. "Are you all right, Mr. Davis?"

"Oh yes, of course. Please call me Clint . . . err Thomas."

"Clint?" she asked curiously.

"No, my name is Thomas, Thomas Davis."

Get control of yourself, he thought. *You've rubbed elbows with the uberrich and beautiful before.*

She raised an eyebrow and said, "I'm having scotch. What would you like?"

"Bourbon over ice, please."

"Blanton's?"

"Of course. One of my favorites."

"And just one ice cube. I overheard your drink order on the plane after you dealt with the hijackers."

When Jarrett's eyes finally left her, the living room came into focus.

Except for the polished, beige tile floors, the room was a colorama of Egyptian royal blue and gold. One wall had hieroglyphic panels, another a painting of the great pyramids with camels in the foreground, and the third a Luxor column bookcase on either side of an upright sarcophagus. The coffee table was a glass panel held up by a three-headed sculpture of Tut. The room was spectacular, but tasteful.

She fixed his drink and sat down next to him. When he raised his glass to take a sip, she blocked his arm.

"First a toast," she said clicking his glass. "To Thomas Davis, our national hero."

Jarrett swirled the bourbon in the glass, took a mouthful, and swallowed hard. The whiskey burned his throat jettisoning him back to the moment with a stark reminder that he didn't know this woman. He needed to be careful.

"Thank you. You are kind to have me for dinner."

"It's the very least I can do. Everyone on flight 1645 thanks you, the passengers, the crew, and most of all me. I never saw you after we were evacuated. I wanted to thank you. I understand you stayed on board and defused the bomb."

How did she know? he wondered.

"I did. It was actually pretty easy."

"I must say, the way you took down the hijackers made me think you've had martial arts training."

"Just a little when I was younger."

"I did judo for a while. It's popular in Iran. The way you handled yourself, you must be a black belt. Maybe karate."

Smart lady.

Jarrett smiled, but said nothing.

She shook her head and grimaced. "I am very grateful to you. The thought of rotting in a cell in north Africa was not appealing. The Saudis are real bastards."

How did she know the hijackers were Saudis?

"Well, I did only what I had to. Weekending in Somalia didn't appeal to me either."

"So tell me about yourself. You represent a medical equipment company?"

How did she know that? We never talked on the airplane.

"Yes, I'm in sales. Body scanners. I'll make calls on hospitals."

"Is this your first trip to Tehran?"

"Yes. It's not quite what I expected."

"What *did* you expect?" she asked, a slight edge to her voice.

"A city less cosmopolitan and a lot less friendly," Jarrett said.

"Most Iranians are lovely people. We fear domination by the U.S. But you have to remember, you're our national hero, so you'll get special treatment."

"I thought Iran sought destruction of America."

"No. That's the radical government and the crazies in the streets. The Iranian revolution was necessary to end the puppet relationship with the U.S. Unfortunately, since then we haven't done well. To say the least. And with the sanctions, we're struggling. Like most people in Iran, I'm vehemently against theocratic governance. A democracy like the U.S. with separation of religion and state is best. We'll have it one day, I hope and pray." She touched his arm. "Sorry, Thomas, I don't mean to lecture you. This topic is very dear to my heart."

"I understand." He looked around. "Your apartment is beautiful. I feel like I'm in an Egyptian museum."

"You are . . . sort of," she said smiling. "I majored in anthropology in college with a focus on Egyptology, specifically the Twentieth Dynasty and Ramses VI. My doctoral thesis was an interpretation of one of the panels in his tomb. As a matter of fact, that one," she said pointing to the wall behind Jarrett. "What did you major in?"

"I didn't go to college," he lied. "I enlisted in the military after high school."

Her eyes suddenly dropped, and she forced a smile.

"So you *do* have special training. I thought so."

"A little. Everyone in our military has combat training."

"You must be famished, Thomas. Let's eat. Bita prepared a traditional Iranian dinner for you. Come."

CHAPTER 23

The dining room table and sideboard were gold, the high-backed chairs upholstered in lush blue velvet. Spectacular hand-painted desert murals covered the walls, and the ceiling looked like the night sky with tiny pinpoints of light. For an instant Jarrett imagined he was a pharaoh crossing the desert under the stars with his beautiful queen.

Bita was a culinary wizard. She whisked in an out of the kitchen, serving kabob seasoned with turmeric accompanied by *doogh*, a mix of yogurt, mint, and diced cucumber. Side dishes included charred tomatoes, rice sprinkled with sumac, a parsley salad, and flatbread. And for dessert there was homemade Persian ice cream—*bastani sonnati*. Jarrett's housekeeper cooked Iranian dishes. He knew the fare well.

After dinner they sat in the living room, where Bita served *arak* over ice. With each sip Ziba nudged closer to Jarrett until their thighs touched.

"You speak our language fluently, Thomas. And Arabic. I heard you on the plane."

"My mother is Lebanese. When I was growing up our housekeeper was Persian. They taught me."

"They taught you well." She turned to him and playfully pinched his thigh.

"Are you trying to bring back bad memories of the plane, Ziba?"

"Just trying to get your attention again."

They laughed.

"That's the first time you've used my name. I love the way you say it."

Sedgewick was right. It's a honey trap.

"Well, Ziba, I'm glad you like it." He deliberately spoke her name again.

"You're quite the enigma, Thomas."

"Why?"

"You speak two difficult languages fluently, although you never went to college. You're a martial arts master, no matter what you say. And you look like a movie star. I see a lot of Clint Eastwood in you, back when he played Dirty Harry. You're tall with long, wavy hair and you have that don't-fuck-with-me aura about you. And I'm told a lot more went on after you defused the bomb."

"You flatter me, undeservedly." Then Jarrett looked at her and grinned. "You're an enigma as well."

"I am? Why do you say that?"

"You weren't very friendly on the plane."

"I was scared to death, Thomas, if you want to know the truth. And you were sound asleep."

"I wasn't asleep. I was listening to music," he said.

"When I saw those two in the galley, I thought I was going die. I had to do some yoga relaxation techniques."

"Alternate nostril breathing?"

"You noticed. It helps. And I was worried after you throttled the two that there were other bad ones on the plane."

"You were right."

"But you took care of them as well. I must confess, when I'm out and about I have a protective wall around me. I don't like to get hit on by men. I was in Paris shopping the last couple of days and I had two different men, both nice-looking and well-dressed, walk up to me on the street and ask me to have a drink. When I'm seated next to a man on a plane, it can get awkward. I wear a wedding band and diamond to make it look like I'm married. It helps to hold off the wolves. You must have the same problem with women."

"Occasionally. Some women can be very aggressive. But you weren't one of them. As a matter of fact, you were very aloof."

A sheepish grin came across her face. "That was then, Thomas, this is now." She stroked his arm. "I have another question for you, if you don't mind."

"Of course."

"Are you married?"

"You're right." Jarrett smiled. "You *are* being a little more aggressive now than you were on the plane."

"Of course. Like I said, that was then, this is now. Different circumstances. I know who you are, at least I think I do, and you're not hitting on me. I suppose you could say I'm hitting on you."

"I'm not married. I came close once, a long time ago."

"I find it hard to believe that some woman hasn't sunk her claws into you. Are you in a serious relationship?"

Jarrett's life since college had been nothing but casual relationships and a bunch of one-night stands.

"No. Are you married?"

"No. Divorced. Two years now. Before you ask, no children."

Jarrett was beginning to feel uneasy. This conversation was going where he didn't want it to go. He stood and looked down at her. "I'd better run now. I have a busy day ahead of me."

"How about a tour of our city tomorrow? Tell you what, I'll be at the Espinas at one o'clock. That way you won't have to worry about coming here."

Mogadan told her where I'm staying.

Jarrett thought for a second. He needed to stay focused on Demus, but this woman intrigued him. *Who is she?* "Like I said, I have a busy day tomorrow. Sorry."

"Doing what, Thomas?"

"I'm going to visit a few hospitals."

"Which ones? I have contacts. I can help you."

"Oh, I have the list in my room."

"Okay," she said with an incredulous look. "A friend is stopping by tomorrow evening for drinks and dinner. I'd love to have you meet him. And we can do the tour the following day."

"That'll work." Although he was wary of her, his curiosity had taken over. "Thanks for dinner and a wonderful evening."

"Seven o'clock tomorrow night then," she said as she stood up.

She took his hand and they walked to the elevator. When the door opened, she turned to him and looked into his eyes.

"Kiss me goodnight, Thomas. And hold me tight."

CHAPTER 24

Sedgewick had forwarded the CIA contact's e-mail. The transfer of the secondary legend and kit would occur at 10:15 a.m. in the same train station. Jarrett would have to shake the babysitters.

Mogadan and his agents knew that Jarrett only had a carry-on bag. Strolling into the Espinas with a full-sized suitcase the day after his arrival would raise eyebrows. Even if he got by the babysitters through a side entrance, cameras monitored the hotel.

Transferring a mission kit in a foreign country presented two problems for Jarrett.

The first was discovery. It meant arrest, a diplomatic brouhaha, and a mug shot on cable news.

The second was the possibility the contact would recognize him from his time with JSOC. With Jarrett's military record expunged from all government databases, only Sedgewick and the president knew who he was, and he wanted to keep it that way.

Jarrett was curious about Demus, so he accessed the tracking history in his phone. Demus had left the airport shortly after 6:00 p.m. and traveled to the Parsian Hotel on Chamran Highway. He'd stayed at the hotel until 8:30 and then went to an apartment building on Ghandi Street. It took him fifteen minutes to get there. At 9:15 he was in the Tong Café three blocks west on Ghandi. He'd left there at 10:45 and was still at the Ghandi Street address. It was now after midnight.

The first call Demus had made to Tehran before his trip was to a residential landline. He'd left a message. Jarrett wondered if the call had gone to an apartment in the Ghandi Street building. Perhaps to a lady friend?

Jarrett googled the Parsian Hotel and found glowing reviews. Directly across from it was a three-star property called the Grand Hotel. He wrote down the address and telephone number.

Although he'd found no bugs in the room, he went into the bathroom, closed the door, and turned on the shower. It was late afternoon in Washington. Sedgewick would probably still be at Langley. He dialed his cell.

"Jarrett, you caught me going out the door. What the hell is that noise? Sounds like Niagara Falls."

"I'm in the bathroom. Shower's running, just to be safe. You in the office?"

"Yes. Why?"

"I need the name of my secondary legend."

"Let's see. You're Marwan Elias from Ankara. Deal in carpets. Wholesale only. You're traveling to Tehran by train. You enter at the Kapitoy Gate. Well, I'll be damned, you're on the train right now." Sedgewick laughed. "I thought you might prefer a train after all the trouble you had on the flight from Istanbul. We've picked up more intel on it. Seems four terrorists died. You were a busy man, Jarrett."

"I told you what happened. I don't remember defusing the bomb or leaving the plane."

"You were in a fugue state. Killed the other three. Another possibility of course is the Iranians did it, and they're giving you credit to cover themselves."

"That's a thought. What time does the train arrive?"

"Nine forty a.m."

"Perfect," Jarrett said.

"How's the Persian gal?" Sedgewick asked.

"Stunning. Much more friendly than on the plane. Knows how to dress and put on makeup. And she's quite the lady. To use your words, a showcase of femininity."

Sedgewick laughed. "Ah, yes, another Julie Crichton. The rich snob from Carnegie Hill. The only woman ever to jilt Clint Jarrett the Ivy League hockey stud."

At the mention of Julie, Jarrett's spirits sank. She was the only woman he had ever loved . . . or thought he loved. They were classmates in college and were engaged in Manhattan over Christmas break their senior year. Jarrett had been playing in a hockey tournament in Madison Square Garden.

Her uberrich family had thrown a memorable engagement party at Daniel for a hundred guests. Julie had called off the engagement in April after months of unsuccessfully trying to convince Jarrett to work for her father. She'd even agreed to quit smoking if he moved to New York after graduation. Jarrett had been crushed. A week later he'd enlisted in the air force.

"I didn't want to live in Manhattan and be one of her father's gofers. And she wouldn't move to South Dakota and live on the Capistran Ranch."

"You'd be a gizillionare now, pal, running the Crichton empire. Her father just died. It made *The Post*. He was an older gent, in his fifties when she was born. And she was an only child, like you."

"That's too bad about her father. He was a nice man. I've got a busy morning tomorrow with the kit transfer. Then dinner again at Ziba's. She wants me to meet a friend of her's."

"Be careful. It sounds like she's working you pretty good."

"Have you got anything on her yet?" Jarrett asked.

"Nothing. And that's surprising. We could dredge up dirt on the cleaning lady in your hotel if we wanted to."

"Maybe because she's in the secret police. She knows my entire Davis legend, what happened in the plane after I dealt with the hijackers, and my new hotel."

"Like I said, be careful."

"I will."

Jarrett called the Grand Hotel and made a reservation for Marwan Elias. He explained he would arrive by train from Ankara in the morning and would stay for seven days. He asked for a room facing the street. There was one available on the third floor.

CHAPTER 25

Jarrett was up early.

After two cups of black coffee in the hotel he converted four hundred dollars to rials at the front desk. At thirty-one thousand for each dollar he had twelve million rials in his pocket.

I'm a millionaire, he thought, as he walked out of the hotel with two babysitters behind him.

Across from the hotel was an upscale, four-level shopping mall. He causally strolled the perimeter and discovered a men's shop that had an outside entrance on a side street. There was a taxi stand nearby.

He circled the block and walked into the mall. There were elevators and escalators at each end of the atrium. Half the stores were boarded up and very few shoppers were about.

Maybe the sanctions were working after all, he thought.

After studying the mall directory, he bought a baggy white sweater and a black scarf in a department store. The babysitters stood nearby, not particularly attentive. After all, their national hero was within reach. One was a chain-smoker and the other played with his cell phone.

He purchased a burner on the fourth level making sure the babysitters saw him. After an escalator ride to the main floor, he went into the men's shop. The window displays blocked the view from the mall's atrium.

The babysitters upped their game, stationing themselves at the shop entrance—one on each side of the door.

After a few minutes perusing shirts, Jarrett slipped into a changing room. He put on the white sweater and wrapped the scarf around his head. He was in a taxi before the babysitters realized he was gone.

* * *

At 10:13 a.m., Jarrett sat opposite a newsstand in the train station, looking up at the giant wall clock. When the clock struck 10:15, he dialed a number on his new burner.

The phone rang four times, followed by three beeps, and then a recording. He heard, "You have reached 031-77514832. This number has been disconnected."

The number wasn't the one he had dialed. He added a one to each of the last four digits and dialed that number. A man answered and said, "Thirty-seven," and the call disconnected.

The second call went to the contact signaling that Jarrett was in the terminal.

Jarrett waited ten minutes then hustled across the main lobby and followed a side corridor to a men's room with a "Closed for Cleaning" sign at the door.

Despite the sign Jarrett entered the bathroom. It was empty. A tiny black dot in the right upper corner of the mirror over the sink signaled the pickup was a "hot go."

He found a key taped under the sink. The number stamped into it had been filed off.

He found locker thirty-seven in the basement, opened it with the key, and retrieved a suitcase.

* * *

Jarrett registered as Marwan Elias at the Grand Hotel and paid cash for seven nights. After the clerk copied the first page of his Turkish passport, Jarrett tipped him and was upgraded to a junior suite on the street side of the hotel.

The room was small with a double bed, a table with a single chair, and a tub-shower combo in a small bathroom. Jarrett groaned when he discovered the showerhead was at the level of his Adam's apple. If this was an upgrade, he wondered what the regular rooms were like. But there was an excellent view of Demus's hotel across the street.

He carefully removed the electronic sniffer from the bag. It was designed to look like a cell phone. He turned it on, feigned making a call, and walked about chattering into it. The room was clear of electronic devices.

In the bag were four full changes of clothing, boots, and a full complement of toiletries. The cobblers at Langley had thrown in a worn, leather-bound copy of the Koran with a faded signature in Jarrett's hand inside the cover. He put it on the bedside table in plain sight.

A Leatherman tool, a roll of Scotch tape, a pair of binoculars, a 9mm Glock with a suppressor, and a box of fifty hollow points were also in the kit.

The handgun was a problem. It was best left in this room.

A small refrigerator inside a freestanding cabinet caught his eye. He pulled it out and found a screw-on metal back.

He removed the back with the Leatherman and tucked the gun, suppressor, and box of ammunition alongside the cooling coil. He replaced the back, slid the refrigerator into the cabinet, and pushed it against the wall.

Jarrett hadn't checked on Demus yet today, so he opened the tracking program on his phone.

Demus had spent the night at the Ghandi street address and had returned to his hotel at 9:00 a.m. There was no doubt in Jarrett's mind that he had a lady friend. Thirty minutes ago he'd left the hotel and traveled in the opposite direction to the Ghandi Street address.

Was he meeting with his contact?

CHAPTER 26

Demus was at 161 Khojastek.

He had traveled north on Chamran Highway, and then through the university district, probably in a taxi. Khojastek was an alley closed to traffic, and there was no name on the map attached to the address.

That meant the location likely wasn't a government building. If Demus was meeting with his contact, Jarrett would have a chance to take a photograph of him.

Jarrett took a taxi from the Grand to an intersection two blocks from the address. There was no need for evasive maneuvers.

With clear skies and mild temperatures, the university district bustled with young people. Jarrett fit in as if he were hustling to meet a lady friend for lunch.

Demus and the contact sat in a cloud of smoke outside a small, nameless café tucked between a bookstore and a bakery. The other tables had young people drinking coffee and smoking. The smell of *sangak* got Jarrett's juices flowing.

Demus faced the alley just ten feet away as Jarrett walked past the café. The messenger bag was at his feet. Between mouthfuls of salad, he was munching on a chunk of barbari bread. He seemed to be doing most of the talking.

The contact was bald on top, but had scraggly tufts of gray hair touching the collar of his dark suit. He sipped from a tall mug and puffed on a cigarette like it was his last. Jarrett couldn't see his face.

At the end of the block, Jarrett turned and walked back toward the café. He stopped at the bookstore and perused the window display.

A waiter was refilling the contact's coffee mug, while Demus trimmed the end of a cigar.

Jarrett moved quickly, following the waiter into the café. He sat down at a small table facing a hallway that led to restrooms. He was the only patron inside, and he ordered a glass of *torsh Ab Anar*—sour pomegranate juice.

The contact was on his second cup of coffee. He would have to use the restroom before he left, or at least Jarrett hoped he would. After adjusting the zoom on his phone's camera, Jarrett balanced it between his knees and angled it upward toward the hallway.

Just as Jarrett swallowed his last mouthful of juice, the contact appeared. Jarrett snapped a photograph of him walking to the men's room. The upper half of his head was cropped in the frame, so Jarrett made a slight upward adjustment to the phone.

By the time the man reappeared, Jarrett's thighs were spasming, but the photograph was nearly perfect. The top of the man's forehead was at the upper edge of the frame and the tip of his nose just left of center.

Jarrett dropped cash on the table. As he walked out of the café, Demus was putting a manila envelope into his messenger bag.

Jarrett figured Demus and the contact would walk to the nearest cross-street and hail taxis.

They did walk to the nearest intersection, but they both got in the taxi Demus hailed.

Jarrett was curious about the contact. Very curious. He planned to follow him and waited nearby in a taxi.

He gave directions to his driver to follow Demus's taxi.

The taxi retraced Demus's route to the meeting, before abruptly turning onto Enghelab Street. After a short distance it stopped, in an area with tall buildings interspersed with stores and restaurants and lots of pedestrian and vehicle traffic.

Jarrett had his driver stop a half block back. He paid the fare and hustled toward Demus's taxi. As he approached, the contact stepped out and walked off, and the taxi disappeared in traffic. Jarrett was sure he hadn't been seen.

The contact lit a cigarette and walked five blocks to an unmarked eight-story building. The featureless structure encompassed the entire block and looked like a library that hadn't aged well.

As he approached the building, he stubbed his cigarette underfoot and hung an ID badge around his neck.

Jarrett snapped a photograph of the building.

CHAPTER 27

Jarrett was back at the Grand by 2:30 p.m.

The tracking program showed Demus had gone directly to the Ghandi Street address.

With a facial photograph of the contact, Jarrett should have felt good, but he didn't.

The meeting raised questions. Lots of questions.

He studied the photograph of the contact again. The man looked Russian, like an accountant or school teacher. He had narrow-set eyes, wire-rimmed glasses atop a thick nose, thin lips, and a square jaw. Jarrett had expected a typical middle-aged, well-dressed Persian, with the smug, confident air of a bureaucrat.

The contact didn't fit the stereotype of an agent of the Revolutionary Guard. Who was he then?

Why had they met at an out-of-the way café? Why not at the contact's office? And why had the contact been dropped off five blocks from his office building?

It had to be because he didn't want to be seen with Demus. But why?

The building required a badge for entry like many office buildings. If it housed the Revolutionary Guard, it would be an armed fortress like the Pentagon. But it wasn't. So what was it?

And what was in the manila envelope the contact had given Demus?

Demus had convinced the Iranians an ethereal American agent tagged Paladin had learned the spy's identity. Demus had the book on Paladin. He knew who he was. Where he lived. And his CIA handler. Everything. But when the deal was struck the Iranians knew nothing about Paladin. All they brought to the table was a boodle of cash from the U.S. nuclear treaty. And they still knew nothing about him. Whatever was in the envelope had nothing to do with the contract on Jarrett.

If Demus was the same Dietz Meyer who was on the CIA's watch list, he was an international bad guy involved in arms dealing, drugs, and human trafficking. Anything was possible with him.

Jarrett asked himself the key question, the question he should have considered *before* leaving Scotland. Why had Demus traveled all the way to Tehran to discuss the contract? There was no reason.

Demus was here for something else. He and the Russian-looking guy were working a deal.

Jarrett e-mailed the photographs of the contact and the building to Sedgewick, jostled the bedding, attached a tiny sliver of tape across the doorjamb, and left the Grand.

CHAPTER 28

The lobby of the Parsian Hotel was a world nicer than the Grand, but still the décor seemed oppressive and outdated. Surprisingly spacious, it bustled with well-dressed business types. Jarrett wondered why Demus had chosen it.

He got directions to the spa and rode an elevator to the second floor. As he neared the registration desk, he reached into his pants pocket and began shaking his head.

With a perplexed look he said to the attendant, "Hi. I'm Mr. Meyer. I'd like to work out, but I left my key in my room."

"That won't be a problem. How do you spell your last name, sir?" the man asked.

Jarrett spelled it.

"One minute, sir." The attendant looked down and began typing.

"Ah, yes, Mr. Dietz Meyer. Room 1213," he said, handing Jarrett a numbered key on a wristband. "The key will open your locker in the spa changing area. You'll have to go to the reception desk in the lobby to get a replacement room key."

"Thank you. By the way, could you make a reservation for me for a massage tomorrow?"

"Let me see. I have slots open at two and five. Unfortunately, we only have male therapists tomorrow."

Jarrett frowned.

The attendant smiled. "I can direct you to a nearby private spa with female therapists if you like. You'll find the facility very accommodating."

"I'll stick with the hotel, thank you. The 2:00 p.m. time is fine."

The man handed Jarrett a reservation card with Dietz Meyer's name, his room number, and the date and time of the massage.

"Thank you. Oh, I'm sorry I never got your name," Jarrett said handing the man two hundred thousand rials.

"Sayed is my name. Thank you, Mr. Meyer."

* * *

After an hour workout, a self-guided tour of the hotel, and an hour reading in the lobby, Jarrett went back to the Espinas Hotel.

Although he found no bugs when he checked the room, the sniffer detected a camera in the housing of the ceiling fan in the living room and one in the recessed lights over the bed. Microphones were built into the coffee table and the headboard of the bed. The Iranians had done a masterful job of concealing them. The bathroom was clear. At least he could use it in peace without someone watching or listening. He closed the bathroom door, turned on the shower again and called Sedgewick.

"You're in the bathroom again."

"The rest of the damn suite is bugged."

"Doesn't surprise me. I got your photos. We're working on them. How did you get such a good one of the contact?"

"It wasn't easy. My cell between my legs."

"Clever. Why the pic of a building?"

"I want to know what it is. The guy Demus met with works there. Their damn meeting isn't sitting well with me."

"Why?"

"The guy isn't Persian. He's Russian."

"Well that fits. Demus called a blocked number in Tehran and had a conversation in Russian."

"Exactly." Jarrett went on to describe the meeting in detail. "The building can't be the Guard's headquarters."

"It's not. I can tell you that much," Sedgewick said.

"It doesn't make sense. If the guy's handling the contract on me, he should be in the Guard. Demus is working for them. There's no reason to meet in secret."

"Maybe this meeting wasn't about you. Demus might be cooking up something else with the Iranians. He's a dealmaker. A dirty dealmaker. Could be the guy handling the deal for the Iranians just happens to be Russian."

"I can buy that, but there's still no reason to meet secretly. Why not in a government office? And I've asked myself the key question, the one I should have considered before I traveled here. Why the hell did Demus come all the way to Tehran to talk about the contract on me? There's no reason."

"Who the hell knows why these assholes do what they do? But remember, because he made the trip, we were able to identify him and you'll have an opportunity to deal with him. Who knows, maybe his primary reason was to see his lady friend."

"No. He came here to meet with the Russian," Jarrett said. "I'd bet he has a girlfriend in every damn city in Europe."

"Good for him. It'll probably take us a little time to identify the Russian guy. The building should be easy. There's a ninety percent probability that your Dietz Meyer is one and the same as our Dietz Meyer."

"I'm curious now why Demus is here, if it's not about the contract. Once I get a chance to talk to him, he'll tell me everything. I assure you."

Sedgewick laughed. "I'm sure he will. Then it's bye, bye Demus."

"Maybe I'll learn something of value for you, if he's up to no good with the Russian guy."

"That'd be great. Getting intel out of there is a pain in the ass. Tell you what. I'll get POTUS to sanction Demus for you. One call and it's done. Make you feel better."

"I don't need to feel good about him. He sent assassins to kill me."

"When's the party with him?"

"Soon. I'll find out who the Russian guy is and why they met. If he's not Demus's contact in the Guard, I'll be sure to squeeze the contact's name out of him too. I'm going to need it."

"What about the Persian lady? We still haven't come up with anything on her. Do you want me to stay on it?"

"Yes. There's a lot she's not telling me."

"Will do. Good luck with Demus."

"Thanks. I'll be in touch."

CHAPTER 29

Ziba kissed Jarrett on the cheek and squeezed his hands.

A short, curious-looking man stood next to her.

"Thomas, meet Tony Mahdavi."

As they shook hands, the man laughed. "My name is Mohammad, but I go by Tony."

Tony was in white—sweater, slacks, and shoes—with a diamond-studded Rolex on his wrist and a heavy gold chain around his neck. His head was shaved and he had effeminate features. His eyes were outlined with mascara and he had a flirtatious smile.

Ziba looked like an Egyptian goddess who had time-warped five millennia. Jarrett couldn't stop staring.

"Well, Thomas, what do you think?" She pirouetted with her hands over her head.

"Are you going to an Egyptian costume party?"

"No. I thought I'd dress like a queen for you."

"When does the pharaoh arrive?" Jarrett asked.

"He just did," she said, pointedly raising her eyebrows.

She led them to the living room and poured Blanton's over ice for Jarrett. Tony drank Tito's straight up, while Ziba sipped Lagavulin.

"Tony has to leave soon," Ziba explained. "We'll munch on finger foods and pass on dinner."

"Sounds good to me." Jarrett nodded.

"I've heard a lot about you, Thomas. You're everything Ziba said you were." Tony inhaled and his eyes went up and down Jarrett. "I like big men. My partner is almost as big as you, but nowhere near as buffed or good looking."

95

"Tony, he belongs to me."

"I'm just kidding of course, but there's nothing wrong with looking."

Ziba laughed and glanced at Jarrett. "Just no touching. I'm Tony's cover sometimes when he goes out with his partner."

"It's not so bad . . . as long as I don't get caught. I travel a lot, France and Italy mostly. People are understanding there. How was your day, Thomas?"

"Worked at my hotel in the morning, then made a few calls. I like to walk to them when I can." Jarrett opened his phone and brought up the photo of the building. "I passed this building. It looks like a library."

Tony's eyebrows rose when he looked at it.

"That was a museum under the shah. Now it's the headquarters of the Atomic Energy Organization," he said.

A cold chill shot through Jarrett.

Did the man who'd met with Demus work for the Atomic Energy Organization?

"What were you doing there?" Ziba asked curiously.

"Like I said, I walked by and was curious. There's been a lot in the news about Iran's nuclear weapons program. I suppose it's a hot topic around here, too."

"Always," Tony said. "I'm against it. We should use our money to better the economy and get rid of the sanctions. They're literally strangling us. But our exalted leader wants the bomb and he won't hesitate to use it. He'd start nuclear World War III without giving it a thought."

"I agree with Tony. Most Iranians are against nuclear weapons. There's an active anti-nuclear underground in Tehran. It's the crazies who want a bomb."

"At the top of the *I want a bomb* list is your uncle," Tony remarked, giving Ziba a sideways glance.

Jarrett turned to Ziba. "Your uncle? Who's . . . "

Tony interrupted, "Ziba's father is a mitigating force, thank God, and a wonderful man. But unfortunately he stands alone. We need a democracy here with him as president."

"Who's your father, Ziba?"

She raised her eyebrows and glared at Tony, but said nothing.

Tony stood. "Well, I guess I'd better run now. Talk of nuclear weapons gets my blood pressure up. If our exalted leader heard me ranting like this, he'd have me shot. It's been nice meeting you, Thomas. Take care of Ziba. She's very special."

Ziba and Tony embraced and said goodbye.

After he was gone, Ziba said, "Tony's wonderful. He loves his country, but like many of us he hates the theocracy."

"Who's your father?

"It's not important at this point. Why did you take a picture of that building? Seems kind of strange to me. There's lots of buildings in Tehran. Why that one?"

"It's architecture just struck me. I took some other pictures as well."

"Which hospitals did you visit?"

Jarrett took a sip of his drink and smiled. "It's not important at this point."

She smiled. "We have a date tomorrow. I can't wait. Lunch and a tour of the city. I'll pick you up at your hotel at noon. That'll give you the morning to make a few calls. Like I said, I have contacts in high places. I can help you."

I'll bet you have contacts in high places, Jarrett thought.

CHAPTER 30

J arrett's self-guided tour of the Parsian Hotel was in fact carefully executed reconnaisance.

The hotel elevators required a room key to access floors above the mezzanine. Two side entrances were locked from 8:00 a.m. until 11:00 p.m. but could be opened with a room key. During the night they were secure and could not be opened from the inside or outside. A comfortable lounge with a flat-screen television and a good view of the lobby was opposite the spa on the mezzanine. At both ends of the building a stairway ran from the top floor to the basement. Separate staircases that weren't visible from the lobby led from the mezzanine level to the side entrances.

At 4:00 p.m. a man and a woman came on duty at the reception desk.

Jarrett saw no surveillance cameras anywhere and wondered if Demus had chosen this hotel for that reason.

At the meeting with the Russian, Demus had worn a beige summer suit, an open-collared white shirt, and the straw fedora with a black band. The hat was an eye-catcher.

Jarrett was two inches taller than Demus, about the same breadth across the shoulders, but a lot narrower at the waist.

He was counting on the personnel at the reception desk to associate the fedora and beige suit with the burly guest who habitually returned after midnight. He also counted on Demus—a paranoid bad guy—to have minimal interaction with the hotel staff.

* * *

Jarrett strolled into the Parsian Hotel lobby at 10:30 p.m.

He was dressed like Demus in a beige suite with a fedora low on his brow and a messenger bag slung over his shoulder. A decent look-alike, but not perfect. He had purchased the hat, the suit, and the bag after his reconnaisance of the hotel.

The male clerk was at the desk; the woman was in the back office. As Jarrett walked briskly across the lobby to the elevators, the clerk looked up but said nothing. Jarrett rode an elevator to the mezzanine.

There was no one in the lounge area. Jarrett sat down and focused on the front desk.

When the woman appeared, he rode an elevator back to the lobby and walked quickly toward her. He always did better dealing with women.

The woman looked up and smiled. "May I help you, sir?"

With his best smile, he said, "Good evening. I'm Dietz Meyer in Room 1213. I was just going out and realized I left my key in my room. Could you give me a spare, please?"

"One second sir," she said and began typing. "Yes, I see you're in room 1213, I will need . . ."

Before she finished, Jarrett handed her the massage appointment card and said, "Sayed made an appointment for me for a massage tomorrow at 2:00 p.m. Would you mind changing it to five? He told me there was time available then."

She looked at the card and then at Jarrett.

"Of course, Mr. Meyer, I would be happy to do that for you."

She began typing again. Seconds later, she handed Jarrett the room key and her personal business card.

"You're scheduled for five o'clock. I love your hat Mr. Meyer. If there's anything else you need, anything at all, please let me know. My name is Anahita."

Jarrett left through the front entrance. He used the key to unlock a side entrance and hustled up the stairs to the mezzanine level. Although he was sure Demus would be out until midnight, he checked the tracking program. *Damn it.*

Demus was in route to the hotel. Jarrett had figured he'd stay at his lady friend's until after midnight. Jarrett had under fifteen minutes. He rode an elevator to the twelfth floor.

A tiny piece of masking tape was stretched across the top of the doorjamb. Jarrett slipped on a pair of latex gloves, peeled back the tape, and opened the door with the key.

Although the room smelled of cigars, Demus was a neat freak.

The German in him no doubt.

The purpose of the visit was to get the lay of the land, specifically where the bed and light switches were in relation to the door.

After searching the room quickly and finding nothing of interest, Jarrett replaced the tape across the doorjamb and took an elevator to the mezzanine level. The tracker showed Demus was at the hotel.

The male clerk was at the reception desk. He didn't look up when Demus walked past him with the messenger bag slung over his shoulder.

Jarrett took the stairs to the side entrance and left five minutes before the doors locked for the night.

CHAPTER 31

Jarrett's room at the Grand was as he'd left it. No one had visited.

He retrieved the Glock from the back of the refrigerator, screwed the suppressor in place, and filled the magazine with cartridges. He opened the second operating program on his phone and noticed a text from Sedgewick. "Call ASAP. Important." The tracking program showed Demus was at the Parsian.

Jarrett shrugged. When he was in kill mode he was like a guided missile. Nothing could veer him off course, not even Sedgewick. He would call his friend when he finished with Demus.

At 12:30 a.m. Jarrett walked into the Parsian lobby in his Demus look-a-like garb with the Glock in the small of his back.

Luckily, the woman was at the front desk.

She saw him and said, "Mr. Meyer, I put your massage change in the computer, but please double check with Sayed in the morning."

"Thank you, Anahita," he said.

He took an elevator to the twelfth floor. When he stepped off, a man brushed by him. He was moving quickly, and Jarrett kept his head down and said nothing. The man disappeared in the stairwell with an unmistakable odor of cheap cologne trailing him.

A Do Not Disturb sign was on the door to Demus's room.

Jarrett slipped on latex gloves and found the tape over the doorjamb torn. *That's odd*, he thought.

He used the key to open the door.

The room was silent and dark except for light from the bathroom. The air still stank of cigars, but now something else was mixed with it.

Demus was in bed, covered with a sheet. *A quiet sleeper.*

Jarrett turned on the lights, withdrew the Glock from his waistband, and walked to the foot of the bed.

The gun was for intimidation only. Jarrett wouldn't use it. He never did. When he was done it would look like Demus died in his sleep. But first they would talk, the gun against Demus's forehead—a not-so-subtle form of enhanced interrogation.

"Wake up, Meyer. You have a visitor."

Demus didn't stir.

Jarrett shook him. "Wake up, asshole."

Still Demus didn't move.

Jarrett pulled off the sheet. Demus was in a T-shirt and undershorts lying on his side.

His skin was warm but ashen. He wasn't breathing.

Jarrett examined him for signs of injury and needle sticks. None.

The new odor in the room was the same one he'd smelled trailing the man in the hallway.

He had killed Demus. Just seconds ago.

Jarrett searched the room.

Demus's wallet, Iranian burner, and cigar cutter were on the nightstand next to the bed. The messenger bag and manila envelope were gone.

Jarrett opened the burner. No password was required. He went to recent calls.

At 12:02 a.m. Demus had received a call from a blocked number. The call had lasted fourteen seconds. That meant he was alive shortly after midnight, or the killer had answered the phone.

There was another call from a blocked number at 10:25 p.m. Demus had talked for eleven seconds.

A thought ran through Jarrett's head.

He found an open bottle of expensive French men's cologne in the bathroom along with three unopened bottles of hotel complimentaries. He opened the cologne bottle. It had the same fragrance he'd smelled in the hallway and in the room.

Jarrett left Demus as he'd found him and took an elevator to the mezzanine level. No one was at the reception desk. The lobby was empty.

He hustled down the stairs and out the front entrance.

He had a lot to think about

CHAPTER 32

Demus was dead. Murdered.

Jarrett was surprised and perplexed.

After hiding the Glock in the refrigerator at the Grand, he sat down and took a few deep breaths. He was still in kill mode. He had to unwind and think. *What was going on here?*

The man he'd passed in the hallway had killed Demus. He'd done it to look like Demus died in his sleep. But why? The messenger bag and manila envelope were gone. The man had taken them. The tracker was on the bag.

He opened the phone to check the tracking program and found a second text from Sedgewick. "911. Call me."

Shit.

He made the call.

"Jarrett. Goddamn it, I've been trying to reach you. Don't kill Demus!"

"He's already dead."

"No! You didn't!" Sedgewick cried.

"No. I didn't. I passed a man in the hallway outside Demus's room. He killed him. I'm sure of it."

"How do you know?"

"He left a cloud of cologne in his trail. The same odor was in the room. I checked Demus's bathroom. He had his own cologne. The hotel complimentary cologne bottle was unopened. I opened it, and it had the same smell as in the hall and in the room. The killer must have had it on him. And Demus's messenger bag with the tracker was gone."

"Maybe Demus left the bag at his lady friend's place."

"No. I saw him with it in the lobby. When I passed the guy in the hall I never looked at him. He had the messenger bag. Why the urgent order not to kill him?"

"Demus worked for Mossad," Sedgewick said.

"What?"

"It's a complex narrative like everything else involving the damn Israelis. You remember the call I was going to make to get Demus sanctioned for you? Well, when I made it, all hell broke loose. Within the hour I was choppered to the White House from Langley. Met with the president. Turns out we have an asset in Mossad. He got a handwritten note to our embassy in Tel Aviv. Important enough for our ambassador to fly to Washington and hand deliver it to the Oval Office. A hot piece of intel, probably the hottest to hit the White House in years. Maybe ever.

Sedgewick took a deep breath and continued. "The Iranians are selling a nuclear weapon to Hezbollah. There's an intermediary in the deal representing Hezbollah. Somehow the Israelis got to him and turned him. That was our friend Demus. POTUS ordered me to stop the assassination. I called you from the White House."

"Whoa!" Jarrett was stunned. "Better for a bomb to be in Israeli hands than Hezbollah's."

"For sure."

"I thought Iran hadn't developed one yet."

"They haven't."

"Well, where the hell did they get it then?" Jarrett asked.

"Where do you think? The Russians. The note said the Russians gave Iran two devices. One's the size of a suitcase. I did a little research. The Russians had built 250 suitcase-sized nuclear devices. They're called RA-115. About six kilotons each. Not big by today's standards, but big enough to do a helluva lot of damage. Years ago they were going to plant them in key cities all over the world, including in the U.S. None in the Black Hills of South Dakota, though."

"Thank God," Jarrett said.

"The device requires an electric power source and has battery backup. The bomb itself isn't much bigger than a carry-on, but with the battery pack it's the size of a large suitcase. It weighs only fifty-five to sixty pounds. A hundred of them went missing."

"And one of the missing ones is in Tehran," Jarrett added.

"Right, along with a second device. And there's more. You'll be happy to learn your suspicions were right about the guy Demus met with. We identified him from the photo. Name's Omid Mohsen. He's Russian. The number two nuclear scientist in Iran's Atomic Energy Organization. He must have told Demus where the Iranians got the devices. Demus passed it on to Mossad."

"It all makes sense now," Jarrett said. "Demus flew to Tehran to meet with an Iranian nuclear scientist, this guy Mohsen, to discuss the sale of the bomb. It had nothing to do with me."

"Right. Remember the late Qassem Soleimani, the former head of Quds? He went to Russia right after we signed the nuclear treaty, the one that's now defunct. It was all over cable news. What do you think he did when he was there?"

"Finalized negotiations for the bombs, I suppose. How did the Israelis find out about the deal with Hezbollah?" Jarrett asked.

"Mossad has a spy in Hezbollah."

"A Jew in a Muslim terrorist organization in Lebanon?" Jarrett could hardly believe it. "He must have one big pair of cojones."

"He does, for sure. So the spy tells Mossad that Hezbollah is buying a bomb from Iran and using Demus as an intermediary. The wily Israelis get to Demus and up the ante. Demus is a whore who sells out to the highest bidder. If he gets the device for Israel, it proves the Iranians have them. And prevents Israel's neighbor from being armed with a nuclear device."

"But why use an intermediary? The Iranians support Hezbollah. Why not just do a direct deal?" Jarrett asked.

"That's a good question. I suppose Iran wants to protect itself in the event the deal's uncovered. They'd claim they don't have a bomb and the whole thing was a scam. Mohsen would be accused of being a rogue scientist trying to make some fast money. They might even sell out their friends in Moscow by implicating Mohsen as the intermediary between the Russians and Hezbollah. And Mohsen's Russian."

"Incredible. A nuclear weapon in the hands of Hezbollah would be disasterous. Israel would bomb Iran and Lebanon. It would be war in the Middle East. Nuclear war," Jarrett added.

"Exactly," Sedgewick said.

"Demus is dead. The Mossad caper is kaput." Jarrett said.

"It'll be interesting to see how this plays out on the international stage. The Israeli's know Iran has Russian nuclear devices. They know Iran was going to sell one to Hezbollah come hell or high water. Now we know, too."

"Iran will deny having a bomb. Russia will say they never sent devices to the Persians. No way to prove it. I'll be curious to see how the Oval Office handles this," Jarrett added.

"There'll be talk, talk, and more talk. A high-level meeting is going on right now."

"I'm still bothered by Demus's murder. And what was so damn important in the manila envelope?"

"Maybe his lady friend has a jealous husband."

"No. It has something to do with the nuclear transaction. Like I said, Demus's messenger bag with the manila envelope was gone."

"You may not know who killed Demus, but you know where he's staying, if you're right about the hotel cologne."

"Give me a minute."

Jarrett switched to the tracking program.

Then back to the call.

"The bag's in Demus's hotel," he told Sedgewick.

"Jarrett, you missed it in his room."

"No way. The guy who did Demus has the bag and the manila envelope. He's staying at the hotel, like you said. He uses the hotel's cologne."

"Why do you care who killed him?"

"I'm intrigued," Jarrett replied. "Demus had a blocked call on his burner at 12:02 a.m. and one at 10:25 p.m."

"I'll bet the first call was to get him back to the hotel from his lady friend's place. The second was to get him out of the room. The killer grabbed Demus, escorted him back to his room, and did the dirty deed. It had to be done in the room to make it look like he died in his sleep. What are you going to do about the contract?"

"I don't know. I'm out of the box now. After I took care of Demus, I was going to pose as his partner and fill in for him. I suppose I can still do that, but I'll have to figure a way to introduce myself to the Guard. I don't know who to contact."

"You already have a Turkish legend and a base of operation at the other hotel," Sedgewick reminded him.

"Why Demus was murdered is gnawing at me. If I posed as his partner, I might meet the same fate. Dead in bed. So I've got to weigh my next move carefully. And I'm curious about Ziba Vijany and why she's so interested in me. She's somebody very important."

"Be careful with her, Jarrett. And stay away from the nuclear deal. It has the potential to be an international crisis with horrific ramifications. Hezbollah has its sights on the bomb. Iran wants them to have it. God only knows where the Russians stand. And Mossad is going to go ballistic when it finds out about Demus. I need to pass on the bad news to POTUS. Try to get the Iranians off your back if you can and get the hell out of there."

"You're right, as always," Jarrett said.

"Talk to you soon."

* * *

Jarrett *had* stumbled on a real mess.

He understood now why Demus had flown to Tehran—to meet with an Iranian nuclear scientist to discuss the sale of a bomb to Hezbollah. And he understood why Demus's contact didn't look the part. He was a Russian nuclear scientist, not an agent of the Guard.

But what didn't fit the narrative was why Mohsen had chosen to meet in secret. And why Demus had been murdered.

Something else was going on. Whatever it was, Mohsen was at the heart of it.

He had a date with Ziba Vijany tomorrow. She was pro-democracy and anti-nuclear. And maybe even better connected than he had figured.

CHAPTER 33

Jarrett was in the lobby at 11:45 p.m. After spending a few minutes looking at the pictures in an Iranian travel magazine, he walked outside. The babysitters jumped out of their chairs, but stayed inside the doorway maintaining visual contact.

A black Mercedes sedan with dark tints pulled under the portico. A burly man in a black suit with an open-collared shirt got out. He had a flesh-colored earbud and a bulge under his arm.

The jig's up, Jarrett thought. *Mogadan's agents are here to take me away.*

The man opened the back door and gestured to Jarrett.

Ziba sat against the far door blowing curls of smoke out her window. When she saw Jarrett, she flipped the cigarette. "A bad habit I picked up in the U.K. I hope you don't mind. You're early."

"I do mind." Jarrett said. His voice was silky smooth with a hint of sharpness.

She put a mint in her mouth and began to laugh. "I guess I just quit."

"Not for my sake Ziba, for yours," Jarrett said.

"For ours, Thomas, if that's okay?"

"That's okay, Ziba."

Today she wore a mustard-colored ankle-length dress with a high collar, long sleeves, and a sash tied at the waist. With a black silk scarf and designer sunglasses, she looked like a fashion-forward, rich Muslim chick, maybe one on the prowl. Jarrett liked the look.

"How about lunch first, then a quick tour of the city?"

"Something light, like a salad would be nice," Jarrett replied.

"I thought we'd make a full day of it, if you don't mind. I made a reservation for dinner for us at a great place with wonderful Lebanese food."

"Lebanese food is my favorite."

When the car pulled away, Jarrett looked back. The babysitters stood under the portico looking after them. They were content with Jarrett driving off with Ziba Vijany.

She's one of Mogadan's agents, so there's no need for them to follow us, Jarrett thought.

They traveled north out of the city on the Navvab Expressway then on to Chammran Highway. Ziba pointed out the University of Tehran with its wing-shaped entry gates and Imam Sadiq University, the center of conservative Islamic thought in Iran. Soon the traffic thinned and they were on a country road. The Abloriz Mountains stood in front of them. Mount Damavan, the highest peak in Iran at nearly six thousand meters, dominated the skyline.

They passed through Darakeh, a popular tourist area for hiking and climbing. A new high-rise was under construction, but on balance the buildings looked old and showed years of neglect.

Soon they were on a winding road that led to a broad-mouthed canyon lush with trees and flowering bushes. Climbing upward they negotiated a series of switchbacks with one-lane bridges crossing a stream cascading down the mountain. Jarrett imagined that water from the receding glacier had sculpted the canyon.

The road ended at a two-story stone building at the base of a cliff. Tall windows were framed in colorful tile, and a wide entry led to a courtyard with tables set among trees and flowering shrubs. A tangle of vines with clusters of grapes hung from an eye-catching central lattice. The stream rippled through a raised vegetable garden dotted with flowers and fruit trees on the far side of the building. The setting was lovely.

The guard in the passenger seat went into the building with a paper sack. Ziba cuddled next to Jarrett, who was looking over his shoulder.

"Thomas, no one followed us."

Jarrett said nothing.

"The two agents stayed at your hotel," she reminded him.

"Why? They've been following me since I checked in."

"You're a hero in our country. They're your protectors."

The guard reappeared and opened the door. "Your table is ready, Miss Ziba."

"Thank you, Favad."

CHAPTER 34

The maître d' greeted Ziba and escorted them to a quaint room with doors open to the garden. He seated them in high-backed chairs at a small table with a bouquet of flowers. A chiller bucket with a bottle of wine and two glasses sat nearby on an antique sideboard. Between the fragrance of flowers and the sound of water cascading down the cliff, Jarrett thought he was in heaven.

If this is a honey trap, I might as well sit back and enjoy it. What the hell, he thought.

The driver stayed with the car and Favad sat in the courtyard with his eyes fixed on Ziba. After a young man took their orders, the maître d' poured wine.

Jarrett took a sip. "Chardonnay. Californian chardonnay if I'm not mistaken."

Ziba smiled. "You're right, Thomas. Chateau Montelena. My favorite. This is Café Babul. The owners are friends of my family. It used to be their summer retreat before the revolution. Now they run it as a restaurant. No menus. Everything's made to order. Your Caesar will be the best ever."

And she was right—with a hint of wasabi and topped with chunks of fresh-seared albacore, it was delicious.

Ziba talked about the pharaohs, the pyramids, and the Valley of the Kings. Jarrett was not paying attention, but occasionally asked a question to keep the conversation going. She was passionate and babbled on unmercifully.

By the second glass of wine, Jarrett had filed away his worries about the contract, Demus's murder, and the honey trap. But his curiosity about Ziba was bubbling over—she was beautiful, rich, educated, and on top of that just plain nice. Who was she? And why the armed bodyguards?

Jarrett interrupted her as she was describing how Howard Carter had discovered Tut's tomb. "I don't understand your interest in me, Ziba."

She looked at him curiously. "That came out of the clear blue . . ."

"I'm sorry, but I'm just very curious."

"Well, you're the most intriguing man I've ever met. Let me tell you, that covers a helluva lot of men. If you're Thomas Davis, a salesman from Canada, I'm the queen mother."

She winked.

Jarrett couldn't help but laugh. "You have bodyguards with radios and guns. Why do you need them? And why do you live in a fortress?"

"My father insists. Our country is not as safe as we would like."

"Who is your father?"

Ziba's left eye began to twitch and she rubbed the back of her hand across her cheek. She glanced at Favad and nodded. Lunch was over.

She put on her dark glasses and stood. "When you tell me who you are, I'll tell you about me. Fair enough? It's getting late. There'll be traffic. I promised you a tour."

"Let me pay before we leave," Jarrett said.

"It's been taken care of. You're my guest, Thomas."

* * *

Jarrett would remember very little about his tour of Tehran, even less than his lecture on Egypt. He didn't give a damn about the city, and his mind was back on Demus.

Their first stop was the entry to the Grand Bazaar. Ziba said it was a hotbed of support for the revolution, because the bazaaris would suffer as the country industrialized under the shah.

Next was the Golestan Palace which looked like an old brick and tile dungeon.

Then the Azadi Tower, forty-five meters of white marble. When Ziba said its architect had been expelled from the country after the revolution, Jarrett wondered why the tower hadn't been knocked down. The grounds around the grotesque structure were scarred by dirt paths weaving a pattern of odd-shaped grass hexagons desperately in need of water.

Jarrett perked up when the car pulled to the curb near a building with a hand-painted mural of the Statue of Liberty with a skeleton face.

"This was the U.S. Embassy, Thomas. It was taken over in 1979 by a group of crazed students supported by the ayatollah."

As they idled along, Jarrett recognized the defaced emblem of the United States of America. A column of bile rose in his throat.

"What's left of the embassy is called the Den of Espionage," Ziba told him. "It's a disgrace to the Iranian people, emblematic of the theocracy we live under and its hatred of America. I show it to you only to point out it doesn't reflect the sentiments of most Iranians. The Iranian people are warm and friendly. They hate no one."

Except the tens of thousands who march in the streets shouting, "Death to America," he thought.

"What's the compound used for now?"

She hesitated, then said, "It's a government facility."

Jarrett felt physically ill. He had seen enough. The Den of Espionage had put a bad taste in his mouth despite Ziba's claims that the Iranian people were warm and friendly.

"I'd better get back to the hotel. I have a little work to do before dinner."

With a wry look she asked, "What work, Thomas?"

"Oh, just the usual business matters."

"I'll pick you up at nine o'clock," she said.

CHAPTER 35

A few minutes before 9:00 p.m. Jarrett walked past the agents in the hotel lobby, smiled, and waved. Ziba's sedan was idling under the portico.

"Please allow me, Mr. Davis," the guard said opening the car door.

Ziba was dressed in black for a serious night on the town.

Her hajib was a complicated arrangement of folds that hung well below her neckline. With light gray eye shadow and sparkling, garnet-red lipstick, the only way to describe her was Hollywood glamorous.

"You look beautiful," Jarrett said.

She kissed him on the cheek. "Thank you. I thought I'd look extra special for you. The restaurant is in an upscale hotel not far from here."

After a short ride down Keshavarz Boulevard they turned into a driveway with valet parking.

The guard in the passenger seat left the car, but soon was back to escort them inside. They walked down a long corridor lined with boutique shops. Just before three steps that led to the restaurant entrance was a hallway with a sign that read Hotel Markazi.

The dining room was splendid with an amber chandelier and only eight tables. Only one was occupied by a young couple holding hands. While a gushy maître d' escorted them to a corner table, the guard sat down near the entrance. For some reason the maître d' gave Jarrett the willies.

It was a seven-plate dinner, more American than Lebanese, but excellent. There were two fish plates, three meat plates, two vegetable plates, and a vanilla souffle for dessert. Ziba pushed away one of the meat plates suspecting it was pork.

Midway through the fifth plate the maître d' seated two young men near the door.

At first glance there was nothing of concern about them. They were nicely dressed and well barbered with neatly trimmed beards. But when one of them clumsily knocked over his water glass, Jarrett glanced at his hands. They were heavily callused with dirty fingernails. The index and middle fingers of his right hand were stained with nicotine.

An alarm went off in Jarrett's head.

Those hands don't fit the venue.

His gaze swung to the young couple who were still eating. The woman's eyes were locked on him. He was used to women staring, but this wasn't that look; it was something else. When their eyes met, she quickly looked away.

After coffee Jarrett called for the check. When the maître d' came over, the young man abruptly got up and left without saying a word to his lady friend.

After the maître d' told Jarrett that the check had been put on account, Jarrett glanced at the guard. His hand was cupped over his earbud and his lips were moving excitedly. His eyes shot to Ziba, and then he ran out of the restaurant.

Simultaneously, Jarrett heard a muffled cannonade outside.

Shit.

He leaned forward. "We've got to get out here. Go to the hotel. Find a safe place to hide. Wait for me there."

"What's happening?" There was fear in Ziba's eyes.

"I'll take care of it."

They stood and left the dining room. When they reached the bottom step, Ziba squeezed Jarrett's hand and said, "Thomas, please be careful."

"Go! Now!"

Ziba ran down the hallway with the hem of her dress in her hands and her heels plopping.

Jarrett walked toward the valet parking.

Halfway down the corridor Hand Holder waited with his hands on his hips. Dirty Fingers had hustled down the steps behind Jarrett.

Jarrett continued to walk toward Hand Holder. Time slowed. It always did. In his mind's eye he saw his fate—*an execution. Up close. But why?*

Hand Holder was nervous, breathing heavily, beads of perspiration streaming down his brow, barely shoulder height on Jarrett.

An amateur. Unpredictable. The worst type to go against.

Dirty Fingers had closed on Jarrett and was at his heels.

Hand Holder pulled out a gun. "Put your hands up. Don't try anything."

Jarrett stopped, slowly raised his hands shoulder high and locked his eyes on Hand Holder's.

Behind him Dirty Fingers shouted, "She ran into the hotel!"

The foul odor of tobacco and alcohol wafted across Jarrett.

Hand Holder was wild-eyed and his gun hand shook. "We'll take this guy down and then go after her."

As the words left Hand Holder's lips, Jarrett exploded.

He spun like a top and landed an elbow in Dirty Finger's face. *Crack.* The man's knees buckled and he stumbled.

Hand Holder hesitated a split second.

Jarrett grabbed Dirty Fingers by the shoulders and threw him into Hand Holder.

Boom. An ear-shattering muzzle blast echoed through the corridor.

Dirty Fingers gasped and his body went limp. The shot had hit him in the chest.

The two assailants crashed to the floor in a tangle of arms and legs, Dirty Fingers sprawled across Hand Holder.

Hand Holder struggled to gather himself. For an instant he was catatonic, aghast, his mouth hanging open. His handgun waved wildly. He fired it again. The shot was way wide of Jarrett and hit the ceiling.

As he pushed Dirty Fingers off him, he screamed, "Albie. Help!" His voice cracked with the words. They would be his last.

Jarrett was on him in a flash. Pinning the arm with the handgun against the floor with one hand, he rained down hammer strikes with the other. Jarrett's fist was like a piston firing up and down with incredible speed and power. Hand Holder could do nothing to block the punches.

In a matter of seconds it was over. Hand Holder grunted and spit blood, his eyes locked in a death stare.

Jarrett retrieved the handgun—a Russian P-96—and put a round in each man's head.

He looked in both directions.

No Albie.

Where were Ziba's bodyguards?

He remembered the noise outside.

All was quiet now. Deathly quiet.

Jarrett inched along the wall to the end of the corridor and peeked around the corner.

A white van blocked the driveway. Three bodies lay on the ground under the portico. A man with a gun stood near them, his eyes roving up and down the boulevard.

Albie. The lookout.

Jarrett fired a round into the back of his head. The man's face exploded and he collapsed.

Bye, bye Albie.

Jarrett quickly circled behind the van. The driver was getting out. When he turned, Jarrett shot him in the face.

The portico was a puddle of death. Ziba's driver and the valet attendant had taken execution-style head shots. The guard from the restaurant had two bullet wounds in his chest. His gun was still in his hand.

Jarrett heard sirens in the distance as he ran back to the restaurant.

The maître d' cowered under a table. The woman and the other man were gone.

"Where'd they go?" Jarrett shouted.

The man pointed to the kitchen door. Jarrett hesitated for an instant. The maître d' was part of this. He had to be. Jarrett shot him in the knee and lunged through the door.

No one was in sight.

Where was the staff?

An exit door was directly ahead. The two accomplices had planned to use it to escape.

Jarrett ran to it, pushed the bar. Locked.

Where were they?

Then he heard a woman sobbing. He stepped back and looked down a long, narrow aisle lined with cabinets into an alcove with stoves and ovens.

The third bad guy and Hand Holder's lady stood with their backs to an oven. A baby-faced young girl in a white uniform with a stocking cap stood in front of him.

The kitchen staff—an older man with a toque blanche and a teenage boy—and the waiter knelt on the floor in front of them.

Jarrett walked toward them with long, measured strides holding the gun at his side. No hurry. The corridor was stifling with an earthy, mustard-like aroma of turmeric mixed with roasting garlic. He stopped ten feet from the bad guy who held an old-style revolver at the young girl's head.

"Give me key, or I'll kill her," he growled.

Jarrett searched his memory. How many rounds in a Russian P-96? The chamber was still closed. He had at least one left.

The man was perspiring profusely and gritting his teeth like a rabid dog. The knuckles of his gun hand were blanched. Hand Holder's lady glared at Jarrett with dark, beady eyes, an unsettling calm about her.

She's the leader of this merry band, Jarrett decided.

The young girl was a head shorter than the man. Tears streamed down her cheeks and she wrenched her hands uncontrollably.

"Your friends are dead," Jarrett said. "All four of them. Drop the gun. I'll let you go."

The man glanced at Hand Holder's lady for a split second as if seeking direction, but her eyes stayed locked on Jarrett.

"Okay. I'll have them give you the key," Jarrett said.

Staying focused on the man, Jarrett said, "Whoever has the key, give it to him."

The chef's face was as white as his toque. He reached into his jacket pocket and produced a key. When he held it out, the man glanced down.

Jarrett swung his gun up and fired.

Boom.

The man's left eye exploded spattering the oven with blood and bone.

The young girl collapsed in a dead faint, and the other hostages scurried like scared rabbits.

Hand Holder's lady stood frozen continuing to glare at Jarrett.

Jarrett's P-96 was empty, the chamber open and smoking. He tossed it aside, lunged forward and hit her in the face with a straight left. With his full weight behind the strike her head smashed into the oven with a sickening thud shattering the glass door.

Jarrett heard sirens approaching outside.

He imagined he heard shouting in the restaurant.

The chef was glad to give up the key. The door led to a narrow service corridor between the restaurant and the hotel.

Traffic was beginning to back up on the side street, irate drivers leaning on their horns. He hustled to the street, turned left, and ran toward the boulevard fronting the hotel.

The night sky was alive with red and blue lights, the air filled with a cacophony of sirens approaching from every direction.

A gaggle of firemen and uniformed police with a few curious onlookers milled about. No one seemed to know what to do. An alarm blared in the hotel. Guests in night wear and robes filed out.

A military transport sped down the boulevard and crossed the median, knocking over shrubs and side-swiping two vehicles. It stopped on the sidewalk. A squad of soldiers in full combat gear jumped out and ran toward the hotel.

Jarrett weaved his way to the entrance. A policeman stopped him. "No entry! Bomb!"

He dodged the officer and pushed past the hotel guests into the lobby. Ziba was nowhere in sight.

The elevators were out of service, and hotel guests were streaming down a broad staircase in the center of the lobby. An imperious man in a gray suit with a name tag "Mohammed" directed them toward the exit.

Jarrett ran to him. He screamed over the alarm, "Mohammed, a young woman in black, where is she?"

The man surveyed Jarrett for an instant then pointed to the office behind the reception desk.

Jarrett hurtled over the counter.

"Ziba!"

"Here, Thomas." She stepped from a small storage room, a perplexed look on her face. A woman dressed in a gray business suit with a matching head scarf trailed behind her.

"You're okay. Thank God!"

"I was worried, Thomas," she said

"We have to get out of here. The lobby's jammed."

The woman in gray said, "Follow me, Miss Abassi."

CHAPTER 36

*A*bassi?

The woman led them down a narrow corridor to the employees' entrance. After she unlocked the door, Ziba hugged her and led Jarrett away from the hotel. They scurried three blocks on a dark street and were met by a soldier in full combat gear. He leveled his rifle at Jarrett's chest. Serious business.

With the threat of a terrorist bombing, a five-block area around Hotel Markazi had been cordoned off. No one came out without being questioned and no one went in. No exceptions.

Ziba stepped between Jarrett and the no-nonsense corporal, explaining that she and her friend were just out walking. When he asked to see their identification, she leaned into him and whispered. He snapped to attention, nodded apologetically, and ran to a makeshift command post a block away. An armored military vehicle appeared with two soldiers.

On the drive to her condo the soldiers chattered about a bomb in the Hotel Markazi. Jarrett held Ziba in his arms. Gradually her trembling subsided.

The guards in the lobby were on high alert, standing near the elevators with serious looks.

When they were in the safety of her living room, Ziba growled, "Shit," pulled off her scarf, twisted it into a knot, and tossed it on the sofa.

She hurredly fixed them drinks, downed hers in two gulps and said, "Let me change. Then we'll talk."

Jarrett sat on the sofa, pulled off his boots and stared down at the amber liquid in his glass.

The first taste of the carmel-vanilla bourbon brought back a wave of memories. On his eighteenth birthday Jarrett's father had toasted him and said, "To bourbon whiskey, amber liquid, sweet and clear, not as sweet as a woman's lips, but a damn bit more sincere."

He chuckled. His father had been right.

And in the fall of that year at a fraternity rush party, Jarrett and Sedgewick had split a handle. It was a memorable drunk—the first of many.

He shook his head and came back to the present.

How crazy was this?

He was a deep cover agent on a mission in a hostile country. He was in a world of trouble. Eight people had died tonight, five bad guys at his hand and likely a sixth—the woman.

The assailants were Persians not Arabs, and like the Saudi hijackers, they were bumbling amateurs. They were after Ziba. *Was she the target of the airplane hijacking too?* Jarrett wondered.

The woman in the hotel had called her, "Miss Abassi." Whatever she'd said to the soldier who asked for identification had gotten his attention.

Who was she?

Ziba appeared behind him and began stroking his hair.

"Thomas," she said softly, "what happened outside the restaurant? There was shooting."

She was barefooted wearing a white tank top with blue jeans. She poured another drink for herself and sat next to him.

"I took care of them, just like I did on the airplane," Jarrett said matter-of-factly.

"You killed them?"

"Yes. They shot your bodyguards and the valet attendant. They were after you, Ziba."

She sighed and looked away. When her gaze returned she said, "Who are you Thomas? You haven't made any appointments at hospitals in the city."

"This isn't about me Ziba. This is about you. The bad guys at the restaurant were after you."

"Yes," she said, her voice dropping.

"They knew you would be there. When you made the reservation, who did you talk to?"

"The maître d' who seated us. He's new. I've never seen him before."

Jarrett was right. The maître d' had set up the hit. It would be a while before he seated anyone again.

"Were you the target of the hijacking too?"

"Yes. They wanted to take me to Somalia, collect a ransom from my family, then put a video on the internet of my beheading."

Jarrett sighed. "Who are they?"

"People from my past."

"What people? Damn it, tell me."

She sighed. "MEK. The Mujahadeen-e-Khalq, or the people's holy warriors. They're a radical Islamic political movement dedicated to Marxism. They've been battling our government back to the shah's time. The Saudis on the airplane were their hired agents. Some think the Saudis support them. The Iraqis supported them in the past. If the men tonight were Persians, they were locals."

"Why you?"

She hesitated, her eyes dropping. "Because of my father. By hurting me they hurt him."

That didn't make sense. Why not just assassinate her father? Then Jarrett remembered his father telling him that the worst thing that could happen to a man was to lose a child.

Ziba's cell phone rang. When she saw the number she said, "I have to take this."

Jarrett disappeared to the bathroom.

CHAPTER 37

When he returned, she said, "That was my father. He heard about the shooting. He wants me to leave the country. We have a house in Switzerland. No one knows about it. I told him I couldn't leave. Not now."

"Why?" Jarrett snapped. "Why can't you leave?"

She looked into his eyes and smiled. "Last night I told Bita how I felt about you. She read the Indira cards for me."

"Indira cards?"

"Persian tarot cards developed by Madame Indira in the 1980s. Bita reads them. She's a seer. She said I might have met my soul mate and I should stick with him until I know for sure."

"Know what?" Jarrett asked.

"If you *are* my soul mate and if I'm going to fall in love with you. I know it sounds silly."

"That's fortune telling Ziba. That's really crazy."

She sighed. "I know. But we have fun with it and sometimes it can be helpful. That's the first positive thing she's said about my love life since my divorce. I think she's right. So, I'm not going anywhere until I know. And I suppose I won't know until you tell me who you are."

"You've only known me for two days. You're just on an emotional buzz from what happened on the airplane and at the restaurant tonight."

"Fine. You may be right. But I'm still not going anywhere until this plays out. I never dreamed it could happen so fast. And I don't even know who the hell you are."

Jarrett bit his lower lip.

"You're thinking, Thomas. Tell me. Tell me who you are and why you're here." Ziba's voice was soft, her eyes intent on his.

Jarrett had a suspicion who her father was. If he was right the contract could go away in a New York second. He would need Ziba's help. He couldn't ask for it until he told her his story. But he had to wait until she confirmed his suspicion. Even then it would be a calculated risk.

"Who I am isn't important. I'm here because I'm following an international criminal, reporting what he does in Tehran. He was on the airplane, sitting two rows in front of us. I'll leave when he leaves. It's as simple as that."

"So you *are* a foreign agent. I figured as much. You won't tell me your name?"

"Why don't you ask Bita?" Jarrett countered. "If she's as good as you say, she'll tell you."

"That's not fair. Bita's a wonderful person. She just helps in matters of the heart, nothing else."

"You know now why I'm here. But I don't know anything about you, except that you're rich and educated and this crazy political group is after you."

She shook her head and chuckled. "So here I am, falling in love with a foreign agent who won't tell me who he is. And he'll probably be on his way in the next few days. Great."

"Let's make a deal. When you come clean with me, maybe I'll do the same with you."

"Maybe?"

"Yes, maybe. Because if what you tell me isn't the truth, I will be on my way. End of story."

"You're a real hardass, Thomas, or whoever the hell you are. But I have no choice. I'm not ready to hear goodbye from you. So it's a deal, but only if you stay the night. Even with the guards, I'm nervous about being alone."

"I really shouldn't. Your place is an armed fortress. You'll be safe."

"Knowing you're here makes me feel better. I have a spare bedroom set up for Tony."

* * *

Jarrett stared at the hieroglyphics on the ceiling, wondering what the ancient Egyptians were telling him. Whatever it was had a somnolent effect, like counting sheep backward. The weight of the day was wearing on him and his eyes were heavy. As he turned on his side, the sheets rustled behind him.

Ziba snuggled up to him, her body melding into his, as if they were made for each other.

She slid her hand between his legs and whispered, "Thomas, roll on your back. Let me welcome you to Tehran."

CHAPTER 38

It was an unforgettable welcome. Ziba was incredible—energetic, creative, surpringly uninhibited. And tireless. Three times during the night.

They slept late, had a light breakfast, then a two-hour workout in her gym. Jarrett was taking a breather, leaning on the incline bench, sipping a glass of grapefruit juice. Ziba was still on the elliptical machine, pedaling tirelessly and perspiring profusely, intent on the video screen.

"Yes!" she suddenly shouted.

"What?" Jarrett asked.

"I just summited Mount Toubal! I've been on a trail upward for the last forty minutes."

"Nice going. You're in the Atlas Mountains."

"How do you know?"

"Been there."

"Really? Were you on the job as a spy following someone?"

"Nope. Skied Oukaimeden. A friend of mine wanted to ski all seven continents, so I went to Morocco with her. Long time ago."

"A lady friend?"

"We were engaged at the time. But it didn't work out."

"So you ski."

"I did. And I played hockey in college. Actually had a scholarship and was named All-American three years in a row."

"I knew you went to college. You lied to me."

"All in a day's work."

"Did you lie about being married?"

"No. And I haven't had a serious relationship since I was engaged."

"Now that you're on a roll talking, I'm curious about one thing. You must have serious martial arts training. Tell me about it."

125

"I grew up on a ranch."

"A ranch with cows and horses?

"Yes, an honest-to-God cattle ranch."

"Where?"

"The Black Hills of South Dakota."

"So you *are* American. Not Canadian. I thought so."

"Let me tell the story. It's interesting." Jarrett smiled. This was one memory he loved to share. "When I was eight, my father hired a ranch hand named Matheus, a political exile from Rio de Janeiro. A remote cattle ranch in the United States was a perfect place to hide from the agents hunting him. Matheus was a lawyer and a martial arts master with a black belt in Gracie Brazilian jujitsu. We outfitted a room in the barn with mats and a stove for cold winter nights, and Matheus and I trained faithfully every evening and on weekends. When I was fourteen, I went to my first competition in Denver. I submitted a twenty-five-year-old black belt with an arm bar. By the time I left for college I was fourth degree."

"What happened to Matheus?"

"After I left for college, he moved to Miami. I see him once in a while. He still teaches there."

"It's hard to believe that a man with your talents just follows people."

"I've told you enough, Ziba."

She stepped off the elliptical machine and began toweling herself. "Let's go to lunch."

"Bad idea. MEK is focused on you right now. Failing twice won't settle well with them. They'll be back sooner rather than later."

She shook her head. "Persistent bastards. I'm not going to cower to him. I'm going to live my life. And I know you'll protect me."

"Who's he? Do you know someone in MEK?"

She hesitated and her eyes dropped. "No, but I do know a really good place we can have lunch. Popular with the financial crowd, or what's left of them. Great *kabob-barg*."

"A steak sounds great, but it's too dangerous to go out right now."

"I have a couple of things I need to do. I'll go myself and bring lunch back."

"You're not going out by yourself. If you insist, we can just drive to the restaurant, no reservation this time, then straight home. No other stops."

CHAPTER 39

Shandiz Mashad had crisp white table cloths, plush chairs upholstered in red velvet, and soft lighting. It was crowded with small groups of well-dressed men, but the maître d' recognized Ziba and found them a table. The driver stayed with the car, while the other guard stood in the restaurant, his eyes locked on Ziba.

Jarrett ate a spiced filet mignon kabob with roasted tomatoes; Ziba had spinach salad with braised prawns.

Ziba talked about her friend Tony and one of her nephews who wanted to go to college in the U.S. It was as if she had completely put the MEK bad guys out of her head. Maybe it was her way of coping. But Jarrett was on edge.

A motorcycle had followed them for a short while after they'd left the condo. A second one had sped by when they parked. But crazy drivers on two wheels zooming in and out of traffic were common in Tehran.

"Your mind is somewhere else, Thomas. Will you check in with me, please?"

"The food's great and the ambience here is just right, but I'm uneasy, Ziba."

"Look around. There's no one here to worry about."

"That's all I've been doing . . . looking around and worrying."

"Would you like to shop for something sexy I can wear for you tonight? There's a couple of shops on the way back to my place."

"No. Let's go back. No stops."

* * *

"I wish you could relax, Thomas."

Jarrett sat sideways in the seat, looking ahead for obstructions and behind for suspicious vehicles. His spider sense had taken over.

They were in a bad neighborhood, driving slowly down a narrow street lined with discount shops, greasy spoon cafés, and walk-in rooming houses. On their left a park stretched one full block to the next street. Vagrants were approaching the car, begging for money. The driver and guard were unfazed, but Jarrett wasn't. If they came under attack, escape would be difficult.

"How much longer on this street?" Jarrett asked, looking out the back window.

An older Volvo sedan was behind them. A beat-up, white step-van with its hazard lights flashing appeared behind it.

"This is a shortcut back to my place."

Suddenly the Volvo swerved into the oncoming lane, cut back in front of them, and skidded to a stop.

"Pass it!" Jarrett shouted.

The driver swerved a split second too late. The front of the Mercedes crashed into the Volvo and accordioned in a cloud of smoke. The air bags deployed.

A man dressed in black with a ski mask jumped from the Volvo and ran into the park.

As Jarrett released his seat belt, he was knocked forward. The van had crashed into the rear of the Mercedes pinning it against the Volvo. The rear window exploded, covering them with fragments of glass.

Jarrett shouted, "Draw your guns!" but the airbags had trapped both guards.

He released Ziba's seat belt and pushed her to the floor.

As he turned to peer over the seat, the van's front doors flew open, and the driver and a passenger jumped out. The driver sprinted toward the park, while the passenger lunged toward the Mercedes.

Jarrett's mind raced.

The passenger is the shooter. He's going to spray the Mercedes with steel jackets. End of story.

But he didn't. He frisbeed a package under the Mercedes and disappeared behind the van.

"Bomb! Out of the car. Now!" Jarrett shrieked.

He opened the door and dragged Ziba across the sidewalk. The clock in his head was ticking—one thousand one, one thousand two . . .

The driver was out of the car but stunned. He hadn't heard Jarrett. The other guard was trapped, his door wedged tight from the collision.

Jarrett and Ziba stumbled toward a table stacked with heavy garments. It was under a display window and the door next to it was closed. No one was in sight.

At one thousand three Jarrett pushed Ziba under the table, scrambling to pull the table on its side. When the table tumbled over it became a makeshirt barrier and heavy coats and other garments covered them.

At one thousand six . . . *boom.*

The ground shook violently.

A shock wave of super-heated air thrust the table into them, but its stout legs and the clothes cushioned the impact. The glass window above them and the shop door exploded inward.

The Mercedes absorbed the brunt of the explosion and was hurtled into the air. The gas tank exploded and hot shards of metal and chunks of plastic rained down on them.

The driver landed on the sidewalk ten feet away.

The Mercedes came to rest on its side, a smoldering heap of tangled metal. The passenger guard was still in the car.

The Volvo and the van were destroyed; four other vehicles parked nearby were severely damaged.

Shop windows for a block in each direction had shattered.

Three pedestrians were down, others were screaming hysterically as they tried to escape.

The air was acrid with smoke from burning plastic and rubber.

Jarrett pushed the smoldering clothes off him and peered over the table.

His concern was a shooter—a trailer—left behind to finish the job if the bomb hadn't. But there were no threats in sight, just horrific, senseless carnage.

A horn sounded across the park, *beep, beep, beep,* and a car sped away. *The escape vehicle.*

As sirens began to blare in the distance, Jarrett gathered Ziba in his arms. He ran through the store skirting a man and a young boy cowering behind a cabinet.

Ziba was dazed. "What happened, Thomas?"

Jarrett never heard a word. His ears were ringing, and he was hell-bent to get as far away as possible.

He sprinted three blocks down an alley and stumbled on a taxi.

CHAPTER 40

Back in her condo, Ziba took a long hot shower. She couldn't stop shaking, and it seemed like the only way to rid herself of the stench of death.

After a lengthy absence she walked into the living room and took Jarrett's hands. "Thank you for saving my life . . . again," she said.

Although she was still shaken, there was a thoughtful, cerebral warmth about her that was indescribable.

"No thanks necessary. I'm just glad you're safe. The guards didn't make it."

Ziba sighed. "That's terrible. I didn't even know them. What happened?"

Jarrett explained, then added, "We were lucky . . . again. But I'm afraid our luck's going to run out. The bad guys really want you."

"Yes, unfortunately they do."

"I still don't understand why you're the target. If it's MEK, they would get more by killing your father."

"You're right," she said, pain etched on her face.

"Ziba. You're not telling me something. You know someone in MEK."

She sipped her drink and kissed Jarrett on the cheek. "This is personal, not political. Someone in a splinter group of MEK has targeted me."

Jarrett said nothing.

"His name is Javid Gil. They call him Jago. We met as freshmen at the university. He was handsome, brilliant, and charismatic. A young, starry-eyed eighteen-year-old girl fell for him."

There was sadness in her eyes. A tear trickled down her cheek.

"Jago was a radical, obsessed with overthrowing the government. He preached Marxism. MEK recruited him, and it got darker after that."

Jarrett sat quietly.

"He tried to convert me to his radical ways. He even took me to a retreat in Syria. I guess in America, you would call it a brainwashing."

Ziba began to cry, and Jarrett took her in his arms. After a few minutes she gathered herself and continued.

"It was a month from hell. He physically abused me, and wouldn't let me leave until I agreed to join MEK. I ate nothing but bread and water. Lost twelve pounds. I was a mess. When I came back, I told my father what had happened. I left the university and went to college in Scotland with a fake identity. Jago disappeared. I met a young professor there, and we married. It didn't work out." She tried to smile. "That's where I developed a taste for scotch and cigarettes."

"Why does Jago want to hurt you?"

"He hates me. He wrote me a letter. Said that he'd get even with me for leaving him."

"Why now?"

"That's a good question. We think his group gets support from the Saudis. Jago's become the head of it. He's trying to make a statement. Show how powerful he is."

"Where is he?"

"We don't know. We think maybe Paris. Why do you ask?"

Jarrett remembered that the old Arab on the plane had spent time in Paris. Jago was the mastermind behind the hijacking.

"Just curious."

When Ziba excused herself to use the bathroom, Jarrett checked the tracking program. The messenger bag was still in Demus's hotel, and there was a new voice message from Sedgewick. Jarrett could only imagine what was going on in Washington.

"Would you like a drink?" Ziba asked when she returned.

"Yes. Go heavy on the bourbon. It's time we come clean with each other. I think I know who your father is. Remember the woman in the hotel? She called you Miss Abassi."

"That's my maiden name."

"You're Mir Abassi's daughter. The head of the Revolutionary Guard."

She smiled. "His only daughter as a matter of fact. And I have two brothers. I've wanted to tell you about him and my family."

"Well tell me then, damn it. I need to know."

Ziba sighed and stared at the wall. When her eyes returned to Jarrett, she said, "My father was the leader of the students who seized the American embassy in 1979. He was just a young upstart then who wanted to free his country from the shah's tyranny. During his rise to power he realized what he'd done was wrong. Like his children, he believes no country will prosper under a theocracy. His hope is to have a democracy with elected officials. We can live freely then. I don't like wearing a fucking scarf every time I go out or sneaking a bottle of wine into a restaurant."

"Democracy is a lofty goal."

"It is, but he'll keep trying. He believes it's critical to show the world that we won't develop nuclear weapons. Then the sanctions will be lifted. Iran can prosper." She sighed. "Unfortunately my father has one major adversary."

"Who?" Jarrett asked.

"My uncle. My mother's brother, Ali Mandazi. He became the head of the Quds when Soleimani was assassinated."

"Shit. The head of the Quds is your uncle."

She nodded. "He's the opposite of my father in every way, but he has the ayatollah's ear like Soleimani had. He wants a nuclear arsenal. Remember when you asked me what was in the U.S. Embassy compound? Well, that's where his office is, believe it or not."

"Ziba, you live like a queen."

She smiled "An Egyptian queen, perhaps. But they're all dead." She shrugged. "My family controls major businesses. One of my brothers runs telecommunications and the other petrochemicals. We call them *bonyads*."

Jarrett's suspicion was correct. Ziba *was* Mir Abassi's daughter. He had saved her twice. And she was falling for him. Abassi could rescind the contract on him. End of story.

"So now you know about me. You know it's the truth. It's your turn. The story that you're following someone is bullshit," she said.

Jarrett took a mouthful of his drink and swallowed hard. "Can I trust you?"

"Yes," she said with a glow in her eyes. "You know you can, Thomas."

Here I go. Sedgewick's going to be pissed.

After another mouthful of whiskey, he spit the words out. "My name is Clint Jarrett. I'm the personal assassin for the president of the United States. Why I'm in Iran is a long, complicated story."

"I'm all ears."

He told her everything, beginning with the Iranian contract on him to the nuclear deal between Hezbollah and Iran. He left nothing out. She listened and asked questions, lots of questions. He answered truthfully, and he felt better, a lot better, yet he couldn't believe he had confided in her.

"I knew you were someone special, Clint. I like that name better than Thomas."

"Like I said, the CIA analyst told me there was a spy in the Guard, but he wouldn't give me his name."

"So you don't know the spy's identity. That's good. I'll arrange a meeting with my father. He'll know who you are and what kind of man you are. You have saved his daughter's life three times. And he'll know how his daughter feels about you. He'll look in your eyes and ask if you know the spy's name. When you answer no, he'll lift the contract. It'll be over then."

"I hope it plays out that way."

"It will. I promise."

"I'm perplexed why Demus was killed. And wondering who did it."

"There's an anti-nuc underground in Tehran. They may be responsible. I've heard rumors from them that we have nuclear weapons."

"According to the Mossad spy in Hezbollah, you do. Are you a member of the underground?"

"No. But I have a friend who is."

"Your father must be very upset if Iran has Russian bombs and is sending one to Hezbollah."

"I'm sure he is, but I know better than to ask. We don't talk about it. But if we're sending one to Hezbollah, my uncle is overseeing it."

"Find out if the anti-nucs killed Demus."

"I'll try. Now that I know who you are, I feel so much better."

"Me too. Getting the contract off my back will be a big step. I'll be able to lead a normal life then, without worrying about an assassin lurking around the corner."

"And now I don't need Bita and the Indira cards. I've met my soul mate."

"That makes me happy, Ziba."

"I'm glad." She kissed him.

"I'd better head over to the hotel and clean up." He looked down on himself. "I'm a mess."

CHAPTER 41

When Jarrett got back to the Espinas, he trashed his clothes and took a shower. He couldn't stop thinking about Ziba. He was worried.

Despite his heroics it was just a matter of time until Jago fulfilled his promise. He was a psychopath with assets in Iran willing to put their lives on the line for him. Ziba's only hope was to leave. After he met with her father, he'd take her to the cottage outside of Edinburgh. But after that?

With the Iranian contract lifted he'd be a free man.

But as long as Ziba's life was in danger, Jarrett felt bound to her. Edinburgh was only a temporary solution. His ranch in South Dakota would be permanent safe haven. Sedgewick could have a legend cobbled with bona fides that no one could unravel.

Jarrett told himself to step back for a second. What was he thinking? Did he plan to spend the rest of his life with Ziba Vijany?

He needed to escape these thoughts. It was a good time to call Sedgewick.

"Jarrett, glad you called. I heard about a bombing in Tehran."

"They tried to get Ziba again. With an IED this time. We escaped by the skin of our teeth. There's a psycho in MEK named Javid Gil who's targeted her. Calls himself Jago. It's a personal thing. They had a relationship a long time ago."

"Sounds ominous. And you're right in the middle of it."

"I am, and more than you know. Believe it or not, Ziba is Mir Abassi's daughter."

"You're shitting me. You're involved with the daughter of the head of the Revolutionary Guard? I guess that explains everything."

"She says he's pro-democracy and anti-nuclear. Wants the sanctions lifted so the country can grow. Her uncle is Ali Mandazi and he's managing the Hezbollah deal."

"Mandazi replaced Soleimani. He's the head of the Quds."

"I know. And one more thing, Sedgewick." Jarrett sighed. "I told Ziba who I am."

There was silence for a few seconds, then Sedgewick shouted, "You what?"

"I told her who I am. And the whole damn story of why I'm here."

"You've lost your mind, Jarrett. You've blown your cover."

"I had to. It's the only way I could get her to help. She's going to set up a meeting with her father. She says he'll rescind the contract. Then I'm a free man."

"Why would she do that?"

"Why do you think?" After a pause, Jarrett added, "Because she likes me and wants to help. I told her I don't know the spy's identity."

"This is the Paladin syndrome again. At least I hope that's all it is. You meet a hot chick, she falls for you, then you disappear."

"I won't disappear this time. After my meeting with her father, I'll take her to Edinburgh. Otherwise she's a dead woman."

"Forget the meeting with her father. You're going to Beirut."

"Beirut! Why?"

"To meet with Hezbollah. You're replacing Demus."

"I'm what?" Jarrett shrieked.

"You heard me. You're going to purchase the bomb for Hezbollah, or at least both parties to the deal will think you are."

"No way, Sedgewick!"

"You have to. Orders from the Oval Office. We have to prove that the Iranians have Russian devices."

"You know they do. You have intel from your guy in Mossad. Mohsen told Demus and he told Mossad."

"This is our chance to prove it. If we accuse Moscow of giving nuclear devices to Iran, they'll deny it, like they deny everything else—poisoning the former Russian military officer and his daughter in London and messing with our elections. Iran would back them up of course. But if we get one of their bombs, bingo, we have proof. Do you know what would happen if it got into Hezbollah's hands? They're crazier than the Iranians."

"I know. But I'm an assassin, not a spook. Why doesn't Mossad use one of its own agents?"

"I have the impression that Israel doesn't want a second one of its own in harm's way with Hezbollah. And remember the timeline is urgent. They don't have time to train someone and establish a legend. I told them our top Middle East operative is in Istanbul with a Turkish legend. A little fib of course. I said you're perfect, you can look like an Arab when you want to, you speak the language, and . . ."

"And don't say it again . . . I am one."

"Only half. So they agreed to use you as the intermediary."

"How do I get introduced to Mohsen? I can't just appear out of nowhere."

"Fortunately, Mossad's deep cover has been involved with the deal from the beginning. That's how he learned about Demus. When news about Demus's death reached Hezbollah, the deep cover told them he knew a Turkish guy who worked with Demus. That's you. You were billed as a deal-maker, just like him. Both sides want to get this done as soon as possible. Iran insists on an intermediary. You're the man."

"I get all that, but how will they contact me?"

"You won't be contacted. Everything has funneled back and forth between the spy, Mossad, and me. POTUS is onboard with the plan. Just hours after the deep cover got the okay to use you, he reported back that you'd been contacted and agreed to be in Beirut tomorrow. You have a reservation at Hotel al-Sahia compliments of Hezbollah. It's in the Dahieh district, a Muslim stronghold south of Beirut. We checked it out. It's owned by Hezbollah. Two years ago Lebanese authorities raided the property looking for suicide-bomber vests. But it appears to have travel appeal with a beautiful swimming pool and no two guest rooms alike. But when you get the device it goes to Washington. Not Tel Aviv."

"Why?"

"Because the Oval Office wants it, that's why. In our hands it'll be like a high-profile hostage in a foolproof kidnapping. The Russians are vulnerable with their economy in the toilet. The Iranians are in the same boat with the sanctions. And we don't want Israel to start a war in the Middle East."

"Israel will be pissed," Jarrett added.

"Maybe not. They'd rather us have the bomb than the terrorists. They know we'll use it as a big stick to protect them. And we're in a stronger position out of the gate with the Russians and Persians."

"What happens once we have the bomb?"

"That's up to your friend the president. After your last mission, you two are asshole buddies."

"Do I detect a little jealousy?"

"Maybe."

They laughed.

"If I'm going to replace Demus, whoever killed him might come after me. Any theories around Langley about who did him?" Jarrett asked.

"Some of the whiz kids think it might be the anti-nucs in Tehran."

"That's possible. Ziba knows someone in the underground. She'll try to find out if they're responsible. I have a feeling they're not well-organized, a ragtag bunch of intellectuals and young upstarts. Demus's hitter was a pro. If it was the anti-nucs, it would have been messy. A shooting outside his hotel in broad daylight or maybe even a bomb in his hotel room, something like MEK is doing with Ziba. I suppose the underground could have hired someone."

"The other thought around here is it's the Russians."

"The Russians? That's a stretch. Why would they do it?" Jarrett asked.

"Moscow has no stock in Hezbollah. At least none we're aware of. And they gave the weapons to Iran. If they saw value in Hezbollah having one, they would have sent it to Beirut. They must have a few laying around, the ones that went missing. If Iran sells one to their proxy, it complicates Russia's position immeasurably."

"Nuclear weapons are just what the Iranians need to bully everyone. But to use them as leverage, they'll have to let the world know they have them."

"It'll be a carefully choreographed leak," Sedgewick added. "They'll say they developed them. Makes them look good—smart and capable. The Russians certainly don't want anyone to know they gave the Persians weapons."

"And with the money the Iranians save they build missiles and bolster their army."

"For sure. We're not as worried about the Iranians as we are about Hezbollah."

"The Beirut terrorists have a lot less to lose than the Persians," Jarrett said.

"By the way you pick up the stuff for your new legend—Demus number two, the bomb deal intermediary—in the Beirut airport. It's on a plane over the Atlantic right now."

"Who do I leave Iran as? The Canadian or the Arab?" Jarrett asked.

"E-ticket's in the name of the same guy who came in. The hero. What's his name?"

"Thomas Davis."

"Anything special you'll need?"

Jarrett paused to think for a second. "Nothing other than the usual."

"After Hezbollah contacts you at the hotel, meet with them, negotiate a fee, return to Tehran ASAP, and take possession of the weapon. You'll have an open ticket back to Tehran."

"Simple as that?" Jarrett asked sarcastically.

"Simple as that."

"Then what?"

"Then we get you and the bomb the hell out of Dodge. No pun intended."

"You make it sound so easy."

"It is . . . for you. But you might not enjoy this gig. It doesn't involve killing anyone."

"Someone here doesn't want this deal to go through. They killed Demus. Like I said, they might try to do me."

"But Demus wasn't Paladin. You're invincible, my friend."

"I almost bit the dust on the flight to Tehran and a couple of times since then."

"If you weren't invincible you'd be dead long ago. Keep your phone and laptop with you. Same communication setup."

Jarrett laughed. "That's good. At least something will be the same. I might have trouble keeping track of who I am again, like that last Pakistan job. This'll be my fourth legend since I went black."

"Is the Persian lady anything like the Pakistan ISI agent you were so hot on?"

"I wasn't hot on her. Ziba makes her look like one of my cow dogs."

"Wow. She must be something. I've seen pics of the Pakistani in uniform. Good-looking gal," Sedgewick said.

"Ziba is a classy lady. And nice. She's had a tough time of it with this Jago character."

"Put her out of your head, my friend. And please don't tell her why you're going to Beirut."

"I won't tell her. She doesn't need to know. But before I leave Iran with the bomb, I'm going to meet with her father."

"Tomorrow you'll have a bagel with cream cheese and green tea for breakfast."

"Got it."

"You need to know that POTUS thinks this is the most important espionage mission in our country's history."

"Like I said, I'm not a spy."

"You are now. And remember the eleventh commandment."

"What's that?" Jarrett asked.

"Don't get caught."

CHAPTER 42

That night Jarrett ate Chinese food and drank plum wine at Ziba's apartment.

She had recovered from the bombing, at least on the surface, and looked spectacular—like a fitness model—in a low-cut white tank top, mauve slacks, and sandals.

After dinner they had drinks in the living room. Ziba had been very quiet during dinner. Jarrett wondered if something was wrong.

"You okay? You've been awfully quiet. Is the bombing still bothering you?"

She hesitated then said, "Of course the bombing bothers me. It was scary as hell. If you hadn't acted so quickly and if the table hadn't been there we'd be dead. But to be honest, I'm trying to work through my feelings about you. It's been an emotional roller coaster. Everything has happened so fast. I never dreamt I'd be in love with a . . ."

Jarrett interrupted. "A what?"

Ziba took a deep breath. "An assassin. I'm struggling with a disconnect about it."

"A disconnect?"

"Yes, a disconnect. Damn it. You're everything I've ever dreamed of in a man. But you're an assassin, a professional killer. I'm trying to work through that. When the dark side of the disconnect takes hold, it says I shouldn't be in love with a killer. Yet I am. I can't help myself. I don't know what to do. Maybe it would help if I understood why you do what you do."

Jarrett smiled. He could appreciate her disconnect.

"I went to work for the president because I felt an obligation to help my country fight terrorism and I needed the money," he told her. "After my father died, there was a downturn in the cattle market, and I had to take out a mortgage on the ranch to pay expenses. When the money ran out I faced losing the ranch. So I went to work for the president. I paid the mortgage off and I have a nice bank account now. Every time I travel there's one less bad guy out there."

A forlorn look came across her face. "So, that's it? You're a patriot who had financial trouble? You're such a spiritual man, Clint, so warm and loving and thoughtful. I can't believe there isn't something else driving you."

Jarrett sighed, a sadness settling over him. "You're very insightful, Ziba. There *is* something else. It's not easy to talk about it."

"If you tell me it might help me . . . and maybe it would help you as well."

Jarrett spoke in a calm voice. "His name was Charlie. Charlie Brant. He was my best friend in high school. He was Lakota-Sioux, lived on the reservation with his uncles. His tribal name was *Akecheta*, which means warrior. Both his parents had died when he was a child. We were inseparable, did everything together. He always had a smile on his face. His tribe adopted me, and I learned the Indian ways—hunting, fishing, tracking, and survival in the wild. They called me *Wambleeska*—White Eagle. Charlie enlisted in the army after high school. Special Forces. He couldn't afford to go to college. We didn't have the money to help him."

Jarrett choked up and his eyes were rheumy and pained. Ziba took his hands in hers.

"During his fourth tour in Iraq he was captured by ISIS. He was tortured for weeks, then beheaded . . . by a guy who'd been a colonel in the Iraqi army under Saddam Hussein. But Charlie never gave in to them. Never denounced his country or begged for mercy. He was so strong, Ziba, so incredibly strong. ISIS posted all of it online. It was horrible. One of his uncles committed suicide afterward."

"I'm so sorry, Clint."

"At the time I was in the military myself, running all over the damn Middle East killing terrorists. I always worked alone, like I do now. I used elaborate disguises sometimes. It's a long story, but army intelligence uncovered an ISIS recruiter in Baghdad. We used him to get me into ISIS. After a couple of weeks of indoctrination, I beheaded the guy who killed Charlie.

In the dark of night, I put his head in the town square on top of a barrel. Made an example of him for the rest of those bastards."

"Oh my God. They were so vile. How did you escape?"

"A doctor and his daughter in Raqqa helped me. Two days after I got back to Bagdad, I killed the recruiter and two of his helpers. When I come home now from a mission, I always stop under the archway at the ranch entrance. There's a sign hanging from it that says Capistran Ranch. Charlie and I carved it in a slab of pine one summer. I look up at it and remember him. Sometimes I talk to him. He's the brother I never had, Ziba. There's a place in my heart where he'll always live. Everytime I kill one of the bad guys it's for Charlie. I guess you could say I'm avenging him."

"You *are* avenging him," she said, looking at Jarrett with love and understanding.

"Sometimes the pain of not having him and how he died is unbearable. Maybe one day the pain will be gone, and I'll be at peace. But until then I have to carry on. So now you know why I do what I do."

Ziba smiled. "I understand now. And I knew there was a reason. I feel better now. I hope you do too."

"Actually, I do feel a little better. You and my friend Dodge Sedgewick are the only ones I've talked to about this."

"The disconnect I felt before is gone now, Clint. I feel a deep connection to you, I guess you could say through Charlie." She kissed Jarrett on he cheek.

"I'm glad you feel better. I wish I didn't have to tell you this, but unfortunately, Ziba, I have to fly to Beirut tomorrow. I don't like leaving you," he said.

"Beirut? Why?"

"CIA business. Spur-of-the-moment thing. Nothing major."

"You haven't met with my father yet."

"I'll be back in a few days. I'll meet with him then." Jarrett's plan was to close the deal with Mohsen, meet with Mir Abassi, take possession of the bomb, and get out of Iran.

"I've spoken with him already. He's anxious to meet you."

"We'll have to travel separately to Edinburgh. You should fly by charter, after what happened on Iran Air."

"Don't remind me of that awful experience. Tony has a plane. I'll ask him if I can use it. He'll probably come along and hang out with us for a while."

"We're going to stay at a cottage an hour outside the city. It's a CIA safe house. Best we go there alone, without anyone knowing. Tony can fly you to Edinburgh. I'll pick you up at the airport."

"Why don't we fly together on his plane? That would be fun."

"I have to leave Iran as Thomas Davis, on a commercial flight, the way I came in."

"If it's a CIA safe house we can't stay there forever. I love Scotland. I'll sell this place and we can buy a country house. I have a U.K. passport. It'll be easy."

"I have to get back to my ranch in South Dakota. I've been gone for a couple of months."

"What about me?"

"You'll come with me. I'll get you a new identity."

She looked into his eyes. "What happens then? Do I stay there the rest of my life?"

"That's up to you," Jarrett replied. "You might not like living on a ranch. It's remote and the winters are long and hard."

"No, Clint. It's up to you. You know how I feel about you, but you haven't told me how you feel about me."

"You're in my heart, Ziba." That was the most he could say.

"Do you love me?"

"I have strong feelings for you. But you know who I am, and now you know why I do what I do. I'm not sure what love is at this point. Maybe I'm just afraid of being hurt again."

"You won't be hurt by me," she said. Jarrett felt relieved.

"You'll be safe at the ranch. That's all that matters right now. We'll see how things go. If you don't like it there, you can get a place in Scotland. I can visit you." Jarrett suddenly chuckled to himself with the thought that there'd be a third Middle Eastern woman in the Black Hills of South Dakota . . . at least for a time.

"I want to be with you Clint . . . forever. I'll be your best friend and your lover no matter where we are. I'm even going to learn to cook."

They laughed. "That'll be interesting. You're a special lady, Ziba. I have to get back to the hotel and pack now. Will you hold onto my kit for me while I'm gone? I'll drop it off on my way to the airport."

"Your kit? What's that?"

"It's the stuff I use on a mission. I picked it up at the train station the morning after I got here. It's a suitcase with clothes, an electronic device we call a sniffer for detecting hidden cameras and listening devices, a gun with ammo, and a few other things."

"Of course. But stay the night."

"I've got too much to do. And I need a good night's sleep. Something I won't get if I stay here with you." He winked and kissed her. "Long day tomorrow. I'll be in touch when I get back."

"I love you, Clint."

CHAPTER 43

Jarrett sailed through security at the Tehran airport. He wondered if Mir Abassi had something to do with it. After all, Thomas Davis was a national hero in Iran.

The flying time to Beirut was three hours and thirty-five minutes. The flight landed at 1:10 p.m. local time. He had no problems using the Davis ID at passport control, and his bag wasn't searched at customs.

After he purchased a burner, he rode an escalator to the second floor, walked to the south end of the terminal, turned around, and retraced his steps. In spy parlance this was called the accordion maneuver. He wasn't followed, so he stopped at a small coffee shop, drank a cup of coffee and ate a *bukaj baklava*. The only two patrons were uniformed airport employees.

At exactly 2:30 p.m., he followed a side corridor to a plain door with a sign over it that read Chapel. A hand-scrawled note on the door said it was temporarily closed.

He knocked twice, paused, knocked once, paused, and knocked twice again. A few seconds later the lock snicked.

He let a full minute pass on his chronograph before opening the door.

The small room was draped in shadows. Four rows of benches divided by a center aisle faced a table with flickering votive candles.

A woman wearing a long coat and scarf sat on the front bench staring at a painting of St. Maron on the wall behind the table. She was alone.

When Jarrett sat down behind her, she murmured, "What did you have for breakfast?"

Jarrett replied, "A bagel with cream cheese and green tea."

With that she slid a carry-on bag into the aisle.

146

He took it and removed a wallet and passport from its side pocket.

Inside the passport was a boarding pass for Yusuf Sahin for a flight from Istanbul earlier that day. The Turk had cleared passport control at the Beirut airport after the flight.

Jarrett murmured, "Thank you," and the woman nodded.

He left behind his carry-on with the Thomas Davis bona fides.

The contact never saw his face.

CHAPTER 44

At the arrival level of the terminal Jarrett jumped two taxis, a habit he'd developed after a bad experience in an airport in Afghanistan.

He took the third taxi and gave the driver the name and address of his hotel.

At the first stoplight, the driver closed the privacy screen. The door and window locks snicked seconds later.

Jarrett had an uncanny sense of direction having been to Beirut many times. The driver was going in the wrong direction.

He rapped on the window, shouting, "Wrong way!"

The driver looked in the rearview mirror, sneered at Jarrett, and flipped his cigarette out the window.

Despite jumping two taxis, Clint Jarrett, the vaunted Oval Office assassin known as Paladin, was the victim of a random kidnapping. *Welcome to Beirut.*

The kidnappers would hold him for ransom. Whether it was paid or not, he was a dead man.

They drove through a war-torn neighborhood, the streets and sidewalks littered with trash. Many buildings were windowless, with bullet-scarred walls and gaping craters in the roofs. Abandoned cars with flat tires and soot-covered windshields lined the streets. This was the vestige of an upscale neighborhood bombed into oblivion during the last conflict with Israel.

Jarrett's impression of Beirut was that she was battered and bruised but refused to stay down. This section of the city had missed the remarkable recovery the city center had enjoyed since 2006.

The GPS on his phone showed that this was Haret Hreik, one of Hezbollah's strongholds.

The driver stopped at a plank gate that led to a walled compound. He beeped the horn, and a man with a Kalashnikov opened the gate. The driver pulled into a courtyard, circled what was left of an ornate marble fountain, and stopped in front of a two-story stone building with boarded-up windows. Gardens on either side of the building were overgrown with weeds and littered with rubble and trash.

Jarrett figured this had once been a grand estate.

Three crumbling steps led to a broad landing at the building's entrance. A man dressed in a long black robe with a keffiyeh and a Kalashnikov appeared in the doorway.

The gate-opener walked to the front of the taxi with his weapon trained on Jarrett.

The driver got out, lit another cigarette, and opened Jarrett's door.

"Who are you?" the man in the doorway shouted, as Jarrett got out of the taxi. The driver quickly backed away.

"My name is Yusuf Sahin," Jarrett answered. "From Istanbul on holiday. Peace be with you my friend."

"Come inside Yusuf. We must talk." The man gestured for Jarrett to come forward.

Jarrett had to make his move before they got him inside.

If I don't, I'm history, he thought.

The gate-opener followed him up the stairs.

Jarrett slowed his pace, pausing on each step, to close the distance between them.

The black-robed man stepped across the threshold onto the landing. His rifle sling was around his neck, and he cradled the barrel in one hand and the stock in the other. When Jarrett reached the landing he moved to within arm's reach of him.

The gate-opener was nearly on top of Jarrett, so close that Jarrett could smell his foul breath.

Suddenly a car sped through the gate and came to a screeching stop behind the taxi. When the gate-opener turned at the sound, Jarrett grabbed the black-robed man's rifle. In a blur of motion, he twirled it, locking the sling around the man's neck like a garrote. Using the rifle as leverage, he spun and threw the man into the gate opener.

As the gate-opener tumbled backward down the steps, his firearm discharged. The bullets were off their mark and shattered the overhang. Chunks of plaster rained down in a cloud of dust.

The black-robed man was on his knees tethered by the sling. Jarrett thrust the rifle downward, snapping his neck. As his eyes rolled back, the man's mouth fell open and he gurgled. Jarrett twirled the Kalashnikov in reverse and pulled the sling free.

The gate-opener was sprawled on his back on the steps. While trying to right himself, he fired his rifle again, a frenzied burst that resonated over Jarrett's head. Jarrett tucked the Kalashnikov's stock under his arm, swung the muzzle downward and squeezed the trigger for a split second. *Rat, tat, tat.* Three rounds hit the gate-opener in the face.

Just to be sure Jarrett shot the black-robed man point blank in the forehead.

Suddenly a fusillade of bullets ricocheted off the building's façade. They weren't even close to Jarrett, but spalls of stone stung him.

The driver of the car had emptied his handgun and was hell-bent on escaping. As he turned the front wheels and accelerated backward, Jarrett sprayed the windshield. The vehicle spun out of control and crashed into the wall. The driver slumped over the steering wheel in a wash of blood and glass.

The taxi driver sat on the fender of his car, wide-eyed with his mouth agape. When the mayhem finally registered, he flicked his cigarette into the air and ran like a scared jackrabbit.

Jarrett tackled him just outside the gate.

They went down hard, the driver facedown with Jarrett on his back.

Jarrett smashed the driver's face into the concrete sidewalk, then snapped his neck.

The taxi keys were in the ignition. Jarrett used his phone's GPS to direct him to the hotel and abandoned the car in an alley two blocks away.

CHAPTER 45

The hotel, a rough-hewn stone compound encompassing an entire city block, looked like a medieval fortress. A central courtyard featured a magnificent swimming pool with a waterslide and spacious decking for sunbathing. Boutiques and trendy cafés tucked in narrow passages conveyed the charm of old Beirut. But the complex had a brooding quality, as if it somehow knew it was out of place in this part of the city.

When Jarrett checked in using the Turkish legend, he was told his room charges were covered.

Nice of Hezbollah, he thought.

The room was comfortable and bright with a giant arched window overlooking the pool. A bottle of Lebanese red wine and an assortment of fruits, compliments of the manager, sat on a small table.

His kit was complete and included ten grand sewn into the lining of the bag, but no gun.

Only in special situations did Jarrett need one, and this wasn't one of them. He would meet with Hezbollah, negotiate his fee, shake hands, and return to Tehran. At least he hoped it played out that way.

It was too early for dinner, so he thought a hot shower and a drink at poolside would help him unwind. He wondered how Hezbollah would make contact.

Although he planned to have just one drink, he had a second because the whiskey was just right with a pleasing oak-caramel nose and a cinnamon-spice finish.

The bartender had a generous hand pouring Yellowstone Bourbon from the Limestone Distillery in Lebanon, Kentucky. He told Jarrett there were no bourbon distilleries in Lebanon, but whiskey from a town called Lebanon was the next best thing.

When Jarrett got back to the room he had an alcohol buzz and felt relaxed for the first time in days . . . almost. The tape over the doorjamb was torn, but the Do Not Disturb sign was still in place.

He entered the room cautiously. Nothing had been touched.

A note had been left with instructions to be at the Abu Aziz café at 8:00 p.m. and order the special house salad.

CHAPTER 46

Jarrett walked six blocks to the restaurant with his legend's wallet, a few Lebanese pounds, and his burner. He didn't want to chance losing his passport or sat phone.

He ordered the special salad as instructed and a glass of Chateau Musar wine.

A salacious young woman with dark, mischievous eyes sat alone at the bar sipping a martini. She wore a black sleeveless blouse with three buttons open and no bra, a mid-thigh skirt and black heels. Her body was toned and her skin as brown as a berry, but a dorsal nasal hump stole the glimmer from her otherwise pretty face.

With no shame she brazenly stared at Jarrett with that I'd-love-to-meet-you look. He'd fought off advances from women with fire in their eyes in cities around the world. He hoped she wouldn't walk over to his table. It might complicate the evening.

He finished the salad and half the wine and asked for the check. No one showed interest in him other than the woman. He wondered if she was the Hezbollah contact and if the come-on was an act. If so, she'd make a move when he got up to leave.

Jarrett paid the check with the Yusuf Sahin credit card. The waiter thanked him for the tip and placed the signed receipt on the table face down with the credit card. He tapped the receipt with his finger and winked. Scrawled on it was a street address with instructions to take a taxi.

When the young woman looked over again, Jarrett smiled and shook his head. She frowned and held out her hands, as if to say, "Why not?" Jarrett noticed that she had the hands of a working man—thick, rough-skinned fingers with nails crusted with dirt. He shook his head again and left.

The restaurant was in a bustling neighborhood with boutiques, eateries, and movie theaters. The street was well-lit with bumper-to-bumper traffic and crowded sidewalks.

Jarrett decided to walk for a while and hail a taxi at random. It would give him an opportunity to determine if he was being followed.

When he paused to peer into a shop window, a man stopped several storefronts behind him. He fit the stereotype of Hezbollah—young with a buzz cut, dark skin, a stubble beard, dressed in a white collarless shirt and black slacks. But he hustled past Jarrett without a glance and disappeared into the crowd.

At the next intersection Jarrett turned onto a narrow side street. He planned to walk to the next main thoroughfare, follow it a few blocks, and hail a ride. If someone was following him they'd have to show.

After just a few steps he realized he'd crossed into one of the no-go zones that travelers were warned about. He should have known better.

The street was dark with boarded-up storefronts that reeked of stale urine. There was no pedestrian or vehicle traffic. Tiny creatures with high-pitched squeals scurried at Jarrett's feet and the sidewalk was littered with trash.

He decided to backtrack. As he turned, a man stepped out of a storefront behind him.

He was big, nearly six feet tall and wide at the middle. Jarrett couldn't see his face.

A second man brandishing a knife appeared from the shadows. He had long, straggly hair, coarse features, and pockmarked skin. Wide-eyed and agitated, he was unsteady on his feet.

Welcome to Beirut, Jarrett thought for a second time.

He stopped and faced the knife-wielder.

"Your wallet and phone," he said, his words garbled.

The big man joined his partner slapping his palm with a blackjack. His breathing was heavy, and sweat covered his brow.

"You can have my cash. I keep my wallet."

"We'll fuck you up."

"You have a choice pal. Walk away with the cash or else."

The knife-wielder repeated his demand.

This was a bad setup for a shakedown. They were amateurs—drug addicts—standing elbow to elbow and they were about to get their butts kicked.

When Jarrett shook his head, the knife-wielder lunged, thrusting the blade at Jarrett's mid-section.

The man was slow and unsure of himself. Jarrett effortlessly sidestepped and grabbed the outstretched forearm at the wrist. He twisted the arm and thrust his knee upward into it.

Crack.

The man yelped in pain and dropped the knife.

The big man screamed, "You bastard!" and swung the blackjack. Jarrett blocked it with his forearm and delivered a punch to the man's midsection. Although the man was soft, he took the blow standing and swung again.

Jarrett ducked a split second late, and the blackjack grazed his shoulder, sending an electric shock down his arm. He pirouetted and swept the man's leg with a full-power side kick. When his boot hit the man's lower leg, the ankle popped and the man growled like an injured bear. As he stumbled sideways, Jarrett kneed him in the face.

The knife-wielder was enraged, his eyes crazed and his teeth bared.

He had retrieved his knife and swung at Jarrett in a wild scything motion with his good arm, screaming, "I'll kill you! I'll kill you!"

Jarrett lunged backward, but the blade grazed his arm.

A surge of anger exploded in Jarrett. "You shouldn't have done that, asshole."

He circled the knife-wielder to parry the attack, waiting for an opening. When the man stumbled on a broken bottle, Jarrett caught him with a perfectly timed uppercut.

It was lights out instantly.

Jarrett stood over the two assailants and mumbled, "Sorry guys. You should have taken the money."

After a short walk back to the busy street, Jarrett hailed a taxi.

He gave the driver the address and asked, "Do you know where that is?"

The driver punched the address into a GPS on the dash. "Are you sure you want to go there?" he said shaking his head. "It's a bad area, if you know what I mean, sir."

Jarrett knew exactly what he meant. "Yes, that's where I'm going."

"I'll have to drop you off three blocks away. Don't want to drive down that street."

"That'll be fine."

As the taxi drove off, Jarrett slumped in the seat, chiding himself for leaving the busy street. Was he suffering from what Sedgewick called the Indiana Jones syndrome? In the classic action-thrillers the daring archaeologist regularly extricated himself from death traps he'd unwittingly stumbled into. Since the flight to Tehran, Jarrett had experienced nothing but trouble, and he had a feeling the worst might be just ahead.

CHAPTER 47

Jarrett paid the driver with a hefty tip.

Like much of south Beirut, this was a neighborhood in transition, struggling mightily to recover but with modest success at best. Older cars, many dinged and some with flat tires, were parked bumper-to-bumper along the street. Most of the refurbished buildings had small businesses on the first level and walk-up apartments on the second. The most eye-appealing was a shop with sacks of coffee in the window and a welcome sign on the door. It seemed to offer a modicum of encouragement that the neighborhood was headed toward resettlement. But the shop was closed like every other one.

The street name was etched on a building at the second intersection. He found the address in the middle of the next block. It was a creepy, two-story, war-torn building with cracked and pocked stucco and a flat roof. Light peeked around blinds on the first level, but the windows on the second were dark. Two crumbling stone steps led to a door with a lock and a catawampus door handle. Four door buzzers were dark with their brass name holders empty.

As Jarrett walked up the steps, the door swung open. The girl from the restaurant stood in front of him with a winsome look.

He stepped into a small foyer cluttered with cardboard boxes and broken furniture. Makeshift beds dotted with personal items lined the floor along the wall. An open central staircase led to a second-story landing.

A man dressed in a black shirt and black harem pants with a Kalashnikov stood at the top of the stairway.

A dark-skinned man wearing a white keffiyeh trimmed in red and a black jellabiya stepped through a door into the foyer. He had a pronounced limp with a drooped shoulder as if one leg was shorter than the other. His obsidian eyes held unimaginable malevolence and sent a chill through Jarrett.

"I'm Yusuf Sahin from Istanbul. An associate of Dietz Meyer," Jarrett offered.

The gun-toter on the stairs descended halfway down and trained his rifle on Jarrett, while the evil-eyed man growled, "On your knees. Hands behind your back."

Jarrett glanced at the man with the Kalashnikov. He was used to fighting his way out of situations like this, but tonight this would end badly. He had no weapon. The stairway shooter was pivotal. The bad guys had planned well. This was a perfect setup to take him hostage.

Jarrett kneeled.

The girl secured his hands behind him with a nylon friction tie and dropped a hood over his head.

Jarrett's heart began to race.

He abhorred hoods. It made him feel like he was drowning. He'd been hooded twice in the past, once in Bagdad and recently in Maryland. Both times things had ended badly for the kidnappers.

Worse yet, this hood stank. The odors of cigarette smoke and cooking grease were nauseating.

The girl whispered, "Night night."

Jarrett felt a sharp prick on his neck.

His eyes began to spin.

Then everything went black.

CHAPTER 48

Jarrett felt as if he were floating in a murky fog.

He heard dogs growling.

Light began to peek around the edges of his vision. Then suddenly everything was bright. Glaring. His eyes burned and he blinked hard, again and again, trying to focus. As he shook his head back and forth, he began to shiver.

I'm alive, he thought.

His head was pounding unmercifully, worse than any hangover imaginable. His shoulders throbbed, his arms stretched to their limits. And his legs felt heavy as if lead weights hung from them. The balls of his feet barely touched the floor.

The hood was gone. He was stripped to the waist. Beads of perspiration streamed down his chest.

He looked up, his eyes fluttering as they adjusted to the fluorescent lights overhead. He saw ropes tied to his wrists looping through pulleys attached to a rusty steel beam on the ceiling.

The room was cavernous. The walls appeared to be cut out of bedrock and the terra-cotta tile floor had a spider web of cracks. The musty, cool air told Jarrett he was underground, and he felt like a massive structure loomed over him.

Two men stood ten feet away.

The evil-eyed man with the limp held two snarling dogs. They looked starved and sick, tugging on their leashes with bared teeth.

The other man was dressed to the nines—a tailored black suit with a starched white shirt open at the collar, gold cuff links, and Italian loafers. With a full head of salt-and-pepper hair, a black mustache, and a paunch, he looked like an overweight Omar Sharif.

The man lit a cigarette with a gold lighter and inhaled deeply. "You're finally awake. Who are you?"

Jarrett pushed upward on the balls of his feet. His shoulders were in excruciating pain, and his hands were numb and swollen. After a few seconds his thighs began to burn, and he had to let the ropes take his weight. He wondered how long he could endure this.

"My name is Yusuf Sahin. From Istanbul. I'm here to replace Dietz Meyer."

The evil-eyed man lashed Jarrett three times with a quirt. He winced in pain, as his abdominal muscles tensed. Red welts began to appear.

"Who's Dietz Meyer?" the man in the suit asked.

"The man you hired to do a deal in Tehran. He's called Demus."

Jarrett got three more lashes. Tiny rivulets of blood began to trickle down his abdomen.

"You're lying."

Jarrett fought to compose himself. "I'm not."

After three more lashes the man in the suit said, "Tell me who you are, or the dogs will feed on you."

Blood had pooled in Jarrett's legs, and he felt light-headed. Once he passed out it would be over. The dogs would have at him.

"You have my wallet. It has my driver's license and credit cards."

"You're a spy. You work for the Zionist pigs."

"No, I'm Turkish. I worked with Meyer in the past."

Jarrett's abdominal muscles were in spasm, the worst cramping imaginable. The pain was unbearable, and he was having trouble breathing.

"Who contacted you?"

"He didn't give me his name. Let me down. We can talk," Jarrett pleaded.

"Do you believe in Allah?"

"Yes. And I believe in your cause."

Jarrett shook his head to fend off a gray curtain closing over his vision.

"You're lying. Let the dogs have at him."

The evil-eyed man stepped forward, the dogs lunging at Jarrett.

Then a voice shouted over the snarling animals. "Stop! He's the one."

A shadowy figure waved something in the air.

Jarrett tried to focus.

"I have his . . ."

The voice echoed in the distance, as Jarrett tumbled into darkness.

CHAPTER 49

Jarrett awakened on the floor in a fetal position. The ropes were gone, and he was shaking. His abdominal muscles were in knots, and his hands were swollen, but he could move his fingers and the sensation was returning. The room was swirling about him and his vision was clouded.

As he sat up someone said, "Here's your shirt, Yusuf. We have a short walk to my office, then we'll talk."

He put it on and was hooded again and helped to his feet. A hand grasped his arm and he was led out of the room to a passage that smelled of earth and fresh concrete. At first he could barely walk, but with each step he became stronger and his head began to clear. But with the hood on he imagined he was having trouble breathing.

After a short elevator ride, the hood was removed in a nicely appointed office with deep red carpet, colorful wall hangings, and blackout drapes. A huge desk with a PC monitor and a clutter of papers and magazines took up the center of the room. Jarrett sat down with the torturers and a third man on an L-shaped sofa near a coffee table with carved legs. The soft cushions were welcome after the ropes.

With a clear head he recognized the man in the suit across from him. Nassim Alfour. Hezbollah's number one. Jarrett knew all about him.

He was Shiekh Nassim to his followers, and in the complex web of terrorism in Lebanon he was the spider. A lawyer by training, he'd joined Hezbollah in 1984 and quickly became head of international operations. After a failed assassination attempt on the Lebanese prime minister in 2004, he'd escaped capture with help from the Iranian Revolutionary Guard. He was also suspected of masterminding several suicide bombings in Israel.

Alfour, like Osama bin Laden, reeked of sociopathic charisma—an amalgam of focus, vision, kindness, and authority—that drew naïve young Muslims to terrorist organizations. With a boyish smile he was forceful and direct, yet at times he could be gentle and soft spoken. Known to be masterful at getting what he wanted, Alfour was all apologies at the outset.

"Yusuf, I'm sorry."

He touched Jarrett's arm.

"I was led to believe you were an Israeli spy. I'm Nassim Alfour. These are my associates." He pointed to the evil-eyed man. "Abu is my deputy in arms." The man nodded to Jarrett, while Alfour gestured to the third man. "This is Rami, one of my new men."

Rami was clean-shaven with finely chiseled features and a lean runner's build. His eyes were locked on Jarrett and he nervously fidgeted with a heavy black cloth. He shook Jarrett's hand with a strong grip and said, "Rami Monsour."

"Rami saved the day," Alfour continued. "He got your passport. It confirms you're a well-traveled Turk. Your boarding pass shows you left Istanbul this morning."

Jarrett wondered if the passport had changed their minds, or if they were hell-bent on a little sadistic fun before they sat down with him.

"Meyer died in Tehran. I was contacted to replace him," he said.

"I contacted you," Monsour interjected. "You came highly recommended."

Alfour glared at Monsour like a father at a son who had spoken out of turn.

So Monsour was the Mossad agent.

He had broken into Jarrett's hotel room, stole his passport and boarding pass, and brought them to the torture room. His was the voice Jarrett heard before he passed out.

By recommending Jarrett as Demus's replacemnt, Monsour had put his life on the line. It was the end move for him. His days with Hezbollah were numbered. If he was still in Beirut when Hezbollah learned the fate of the bomb, he would be tortured and killed.

And Jarrett's life was in jeopardy as well. If Mossad exfiltrated Monsour before Jarrett took possession of the bomb, Ziba's uncle would swoop down on Yusuf Sahin. Jarrett would be a dead man in Tehran.

Monsour's escape had to be timed perfectly with Jarrett taking possession of the bomb. Monsour had saved Jarrett's ass. He would return the favor. It was all about timing.

"I don't even know what the deal is about," Jarrett said.

Alfour lit a cigarette, inhaled deeply, and blew smoke through his nose. "We're purchasing a nuclear bomb from the Iranians."

"What?"

"You heard me, Yusuf. You will represent us in the deal."

"A bomb! You must be kidding."

"We do not kid about such things."

Jarrett looked from Alfour to Monsour and back hoping to convey a sense of disbelief.

"Why not deal with them directly?" he asked.

"It can't be done that way. But if we did, there'd be no need to pay you an exorbitant fee."

Jarrett grinned. "I need $250,000 American."

Alfour took a deep drag on his cigarette. His eyes bored into Jarrett. "Too much. Way too much."

"This is a dangerous deal with potential for international fallout," Jarrett retorted.

"The fallout should be none of your concern, Yusuf."

"It will be if the Israeli bastards come after me."

"The only people who know about you are the three of us—Abu, Rami, and me—and of course your contact in Tehran. We'll pay you a hundred thousand American."

"Who's the contact?"

Alfour sneered. "Not until we have a deal."

"Two hundred thousand. Half before I leave for Tehran and the rest when the bomb is delivered."

"Our best is a $150,000. Fifty to your hotel here and the rest at delivery."

"It's a deal." Jarrett extended his hand.

As they shook hands Jarrett glanced at Monsour and noted a subtle change—the muscles around his eyes and mouth had relaxed. In poker jargon this was the tell. Monsour had just engineered a deal for his country to steal a Russian nuclear bomb from the Iranians. Little did he know, the bomb would go to Washington instead of Tel Aviv.

"What's your top number for the bomb?" Jarrett asked.

"The Persians are reasonable partners. We'll pay the asking price," Alfour said.

Jarrett figured that meant the Iranians would give the bomb to Hezbollah.

"How will I tell them you'll transfer the money?"

"Don't worry about that. We have established routes."

"That makes it easier," Jarrett said.

Alfour handed Jarrett a card with Omid Mohsen's name and phone number and an internet address.

"That's your Iranian contact's name and cell number. And the address is where you can reach me." A sly grin came across his face. "There's one thing that will be a challenge for you, Yusuf. Part of the deal is for you to deliver the bomb to us."

"What?"

"It's the size of a large suitcase."

"Are you serious? I thought nuclear bombs were huge."

"Some are. Just not this one. But it packs one helluva punch." Alfour glanced at Monsour and laughed.

"Where do I deliver it?" Jarrett asked.

"The Iranians will tell you."

CHAPTER 50

Jarrett was hooded again. Same sack. Same disgusting smell. And the same sense of breathlessness.

Abu drove him to the hotel. It seemed like an eternity, countless stops and turns, around and around. Jarrett was disoriented. A block away Abu pulled over, removed the hood, and gave Jarrett the Turkish passport. Jarrett left him without a word and hustled back to the hotel gulping fresh air.

As expected, the tape over the doorjamb was gone.

Jarrett checked on Demus's messenger bag, then called Sedgewick.

"How goes it?" Sedgewick asked.

"I'm Indiana Jones. A cab driver at the airport kidnapped me, two druggies tried to rob me, I was strung up by Hezbollah, and whipped . . . all in one day. My belly's crisscrossed with welts."

"You've been a busy boy. In your next kit you'll get a fedora, a leather jacket, and a whip. Too bad you don't have Spielberg telling you what to do." They laughed. "Where do you stand with the deal?"

"It's on. The contact's Mohsen, as expected. I'll fly tomorrow."

"Good."

"I met Nassim Alfour."

"You're kidding. Shiekh Nassim. A bad dude, one of the worst."

"Before I left Tehran I did a little research on Hezbollah. Nassim's their poster boy. Actually he's rather charming and reeks of charisma. He told me not to worry about the price for the bomb. They'll pay whatever the Iranians ask."

"That means the Iranians will give it to them."

"For sure. I'm to be paid a $150,000, fifty before I leave, and the balance on delivery."

"Wow. You can keep the money," Sedgewick said.

"No way. It's blood money. I'll give it to the guys at the CIA station here. They can do what they want with it. Maybe give it to a charity."

"I'll have them contact you and set up a transfer."

"This mission isn't settling well with me. Why do you think Hezbollah tortured me?"

"Alfour probably thinks Mossad took out Demus. He doesn't know Demus was on their payroll. We have intel that Hezbollah suspects they have a spy. They may have thought you're a plant after Demus was killed. They figured with a little pain, you'd spill the beans."

"I wondered if Hezbollah was worried about a spy," Jarrett said.

"These assholes always worry about spies, like everybody else."

"Suppose Mossad did kill Demus?"

"For God's sake, Jarrett, he worked for them," Sedgewick said.

"Like you said, Demus was a whore. If Hezbollah paid him more than Mossad, he'd jump ship a second time," Jarrett said.

"I don't think so. Demus was a whore but a damn smart one. He could get away with double-crossing Hezbollah, but not Mossad. The Israelis would track his Russian ass down and kill him. And they'd recruit us to help." Sedgewick snickered. "So tell me how the deal with Alfour went down."

Jarrett explained, then added, "Monsour is the Mossad spy."

"Sounds right. We don't know who he is. I bet very few people do."

"When Hezbollah learns the bomb is in American hands, Monsour's a dead man, if he's still in Beirut," Jarrett said.

"We should let the Israelis know and get him out."

"Not yet. When I have the bomb in hand they can exfiltrate him. Not before. If it's done prematurely, the Iranians will know I'm on the other team. I was recruited by him. His homecoming has to be timed carefully."

"Gotcha. When you have the device, I'll tell Mossad to make its move."

"How do I get out of Iran?" Jarrett asked.

"I'm working on that now. When you take possession of the device call me."

"Well you'd better put a plan together soon. I'll have the bomb in a few days."

"Relax. I'll take care of it. You know for security reasons we never discuss exfiltration plans beforehand."

"By the way," Jarrett added, "Demus's bag is still in the Parsian Hotel. That means the cheap-cologne assassin is still there."

"Where will you stay in Tehran?"

Jarrett thought for a minute. "It won't matter. The assassin will find me. I'll make it easy for him. I'll stay at the Parsian. Maybe I can flush him out and find out who he works for."

"He's in for a rough ride targeting you. Are you going to contact the Persian gal?"

"She doesn't know what I'm doing. I told her I was on routine CIA business. But I'll have to at some point. I still have to meet with her father."

"Suppose he finds out you're the culprit who stole the bomb and it's on its way to Washington?"

"I'll be long gone when he finds out. But Ziba tells me he's anti-nuc. He'll be glad I stole it." Jarrett heard knocking on the door. "Someone's at my door. Catch you later."

CHAPTER 51

The Hezbollah woman delivered the money.

With a saucy smile, as if nothing had happened, she invited herself in for a drink. Jarrett smiled, shook his head, and closed the door in her face.

He bump-passed Hezbollah's $50,000 to a CIA contact in the Beirut airport.

On the flight to Tehran, his thoughts were on Ziba.

She would be a major distraction, so he decided not to call her until he met with Mohsen and was ready to take possession of the bomb.

He checked into the Parsian Hotel and called Mohsen on the room phone.

The nuclear scientist was surprised that Demus's replacement had arrived so soon. Jarrett wondered why. It implied he knew Demus was dead, and Alfour hadn't contacted the Iranians yet about the new intermediary.

Their meeting was the next day in the same café in the university district. Mohsen said that he would be in a dark blue suit with a gray and white striped tie. The authentication question was, "Do you enjoy coffee?" The answer was, "No, I prefer Silver Needle White Tea."

* * *

Mohsen was waiting at the same table outside the café. After the authentication question, they shook hands. Mohsen's palm was sweaty and his grip loose. A wet-fish handshake. Jarrett sat down across from him in Demus's seat.

Déjà vu. Bad sign.

For a small man Mohsen had huge hands with thick fingers. He spoke perfect Farsi, although Jarrett detected an accent with a few words. Jarrett ordered ice tea and a chickpea cookie; Mohsen sipped coffee.

"I'm Yusuf Sahin. Here to replace Dietz Meyer," Jarrett began.

"How did you know Meyer?" Mohsen lit a cigarette and puffed on it nervously.

"A mutual friend introduced us. We've done projects together in North Africa and Syria."

"And now Iran. Who contacted you?"

"An operations deputy in Hezbollah. He said it was urgent."

"Did they tell you what the transaction involved?"

While they talked, Jarrett assessed the restaurant for threats.

Two young men were chatting over lunch. A young couple was celebrating the woman's birthday with cell phone pictures. No one posed a threat.

"Yes. A nuclear bomb about the size of a suitcase. I'm to transport it to Beirut. I was told you would know its final destination there."

"The price is five million American. Non-negotiable," Mohsen blurted.

Mohsen's demand for money took Jarrett by surprise.

"I'll have to consult with my clients."

"Of course. When they agree, I'll give you instructions for transferring the money."

"I'll contact you. We can meet again, perhaps over dinner," Jarrett said.

"Dinner is fine."

Jarrett paused to work a concerned look on his face. "It's really too bad about Meyer. Any word on how he died?"

Mohsen's jaw tensed and his eyes cast downward. "I was told he died of natural causes in his hotel room."

He's lying, and not hiding it well, Jarrett thought.

"I was surprised. He was healthy, as far as I know. Any chance of foul play?" Jarrett asked.

Mohsen looked around as if about to share a secret, but he was a bad actor.

"Yes. There's one possibility. An anti-nuclear group doesn't want us to have nuclear devices, let alone sell one to a proxy."

"Anyone else who might want Meyer out of the way?"

Mohsen's eyes locked on Jarrett for the first time. "Someone who wanted to take over the deal and collect a fat commission. That would be you, Mr. Sahin, wouldn't it?"

"Meyer was a trusted colleague," Jarrett replied.

Mohsen snickered. "I guess there's honor among thieves."

"You haven't developed a nuclear device yet. Where did this one come from?"

"It didn't come from the U.S., that's for sure." Mohsen sneered at him.

"China or Russia?

"We are very friendly with the Russians. I need your cell number," Mohsen said.

Jarrett's Iranian burner was in his kit at Ziba's condo.

"I don't have one yet. I'll call you."

When they shook hands again, Mohsen's palm was even more moist.

Why is he stressed? Jarrett wondered. *He's in the driver's seat.*

Jarrett paid the check, and they left.

It was a glorious afternoon with clear skies, comfortable temperatures, and just a skosh of smog. Jarrett wondered if he had been followed. With the sidewalks bustling with people, it would be a challenge to identify surveillance.

At a busy boulevard he darted across two lanes to the median, turned around, and hustled back. As he stepped on the sidewalk, a man walking toward him stopped to look into a store window. He carried a shopping bag and wore a red cap, a plain black T-shirt, and black slacks.

Jarrett walked past him and glanced at the man's feet—blue cross-trainers.

After a short distance, Jarrett feigned stumbling and looked over his shoulder. The man was behind him.

On the next block Jarrett went into a gelato shop and lingered a few minutes. When he came out, he paused on the sidewalk. The man in the cap was nowhere in sight. But two store fronts away a man with a white T-shirt and dark glasses leaned against an electrical pole and played with his cell phone. He had blue cross-trainers on his feet.

Jarrett lost the blue-shoed man with a series of simple evasion maneuvers.

He's an amateur, Jarrett thought.

As Jarrett got into a taxi, he looked around. His sixth sense was tugging at him. He'd lost the blue-shoed guy, but was someone else following him?

CHAPTER 52

The Do Not Disturb sign hung on Jarrett's hotel room door; the sliver of tape he'd put across the jamb was undisturbed.

He sent an e-mail to Alfour about the five-million-dollar price tag.

The tracking program showed the messenger bag was still somewhere in the hotel.

With the adrenaline rush from the meeting waning, Jarrett's body began to ache. He was a mess.

The welts on his abdomen looked like multi-colored railroad tracks. His shoulders felt like they'd been dislocated and the rope burns on his wrists had blistered and were weeping clear fluid. He decided a massage might help, so he called the spa. Luckily Sayed was on vacation. When he asked for a female therapist, he was surprised to learn one was available in the morning.

He took two aspirins and stretched out with a cold cloth on his abdomen. He always did his best thinking flat on his back staring at the ceiling with his hands clasped behind his head.

Mohsen was an intriguing character. He left Jarrett uneasy. And the bomb deal wasn't sitting well with him. Both raised questions.

Why did Mohsen have a Persian name if he was Russian?

Why had he been so nervous during their meeting?

Why did he demand five million dollars?

Why would he give Jarrett wiring instructions, after Hezbollah agreed to the price? Alfour had said that the system for moving money was in place.

How did Mohsen know Demus was murdered? Mohsen had lied when he'd said Demus died of natural causes in his hotel room.

What was in the envelope that Mohsen had given to Demus?
Was Demus's murder somehow related to the envelope?
Why did the killer take Demus's messenger bag and the envelope?
Why was today's meeting—like the one with Demus—in secret?
Questions, questions, and more questions.
But no answers.

* * *

While Jarrett ate a light dinner in the hotel dining room, he worked at convincing himself that the deal with Mohsen was on the up-and-up. That meant concocting a narrative that fit the bomb deal and answered the questions surrounding Mohsen. When it finally came together, it wasn't complicated. If anything, it was pretty simple, and everything fit . . . almost.

Mohsen was representing the Iranian government in good faith. He was Russian, had married a Persian woman, and had taken her name.

The anti-nuclear underground had learned that the Iranians had nuclear bombs, were selling one to Hezbollah, and that Demus was the intermediary. They had a spy in the Atomic Energy Organization.

The anti-nucs had hired a professional assassin to execute Demus.

The manila envelope had specs for the bomb. The ant-nucs had instructed the killer to steal it.

The Iranians figured out that Demus had been murdered. Jarrett had sorely underestimated their intelligence capability.

The meetings with Demus and now Jarrett were held in secret because the Iranians feared a spy in the Atomic Energy Organization. Their suspicions were right. A spy was feeding intel to the anti-nucs.

Mohsen was privy to everything. He knew the anti-nucs had killed Demus. He was a nervous Nellie, because he feared for himself.

End of story.

Enter Yusuf Sahin.

On with the Hezbollah deal.

When Jarrett returned to his room, there was a two-word e-mail from Alfour, "Agree. Proceed."

CHAPTER 53

Jarrett was in the hotel spa at ten o'clock the next morning.

Before leaving his room, he'd called Mohsen and scheduled a meeting for that evening.

He checked on Demus's messenger bag. It hadn't moved.

After an hour with free weights, Jarrett went full blast on a treadmill for thirty minutes.

There were only two other men in the gym. They were older with big bellies and toothpick legs, and were intent on their workouts.

As he stepped off the treadmill, a man dressed in a gray shirt and matching pants walked through the gym. He was small and looked like a hotel maintenance worker. There was nothing threatening about him, but his bearing caught Jarrett's eye. With all that had occurred, Jarrett's paranoia was off the charts.

The masseuse was a chatterbox. While working on Jarrett's back she asked about the ugly, boomerang-shaped scar on his shoulder. He told her he'd fallen on a picket fence when he was a child. It was really a healed knife wound from a tussle he'd had with a Bedouin chieftain in western Jordan. He was careful to keep the welts on his abdomen covered. When she asked, he said he had a bad scrape from a fall. She worked out the knots in his neck, shoulders, and back, and he left her a hefty tip.

After his massage he walked to the men's changing area, rinsed off in the shower, and stepped into the sauna with a wet towel draped around his neck. He felt good, for the first time in days.

As the first beads of perspiration trickled down Jarrett's forehead, the door opened. Cool air streamed over him and he looked up. A man stood in the doorway with a white robe snug around his neck and blue cross-trainers on his feet.

As the man reached in his pocket, Jarrett grabbed the end of the wet towel and snapped it.

Crack.

The towel stung the man's face like a whip, and he yelped. When he instinctively reached up to protect his eyes, a gun flew from his hand.

Jarrett sprang from the bench. With the full force of his weight behind him, he struck the man in the breastbone with his fist.

The man flew backward and crashed to the floor. His head bounced on the tile with a horrible *thud*, and he lay motionless with his eyes rolled back in his head.

Jarrett tossed him in the sauna with the gun.

No one was in the changing area. There were just two exits, one to the spa and the other to the registration desk. Jarrett figured there was a lookout.

A yellow sign—Closed for Cleaning—sat outside the door to the spa. The same sign was outside the other door. The man in the gray uniform stood next to it, facing away, intent on the hallway to the registration desk.

In three quick strides, Jarrett was behind him. He locked on a rear naked choke hold and lifted the man off the floor. The man kicked and punched to no avail. He tried to cry out, but was only able to muster a raspy gurgle. In a matter of seconds he was limp, and Jarrett snapped his neck. After an agonal grunt, he stopped breathing.

Jarrett carried the man and the sign into the changing area. He threw the body in the sauna, and propped the sign in front of the door.

Dressing quickly, he exited the changing area.

Luck was with him. There was no one at the registration desk. He took the stairs to his room.

CHAPTER 54

There was an envelope under Jarrett's door.

The fragrance of Caron's Poivre, an expensive French perfume, was in the air.

Ziba's favorite.

Jarrett had teased her that it was the fragrance of an Egyptian queen. Just a spritz behind each ear worked magic on the pharaoh.

A handwritten note inside the envelope read, "You're back! Please call." And two voice messages were on the hotel telephone.

How did she know I was registered as Yusuf Sahin?

He shrugged. The card and messages were a godsend. After his escapade in the spa, Ziba was front and center in his thoughts. He needed her help.

He called her. It was a short conversation.

"Clint, why haven't you called me?" she asked with breathy excitement in her voice.

"I need your help," Jarrett said in earnest.

"My car is on its way."

* * *

Ziba was waiting for him.

When the elevator opened at her condo, she ran into his arms.

"I missed you, Clint. I'm so glad you're back."

Bita served Ziba and Jarrett each a frosted glass of orange juice with a sprig of mint. Ziba had been exercising and was in a white silk T-shirt and shorts.

With a wry smile on her face, she asked, "So tell me what's going on with Yusuf Sahin."

Jarrett shook his head. "It's a long story. Before I get into it, I have a question. How did you know I was back in Tehran?"

"You are a very intriguing man." She smiled. "Your comings and goings are surreptitious, but not beyond my father's reach. When you left Iran, you used your Canadian passport. When you checked into the Parsian Hotel as Yusuf Sahin your picture was taken. You were identified as our national hero, Thomas Davis. My father called his morning. I contacted you right away." She laughed. "Big brother Mir is everywhere."

"A man tried to kill me this morning in the hotel spa."

"Oh my God! Trouble follows you. It must have something to do with why you're back."

"It does. I'm here to fill in for Demus."

"You're kidding. Why?"

"Because my government doesn't want a bomb to fall in the hands of a terrorist organization. I had a meeting with Mohsen yesterday."

"What's your plan?"

"Mohsen will turn the bomb over to me. It won't go to the terrorists. It'll find its way to Washington."

"That's why we're traveling to Scotland separately," she said.

"Exactly. I didn't want to tell you until I got back from Beirut. When I have the bomb, the CIA will get me out of Iran with it. You and I will rendezvous in Edinburgh."

"But Clint, your life is in danger," Ziba protested. "Someone doesn't want the deal to go through."

"It's the anti-nucs. The guy who tried to kill me this morning followed me from my meeting with Mohsen. I don't understand how they found out about it so fast. They must have a spy in the Atomic Energy Organization."

"I'm still waiting to hear back from my friend in the underground. He's traveling and I can't reach him. When I hook up with him, I'll try to find out how they knew about you and if they were responsible for the attack this morning. I'll ask about Demus too."

"A skilled assassin killed Demus. If the underground hired him, why send a team of amateurs after me?" Jarrett asked. "Why not use the same guy that did Demus?"

"I'll do my best, but no guarantees." Ziba shook her head. "How about dinner tonight?"

"I have another meeting with Mohsen. It's early, so I'll pass by afterward. You'd best stay close to home."

"I'll be waiting for you, Clint."

CHAPTER 55

When Jarrett got back to the hotel, he used a side entrance and took the stairway to the mezzanine. The lobby was alive with police responding to the trouble in the spa. His name was in the registration book and the masseuse would remember him. It was just a matter of time until the authorities tracked him down for questioning. He rode an elevator to his room and spent the afternoon reading and napping.

Shortly before 6:00 p.m., he walked ten blocks to a small café in the atrium of the Kourosh complex. He was confident no one had followed him.

Mohsen waited at a table with his briefcase at his feet. After they shook hands, Jarrett sat down across from him.

"I'm not hungry," Mohsen said curtly.

Jarrett ordered a spinach salad and flat bread with spicy cheese spread. He surveyed the restaurant for threats, but saw none.

"My client has agreed to the price," he told Mohsen.

"Good." Mohsen handed Jarrett a manila envelope similar to the one he had given Demus.

"There's a picture of the device, basic specs, and routing instructions for the money."

Jarrett opened the envelope and studied the picture. The bomb was in an aluminum case with two handles and a lock. From the picture he couldn't tell how big it was, but he remembered Sedgewick saying that with its battery pack it was the size of a large suitcase.

Mohsen added, "It weighs only fifty-eight pounds."

"That's amazing."

There were also three pages of specs on the device that Jarrett didn't understand and a page of routing instructions.

"The money will pass through ten locations before it reaches Minsk," Mohsen explained.

"Belarus? Why Belarus and not Tehran?" Jarrett asked.

He wondered if any money would be transferred. An intriguing thought passed through his head. Maybe the Iranians had purchased the bomb from Moscow. Maybe the five million was an installment sent to the Russians via Belarus.

"We have good connections there. It'll keep the deal secret," Mohsen said.

"How will the money get to Iran then?"

For the first time, Mohsen made eye contact. "That's none of your business, Mr. Sahin. The wiring instructions must be given to your client precisely. No mistakes."

"I'll e-mail them as soon as I get back to my hotel. I'm supposed to deliver the bomb. I was told you would know where."

"When you take possession, I'll tell you."

"I need to know to make plans."

"I understand. When the money reaches Minsk, I'll contact you. We'll meet again."

"My client is anxious. I'm sure the money will go out in the morning. Let's schedule a lunch meeting for tomorrow."

"No meeting until the money is there," Mohsen said.

"I'll wait to hear from you. Call me at my hotel."

"I will." Mohsen stood, shook Jarrett's hand and hustled out of the restaurant.

* * *

After a taxi ride back to the hotel, Jarrett sent the routing instructions to the Hezbollah drop box. There were ten stops along the way: Egypt, Liberia, Mexico, Nicaragua, Turkey, Morocco, Pakistan, Cuba, Argentina, Tajikistan, and finally Minsk, Belarus.

If the electronic transfer was initiated early in the morning, the money should be in Belarus by midday if there were no glitches. With luck Jarrett would take possession of the bomb late tomorrow.

He had to contact Sedgewick tonight to finalize his exfiltration, and he had to schedule a meeting with Mir Abassi.

Ziba had left a message that she had information for him and would send her driver.

Jarrett took the stairs to the mezzanine, exited through a side door, and walked several blocks before hailing a taxi. He wasn't sure why, but it seemed like the right thing to do.

CHAPTER 56

Bita put out a tray of treats, while Ziba fixed drinks. She looked sensational in an ankle-length white dress, belted at the waist with a plunging neckline.

The sexiest Muslim woman on the planet, Jarrett thought.

"You look beautiful. Do you have a date?" he asked her.

"Yes, indeed. He just arrived. And he'd better hold on to his socks, because he's in for a workout."

She pointed to the bedroom, and Jarrett felt a bolt of electricity surge through him.

"So how was your meeting?" Ziba asked.

"As expected. Short and not so sweet. Did you learn anything?"

"I did indeed. Believe it or not, Omid Mohsen's secretary is my contact's aunt. She's the one feeding the underground information."

"That's crazy. I thought there must be a spy."

"My contact's a young professor at the university. His family is friendly with mine and he went to high school with one of my brothers. He doesn't know if the anti-nucs tried to kill you this morning, or if they killed Demus. He did say there's a militant faction, mostly students. He wouldn't put it past them. They know you're the Turk named Sahin and where you're staying. They took a photo of you at your first meeting with Mohsen."

Jarrett shook his head and laughed. "There was a young couple in the restaurant snapping pictures with their phones."

"Pretty clever," Ziba said.

Clever of them, but stupid of me.

A thought popped into Jarrett's head. "Is Mohsen acting on behalf of the government?"

Ziba looked at him curiously, as she mixed another round. "What do you mean?"

"Well, is he acting on behalf of the Iranian government or himself?"

"My contact's aunt passes along information about Mohsen's meetings. I imagine if she knows about the meetings, he's acting on behalf of the government. If he were on his own, she wouldn't know. He'd want to keep it secret."

"Why do you think the anti-nucs don't just kill Mohsen?" Jarrett asked.

She pondered for a minute. "That's a damn good question. I suppose they view him as a go-between, a pawn of my uncle's. If they killed him, there'd be an ugly backlash. Mohsen would be replaced with someone else. The new man might have a different secretary. They'd have no source of info then."

"That makes sense. Mohsen's nervous as hell and seldom makes eye contact. I suppose he's afraid of the underground."

"I would be too. You won't be safe in any hotel in Tehran now. But you're safe here with me."

"Yes, we're both safe inside these walls, but the minute we go outside we're targeted, you by MEK and me by the anti-nucs. I have to find someplace else to stay. Tomorrow the authorites will be looking for me after what happened in the spa. But I want one more night in the hotel."

"How about Tony's?" Ziba suggested. "He has a beautiful home outside the city. His partner is away. It's perfect."

"What does Tony do for a living?"

"Manages his businesses all over the world. He's into everything imaginable. If you think I have tight security wait until you see his place. Will you stay with me tonight? We can go to Tony's in the morning."

Jarrett shook his head. "I've got some things to do at the hotel. Like I said, I want to spend one more night there. I'll leave the hotel early tomorrow morning. We can relocate to Tony's then."

"Sounds risky after what happened this morning. And they know who you are and where you're staying. But you know best."

"Right now, I'm more concerned about the authorities. I noticed you sketch."

"I dabble a bit. It's relaxing. I'm not very good."

"Can I have a pencil and a pad of paper?"

She looked at him curiously. "For what?"

"I like to doodle once in a while myself. I need to take something from my kit with me too."

CHAPTER 57

Jarrett breathed a sigh of relief.

No one had been in his room, and there were no messages that the authorities were looking for him. He would quietly disappear from the hotel early in the morning.

Jarrett's doodling during the ride from Ziba's amounted to just that—a simple drawing with a black pencil on a sheet of white paper. He wasn't much of an artist, but the rendering would hopefully serve its purpose.

An e-mail from Alfour said the money would go out in the morning.

He scanned the room with the sniffer from his kit and found it clean. He had to call Sedgewick but didn't want to leave the room.

"How are things?" Sedgewick asked.

"The bad guys took a run at me this morning in the spa."

"What bad guys?"

"The anti-nucs. Ziba has a contact in the underground. A young professor at the university. A family friend. Believe it or not his aunt is Mohsen's secretary. That's how they knew about the meetings. They know I'm Yusuf Sahin, where I'm staying, and that I'm here representing Hezbollah. The contact didn't know if the anti-nucs were the ones in the spa this morning or if they did Demus. But they had to be."

"You've talked to her about this? What you're doing in Tehran is top secret."

"I told her I'm replacing Demus."

"You've lost your mind, Jarrett. This mission is critical. You should never have discussed it with her."

"Maybe so. But I need her help and I trust her."

"Famous last words. In our business the watchword is trust no one," Sedgewick said.

"I hear you, but it's done." Jarrett quickly changed the subject and described his meetings with Mohsen and the contents of the manila envelope. "The envelope looks like the one he gave to Demus. The bomb's in an aluminum case."

"I know. We have photos of it," Sedgewick said.

"The money goes through ten stops and lands in Minsk, Belarus."

"Belarus? Why Belarus?"

"He said it was the safest way to move the money. They have contacts there."

"Maybe so, but it's odd. I suppose transferring that amount of money into Iran is a problem these days with the sanctions and all. Someone would probably have to fly from Belarus to Tehran with a suitcase full of cash."

"I should have the device soon. How do I get out of here?"

"The plan is set. Call me when you have the device in hand. Then away we go. It'll be a car ride, then a small boat to a rendezvous with one of our subs."

"Damn it. You know I don't like to be underwater," Jarrett said.

"It'll be a short trip."

"I'm relocating tomorrow to the home of a friend of Ziba's. An uberrich guy named Tony."

"You don't sound good, Jarrett. I know this gig is different. You're not just flying in, taking out a target, and vanishing."

"I'm uneasy," Jarrett admitted. "I have a feeling there's trouble lurking. I don't mind a fight as long as I know who I'm up against. And this Mohsen character bothers me."

"Why?"

"He's nervous as hell. When I shake his hand I feel like I'm grasping a fish. He has nothing to fear. It should just be a transaction for him. We met in secret, and he told me Demus died of natural causes. His eyes and body language told me he was lying. That means he has another source."

"The Iranian authorities probably figured out Demus was murdered. They told Mohsen, and he's nervous, because he thinks the anti-nucs will target him," Sedgewick said.

"You're probably right. I might not be giving Iranian intelligence enough credit. Mogadan is a smart guy."

"I'd bet your meeting was in secret because Mohsen and the Iranian authorities are suspicious of a spy. Little does he know it's his secretary."

"If things hold true, the guy who did Demus will visit me tonight."

"The cheap-cologne assassin?"

"Right."

"Why tonight?"

"Demus was killed right after he got the envelope from Mohsen. I got mine today."

"What's with the envelope? You're focused on it."

Jarrett thought for a second. "I know I am. I think it has to do with the instructions for the money transfer."

"How so?"

"I haven't figured that out yet. But I'll be waiting for him."

"You're the man when it comes to the dark stuff. Wouldn't want to go up against you."

"Dig into Mohsen some more," Jarrett said.

"All we've done so far is identify him from your photo. I'll see what I can come up with. Not to change the subject or anything, but how about a pic of Ziba?"

"Google princess Fathima of Saudi Arabia," Jarrett replied. "Ziba looks like her sister only sexier."

As the words left Jarrett's lips the landline phone rang.

He ended with Sedgewick and picked up the call. It was Ziba.

"Are you okay? Jarrett asked.

"No, I'm not," Ziba said.

"What's wrong?"

"I can't sleep. I'm tossing and turning. I want you here."

"We'll be together tomorrow morning. And as soon as I finish, we'll meet in Scotland."

"Clint, I've fallen for you, harder than I could ever imagine. I'm used to getting what I want. But you're a mystery cowboy." She laughed softly.

"Maybe that's the appeal. When all this is over, you'll find I'm a pretty simple guy. Not very exciting."

"It just gets worse, Clint. The more I'm with you, the more I want you. Come over, we can talk and then . . ."

"I'm already in bed. I was asleep when you called," he lied. He was readying himself for the late-night visitor.

Suddenly he heard the door lock snick.

His eyes shot toward the noise. Until he was ready, he had wedged a chair under the door handle in case his visitor had a key.

"Someone's here. I'll call you back," he whispered.

CHAPTER 58

"Room service, sir."

Then another knock.

Jarrett approached the door cautiously, staying out of a shooter's line of fire. He leaned against the wall and held out the sheet of paper with his doodling, carefully positioning it in front of the peephole.

"Who's there?"

As the words left Jarrett's lips, he heard a *pop* and the peephole exploded. A pencil-sized hole appeared in the eye he had sketched on the paper. If Jarrett had been in front of the door—game over.

He stomped his feet to mimic the sound of a body falling to the floor.

After a few seconds, he removed the chair and opened the door. When he peeked around the corner, he saw a big man dressed in black with a buzz cut disappearing into the stairwell.

Jarrett shouted, "Hey you!"

The man turned and stepped back into the hallway—a brute, with a round Slavic face, fair skin, gray eyes, a straight nose . . . and a gun in his hand.

Jarrett ducked back into the room, slammed the door, and ran toward the bathroom. As he dove headfirst across the threshold, a volley of bullets whizzed over his head, shattering the mirror.

He rolled on his back, closed the bathroom door, and held it fast with his feet.

A second volley of bullets on a lower trajectory tore through the door and shattered the sink.

The next volley will rip me apart, Jarrett thought.

The hallway door would have locked automatically when he'd closed it. But even if the shooter didn't have a key, he could easily shoot out the lock. Jarrett was trapped. His gun was at Ziba's. All he could do was wait. And pray.

The shooter's weapon was fully automatic. Maybe an H&K MP5. The bullets had to be armor-piercing. If the plan was to take out Sahin with just one shot, the shooter wouldn't have a spare magazine. Jarrett hoped the gun was empty.

He thought he had smelled the cheap cologne in the hallway. The shooter had to be the same guy who killed Demus. And he looked Russian. A crazy thought ran through Jarrett's head.

Maybe the Russians are trying to nix the deal like Sedgewick said. But they have enough clout to stop it with one phone call.

Jarrett stayed on his back, wedged against the bathroom door, counting the minutes as if they were his last. A lifetime of thoughts rattled through his head.

When he was sure the shooter was gone, he opened the bathroom door. The hallway door was still locked and, like the bathroom door, looked like a used target at a rifle range.

His next move was critical.

The shooter was a pro, hired by the anti-nucs. He'd figure his target—Sahin the Turk—wouldn't risk calling the authorities. He'd run instead. Right away. Now. The only way out of the hotel at this time of night was through the main lobby. The shooter would set up in the mezzanine to finish the job.

Jarrett's mind raced. He called Ziba.

"You hung up on me. What happened?" she asked.

"Someone tried to kill me. Can we go to Tony's tonight?"

"Oh, Clint. You're not safe. Come over. We'll go in the morning."

"No. We have to go now. What's the nearest hospital to the Parsian?"

She thought for a few seconds. "Efran Hospital."

"Pick me up there. Bring my kit with everything including the gun. From there we'll go to Tony's."

Jarrett slipped into a hotel robe and folded the manila envelope into a small square. He stuffed it in a pocket along with his Yusuf Sahin wallet and passport and the electronic sniffer.

He opened the door and tossed a pillow into the hallway. Nothing.

He darted from the room, ran down the stairs to the floor below, and pulled the fire alarm.

The hall lights flashed, and a noxious alarm began to sound.

He waited a few minutes, then followed a stream of befuddled guests down the stairs. A long descent.

At the archway to the mezzanine, he stopped. No Russian shooter in sight. He ran to the overlook to the lobby. It was a sea of confusion below. Firefighters and police huddled with the night manager, while the staff herded guests out the main entrance. But no shooter.

Jarrett waited until the last of the guests had passed, then descended the stairway. He hustled across the lobby to the main entrance.

Outside the hotel, fire trucks and ambulances lined the street.

He targeted the ambulance at the head of the line. A uniformed paramedic stood next to it.

He staggered up to him and said he was short of breath and felt faint. When the paramedic rolled out a stretcher, Jarrett collapsed on it.

CHAPTER 59

Tony's estate was not what Jarrett expected.

A thirty-minute drive from Efran Hospital, it was a sprawling compound with the look and ambiance of a movie mogul's retreat in Palm Springs.

The property was at least five acres with an eight-foot-high, ivy-covered wall. An electric gate with a guardhouse led to a long meandering driveway with trees and reflecting ponds beautifully sculpted into the rolling lawns.

The main house was an ultra-modern two-story edifice built of stone and glass. With security lights aglow it looked like the White House after dark.

The guards waved them through the gate. Tony was waiting at the door smoking an unfiltered cigarette. Exuding unmistakable warmth with a disarming smile, he kissed Ziba and shook Jarrett's hand.

The interior of the house was as impressive as the outside—polished marble floors, an array of modern artwork, and stainless steel furniture upholstered in fine leather.

They sat in the game room, where Ziba explained that there had been several attempts on her life by MEK and she didn't feel safe at her condo. She couldn't sleep, so they'd come in the middle of the night. She mentioned nothing about the shooter at Jarrett's hotel.

Tony was delighted to have them and explained that the house was a fortress—complete with infrared cameras, ultrasonic motion detectors, guards patrolling the grounds with dogs, and a security station in the basement manned 24/7.

"You can't be too safe," he said.

Jarrett glanced at his chronograph and yawned.

Ziba said, "You must be tired, Thomas. You're staying in my suite."

"I'm up early. Sleep in if you like," Tony said.

The suite was a spacious bedroom, sitting area, and bath decorated in royal blue and gold Egyptian décor, Ziba's favorite.

While Jarrett showered, Ziba fussed with her clothes, set out her makeup, and turned the bed down.

When he walked into the bedroom she saw the welts on his abdomen and asked, "What the hell happened to you?"

"I ran into some bad guys when I was in Beirut." Jarrett shrugged. "They strung me up and whipped me."

"Oh my God. Does that have anything to do with the deal with Mohsen?"

"Yes, indeed. I'll tell you the story in Scotland over a bottle of single malt."

"I'm looking forward to Edinburgh. I want you to relax. You've had nothing but trouble since we met on the plane."

Jarrett was asleep before Ziba finished her shower.

He imagined he was having a special teenage-boy dream, until he opened his eyes and saw her.

"Stay on your back, Clint. Let me finish."

When she was done, he thought he had died and gone to heaven.

CHAPTER 60

Jarrett was up early the next morning.

First things first.

He took inventory of his kit. He needed the burner to contact Mohsen.

A closet in Ziba's suite held an array of men's clothes. Jarrett wondered if Ziba had a boyfriend. If she did, he was a big guy, because the clothes fit. In sweats and cross-trainers, he went for an early-morning run.

He did ten laps on a winding path just inside the perimeter wall. Cameras and motion detectors were on the walls, in trees, and tucked under shrubs. Everywhere. He passed a guard with a sidearm and an automatic rifle walking two champagne-colored Persian mastiffs. The guardhouse at the gate looked like a field armory with an assortment of weapons, even a grenade launcher.

Tony was right. His estate was a veritable fortress. They would be safe here until Jarrett took possession of the bomb.

* * *

Shortly after nine Jarrett called Mohsen and left a voice message, then he and Ziba spent two hours in Tony's gym.

Like a fitness model, she was dead serious about her body—a woman on a mission with stretching, free weights, and aerobics.

After a late breakfast Tony gave Jarrett a tour of the house. In addition to the gym, a steam room, and sauna, there was an indoor Olympic-sized pool and tennis court, but the highlight was an underground garage with an array of exotic cars. Tony pointed out a red Audi R8 V10, a McLaren 570S, a Rolls-Royce Dawn, a Ferrari 488 Spider, and a Lamborghini Huracan

LP 610-4-Spyder among others. But Tony's favorite was a restored 1969 Corvette Stingray.

When Jarrett asked what Tony used for his daily outings, he laughed. "An armored Toyota Land Cruiser. I thought about a field-ready Hummer, but that would raise the eyebrows of the ayatollah's gang."

Early in the afternoon the skies clouded over and Ziba thought a nap would be nice after their late-night adventure.

Jarrett's nap turned out to be two double bourbons, a round of incredible sex, a shower, another double bourbon, more sex, and another shower. It was wonderful.

Ziba had an insatiable appetite and could have gone on forever. When she was in his arms, his passion was not of the flesh but of his heart and mind.

After a six-course French-Moroccan dinner, they watched a Jason Bourne movie. Contract assassins were chasing Bourne around the world. A beautiful French woman helped him escape from a particularly tenacious killer. It reminded Jarrett of his last mission in Washington. Before the movie ended he was sound asleep.

After an afternoon of whiskey and hot sex, a fabulous dinner coupled with six different wines, and a movie that brought back bad memories, he was spent.

CHAPTER 61

The next morning there was a voice message on Jarrett's burner. Despite classical music in the background, Mohsen sounded anxious, more so than usual. The five million was in Belarus. They'd meet today for lunch. He gave the name and address of the restaurant.

After breakfast, Ziba said she had a headache. When she excused herself to lie down, Tony said, "Let's go for a walk, Thomas."

The morning air was crisp and perfumed with flower blossoms, the sky crystalline blue without a cloud. With the sun just breaking over the mountains, Jarrett and Tony cast long shadows on the jogging trail.

Jarrett figured this was a setup. He was right.

"Ziba is the sister I never had. I love her with all my heart," Tony began. "She's a wonderful woman."

"I'm worried about her," he said.

"Because of Jago?"

"Yes, and because of you."

"Me?"

"You're a mystery man, Thomas, if that's your name. I don't believe you're a salesman from Canada. You're a high-powered American agent on a secret mission."

Tony paused for Jarrett to respond, but Jarrett said nothing.

"Ziba loves you. I don't know who you are. Which means I don't know what will happen to her. She's had trouble in the past."

"Trouble?"

"Among other things, she had a drug problem. I took her to a clinic in Switzerland myself. It was a situational thing according to the doctors, entwined with her ex-husband in Edinburgh. She's clean now. Drinks a little, but that's all." He shook his head and laughed. "And she quit smoking.

She won't even let me smoke around you. I have to sneak out of my own damn house to have a cigarette."

"How about Jago?"

"He's a psychopath, a madman, and he's fixated on her. Why would he want to kill her if he loves her? We've all tried to convince her to leave Tehran. She's not safe here."

Jarrett weighed telling Tony who he was and what his plans were for Ziba.

"Tony, I'm not Thomas Davis. Who I am and why I'm here is not important." Jarrett chose his words carefully. He didn't want to lie. "I have strong feelings for Ziba."

"Do you love her?"

Jarrett sighed. "I suppose, as much as someone like me can love any woman. When my mission is finished, I'll take her to a safe place."

Tony hand-hugged Jarrett and murmured, "My prayers are answered. I don't care who you are. All I want is for her to be happy and safe. Money is not an object. Whatever you need, you'll have."

"I don't need money, but thank you."

"Let's fly to Nice this afternoon. My yacht's there. We'll celebrate."

"I have an important lunch meeting today." Jarrett gave him the name of the restaurant.

"I know the place. Excellent food, nice atmosphere, fabulous hotel across the street."

"Hey guys, my headache is better. May I join you?" Ziba appeared behind them, walking fast to catch up.

"I suggested we fly to France for a few days, but Thomas has a lunch meeting today."

"I can drop you off," Ziba said.

"Are you leaving us?" Tony asked.

"Are you kidding? I just want to get some things from my place."

"I can pick up Thomas after his meeting. I'd like to show him the National Jewelry Treasury. You can join us, Ziba."

"I love that museum. It's my favorite. You'll see an opulent array of priceless gems, crowns, and other jewels, Thomas."

Ugh.

Tony chuckled and told Ziba, "I'm glad you're coming. I wouldn't want to be seen alone with a hunk like him."

"Remember, he belongs to me," Ziba said with a smile.

CHAPTER 62

On the drive into the city Jarrett explained that his luncheon meeting was to discuss the transfer of the nuclear weapon. He'd have to meet with Ziba's father soon, maybe later that afternoon.

As the car pulled into the valet, Jarrett said, "Be careful, Ziba. Use the guards as shields getting in and out of the car."

"I will. And you be careful too."

Jarrett looked around and smiled. "I doubt anything will happen here."

"Tony will pick you up. I'll meet you at the museum."

The restaurant reminded Jarrett of an upscale New York steak house without a bar. Booths upholstered in dark leather with polished tables and ornate brass swagger lamps lined the walls and two wide aisles. It was half-full. No one looked like a threat.

Jarrett chose a wall booth with a good view of the entrance.

Mohsen arrived ten minutes late, disheveled and anxious, more so than at their previous meetings.

Jarrett ordered a fruit salad and lemonade; Mohsen drank coffee again.

"Everything okay?" Jarrett asked.

"Yes," Mohsen replied still unable to make eye contact.

"The money made it to your bank?"

"Yes. You're not at the Parsian anymore?"

"There was a fire at the hotel. I moved," Jarrett said, his eyes darting between Mohsen and the entrance.

"Where?"

"Another hotel. When will I take possession?"

"We'll have to travel to a secure location."

Jarrett pressed. "You have the money. When?"

"Tonight. An hour by car."

"I'll need transportation back to my hotel."

Jarrett planned to check into a downtown hotel and use it as a base of operation.

"No problem," Mohsen said.

"I need to know if there's anything special about moving it."

"My technicians will explain everything. And we'll let you know where to deliver it. I'll call you later this afternoon to finalize arrangements."

"When you call, I'll tell you where to pick me up," Jarrett said.

Mohsen glanced at his watch and finished his coffee in two gulps. "I have another meeting," he said.

Jarrett called for the check and excused himself. In the men's room he sent a text to Tony. More people had been seated, but no one suspicious.

As he walked back to the table, his cell beeped. Tony was waiting outside with the car.

When Jarrett approached the table, Mohsen was on his phone. He looked up, quickly finished the call, and said, "I'll walk out with you and get a taxi."

Jarrett paid and they walked to the valet parking station.

The traffic was backed up to the street.

"I have to use the men's room. You'll hear from me soon," Mohsen blurted and disappeared.

Jarrett saw Tony hustling toward him, waving like a long-lost cousin. He was in white again with a flat cap and a jacket draped over his arm, his boyish smile on full display.

They shook hands. "We're parked on the street. Didn't want to get stuck in the valet line. Did you have a good lunch, Thomas?"

"It was fine," Jarrett replied as they walked down the driveway. Tony's white Land Cruiser idled at the curb.

Jarrett was on the outside. The sun was over his shoulder. He towered over Tony.

A bright flash suddenly hit Jarrett in the face. He ducked—an ingrained reflex from years of training.

An instant later the air resonated over his head, and he heard an unmistakable sound.

Thu-ump.

A bullet hitting living tissue.

Tony's dark glasses had exploded and his knees were buckling.

Jarrett caught him before he hit the ground. With Tony in his arms, Jarrett ran to a car parked in the driveway and crouched behind it. He looked down at Tony and shuddered. There was a bullet hole above Tony's left eye. The back of his head was a bloody crater, and he shook as if having a seizure. Jarrett closed Tony's eyes and eased him to the ground bunching his jacket under his head.

Jarrett peered over the hood toward the hotel. The flash hit him again, and again he ducked. A split-second later a bullet creased the hood and whizzed over his head. Fragments of concrete spalled from the driveway behind him.

Suddenly it all came together.

The assassin worked for Mohsen. He was set up with a rifle in the hotel across the street. He was the shooter at the Parsian. He murdered Demus. Mohsen was a rogue operator.

Jarrett touched Tony's cheek with the back of his hand. "I'm so sorry my friend."

The valet attendant stood aghast under the portico. Jarrett sprinted past him to the men's room outside the restaurant.

Mohsen was gone. A fire exit next to the men's room was ajar.

Jarrett darted through it to an alley. He saw no one.

Amid a storm of blaring sirens and flashing red lights, Jarrett sprinted aimlessly down the alley, until he could run no more.

He felt a hollow sensation inside of him, as if someone had stolen his soul. If he hadn't ducked, the assassin's bullet would have hit him. Tony would be alive.

It wasn't right.

He liked Tony.

And Ziba loved him like a brother.

She would be devastated.

Out of breath and exhausted, he hailed a taxi. As he slumped into the back seat, he dialed her number.

CHAPTER 63

He found Ziba on the sofa staring into space, her face masked in anguish. She'd been crying and smelled of alcohol. A glass of scotch and a bottle of prescription medication sat on the coffee table in front of her. He kissed her on the cheek.

"Tony's dead?" Her voice was soft and plaintive.

"Yes. I'm sorry, Ziba."

"How did it happen?"

"A bullet meant for me."

After he explained what happened, she said, "It's not your fault, Clint."

"Yes it is, damn it. Tony should be here with you."

"Was it the militant anti-nucs?" Ziba asked.

"No. It was arranged by Mohsen."

"Why would Mohsen want you dead?"

"He's gone rogue. Looking for a big payday. He had me transfer five million dollars from Hezbollah to his bank in Belarus. The money was there, so he planned to kill me. Then escape to Belarus a rich man."

"But he didn't need to kill you. He could have just run if the money was all he wanted."

She's right, Jarrett thought. *Why does Mohsen want me dead? And why did he have Demus killed?*

"That's an interesting thought. It doesn't make sense. Unless . . ."

Ziba interrupted. "Mohsen ordered Tony's death." There was a coldness in her voice.

"He hired the killer," Jarrett said.

"What are you going to do now."

"Payback. Mohsen and his assassin. When it's done, it'll look like they died of natural causes. Then, I'll let my client know that the nuclear scientist handling the deal died unexpectedly. And he stole their money. They'll be pissed. They'll contact Tehran. Hopefully, your uncle will assign someone new to replace Mohsen. Can you get Mohsen's home address, the make of the car he drives, and a tag number?"

"Of course." After wiping tears from her eyes and blowing her nose, she dialed a number. "Hi, it's Ziba. Is my father there?" While Jarrett began mixing a drink, she said, "Please ask him to call me as soon as possible."

"He's not there?"

"In a meeting. He's good about calling back, though."

"My kit's at Tony's. I need it."

"I have some things there as well. It'll be hard to go to Tony's. But I have to face it sometime."

* * *

The gate was open.

A half-dozen cars were parked in Tony's driveway including two police vehicles. The security personnel milled around the front entrance with confused looks.

Ziba went into the house with one of her guards. While Jarrett waited in the car, he found a message to call Sedgewick ASAP.

After a few minutes the guard returned with Jarrett's bag and two others.

Thirty minutes later Ziba came out. She looked shaken.

"What took so long?"

"Tony's lawyers were there. Thank God his new partner wasn't."

"And?"

"I'm the executor of his estate. Tony has no family. The partner he just split with gets a little money and one of the cars in the garage. The new one gets nothing. I get everything else. It'll be a few weeks before the will is read. That's the gist of it."

"That's pretty amazing, Ziba."

"Do you know what that means, Clint?" she asked, her voice echoing with sadness.

"No."

She began to choke up. "I'll be a billionairess several times over. But I don't want a fucking penny. All I want is Tony back."

CHAPTER 64

They drove back to Ziba's condo.

While she made calls to her family and friends, Jarrett disappeared into another room and called Sedgewick.

"Glad you called. What's up?" Sedgewick asked.

"Nothing good. Lots of trouble."

Jarrett described the shooting and explained that Mohsen was behind it. The shooter was the guy who had tried to kill him at the Parsian. He'd killed Demus. Mohsen was a rogue operator looking for a big payday.

When Jarrett finished, Sedgewick said, "That's too bad about Ziba's friend. He sounds like a good guy."

"What I don't understand is why Mohsen had Demus killed and tried to kill me. He could have just taken off. The money was in Belarus."

"Reminds me of that song, 'Take the Money and Run' by Stevie 'Guitar' Miller. Great tune. One of my favorites," Sedgewick said. "So we took a harder look at Mohsen. I'm kicking myself, because I should have done it at the get-go. What we came up with explains why he had Demus killed and why he tried to have you killed. It took some digging to find out who he is, or should I say, who he was. From our contacts at Cal Tech, we got a full dossier on him. He's Russian."

"No shit. We know that," Jarrett said snidely.

"But a special type of Russian. His given name is Mohammed Umarov. Born in Argun, Chechnya. He was a brilliant student—genius caliber—and got a full ride to Cal Tech to study chemistry. Met a Persian woman there, also a student, named Usma Mohsen."

"And?"

"And Usma Mohsen just happened to be the niece of the Grand Ayatollah Sayyid Rubollah Musavi Khomeini."

"He started the revolution," Jarrett said.

"And he looked like Sean Connery with a beard and a turban. But think about this for a minute. The grand ayatollah finds out his niece is sweet on a brilliant student studying chemistry at Cal Tech. The Persians desperately need nuclear scientists. The next thing you know Umarov switches majors to nuclear physics, marries the ayatollah's niece, finishes his studies, and moves to Tehran. And of course he has to become a Shite, because he was brought up Sunni in Chechnya. And he changes his name to his wife's. They had no children we're aware of."

"What's so unbelievable about that?"

"Please, don't interrupt when I'm on a roll. Most intriguing is his relationship with the Chechen rebels. The bad Muslim dudes who fight with mother Russia for independence. Their longtime leader is Bworz Umarov, Mohsen's younger brother. You get the picture?"

"Aha. So if the rebels get a bomb, they'll have a bargaining chip with Moscow. A super-duper bargaining chip," Jarrett said.

"You got it, my friend. From Washington's perspective, a nuclear weapon in the hands of the Chechen rebels isn't so bad. Certainly a helluva lot better than one in the hands of Islamist terrorists in the Middle East."

"And there's five million bucks in Belarus," Jarrett said.

"A nest egg for the rebels when Mohsen joins his brother."

"The little twerp is pretty clever, but not a very good actor," Jarrett said. "I think it went down like this. The Russians secretly gave Iran two nuclear devices, one a storied suitcase bomb. The Iranians decided to donate one to Hezbollah. Mohsen was assigned to manage the deal. He saw a golden opportunity to help his brother with a bomb and a whole lot of cash to the Chechen rebels. To protect themselves the Iranians demanded that Hezbollah use an intermediary. Enter Demus representing Hezbollah, but really working for Mossad. He's given a demand for cash and wiring instructions at a secret meeting. Just hours later Demus is murdered by the cheap-cologne assassin. Mohsen was going to substitute a Chechen for Demus. The Iranians would think the bomb was on its way to Beirut. But bingo, it winds up in Chechnya in the hands of the rebels. And Mohsen hightails it with five million waiting for him."

"Neat little deal," Sedgewick said.

"It was perfect because on the Iranian side only Mohsen knew what Demus looked like. That's why the meetings were secret. But Demus was killed before he sent the routing instructions to Hezbollah. He went directly from the meeting with Mohsen to his lady friend's place. I had it on my tracker. He spent the day with her instead of e-mailing the instructions. A few days later Yusuf Sahin shows up."

"Mohsen needed an intermediary to have the money wired."

"Exactly. Someone sent by Hezbollah. Someone they knew and vetted. I was surprised that Alfour agreed so quickly to the price and wired the money," Jarrett said.

"He might have thought he'd get his money back, because the payment was just part of the facade his friends the Persians were using to cover themselves. If the deal was uncovered, they'd claim they didn't have weapons and Mohsen was just a rogue operator looking for a big payday."

Jarrett laughed. "In fact, that's what he was, a rogue operator. It's more likely they didn't even know there was money exchanging hands. They trusted Mohsen and Alfour had to work through an intermediary. Can you imagine what the Russians would do when they found out a bomb they gave to Iran wound up in the hands of the Chechen rebels?"

"They'd deny everything and then come down on Iran. What's up next with Mohsen?" Sedgewick asked.

"He doesn't know Yusuf Sahin is a plant. After two attempts on Sahin's life, he'll figure the Turk is spooked and will cut and run. His cash is in Belarus. He can replace Sahin with a Chechen, transfer the bomb, and hop a plane home. But he has to move quickly, because he knows Sahin will tell his client—Hezbollah—that the Iranian scientist handling the deal is trying to kill him. That will stir up a hornet's nest in Beirut and Tehran."

"All you have to do now is meet with Ziba's father and be on your way," Sedgewick said.

"Don't you guys still want the bomb?"

"Are you kidding? Of course."

"I'll deal with Mohsen and the shooter," Jarrett said. "Make it look natural like always. Then I'll tell Alfour that the nuclear scientist handling the deal died unexpectedly. Hopefully a replacement for Mohsen will be assigned. Then we can pick up where we left off."

"Sounds like Dr. Omid Mohsen's not long for this world."

"He's not. I'll be in touch after I finish with him and the assassin."

"Good luck, Jarrett."

CHAPTER 65

"**M**y father returned my call. He accessed Mohsen's personnel file. Mohsen drives a white Avtovaz sedan. I'm not surprised he has a Russian car. I got his tag and home address, too."

"Did your father ask why you wanted the information?"

"Yes," she replied sheepishly.

"What'd you tell him?"

"Everything. He already knew about Tony. He's very upset. He admitted we have nuclear weapons, but he knew nothing about the Hezbollah deal. That means I was right. My uncle's managing it secretly for the grand ayatollah."

"You told him I plan to kill Mohsen and the assassin?"

"I had to tell him everything, Clint. He'll help in any way he can. And you were right. Mohsen's not Persian. He's Chechen. He married Khomeini's niece."

"I was just on the phone with Sedgewick. There's a lot more than that." Jarrett summarized the conversation.

"Oh my God. The Russians will go crazy if a bomb gets in the hands of the Chechen rebels. God only knows what they'll do to us." She brightened. "But if you deal with Mohsen that won't happen."

"Only if I get to him before he transfers the bomb and leaves Iran. I'm sure he'll move quickly."

"What's the plan?"

"A visit to Mohsen's house. I'll take care of him and get the name of the shooter. He's staying at the Parsian Hotel."

"How do you know?" Ziba asked.

"I put a tiny tracking device on Demus's bag on the airplane. You remember that flight from Istanbul."

"Don't remind me of that flight," Ziba said chuckling.

"The assassin took the bag when he killed Demus. Mohsen didn't want the authorities to find it. It had a picture of the bomb and the routing instructions for the money. The tracker shows the bag is in the hotel. Does Mohsen live in a house or an apartment?"

"I knew you'd ask." She pointed to her laptop. "According to Google Earth, it's a single house in a middle-class neighborhood, not far from here. Across the street is a vacant lot."

"Good. He probably drives to work."

"I suspect so."

"He has no children according to Sedgewick."

"My father says the scuttlebutt is that Mohsen's wife is sick. The marriage is on the rocks."

"A good time for him to go home to Chechyna. Best place for me to confront him is at his house. But I don't want to involve his wife."

"If she's sick and the marriage is bad, she might not be there," Ziba said.

"I hope that's the case. Can you find out if there's a parking garage at his office?"

"Let's take a ride," she said.

CHAPTER 66

There was a garage behind he building.

They found a parking spot on the street near the exit.

"We'll follow him tonight. Time is critical," Jarrett said.

Ziba looked at her wristwatch. "He gets to work at 7:30 a.m. and leaves at 7:00 p.m. like clockwork every day except Sunday."

"How do you know?"

"My father. Mohsen uses a security badge. When he signs in and out it's recorded. My father accessed the security records. It's almost quarter of seven now. We can just wait."

* * *

Shortly after seven o'clock Mohsen exited the garage, alone and puffing on a cigarette. No doubt it had taken him a few minutes to badge out and walk to his car from his office.

Ziba's driver was an ex-intelligence officer who had no problem staying two cars behind the Russian sedan. There was no indication that Mohsen suspected he was being followed.

He took a direct route to a major highway, and then followed residential streets. Along the way he stopped at a grocery store in a shopping mall with a six-level, open-air garage.

Jarrett instructed the driver to slow as they turned onto Mohsen's street. The timing was perfect.

As they passed the house, Mohsen was pulling into the garage. Other than the garage light, the house was dark. There were no other cars in the driveway.

The house was a two-story with a short driveway leading to an attached garage. There was a construction trailer on a vacant lot across the street.

They drove back to the mall. Jarrett directed the driver to the top level of the parking garage. It was a weeknight and it was empty of cars. After Jarrett surveyed the structure, they drove to Ziba's condo.

* * *

Over dinner, Jarrett shared his plan.

"You'll drop me off one block from Mohsen's at 7:15 tomorrow night. Then drive to the mall, park, and call me when he passes. I'll meet you after I'm done."

"How will you get there from Mohsen's?"

"Don't worry, I'll find a way. We can't forget about MEK. They know where you live, so they may be watching your building. We have to be careful. Maybe you should stay here."

"I have to be part of this, Clint. Mohsen tried to have you killed. He's responsible for killing Tony. It might help with closure."

Jarrett thought for a minute. "Do you have access to a second car?"

"Of course. One call, and it's done."

"Are there women in the building who go out veiled?"

"Of course. This is Iran."

"Do they use taxis or cars with drivers?"

"Both. Some use taxis, others have drivers."

"I'm worried about MEK following us and trying something crazy again. We can run a diversion."

Before he was out of the shower Ziba was sound asleep. She had taken a sleeping pill on top of two double scotches.

Jarrett had a good night's sleep as well—the first since he had arrived in Tehran.

CHAPTER 67

At 6:45 the next evening a stylishly dressed woman with a head scarf and dark glasses left Ziba's building in her car. Minutes later a veiled woman left the building in a taxi.

As the taxi pulled away, Jarrett exited the building through the service entrance and walked six blocks to the Ferdowski International Grand Hotel. Ziba was waiting for him in the lobby. They met her second car at a side entrance to the hotel.

Ziba's car took Bita back to the condo. Despite the risk, she had gladly agreed to be Ziba's body double.

* * *

At 7:15 Jarrett disappeared behind the construction trailer across from Mohsen's house. There was a faint glow in an upstairs window. As he sat down on a stack of lumber, he thought about Ziba.

After two hours of exercise, they'd showered and eaten a late lunch. Ziba had reminisced about Tony and asked questions about the ranch in South Dakota. How big was it? What was the house like? How did Jarrett spend his days? What was the nearest city? Did it have a movie theater? Would the people in the ranching community accept her?

Jarrett had listened, but the best he could do was give one-word answers. He was going into kill mode. His focus was on Mohsen to the exclusion of all else.

"Are you okay, Clint?" she'd asked just before they left the condo.

"Just getting my head together for tonight," he'd replied, slipping the Glock under his belt in the small of his back.

"You seem different. I noticed it earlier. It's like you've completely withdrawn."

"I'm sorry, Ziba." He'd looked at her. "This is what happens just before . . ."

"Just before what?"

Jarrett had hesitated before answering. "Just before I kill somebody. I go into kill mode, I become a different person, one I don't necessarily like. There's an emotional vacuum inside me. It started today after lunch. But this mission is different than any other. For once, I'm not alone in some godforsaken hell hole."

"You have a magnetism that is indescribable, Clint, and it's not because you look like a Hollywood A-lister. Lots of men only have looks, believe me, I've met my share. The change in you is unimaginable. Your skin even feels cold to the touch."

"I'm sorry you have to see me like this. But when I'm done, I'll be magnetic me again. I promise." He'd tried to lighten her mood, but her eyes still looked sad. "Are you worried that I won't come home?"

She'd shaken her head and forced a smile. "I know you'll be okay."

Jarrett glanced at his chronograph and was jettisoned back to the moment. Mohsen was late.

He called Ziba.

"Have you seen him?"

"No. Maybe he took a different route."

"I doubt it," Jarrett said. "He's a creature of habit. There's a light on in the house. I wonder if his wife's home."

"Maybe he came home early."

"If he was home, there'd be other lights. We'll wait. Patience isn't one of my virtues."

"I'm glad we talked this afternoon, Clint. Now I understand what you go through. I'll be happy when I have my Clint back."

"Me, too, Ziba."

After half an hour, Mohsen still hadn't shown. Jarrett called again.

"No sign yet?"

"No."

"Can you call your father? Find out what time Mohsen left work?"

"I'll try."

A few minutes later Jarrett's cell vibrated.

"Mohsen left at five o'clock."

"Five? That's two hours earlier than usual."

"That's what my father said. Wait. He just drove by. But Clint, someone is in the car with him."

Mohsen's passenger no doubt was his wife, Jarrett thought. *That'll complicate things.*

CHAPTER 68

There was no one in sight, so Jarrett crossed the street and hustled up Mohsen's driveway. He crouched behind a shrub along the garage and slipped on a pair of latex gloves.

A few minutes later he heard the garage door opening and Mohsen pulling into the driveway. From his hiding place he couldn't see the car.

After Mohsen drove into the garage, Jarrett slinked to the corner of the house. The garage door started closing. When it was halfway down, he ducked under it and crouched behind the car.

Mohsen was jabbering in Russian, his voice animated and full of energy. He sounded almost happy.

Jarrett had taken Russian classes during his JSOC training, and recognized a few words—package, car, and danger.

Was Mohsen talking to his wife in Russian about the bomb?

When Jarrett heard the house door close, he withdrew the Glock and inched around the car. He waited a few seconds, then opened the door.

Mohsen stepped back with a start. A second man stood next to him. He had an unsettling calm about him.

Jarrett trained the gun on them, stepped inside, and closed the door behind him.

"It's you!" Mohsen blurted.

"We meet again, in your kitchen no less. Who's this guy?"

"I knew there was something about you."

"Answer my question. Who is he?

"A friend."

The man was much younger than Mohsen and a full head shorter than Jarrett. With a muscular, compact wrestler's build, he had coarse Slavic features and thick, brown hair brushed across his forehead. In a loose-fitting suit with an open-collar shirt, he looked like the streetwise twin of the infamous Midwest governor serving a sentence in federal prison. There was a suitcase at his feet.

"Who are you?" Jarrett asked.

With a confident smirk, the man said, "A friend of Dr. Mohsen."

"Let me see your passport."

"I don't have one," he said.

"Take off your jacket. Put it on the counter."

When the man hesitated, Jarrett put the Glock to Mohsen's head. "Do it."

Mohsen began to hyperventilate. "Do it *nefyoo*," he said.

Jarrett found a Russian passport, a visa for Iran, and two boarding passes. The man's name was Kemsi Umarov, born in Grozny, Chechnya. One boarding pass was for a flight from Grozny to Istanbul on Aeroflot, the second for the infamous Iran Air flight 1645.

Jarrett chuckled to himself.

Kemsi Umarov was a relative of Mohsen, Sahin the Turk's replacement from Chechnya.

Jarrett looked at Mohsen. "Your given name is Mohammed Umarov. You were born in Chechnya. This man is Chechen. He has the same name."

"He's my nephew."

"Your brother Bworz's son?"

Mohsen nodded.

"What's he doing here?"

"Visiting," Mohsen replied.

"Wrong answer. Your nephew is here to replace me. He'll deliver the bomb to Chechyna."

Mohsen's nephew glared at Jarrett. "I'm visiting my aunt. She's dying of cancer."

"Is she upstairs?" Jarrett asked.

"No. She's with her sister," Mohsen replied, shaking his head nervously.

With Mohsen and his nephew standing in front of him, Jarrett had a golden opportunity to slam the door shut on the Chechen deal.

"Mohsen, do you have a gun?"

Mohsen was unglued, while his nephew stared at Jarrett with a blank look shifting his weight from one leg to the other.

"Yes. In my office."

"Get it."

Jarrett followed Mohsen and his nephew into a small office.

As Mohsen opened a desk drawer, the nephew stepped to the side.

"Don't do anything stupid, Mohsen. Put the gun on the desk." Jarrett glanced at Umarov. "And don't you move."

Mohsen did as he was told.

The revolver had a knurled wooden grip and a five-point star where the latch for the cylinder should be. It looked like an old Smith & Wesson.

"What kind is it?" Jarrett asked.

"Nagrant-M1895. Belgian-made. Built in 1910. It was my father's." Mohsen looked at his nephew. "Your grandfather's."

"Loaded?"

"Yes. Seven rounds."

Jarrett checked the gun. It *was* loaded with old flat-tipped lead bullets.

"When were you to give him the bomb?"

"Tomorrow," Mohsen answered.

"Shut up, uncle."

Jarrett glanced at Umarov. "Where did you learn Farsi?"

"Fuck you," he said.

"He lived with us during the wars in Chechnya."

Umarov clenched his fists and his jaw tightened. "I said, shut up."

"It's over Kemsi," Mohsen muttered. "This man was supposed to represent Hezbollah. But he's a foreign agent, Israeli or American."

Jarrett noted an expensive-looking pen in Mohsen's shirt pocket.

"Do you have stationery?"

"Yes."

"Use your fancy pen to write, 'Allah, I beg forgiveness for my wrongs.' And sign it."

"Why?" Mohsen asked.

"Because I said so and because you need forgiveness for being a traitor and killing Dietz Meyer and my friend."

Jarrett's eyes followed Mohsen as he sat down at the desk. Suddenly a blur filled his peripheral vision, and a shock wave shot up his legs.

Umarov had thrown a side kick into the back of Jarrett's thighs, buckling his knees.

Umarov quickly followed with two punches to the side of Jarrett's head.

Jarrett tumbled on his back, and the Glock flew out of his hand. A starburst of white flashes filled his vision.

"I'll kill you!" Umarov screamed as he mounted Jarrett and began to rain down punches.

Instinctively, Jarrett raised his arms to block the strikes. Umarov's fists glanced off Jarrett's hands and forearms, buying precious seconds. As Jarrett's head began to clear, he saw Umarov glaring down at him in a rage, shouting, "Take that! Take that!"

Jarrett thrust his hips upward rocking Umarov to the side. While Umarov tried to rebalance himself, Jarrett wrapped his right arm around Umarov's neck and pulled down.

The Chechen did what Jarrett hoped he'd do. He pushed his hands against Jarrett's chest, but Jarrett had him locked tight and was stronger. Unable to gain separation, Umarov pushed up from the floor.

In the blink of an eye Jarrett set a kimura lock. He wrapped his legs around Umarov's waist and rocked hard to the side.

Umarov's shoulder separated with a loud *pop*, and he shrieked like a wounded animal.

With the Chechen disabled, Jarrett set a guillotine choke hold. As he cranked it tighter, he looked up.

Mohsen stood over them with a bewildered look. The handgun was aimed at Jarrett's chest, the hammer was cocked, and Mohsen's outstretched arm was shaking wildly.

In a flash Jarrett rolled, pulling Umarov on top of him while holding the guillotine in place.

Bang. The gun discharged.

In the small office the sound was deafening.

The lead bullet hit Umarov between the shoulder blades and exploded inside of him.

Mohsen screamed, "No! No!" as the recoil threw his arm upward.

Jarrett reacted instantly, slinging Umarov's body into Mohsen's legs. It knocked him backward, and he careened off the desk and landed facedown.

Jarrett pinned him to the floor and twisted his gun arm behind him.

"Let go of the gun," he ordered. "Damn it. I'll break your arm. You saw what I did to him."

Mohsen grunted, "He's a Systema Master," and released his grip.

Jarrett took the gun and retrieved his Glock. He stood up and helped Mohsen to his feet.

"Kemie. Kemie. I'm sorry. It was an accident," Mohsen cried.

He knelt down next to his nephew, but Jarrett pulled him away. "Don't touch him. Leave him. Finish the note."

While Mohsen wrote, Jarrett pulled Umarov's arm—straight down with a firm tug. The shoulder popped back into place.

A pool of blood was spreading under Umarov.

He grunted and took his last agonal breaths.

CHAPTER 69

Mohsen's Russian sedan was the only vehicle on the sixth level of the parking garage. He was behind the wheel; Jarrett sat in the passenger seat. The skies were gray and overcast with light rain.

Jarrett had left Mohsen's handgun on the desk. Investigators would conclude that Mohsen killed his nephew . . . which he had.

Jarrett had Mohsen's handwritten note in his pocket.

"I have questions," he told Mohsen. "If you don't answer them, I'll hurt you. Believe me I know how to inflict excruciating pain."

"No pain. Please, not after all I've been through. My life is over. My wife is dying. I killed my nephew. He was like a son to me. We have nuclear weapons now. My work is finished. I have nothing to live for."

"Tell me the whole deal from start to finish."

Mohsen began without hesitation. "The Russians gave us two devices."

"Gave you? Or sold you?"

"Gave us. No money."

"Why?"

"Why do you think?"

Jarrett glared at Mohsen. "Don't answer my question with a question."

"Because they're Iran's allies. And because it shifts the balance of power in the Middle East. The Jews can't push Iran around anymore. And Iran can honor any agreement with the U.S., because it doesn't need to develop weapons. It already has them." Mohsen snickered. "With the money Iran saves, it builds up it's military and advances rocket technology. Iran wants to be a superpower. Russia wants to dominate the world. In the end the United States suffers on the international stage."

"Why give a weapon to Hezbollah?"

"It was Mandazi's idea."

Ziba's uncle, Jarrett thought.

"I hate the bastard, but he's clever, just like Soleimani was. In order for Iran to flex its muscles, the world has to know it has a bomb. So the suitcase device goes to Hezbollah. As part of the deal they're told to make a video of it. When the video goes viral on the internet, the terrorists say they got the bomb from Iran. The world knows then Iran has nuclear devices. The Persians claim they developed them. Israel goes crazy. The Russians deny everything and avoid trouble with the U.S."

"You had Dietz Meyer killed?"

"Yes. My plan was to replace him with Kemie. I told my boss the Hezbollah contact for the deal died in his hotel room of natural causes. A replacement would be sent. That was going to be Kemie. But Meyer never had the money wired. I needed an intermediary from Hezbollah to do it. You showed up, sooner than I had figured. After you had the money wired, I had to get you out of the way so I could replace you with Kemie."

"What about the money that went to Belarus?"

"The account's in my name and my brother's."

"So the Chechen militants get a bomb and a whole bunch of cash."

Mohsen said nothing. With a blank stare and his hands in his lap, he looked like a condemned man in the last moments of his life.

"Who's the Russian assassin?"

"Ex-Spetsnaz GRU."

That meant Russian special forces intelligence, highly trained black ops agents who specialized in espionage and assassination.

Very bad dude, Jarrett thought.

"His name?"

Mohsen hesitated then sighed. "Vasily Kuznetsov."

"Where's he staying?"

"The Parsian. Same place Meyer stayed. And you."

"Is he registered under that name?"

"Yes."

"Get out of the car."

"I know what you're going to do. I have nothing to live for now. Just no pain. Please."

"You had Demus killed. You're responsible for killing a friend of mine. You tried to kill me twice."

Jarrett directed Mohsen to the wall at the edge of the garage.

He leaned Mohsen into the concrete and locked his right arm around Mohsen's neck. It was eerie setting a rear naked choke hold without a struggle.

He pushed Mohsen's head forward occluding the flow of blood to his brain.

Mohsen stayed calm. In a matter of seconds he was unconscious.

No pain.

Jarrett snapped his neck and threw him over the wall.

He put Mohsen's note on the car dash, walked to the garage stairwell, and dropped his latex gloves in a trash bin.

The night sky had darkened, and there was a chill in the air. Jarrett began to shiver.

He took the stairs to the ground level and exited the garage. As he walked toward Ziba's car, a bad feeling came over him.

Mohsen had been disgruntled. His wife was terminally ill, his marriage was on the rocks, and he just killed his nephew. His career had stalled. With nuclear devices in Iran, there was no need to expend precious resources to develop them. And Jarrett had just foiled his plans.

But Mohsen wasn't a threat to anyone, except the Russians. Killing him wasn't the same as assassinating a high-value target. It was an execution. Plain and simple. Jarrett was an assassin, not an executioner.

Suddenly lights flashed all around Jarrett.

A car pulled behind him, one in front of him.

Armed men jumped from the vehicles.

He was surrounded.

Instinctively, he reached for the Glock. Then dropped his hands.

A voice shouted, "Halt. You're under arrest. Hands over your head."

He saw Ziba's car in the distance.

She had betrayed him.

CHAPTER 70

*E*vin Prison.

Jarrett recognized the expansive, white complex. Concertina wire topped tall masonry walls and gun towers edged against the magnificent Alborz mountains.

Evin was a hotbed with a long history of human rights violations—mass executions, torture, and horrid living conditions.

Jarrett rode with two agents to the prison. After an endless series of security checkpoints, the agents escorted him down a long corridor with institutional white floors and green walls to an interrogation room. The air was hot and thick with a putrid amalgamation of disinfectant and body odor.

His mind swirled around Ziba. Why had she betrayed him? How had he made such a terrible mistake trusting her?

The room was twenty-feet square with one mirrored wall. At the center a metal chair was bolted to the floor. A spotlight on the ceiling bathed it in bright light. Jarrett wondered if the dark stain around a drain under the chair was dried blood.

The agents zip-tied Jarrett to the chair and left without a word.

The room was silent except for humming from an air vent. Jarrett imagined he heard hollow screams in the distance. He braced for the worst.

After a few minutes the door swung open. A man dressed in a tailored black suit with a starched white shirt and striped tie stood in the threshold. He had a trim build, fantastic jet-black hair brushed straight back from his forehead, and a movie star's chin. Soft blue eyes and a relaxed purposeful-ness belied an indefinable aura of power. A mischievous smile spread across his face.

"Clint, please forgive me for all the drama. With your extraordinary reputation, I thought this was the best venue for us to meet. I'm Ziba's father, Mir Abassi. It's an honor to finally meet Paladin, or Jenni as you're known in our world. Ziba told me you speak Farsi perfectly. With your permission, I'd prefer to talk in English. I don't get a chance to practice it unless I'm with my children, which unfortunately is all too infrequent these days."

Jarrett was flabbergasted.

Finally, he mustered words. "It's my pleasure, Mr. Abassi. You know a lot about me."

Abassi chuckled. "I do, indeed. Ziba speaks very highly of you. Please call me Mir, everyone does except my children and grandchildren."

"English is fine. I haven't spoken much Farsi until recently."

"I suppose you speak it when you assassinate one of my agents."

Jarrett smiled. "I'd love to shake your hand, but . . ." He nodded at the restraints.

"I understand your hands are lethal. I'm not armed. If you promise to behave, we can adjourn to a more comfortable venue. I find this room, this whole facility, rather depressing. The odor is . . ."

Jarrett interrupted. "I promise."

CHAPTER 71

After a long walk and two elevator rides Jarrett and Abassi sat at a long table in a musty room that looked like an old library. Shelves crammed with books in aged leather bindings lined the walls, and there was a spectacular view of the mountains from the windows.

Abassi explained this had been the library of the estate of the Iranian prime minister in the 1920s.

"This is the only room in the whole complex that isn't bugged," he added. "What I have to say to you this evening would put me in front of a firing squad."

"I'm all ears," Jarrett said.

"We have a lot to talk about, Clint, but first let me thank you for what you've done for Ziba. I will be forever indebted to you." Momentarily, he had the look of a beleaguered father who adored his daughter. "But more about that later. Let's talk business first. You know who I am."

"I do. You're the head of the Revolutionary Guard, the most powerful secular in Iran."

Abassi sighed. "In official matters I must toe the line, to use your American vernacular. I am a Muslim and I will die a Muslim, but I'm not an Islamist. I don't believe Sharia should be the rule of law. And I'm not an Islamist terrorist, someone who believes violence in the name of Islam is the road to a caliphate. I am a man of peace, vehemently opposed to nuclear weapons. When the sanctions imposed by your country are lifted we will grow and prosper. With Allah's help, perhaps one day even embrace democracy. I greatly admire American capitalism, but I fear you are gradually veering off course."

"Why are you telling me all this?"

221

"I know I sound pedantic, but be patient with me, Clint. The short answer to your question is that I don't want a nuclear weapon in the hands of Hezbollah."

"Why don't you just stop it then?"

Abassi shook his head. "I can't. If I tried, I'd lose everything. It would destroy my family. We'd have to leave Iran. My children and their little ones are the most important things in my life."

"It's hard to believe you can't stop it," Jarrett said.

"I'm powerless because of my wife's brother, Ali Mandazi. He's the chief protagonist for our nuclear program after his predecessor was assassinated by the Americans. Soleimani got the Russians to give us two devices without my knowledge. Ali and the ayatollah want one in the hands of the terrorists in Lebanon."

"Why?"

"This Islamist regime hates the Jews. It's a black hatred, the deepest, darkest hatred imaginable and it's woven into their DNA. I don't hate anyone, Clint. I realized a long time ago that hate is self-destructive. As someone once said, perhaps Churchill, hate is a stimulus for pugnacity. A nuclear device in the hands of Hezbollah would push Israel over the edge."

"It would shift the balance of power in the Middle East for sure," Jarrett said.

"It would bring war. The U.S. would side with Israel. The Russians are bullies, but cowards. They would do nothing to help us. My country would be destroyed, simply because the leaders here hate the Jews."

"You're right, I fear."

"War is meaningless destruction. Your country fought two costly wars against Germany and one against Japan. You used nuclear weapons on the Japanese. You're allies now. We must not fight a bloody war with Israel to gain enlightenment. Two countries don't need to love each other to get along and prosper. A nuclear bomb in the hands of Hezbollah would ignite World War III, and it would be a nuclear war. This bomb must not reach Beirut. You can stop it with the help of the CIA."

"Me?"

"Yes, you. You'll assure world peace, Clint." Abassi leaned toward Jarrett as if he were about to share a secret. "I have a spy in Ali's office. The decision to deliver the device to Beirut was made this afternoon."

"Without an intermediary?" Jarrett asked.

"Yes. I suspect Ali's frustrated with Mohsen. He'll be glad to hear he's dead. You have to stop it, Clint."

"How?"

"Seize it and turn it over to your government."

"That would be bad for you."

"For the crazy theocracy yes, but best for my people in the long run. Trust, me Clint. When your president gets the bomb, he'll have proof that we have these evil devices. We have another one, bigger of course. He'll force us to turn it over."

"To the Russians?"

"No. To the U.S. for safekeeping. Then hopefully we'll sign an agreement and the onerous sanctions will be lifted."

"I'd need a lot of intel. And someone may die."

"There's often collateral damage in an operation like this. You'll know everything I know."

Abassi's eyes bored into Jarrett. "There are other matters for us to discuss."

CHAPTER 72

"**I** hope one is about the spy in the Revolutionary Guard," Jarrett said.

"Ziba explained that was the reason you came to Tehran." Abassi chuckled. "I was grateful that you were on that flight."

"On a prior mission I learned there was a spy in the Guard. I don't know who it is. That's the truth."

"I believe you. Ali tells me the spy was identified. He and his family escaped."

Good, Jarrett thought.

Abassi continued. "I instructed Ali to rescind the contract on you. He's agreed. His problem is getting our money back. Meyer is dead."

"With the billions you got from us with the treaty, you can afford the loss."

Abassi smiled. "But Ali's focused on it. It's all about symbolism to him. He paid someone to do something and it wasn't done. He wants his money back. Meyer was killed, which complicates the recovery."

"A contract assassin working for Mohsen killed him."

"Ziba told me. You returned from Beirut to replace Meyer. The nuclear device was going to Washington."

Jarrett described Mohsen's connection to the Chechen rebels and explained how he'd planned to have the bomb sent to them with five million in cash from Hezbollah.

"Very clever of him," Abassi said. "Then the rebels could flex their muscles. That would be interesting, and we would have some explaining to do to the Russians. Ali would be embarrassed."

"Exactly. After I had the money wired, Mohsen's assassin tried to kill me. Twice. The second time, Tony took the bullet. I feel bad about it. He was a nice man."

Abassi frowned and shook his head. "Tony was the best. Close to Ziba for many years. Also good friends with my sons. He went to college in London with my oldest. We will miss him."

Jarrett explained what had happened at Mohsen's house, then added, "Mohsen was distraught about everything and tumbled off a six-story garage."

Abassi put his hand on Jarrett's arm and grinned. "Is that what you Americans call an assisted suicide?"

Jarrett frowned. "He wanted to die."

"And he did. You did well. My men picked you up near the garage. Ziba told me you'd be there."

"Yes. I drove there with him. He told me about his plan and about the Russian assassin. His name is Vasily Kuznetsov. He's staying at the Parsian. I have to deal with him tonight."

"What will you need?"

"Just one thing."

Abassi nodded. "I know exactly what it is. A friend of mine owns the property. It'll be delivered to Ziba's tonight."

"Good."

Suddenly Abassi's eyes narrowed and his jaw muscles tightened.

CHAPTER 73

"**Y**ou know who Jago is."

"Ziba told me about him," Jarrett said.

"He brings a bad tast to my mouth."

"Mine, too. He's caused a lot of trouble."

"We can't find him. We think he's hiding in one of those horrid slums outside Paris. The French call them *banlieues*. I'd like to hire you to deal with him. Perhaps enlist the intelligence resources of your country. You'll do my family and our country a great service. Just name your price."

"I'd be happy to take care of him. I'll have the CIA track him down. They'll find him wherever he is. Then I'll pay him a visit. I'll do it for Ziba. There'll be no charge."

"Wonderful."

"I'll need as much intel on him as possible."

"We have a thick file. I'll get it to you."

"The sooner the better."

"And last but not least, let us talk about Ziba. She's a bright, strong woman who knows exactly what she wants. She takes after her mother." He winked. "She loves you. She'll follow you, wherever you go."

"She's wonderful. But you know who I am and what I do."

"Believe me, I know. You have a marvelous life on your ranch in South Dakota when you're not assassinating Muslims. But women will be women, as they say. She'll make you a good wife if you want her." Abassi began to laugh. "Imagine that, Paladin, the ethereal killer of Muslim terrorists, marries the daughter of the head of the Revolutionary Guard."

"Jazeera would have a field day with it for sure." Jarrett grinned.

"Indeed they would. If things work out between the two of you, Ziba will give you many children. I want to be called Poppa Mir."

"When the bomb is on its way to Washington, I'll meet Ziba at a safehouse in Scotland."

Abassi interrupted. "When you meet her, she'll have a zip drive in her purse with Jago's file."

"Great idea. I'll get the file to my friend in the CIA right away. From Scotland we'll go to my ranch. I'll get her a new identity. No one will unravel it. By then the CIA will have a fix on Jago. Then I'll deal with him."

"You've made my day, Clint. I'll let you know what I learn about the transport of the device to Beirut."

"I imagine it'll be on a military plane," Jarrett said.

"I don't think so. Someone will smuggle it into Lebanon. An Iranian military plane landing in Beirut would raise a red flag."

"I hear you."

"One last thing," Abassi said handing Jarrett a card. "This is my personal number. Calls bounce off a Russian satellite, but they're encrypted. You can reach me from anywhere in the world. Anytime. Please let me know how you make out in Beirut."

"It's a pleasure to meet you, Mir."

When they stood Abassi hugged Jarrett, then squeezed his shoulders and looked intently into his eyes.

"You're the only man other than my sons I've ever embraced. Our family is grateful for what you've done for Ziba. Good luck with the nuclear device. Ziba has your Austrian handgun with the custom suppressor. It's a beauty."

"I hope I don't need it."

"And just for your own peace of mind, Clint, I had Cha Mogadan expunge Thomas Davis's file from our intelligence records. I personally checked. It's gone."

"Thank you, sir."

"He told me you were a superstar hockey player in college. He saw you play in a tournament in New York."

"That was a long time ago."

CHAPTER 74

"I thought you betrayed me," Jarrett said.

Ziba kissed him on the cheek.

"Never. My father thought Evin would be safest. The director of that horrible place is a friend of his from the old days. I wasn't sure you'd agree."

"Your father is an extraordinary man. We had a nice talk; he even quoted Churchill. His English is pretty damn good."

"He is a voracious reader. His two favorite world leaders are Winston Churchill and Ronald Reagan."

"It's amazing he's able to survive with his political beliefs."

"He's careful about what he says and does. It's a fine line. He believes he can do more in his position than if he tried to buck the ayatollah. Did you settle the spy issue?"

"Yes. Apparently your Uncle Ali identified the spy, but he escaped with his family. Your father had the contract rescinded."

"That's wonderful. Now we can leave Tehran."

Not yet, Jarrett thought.

"We talked about the bomb. Your father has a spy in Ali's office. He learned that the bomb will be sent it to Beirut. No intermediary."

"Why?" Ziba asked curiously.

"Your uncle's frustrated. He and the ayatollah want the bomb in Beirut. Your father doesn't."

"His hands are tied. What can he do?"

"He's done it."

"What?"

"He asked me to seize it."

"You? How?"

"He'll tell me when and how the bomb is to be moved. Then I'll put a plan together."

Ziba's eyes widened. "Will it be dangerous?"

"I don't think so, but you never know. I have something else to do first. Mohsen gave me the name of the assassin. The one who killed Tony and tried to kill me at the hotel. If he's still at the Parsian, I'll visit him tonight. Your father's sending a room key."

Ziba's cell beeped. She glanced down, then said, "A text from my father. There's an envelope downstairs for you. He hasn't heard anything yet about the device."

Jarrett called the Parsian.

"Parsian Hotel. How may I help you?" the operator answered.

"Good evening. Mr. Kuznetsov's room please," Jarrett replied.

"One moment, sir." A few seconds later the operator came back. "Mr. Kuznetsov is not answering, sir. Would you like to leave a message?"

"No, thank you."

Jarrett hung up and looked at Ziba.

"He's still there. When he learns Mohsen's dead, he'll leave."

"Mohsen's dead? You never told me what happened."

Jarrett explained.

"They're both dead then, he and his nephew?"

"Yes, thank God. To the authorities it'll look like Mohsen shot his nephew and then committed suicide."

"They deserved to die. And so does the fucking Russian." After a moment she relaxed and stroked his arm. "You're my magnetic Clint again. I like it."

Jarrett chuckled. "I morphed while I was with your father."

"When you get to the hotel tonight, you'll be bad boy Clint again. Excuse me, I mean Paladin. My father told me you have quite a reputation for killing Muslim terrorists."

"Unfortunately, the terrorists are all Muslims these days."

"Yes they are. But no one knows who you are."

"That's right. But your father knows all about me. The only way he could have found out was—"

Ziba interrupted. "I told him who you were. You can trust him. He obviously trusts you. Besides when you leave Tehran, I hope you'll quit being Paladin. We can have fun in South Dakota and travel the world. Lots of fun places I'd like to visit. I'll own a jet and a yacht soon. And houses in Nice and Rome."

"Once I retrieve the bomb, I'll turn it over to the CIA. After a few days in Scotland, we'll head to the ranch. When you're settled, I'll go after Jago."

"You're going after Jago?"

"You're damn right I am. Your father hasn't been able to find him. But the CIA will."

Ziba smiled. "By the way. I have your gun. Will you need it tonight?"

"No. Just these."

Jarrett held out his hands.

CHAPTER 75

Ziba was right.

When Jarrett stepped from a taxi two blocks from the Parsian Hotel he was Paladin. Tonight there would be no after-mission remorse. This would be a cold-blooded killing. And Jarrett couldn't wait.

He entered through a side door using the master key from Mir Abassi. He took the stairs to the mezzanine and made another call to Kuznetsov's room. The Russian was still out, so he sprinted up the stairs to the sixth floor.

The Do Not Disturb sign was on the door. He knocked and said, "Room service." When there was no response, he used the key to open the door.

The room was a mess.

Dirty clothes were strewn everywhere and the air stank of cigarettes and cheap perfume. An open bottle of vodka and two empties were on a table with an ashtray full of cigarette butts, some with lipstick. A photograph of Jarrett at his first meeting with Mohsen was under one of the empty bottles.

The Russians sure love their vodka and tobacco, he thought.

The closet held hanging clothes and an array of sex toys. Demus's messenger bag and another shoulder bag hung on hooks.

Jarrett removed the tracking device from the bottom of the bag. Inside he found Demus's passport, a copy of his e-ticket confirmation from Aegean Travel, miscellaneous receipts, two cigars, and a laptop, but no manila envelope. He chuckled thinking Mohsen had probably given him the same envelope he'd given Demus.

In the other bag he found Kuznetsov's Russian passport and the passport for a blonde, thin-faced woman with bedroom eyes. Two hard cases sat on the floor, one was made of molded plastic with a rectangular shape.

Jarrett picked the lock and found a Remington Defense CSR .308 sniper rifle with a Swarovski scope and a box of American-made cartridges. He sniffed the chamber. It had been recently fired.

No doubt the gun that killed Tony.

The second case was aluminum and held the infamous Russian PP-200 machine pistol designed to fire the new Cryrillic armor-piercing cartridges. Jarrett was lucky he hadn't been in the line of fire when the Russian visited his hotel room with this scary weapon.

A loaded 9mm Russian P-96 handgun with a suppressor was tucked under the mattress. Jarrett examined it, wondering how Kuznetsov had smuggled all these weapons into Iran.

He glanced at his chronograph. Four minutes in the room. He had allowed a maximum of five, and even that was a stretch. He had no idea when the Russian would return.

Out of curiosity, he checked the bathroom. A nearly empty bottle of hotel cologne sat on the vanity.

As he opened the door to leave, he heard voices approaching.

The bastard is back, he thought.

He closed the door and looked around wondering where to hide. The closet? The bathroom? Maybe under the bed?

Jarrett chuckled to himself. Paladin hiding under a target's bed was worthy of entry into the believe it or not book of black ops . . . if there was one.

He moved behind the door and readied himself. A man and a woman arguing in Farsi passed the room. He heard a door close a short distance down the hall, and breathed a sigh of relief.

He left the room, placed a tiny piece of clear tape over the top of the doorjamb, took the stairs to the mezzanine, and waited.

A short time later Kuznetzov and a woman strolled into the lobby. He appeared to be staggering and she was holding onto his arm.

They rode an elevator to the sixth floor.

The Russian was back.

Game on.

CHAPTER 76

The tape across the doorjamb was torn.

Jarrett opened the door.

Kuznetsov and his lady friend were in bed. The woman was mounted on him, her head thrown back, gyrating up and down. Kutnetsov was flat on his back with his hands around the woman's waist.

They didn't waste any time getting to work, Jarrett thought.

Both were reeling in the moment, the woman moaning and Kuznetsov grunting words of encouragement. Jarrett imagined it was something like, "Faster! Deeper! Harder, you fucking whore!"

Jarrett slammed the door closed and turned on the lights.

The woman froze.

Oblivious to the intruder the Russian snarled at her.

She pointed to Jarrett and screamed, "Vasy."

"Sorry to interrupt your fun," Jarrett chimed.

Kuznetsov's head rose off the bed and he glared at Jarrett.

"You! The fucking Turk!"

He tossed the woman off him like a rag doll. In one swift motion he was on his feet, the gun from under the mattress in his hand.

"You tried to kill me twice," Jarrett told him. "And you murdered a close friend of mine."

"Now, I finish you."

Kuznetsov was a hulk. Glistening with perspiration, he looked like an aging wrestler with bulky, uncut muscles and a bulging gut. Like most Russian bad guys he was heavily tattooed.

Jarrett pointed at the woman on the floor and gestured to the bathroom. She was short and scrawny with a haggard face smeared with mascara and crude tattoos from her neck to her ankles. *A bad advertisement for Russian ink,* Jarrett thought.

She hesitated at first, but when Jarrett thrust his hand across his throat, she scurried to the bathroom.

Jarrett squared himself with the Russian and said, "The ball is in your court fat boy."

"Arab piece of shit. I fuck you up," Kuznetzov sneered thick-tongued.

Jarrett smiled and stood his ground.

The Russian twisted the gun's suppressor and fired. The gun clicked but didn't discharge. He rachetted it back and fired again. *Click.* He looked at it in disbelief and growled, *"Blyad."*

"Always check your weapon, asshole." Jarrett tossed the cartridges on the carpet.

Kuznetsov threw the gun at Jarrett.

It glanced off his shoulder, but the roundhouse kick that followed found its mark. The Russian's foot smacked Jarrett's midsection with a loud *snap* that sounded like a whip cracking. For a drunken, aging hulk the Russian was incredibly agile, almost balletic.

Kuznetsov lunged forward and threw a combination of punches, his fists fast and rhythmic like a boxer.

Jarrett parried, but one blow caught him in the cheek and he dropped to his knees.

Kuznetsov grabbed a chair and broke it over Jarrett's back. "Take that, motherfucker!"

Jarrett's legs gave way, and he collapsed facedown. The Russian growled, "Bastard!" and kicked Jarrett in the ribs.

A sharp pain shot through Jarrett's chest taking his breath away. When he instinctively rolled on his back, Kuznetsov top-mounted him, balancing his weight perfectly across Jarrett's hips.

Jarrett was trapped under a massive Russian brute who was dripping in perspiration and whose breath carried a sickening stench of alcohol and tobacco.

Punches began to rain down—hammer fists—one after another, like a hydraulic piston.

Jarrett held his forearms and fists in front of his face—the Ali rope-a-dope maneuver. If just one strike found its mark, it was lights out. Game over.

With a surge of adrenalin fueling him, Jarrett's head cleared quickly, but he was breathless after the kicks to his midsection and ribs.

The Russian was a madman, out of control, punching Jarrett in a frenzy, confident he had Sahin the Turk at his mercy.

After a few deep breaths, Jarrett locked his left leg across the Russian's right leg.

Kuznetsov, sensing the end was near for Jarrett, cried, "Yah!" and threw a wild roundhouse right. But the Russian was tiring and had locked his arm at the elbow telegraphing the punch. Jarrett easily blocked it and pulled Kuznetsov's arm inward.

With Kuznetsov's right leg trapped and his right arm locked, Jarrett bridged and rolled the Russian on his back. The perfectly executed mount reversal took Kuznetsov by surprise.

Immediately Jarrett sprang to his feet.

"Get up," he snarled.

Kuznetsov sat up, shook his head, and took a few deep breaths. He balanced his weight with his hands on the floor and rolled onto his knees. As he stood, Jarrett hit him square in the jaw with an uppercut. The Russian's mouth snapped closed and he tumbled on his back.

With a stiff punch jarring his brain, the Russian's eyes were locked in a boozy, thousand-mile stare.

"I said get up, asshole."

Kuznetsov struggled to his feet again, balancing himself against the table. Flat-footed with his legs apart and rocking back and forth, he looked like a drunken sumo wrestler.

Jarrett's fists flashed—left, right, left, right.

After taking the punches to his gut, the Russian tensed his abdominal muscles and flexed his arms like a body builder posing.

"All you got?" he growled.

"No." Jarrett smiled as he swung an axe kick.

His boot hit Kuznetsov in the crotch, so hard that it lifted the wobbly Russian on his toes. Kuznetsov grunted, dropped to his knees, and began retching.

With his mouth hanging open, the Russian gasped, "No more!"

But Jarrett wasn't finished.

He locked his hands behind Kuznetsov's head and thrust a knee under full power, smashing the Russian's face. *Crunch.*

When Jarrett released his grip, Kuznetsov crashed into the table. The bottle of vodka exploded and the ashtray flipped over, showering the Russian with alcohol and cigarette butts.

Kuznetsov's face was unrecognizable—his nose was split down the middle, his eyeballs were bulging, and his jaw was askew.

Jarrett loaded the P-96 and shot him between the eyes. With only a dull *pop*, the Russian suppressor worked beautifully.

He wedged a chair against the bathroom door.

With Jarrett's prints and DNA expunged from the Iranian intelligence files, there was no need to sanitize the room.

As Jarrett opened the door to leave, he turned and muttered, "That was for Tony."

Payback was always a bitch.

CHAPTER 77

Jarrett and Ziba were enjoying a glass of French champagne in her condo. Jarrett had unwound and was relaxed with his legs propped up on the coffee table.

"What happened to you?" she asked. "Your eye is swollen and you're favoring your right side."

Jarrett told her about his encounter with the Russian assassin. When he finished, he touched his right chest and winced. "This is where he kicked me. It hurts like hell."

"How about Demus's bag?"

"I left it there. Took the tracker." He held it up to show her.

It's a tiny little thing," she noted.

"The manila envelope was gone. I'll bet the Russian gave it to Mohsen and he gave it to me. There was an arsenal of weapons in the room."

"How about the woman?"

"Locked her in the bathroom. She'll find her way back to Russia."

Ziba sighed. "I was worried something might happen to you."

"Entry was easy with the key from your father."

"He called. The man taking the device to Beirut is Davoud Ghorbani. He's the top scientist in the Atomic Energy Organization. Mohsen's boss. He'll be accompanied by a Quds agent. My father e-mailed photographs of them. Here . . ."

Ghorbani's face was thin and pale with a long straight nose and narrow-set eyes. His hair was thinning and he was clean-shaven with wire-rim glasses. Other than a pale face, Ghorbani was a stereotypical Persian intellectual.

The Quds agent looked like a street thug, dark-skinned with a nondescript face, wary eyes, a scar under his left eye, and a heavy five o'clock shadow.

Ziba continued, "They're flying to Cyprus tomorrow on Qeshm Airlines flight 1255 leaving at 11:55 a.m."

"I never heard of that carrier," Jarrett said.

"It's a small Iranian airline, operates only in the Middle East. According to my father it's 1626 kilometers to Cyprus with a flying time of two hours and sixteen minutes. You have a reservation on the same flight."

"Your father is very efficient. I have to make a phone call. Excuse me for a few minutes."

She understood that he wanted to be alone.

"Of course. I'll take a shower and wait for you in bed," she murmured. "I have a going-away present for you."

CHAPTER 78

Jarrett opened the second operating system on his phone. There were three calls from Sedgewick. He suspected what they were about and dialed his friend's office number.

"I've been trying to reach you, Jarrett. POTUS wants you to hold off on Mohsen. There's a lot of talk around here about whether to let the Chechens have the nuclear device. A final decision hasn't been made."

"It's too late. I dealt with him and his nephew last night."

"I guess you made the decision for them. You took out his nephew, too?"

"He was my replacement. Mohsen shot him by accident. The bullet was meant for me. And then Mohsen tumbled from the top of a parking garage. Long way down. He wrote a final note."

"I'll bet he was dead before he hit the ground."

"He was distraught. Wanted to die. He went to be with Allah. The Chechen connection is gone. And I took care of the Russian assassin who killed Demus. A tough one. An ex-Spetsnaz, GRU brute with serious sambo training."

"Those ex-Spetsnaz brats are bad. The GRU ones are the worst of the bunch."

"This guy was drunk and probably high on something. Doing a skank when I crashed his room. Skinny as a rail and covered with tattoos. Mascara all over her face. Looked like a Halloween ghoul."

"Not your type, Jarrett. You're into the good-looking ones with big boobs. Tattoos verboten. What'd you do with her?"

"Locked her in the bathroom. He tagged me a couple of times pretty damn good. My ribs hurt like hell and I have a shiner under one eye. After that I had fun with him."

"I'd love to see what he looked like when you were done."

Jarrett sighed. "I was pissed. It wasn't pretty."

"I'll bet it wasn't."

"The bomb is going to Beirut tomorrow."

"What? How do you know?" Sedgewick asked incredulously.

"Mir Abassi, Ziba's father. We met in Evin Prison believe it or not. He's an amazing guy, anti-nuclear and pro-democracy. Mohsen's boss, Davoud Ghorbani, will deliver it to Hezbollah. Ziba's uncle is running the operation."

"That's bad news for us. Worse for Tel Aviv."

"Maybe not. Mir asked me to seize it."

"He did?"

"Long story. Short version is he wants peace in the Middle East. A bomb in the hands of terrorists might ignite a war. And additional sanctions on Iran will have dire consequences."

"And big-time sanctions they'll be," Sedgewick said.

"Mir has a spy in Mandazi's office. Ghorbani and a Quds agent fly to Cyprus with the bomb tomorrow. I'm on the same flight. But that's all the intel I have at this point. I don't understand why they're going there first."

"Doesn't make sense. You'd think they'd have a plan to deliver it directly to Beirut."

"They have a plan, I'm sure. We just don't know what it is. Mandazi's clever. Cyprus is just a stopover for some reason. I'll seize it there."

"Good idea. If the device makes it to Beirut, you'd have to move on it quickly, before it gets into Hezbollah's hands. Once it does, it'll disappear. You'll never find it," Sedgewick said.

"Unfortunately, it'll surface on the internet in a terrorist propaganda video, maybe with an American hostage perched on it."

"What'll you need?" Sedgewick asked.

"A helper. And the usual stuff."

"A helper? You're kidding me, Jarrett. I thought you were *el lobo solo*. You've always worked alone."

"This is different," Jarrett said.

"Does that mean you don't plan to kill anyone?"

"I don't have a clue what'll happen in Cyprus."

"Tell me about the helper."

"Needs to be young, smart, good with his hands, and a crack shot. Maybe a spook who used to be a SEAL. All he needs to know is we're recovering an important package. Give him my Turkish legend—Yusuf Sahin. He mustn't know my identity. Authentication question is, 'Who won the NCAA hockey championship ten years ago?' You know the answer."

"I do indeed. You scored both goals."

"And you tended a shutout," Jarrett added.

"Is that all you need?" Sedgewick asked with a hint of sarcasm in his voice.

"Listen, I'm an assassin, not a spook. I've never done anything like this."

"You'll have everything you need," Sedgewick assured him. "I had a clever plan to get you and the bomb out of Tehran, but I'll work on a way out of Cyprus. It should be a lot easier. When do you leave?"

"Tomorrow. Oh, one other thing. What's the battery life on those tracking devices?"

"The one you put on Demus's bag?"

"Yes. I retrieved it when I visited the cheap-cologne assassin's room."

"The battery is solar. In the dark, maybe two weeks at the most. Indefinitely, if they're exposed to light."

"I've got a few days left on mine."

"What about the contract on you?"

"Mir told me they fingered the spy, but he escaped with his family."

Sedgewick said nothing for a few seconds. "That's odd. I'm glad he got out, but we haven't heard anything from him."

"He's probably hiding some where. You'll hear from him soon. The contract's been lifted. Ziba's uncle wants his money back."

"Too bad about their damn blood money. What will you do about the Persian gal? Take her with you?"

"No. She stays here. The nuclear scientist travels with a Quds thug. This may get a little messy."

"I'll contact you about your hookup with your helper."

"It has to be in the airport in Cyprus. I'll be pulling a carry-on bag with a purple ribbon tied to the handle. Red cap and dark glasses. You've got a lot to do between now and then."

"Are you kidding? Good luck my friend."

"Thanks. I'll need it."

CHAPTER 79

Jarrett was early.

Behind dark glasses his eyes were on the Qeshm Airlines check-in counter. It was 9:30 a.m., and the flight to Cyprus was at 11:55 a.m. According to the departure board it was on time.

The Quds agent stood near the counter with a backpack at his feet. In a baggy, dark suit with a gray T-shirt and scuffed military boots he looked the part—a thug in the service of the Revolutionary Guard.

Jarrett had his laptop with the tracking device attached to its bottom in his carry-on bag.

* * *

At 10:15 a.m. Ghorbani appeared pulling a carry-on with a briefcase riding on it. He was in a gray suit, white shirt, and matching striped tie. A young man dressed similarly with a backpack on wheels was with him, no doubt a technician or junior scientist familiar with the technical details of the bomb. But there was no large suitcase with them.

Jarrett figured Mandazi had made arrangements with the airline to transport the bomb in the cargo hold. Ghorbani would claim it in Cyprus.

Ghorbani, the young man, and the Quds agent checked in and walked to the security hall.

Jarrett waited until their agent was free, then approached him.

"Your destination today, sir?" the man asked.

"Cyprus. I have a reservation," Jarrett replied handing over his Turkish passport.

"Will you check luggage, sir?"

"Not today. I'm traveling with an associate, Dr. Ghorbani. I believe he checked in already. Are there any seats open near him?"

"The flight is a single class of service. It's open, so there should be. Let me see," he said, glancing down and typing. "Dr. Ghorbani is in an aisle seat in row eleven. Nothing in his row, but there are seats in front of him and behind him. Which would you prefer?"

"Behind."

"You're directly behind him," the man said, handing Jarrett a boarding pass.

"Thank you."

Jarrett cruised through security and passport control again.

At the gate Ghorbani, his associate, and the Quds agent were nowhere in sight.

A few minutes before the boarding announcement, they appeared with an airline representative who escorted them onto the plane.

Jarrett removed the tracking device from his laptop and cradled it in his right hand, sticky-side up, then put his laptop in his carry-on.

He planned to attach the device to Ghorbani's briefcase in the overhead bin just as he had with Demus. Jarrett was worried though that Ghorbani would stow his briefcase under the seat in front of him. He wasn't in a bulk-head seat. If he did, Jarrett would have to attach the tracker to the carry-on. It wasn't ideal, since Ghorbani would leave it in his hotel and keep the briefcase with him.

When Jarrett boarded the aircraft, the baggage compartment above Ghorbani was full. Ghorbani's carry-on, his associate's carry-on, and the Qud's agent backpack were in it, but no briefcase.

Momentarily, Jarrett panicked. How would he get the tracker on Ghorbani's briefcase? And he couldn't reach up and put it on Ghorbani's carry-on.

Jarrett stopped at row ten, his mind was racing through his options. When he looked down, Ghorbani's briefcase was on his knees and open, and he was leafing through documents.

Jarrett took two steps and stumbled sideways.

Ghorbani looked up as the tall passenger fell into him.

Jarrett broke his fall by leaning on the aisle armrest with his left hand. His shoulder blocked Ghorbani from seeing him attach the tracker to the bottom of the briefcase with his right hand.

Done.

As Jarrett righted himself, he apologized.

Ghorbani shook his head and sighed but said nothing.

Jarrett put his carry-on in an empty compartment and took his seat.

Using the tracking program, he followed the aircraft's route from Tehran northwest into southern Turkey, across Turkish airspace just north of the border with Iraq and Syria, and then a short distance across the Mediterranean to Larnaca Airport in Cyprus.

The flight took two hours and thirty minutes instead of the scheduled two hours and sixteen minutes. Jarrett figured the aircraft had flown north to avoid the hotbed cities of Mosul, Iraq and Aleppo, Syria.

CHAPTER 80

When they landed, Jarrett followed Ghorbani and his companions to the passport control hall. They had their passports stamped and bypassed baggage claim. At customs, Jarrett's stomach was in his throat, but fortunately only the Quds agent's backpack was opened and inspected. Jarrett passed through passport control and customs without difficulty.

Outside the customs hall Ghorbani made a phone call. Jarrett wondered how a cell phone with Iranian service worked outside the country.

It had to be a satellite phone.

After the call Ghorbani exchanged words with the Quds agent, then the three rode an escalator down to the arrival level and walked out to the street. A black Mercedes SUV was awaiting them.

Jarrett waited inside until the SUV drove off. He put on dark glasses and a red cap and hustled out pulling his carry-on with the purple ribbon.

A black Range Rover, double-parked a short distance away, pulled up. The driver said, "Hi, there. Need a ride?"

Jarrett replied, "I do."

"Who won the NCAA hockey championship ten years ago?" the driver asked.

"Big Red," Jarrett answered.

"Welcome to Cyprus, Mr. Sahin," the driver said with a smile.

Jarrett tossed his bag and cap on the back seat and got in.

The driver extended his hand. "Damocles Nikas. Nick for short."

Jarrett shook his hand.

"Did you see the Mercedes SUV that just pulled away?" he asked.

"Yes, sir," Nikas said. "Three men got in it."

With a formal ring to sir, Nikas had to be ex-military.

"We need to follow it. I placed a tracker on one of their bags. I'm monitoring it on my phone."

Nikas glanced at the phone and pulled away. "Just tell me where to go."

Jarrett studied the color display. "You'll come to a rotary. Take the third exit for the airport frontage road."

After they traveled a short distance on the frontage road, the flashing red ball on the screen stopped moving.

"Slow down," Jarrett said. "They've stopped for some reason. Maybe a light."

There was a chain-link fence on their left, and in the distance the runway undulated with heat waves. Small private planes covered with tarps were parked wing to wing along the fence. On their right was a rental car center and beyond that a service station.

"Pull over." Jarrett pointed to the service station.

After several minutes the red ball hadn't moved.

"They're parked," Jarrett said. "Drive down the road. Where's the binos?"

Nikas pointed to the glove compartment.

After they passed several warehouses, they saw the Qeshm Air Freight building beyond a vacant lot.

The small, single-story structure had a pedestrian door in the middle and a loading dock off to one side. Just beyond the building was a cross street.

"There's the Mercedes," Jarrett said gesturing to the building.

Nikas turned at the cross street. After a short distance, he hung a U-turn and pulled over. They were about thirty yards from the Qeshm Air Freight building with a view of the back of the SUV, but they couldn't see the entrance or the loading dock.

Jarrett was impressed. Nikas knew exactly what to do.

The Quds agent hadn't been particularly watchful in either airport. The Iranian thug felt confident that no one knew about their mission outside of Mandazi's inner circle, so he wasn't concerned about surveillance.

As they waited, Jarrett gave Nikas a once-over.

The young CIA agent was big, over six feet tall and at least 220 pounds. He was broad across the shoulders and chest with weight-lifter thighs, and his forearms and hands were thick and powerful. He had a full head of curly brown hair, a pudgy baby face with bright, hazel eyes and a warm smile that never seemed to leave his face. If Jarrett had to guess there wasn't an ounce of fat on him.

Jarrett had a built-in disdain for spooks. Their condescending attitude and crowing arrogance was part of the narcissistic personality disorder that afflicted most of them. And if you worked at Langley it was highly contagious. Even agency recruits who were well-grounded ex-military types seemed vulnerable to the malady. CIA careerists with their I'm-smarterthan-you attitude grated on Jarrett. Other than Sedgewick, he avoided the Langley brats like the Velvet Fog.

But this Greek brute seemed different. The early vibes from him were good—very good.

CHAPTER 81

"Tell me about yourself, Nick."

"I'm second-generation Greek-American," he answered easily. "Grew up in St. Paul. My father owned a restaurant there. I was a waiter and some-times a cook in high school." Nikas laughed. "Went to Iowa on scholarship, after that a green face for four years, then Langley. I flew in from Athens last night for this mission."

"Can you shoot?"

"I do okay."

Jarrett glared at him. "Just okay? I told Langley I wanted a crack shot."

Nikas's smile disappeared, and he turned to Jarrett. "I was one of the shooters on the DEVGRU mission made into a movie with Tom Hanks."

DEVGRU was the JSOC name for SEAL Team Six. Nikas had killed a Somalia pirate in a small boat bobbing in the Arabian Sea with a single head shot. That was good enough for Jarrett . . . any day.

"How about your hands?"

"I was a wrestler in college, All-American two years running. After that some karate to learn stand-up."

As he spoke, he held up his right fist. Despite his massive body, his hand seemed disproportionately large. His fingers were thick and a jagged scar stretched across the knuckles. For some reason it reminded Jarrett of the meat hooks he used when hanging a side of beef at the ranch.

"I broke this one on a Taliban jaw," Nikas told him. "Had to have pins. I was out of action for a couple of months. It hurts sometimes. But I still can hold my own hand-to-hand."

Jarrett imagined this ex-Navy SEAL *could* hold his own, maybe a lot more than that, and there was no patented Langley arrogance about him. If anything, he had an air of down-home humility. Jarrett was beginning to like Nikas.

"Languages?" Jarrett asked.

"Greek and some Russian."

"Arabic or Farsi?"

"I wish," Nika said shaking his head. "I was surprised when I got the nod for this mission. Some of the guys at the office are fluent in Arabic. Guess it didn't matter. This one's top secret. When it gets its own code name, it must be important."

Sedgewick hadn't mentioned a code name.

"What is it?" Jarrett asked.

"You don't know?"

Jarrett shook his head.

"Little Boy. My orders are to do exactly what you tell me. You're supposedly Turkish, but you sound American. Midwest. I was told not to ask questions. Are those your ground rules?"

"They are," Jarrett replied. "We're to seize a package, a large suitcase, before it gets to Beirut. It was flown here on Qeshm Airlines as cargo. The airline will see that the package isn't opened in customs. It's accompanied by the men in the Mercedes SUV. The tracker I mentioned is on the briefcase of the leader, a guy named Ghorbani."

"They should pick it up here then," Nikas said.

"Right. The package will be delivered to the warehouse. They beat it here."

As Jarrett spoke a white step van with the Qeshm logo pulled into the parking lot and disappeared on the side of the building.

"That must be it. What now?" Nikas asked.

"They'll take it somewhere from here. We'll seize it on the road. They have a Quds agent with them, so it might get a little interesting."

"Then what?"

"Remember your orders. No questions."

"Sorry. Just trying to get my arms around the mission."

"You have everything we need?"

"Yes, sir. Back there." Nikas gestured to a large duffel bag in the back of the Range Rover. "It's your standard mission kit, but I added a few things."

"Where are you staying?"

"A rental twenty minutes from here. That phone with the tracking software is special." Nikas pointed to Jarrett's phone. "It's linked with the CIA network."

Jarrett said nothing.

"Sorry. I know I'm not supposed to ask questions, but only a few guys get one of those puppies."

"Are you married Nick?" Jarrett asked.

"No. Why?"

"If this mission goes south, I won't feel bad if something happens to you."

"Don't worry about me. I can take care of myself," Nikas said.

"That's good to hear."

"If the package is in the warehouse now, why don't we just waltz in and take it?"

"I thought about that. There'll be innocent people inside who work for the airline. If there's a shootout, I don't want any collateral damage. That'd stir up a major brouhaha with the locals."

"Sounds like we're out of the box already."

"We are. We'll follow them. When we come to a quiet stretch of road, we'll force them over. Might cause a little damage to your fancy ride."

"The car can be fixed. There's a 9-mil under your seat. When the time comes, what are the rules?"

Jarrett laughed. In his work there were no rules.

"There aren't any. Seize the package at all cost. Anyone with it is an enemy combatant. The only one we'll have to worry about is the Quds agent. But I doubt he's armed, at least not yet. We should be able to take the package without a whole lot of noise."

Jarrett was antsy. Twenty minutes had passed. His arms were feeling heavy holding up the binoculars.

"I wonder what's taking so long," he said.

Seconds later Nikas pointed to the warehouse. "There's movement."

CHAPTER 82

Jarrett focused the binos on the Mercedes. "The SUV's backing away. I don't see anything in the cargo hold." He checked the tracking program.

"Shit! Ghorbani's on the move. He's already on highway A3 going northwest. That means they're using the Qeshm van to transport the package. There must be a back way from the building to the highway." He glanced at Nikas. "Thank God for the tracker. Backtrack to the rotary just outside the airport, and take the A3 exit. We have to catch up to them."

But they didn't.

They passed the Mercedes SUV on the highway, but the Qeshm van had a head start and was traveling fast.

They followed the van's route northwest on highway A3 to A5 east to a residential neighborhood.

The van was parked in the driveway of an L-shaped rambler with blackout curtains on the windows. It looked like a small tract home in southern California. The house to the left appeared empty and had a for sale sign in the yard. Three young children played in the dusty side yard of the house on the right.

As they drove by, the SUV appeared behind them and pulled into the driveway. The driver was Ghorbani's young companion. He was alone.

They pulled over a block away.

A young woman pushing a baby stroller with a child riding a three-wheeler beside her walked past them. When Nikas waved to her, she smiled and walked on.

"They used the Qeshm van because the package wouldn't fit in the SUV," Jarrett said. "Damn it. We missed our chance. The package is in the house."

Nikas had his cell phone to his ear. "It's Nikas. The address is 1665 Gastroplopis Way on the Salt Sea."

"Who're you calling?" Jarrett asked.

"The station in Nicosia. We need to know if this an Iranian safe house."

Jarrett's eyes darted up and down the street, from the target house to the children playing in the side yard in the next house, to the woman walking with her young ones. Across the street a boy appeared riding a bicycle with training wheels.

"Much as I'd like to storm the place, we can't. There are children in harms way. I'd feel awful if one was hurt. We have to wait until they move it again."

"If this is a safe house you can bet there's a small arsenal inside," Nikas added.

"And we probably wouldn't get the package into this vehicle anyway, which means we'd have to use the Qeshm van. I don't like that."

"I thought you said it was the size of a large suitcase."

"I did, but I'll bet they crated it with a lot of padding. We'll have to intercept it in transit to the step-off point to Lebanon. So, we need a place close by and an unmarked van. We can take turns keeping an eye on the tracking program. Ghorbani will stay with the package until it's delivered. When he moves, we move. Then we'll strike."

"Sounds like a plan. I'll find a place near here and get us a van."

CHAPTER 83

The Olympus House, a small property catering to budget-minded tourists, was less than a half-mile away. They checked into a room with two beds, and exchanged the Range Rover for a nondescript van.

Nikas learned that a Lebanese shell company with ties to Hezbollah owned the rambler. Jarrett was surprised. He'd figured it would trace back to the Iranians.

While they ate pizza, Nikas talked about his family. As he began, his voice cracked and his eyes glazed over. His mother was a grade-school teacher and the guiding force in his life. Despite being treated for depression, she'd taken her life when he was a senior in college. He'd planned to go to law school but instead enlisted in the navy. His older brother ran the family restaurant in St. Paul and was about to open a second in Bloomington. His younger sister had married an older man who was a successful entrepreneur in the Twin Cities. He was a Muslim, she converted, and they had three children. Nikas's father refused to attend the wedding and hadn't spoken to his daughter in more than five years.

"My dad's old-school, tough as nails," Nikas said. "I respect his feelings, but I love my sister. It doesn't matter what religion she is, as long as she's happy."

As Jarrett listened, he saw a lot of himself in Nikas—a man with good values and a strong moral compass, yet one who could flip a switch and become a cold-blooded assassin. Jarrett offered nothing about himself or the mission.

They were both exhausted and alternated four-hour shifts staring at the red ball on Jarrett's laptop. It was mind-numbing.

Jarrett slept fitfully, imagining he heard Nikas clearing his throat and the clock ticking on the bedside table. At least he wasn't dreaming about Jago killing Ziba.

Just a few minutes before 8:00 a.m., Nikas shook Jarrett.

"The red ball's moving."

Jarrett was on his feet before Nikas finished the sentence, and they were on the road in under two minutes.

Nikas drove, while Jarrett focused on the laptop map and gave directions. They wore Kevlar vests under loose shirts with Glocks in the small of their backs. Nikas's go-duffel was in the back of the van.

As they followed the signal from the tracker, a sense of uneasiness settled over Jarrett. Why had the Iranians chosen Cyprus as a stopover? Why hadn't they just flown directly to Beirut on Qeshm Airlines? There were no Iranian airlines that flew from Cyprus to Beirut, and they couldn't risk transporting the bomb on another commercial carrier. The only other way to travel to Beirut was by water. Did that mean a small charter plane or a boat for the last leg of the journey? It had to be one or the other.

Jarrett assumed all along that Mandazi had ordered Ghorbani to stay with the bomb until it was handed over to Hezbollah. If he was right, Ghorbani would travel with it to Beirut.

Nikas was a skilled driver, weaving the road-lumbering van in and out of traffic and flashing his lights to move drivers over. The pulsating blue ball on the phone—their position—was not far behind the red ball. But the route they were following led to the airport.

Was Ghorbani meeting a charter?

If he went to the airport there were two possible scenarios.

The first was that the bomb was with him in the Qeshm van, and he was going to fly with it to Beirut on a charter. If that was the case, he and Nikas would have to seize the bomb in the airport. It could get messy, very messy.

The second scenario was even more problematic. The bomb went directly to a boat in the Qeshm van. Ghorbani was in the Mercedes SUV and would fly to Beirut to rendezvous with it. That meant Jarrett's assumption that Ghorbani had been ordered to stay with the bomb was wrong.

Seizing it in Lebanon would be challenging and fraught with peril. Jarrett would be trapped in a time box again.

Tick, tick, tick.

Locking on the tracker and striking quickly in Beirut would be critical. If they didn't intervene before the bomb was turned over to Hezbollah, it was game over.

As the red ball turned onto the airport access road, the blue ball was closing on it. Nikas circled the rotary on two wheels. He seemed to be having fun. When they passed the turnoff to the Qeshm Air Freight building, the blue ball was nearly touching the red ball.

Jarrett was on the edge of his seat looking for the Qeshm van and planning his next move.

"Damn it, I don't see the Qeshm van," Jarrett said.

"The Mercedes SUV is just ahead of us," Nikas said pointing to it.

"How'd you know?" Jarrett growled.

"Same plate as the one yesterday."

As the SUV pulled over at the departure terminal, Nikas double-parked a short distance away.

Ghorbani had his briefcase in hand when he got out of the SUV. He and his young associate hustled into the terminal pulling their carry-on bags behind them.

The Quds agent wasn't with them.

The SUV pulled away. Its cargo hold was empty.

"I have to call Washington to find out if Ghorbani is flying on a commercial carrier," Jarrett said.

"Our station monitors everyone in and out of Cyprus."

"That'd be faster. Do you see the Qeshm van? It might be dropping off the package at a charter."

"No. I don't see it. And this is a small field. We can see everything from here."

Nikas called his office. In less than a minute he muttered, "Thanks."

With a perplexed look he turned to Jarrett. "Believe it or not, Ghorbani is on the early-morning flight to Tehran on Qeshm Airlines."

"Shit! He's not flying on a charter with the package or commercially to Beirut to meet it."

Jarrett suddenly understood why the Iranians had stopped in Cyprus and why Ghorbani and his companion were flying back to Tehran.

"Hezbollah took possession of the package at their safe house. I should have figured as much, when you told me the house was owned by them. The Iranians wanted to avoid Beirut."

"So what now?" Nikas asked.

"It's going by boat. It's the only way. Where's the nearest marina?"

"Downtown. Larnaca Marina."

Jarrett found the marina's website on the internet and gave Nikas directions.

"The marina's owned by the city," Jarrett said. "Fifty-seven slips catering to monthly rentals, charter boats, and transients with a small store, a fuel dock, and a marine repair yard. According to this there's locked gates and roving security 24/7. The reviews are barely three-star. It looks run-down."

"I know. I took a fishing charter out of there a few months back. The road through it is one-way and full of potholes. If I remember correctly, there's a combination lock on the gate."

CHAPTER 84

Nikas remembered correctly.

He cut the lock on the entry gate, and they drove along a dirt road to the edge of the seawall.

The Qeshm van was nowhere in sight.

A white go-fast boat, long and sleek, idled out of the channel toward open water. Jarrett focused on it with the binos. It looked new, at least fifty-feet long with its top coat sparkling in the morning sun. There were two men in the open bridge and the twin inboards stirred a frothy wake. Fancy gold letters on the transom read *Party Time, Mykonos*. When the boat cleared the channel the engines roared spewing a cloud of black smoke. The bow rose out of the water as the boat accelerated.

The bomb's on its way to Beirut, Jarrett thought.

A man in a white T-shirt, brown shorts and flip-flops approached. His face was mahogany-brown and furrowed from the sun. He spoke to Nikas in Greek, a cigar stub hanging from the corner of his mouth.

After a brief conversation, Nikas said, "He's the dockmaster. Name's George. Wants to know how we got in here."

"Tell him the gate was left open. Find out about the Qeshm van and that boat," Jarrett said, pointing to the go-fast heading east toward the horizon.

Jarrett was beside himself. It was 130 miles from Cyprus to the Lebanon coast. The go-fast cruised at forty knots in calm seas. It would be in Beirut in less than four hours.

While Jarrett surveyed the marina, Nikas jabbered with George.

The dirt road followed the gentle curve of the seawall through the marina. The larger boat slips abutted the seawall and were easily accessible from the road. Rickety wooden walkways on rotted pilings accessed the other docks. If the Hezbollah bad guys had done their homework, they would have moored their transport in a seawall slip.

The slip just ahead of them was empty. Beyond it was an old fishing boat—a gray house on a dirty white hull—with a small cockpit and a half tower. There was no name on the transom and the motors were idling. A man dressed in a black shirt and jeans was on the bow freeing the dock line.

Something suddenly tickled Jarrett's brain. He closed his eyes to pinpoint what it was. When he opened them, the man was gone.

Nikas shook the dockmaster's hand and slipped him a twenty for his troubles.

"The van left a few minutes ago. It was parked there," Nikas said pointing to the road near the empty slip.

"Did he see them off-load the package?"

"No. He saw the van pulling away."

"How about the go-fast?"

"A transient. Came in last night. Spent the night in the empty slip."

"Does he know where it's headed?"

"No, but I got its registration from him."

"If we charter a boat, we'll never overtake it." Jarrett dialed Sedgewick's number.

"Jarrett. You got it?" Sedgewick asked excitedly.

"No. It's on a boat that just left Larnaca Marina in Cyprus. Name's *Party Time* out of Mykonos." Nikas recited the registration number and Jarrett repeated it. "You've got to have it intercepted," he told Sedgewick.

"What happened?"

"Long story." Jarrett recapped what had happened in Cyprus. "The boat will land in Beirut in less than four hours. Once it does the package is lost."

"I'm on it. Sit tight."

The call ended.

* * *

A few minutes later Jarrett's phone beeped.

"Jarrett, I have someone who wants to speak with you."

"Clint, it's Carpenter."

It's nice to hear your voice, Mr. President."

"Likewise. I ordered one of our ships off the Lebanon coast to intercept the Greek boat. And I want to thank you for all you've done for us. Dodge tells me you've had one helluva time. Sounds like it was terror in Tehran for you."

"It was, sir."

"I understand you got the Iranians off your back. Congratulations, son. You'll be able to come home."

"I'm looking forward to getting back to the ranch. There's a lot of work to be done."

"Dodge will be in touch when we have the bomb."

"Thank you, sir." Jarrett hung up and glanced at Nikas, who was gazing quizzically at him.

"Was that President Carpenter?" Nikas asked.

"It was."

"Sounds like you're old friends."

"He views it as a father-son relationship. At the moment it's an employer-employee relationship," Jarrett said.

Nikas took off his sunglasses and continued staring at Jarrett.

Recognizing that Nikas was perplexed, Jarrett said, "I like you, Nick. I'd trust my back to you anytime. When this is over I'll tell you everything . . . about the package, the mission, and me. You deserve that."

"That'd be good." Nikas nodded. "While the navy is intercepting the go-fast boat, let's deal with the bad boys in the Qeshm van."

Jarrett grinned. "Enemy combatants."

"Right. There's probably two. The Quds agent will be one," Nikas said.

"We'll say we were questioning the delivery crew. Things went downhill from there."

CHAPTER 85

The Mercedes SUV was at the Qeshm warehouse. A man was in the driver's seat blowing curls of smoke out the window.

The Qeshm van was nowhere in sight.

Nikas turned on the side street and stopped in the same place facing the parking lot.

Jarrett said, "We beat them back. I bet they stopped for breakfast. They'll drop off the van and drive to the safe house in the SUV."

As Jarrett checked the suppressor on his Glock, Nikas nodded and followed suit. Then he reached behind the seat and handed Jarrett a black mask and fingerless gloves.

"You do come prepared," Jarrett said stretching the gloves over his hands.

While adjusting his mask, Nikas pointed to Jarrett's and said, "Put it on, please."

"Never wore one before."

"I know. But it's broad daylight, and you never know who's going to drive by and video us with their phone."

"You got it, my friend." Jarrett pulled the mask over his head.

"How do you want to do this?" Nikas asked as he slipped on his gloves.

"The Mercedes driver may know nothing about the go-fast, its cargo, or its destination. His job was to drive Ghorbani to the airport. But he's an enemy combatant."

"Right," Nikas agreed.

"The people in the building work for the airline. They're not part of this, might not even be Iranian. You go in. Secure the building. I'll take care of the driver. Then we wait for the delivery crew."

Jarrett gestured for Nikas to drive to the parking lot. "Pull in behind the SUV. Maybe he won't see us."

* * *

He didn't see them. Nor did he hear them. Loud music blared from the radio.

Jarrett approached from behind.

The driver's eyes were closed and his head swayed back and forth. He took a drag on his cigarette and blew smoke out the window.

When the smoke cleared, Jarrett shot him in the head. Blood, bone, and brain sprayed the inside of the SUV, as his body sagged into the passenger seat. Jarrett reached in and righted it.

Two minutes later Nikas joined Jarrett in the cargo hold of the van.

"I love it. You're such a badass," Nikas said with his voice ringing. "You don't screw around." They fist bumped.

"Not when I'm working. I didn't like the music. He blew smoke in my face. He joined Allah. End of story."

"There were two guys inside. Both Greek. Locals I'm sure. I shoved them in the bathroom and wedged a chair under the doorknob. Told them if they came out, I'd shoot them. They were scared shitless."

"We'll approach the guys in the van as they walk to the SUV. I hope you're right that the Quds agent's one of them. I'd like to question him before we . . ."

Nikas interrupted. "Better to deal with them inside. I put the closed sign in the window."

When Jarrett heard the hum of an engine and the crunching of gravel, he peered out the back window.

"They're here," he said.

CHAPTER 86

There *were* two of them.

The Quds agent was looking in the SUV when Jarrett and Nikas closed in on them. The second man was a few steps behind.

"Stop!" Jarrett shouted. "Hands behind your heads."

The second man turned and cried, "They got guns!"

He was younger than the Quds agent, but rail thin with scraggly hair, a long narrow face, and a week's facial hair.

Nikas flanked Jarrett, his handgun trained on the two.

"I'll relieve them of their weapons," Jarrett said.

He tucked his Glock in his waistband and frisked the younger man. There was a gun under his shirt and a knife in his pants pocket. Jarrett tossed them under the SUV.

"Put your hands on the trunk and spread your legs apart," Jarrett ordered.

"What do you want from us?" the younger man asked as he leaned on the SUV.

"Shut up," Jarrett snarled. "Do as you're told."

He approached the Quds agent. "What's your name?"

"Fuck you."

"My friend's weapon is aimed at your head. One move and you're dead."

"Fuck you and your friend."

The Quds agent faced the SUV with his back to Jarrett. His hands were clasped behind his head and his feet were spread apart, but he was coiled and ready.

As Jarrett began to search him, the man suddenly twisted and elbowed Jarrett in the chest.

Jarrett's ribs popped, and he fell to his knees. A sharp pain shot through him, awakening his animal instincts.

"God help you," he muttered.

As the man reached for his gun, Jarrett hit him behind the knees with a stiff arm. Both the man's legs buckled and he fell forward.

Jarrett bounced to his feet and hit the man between the shoulder blades with a straight right. The man crashed into the SUV, breathless and stunned. Jarrett grabbed the man's head and smashed it into the window. Again and again. The sound of bone on glass was horrifying.

When the window spider-webbed, Jarrett spun the man around and pounded his midsection like a punching bag.

Nikas watched the gruesome spectacle with a smile. When he'd seen enough, *pop*, the agent's head exploded.

Jarrett turned to Nikas with rage in his eyes.

Nikas was in the SEAL shooting stance, swinging to his left, toward the younger man who was high-stepping across the parking lot toward the road. Swift afoot and scared to death, he was already ten yards away.

Nikas adjusted his line of sight and his gun spit. The man screamed, "I'm hit!" and tumbled head over heels.

The bullet had shattered his knee.

It was an extraordinary shot, one few of the best could have made.

"Just wanted to stop him," Nikas said. "So we can question him."

When Nikas got to the man, he was rolling on the ground holding his knee and crying like a baby. Using the man's belt as a tourniquet Nikas quelled the bleeding, while Jarrett dumped the Quds agent's body in the SUV. His chest hurt, and it was a struggle.

Nikas dragged the injured man into the air-freight office. Jarrett followed.

When they were inside Jarrett snarled, "Why the hell didn't you shoot sooner?"

"I wanted to see how good you are with your hands."

"Really? Well he hit me right where a Russian brute kicked me a few days ago. The Kevlar didn't help. My ribs popped. I think they're broken."

"Sorry about that," Nikas said holding back a smile. "The vest is good for 9-mils, but maybe not so good for a Quds elbow."

Jarrett sighed. "That was a nice shot."

"I told you, I'm okay with a gun."

More than okay, Jarrett thought. *Amazing.*

While Jarrett checked the air-freight employees, Nikas lashed the young man to a chair with packaging twine. He was rocking back and forth and hyperventilating.

"Who are you?" Jarrett asked.

"I'm bleeding," the man sobbed.

Nikas said, "You're not. It stopped."

"What did you take to the marina?" Jarrett asked.

"What marina?"

"You delivered something to the Larnaca Marina. In the van. What was it?"

When there was no response, Nikas backhanded the man across the face snapping his head sideways.

"A wooden crate," the man said, spitting blood.

"Where's it going?"

"I don't know."

"You're lying," Jarrett shouted, as Nikas backhanded him again.

"Beirut."

"Did it leave the marina in the white boat from Greece?"

"Yes. Yes. The white boat," the man said in earnest.

Instantly Jarrett realized his mistake.

He turned to Nikas and shook his head. "Damn it, I'm not thinking straight."

After beating the Quds agent into oblivion, Jarrett was unhinged. His head was pounding and his body was shaking from the adrenalin rush. On top of that, his chest hurt like hell, like a knife was stuck between his ribs. He needed to cool off and gather his wits.

Jarrett continued, "That's all we'll get from him. Let's get out of here."

Nikas, sensing Jarrett's dismay, said, "I'll finish up here and meet you in the van.

* * *

As they drove away Jarrett asked, "What did you do in there?"

Nikas touched Jarrett's arm. "Like you said, enemy combatants. We'll head over to the apartment now. You can unwind there."

CHAPTER 87

Jarrett was famished.

He washed down a lamb gyro with two bottles of Hula Hop Cyprus, the best of the local IPAs.

There wasn't much said while they ate, except for some small talk about Cyprus and the Greek food. It was the same quiet that often settled between soldiers after a harrowing mission.

Finally, Nikas broke the ice. "You went crazy back there."

"He hit me in the ribs. It hurt like hell, like a knife going through me. All I saw was red. After that I don't remember much, until you shot him. That's only the second time I've lost it. The first was in high school, when I was sucker-punched."

"I wouldn't want to be the guy who suckered you."

"I screwed up back there at the warehouse."

"What'd you mean?" Nikas asked.

"Well, I asked the rabbit if the package was on the white boat from Greece. He said, 'Yes. Yes. The white boat.' I wasn't thinking. I should have asked, 'What boat did you put the crate on?' He would have told us. His quick answer makes me think it wasn't the go-fast. I hope I'm wrong. We'll know soon."

"Your hands were a blur. You've had a lot of training."

"And you, my friend, are an incredible shot with a handgun."

Nikas smiled.

Jarrett continued, "The navy will intercept the boat soon and have the package. I promised you, I'd tell all. It's a nuclear bomb the size of a large suitcase. Given to the Iranians by Russia along with another bomb. The Persians are sending it to Hezbollah. Our job was to seize it."

"My God! I knew it was something major when you got a call from the president. And the mission name—Little Boy—was the nickname for the bomb dropped on Hiroshima. I should have figured it was a nuc. I've heard stories about the lost Russian suitcase bombs."

"If it gets into terrorist hands, it'll turn the Middle East upside down."

"For sure. How did this all come down?" Nikas asked.

"It's a long, complicated story."

Jarrett summarized what had happened in Tehran and everything that had led up to his trip. Nikas was a good listener. When Jarrett finished he asked only one question.

"What's going to happen after we have the bomb?"

Jarrett thought for a few seconds before he answered. "I don't think anyone can predict how things will play out. The Israeli's know the Iranians have nuclear devices. They know where they came from. The Iranians can't deny they have Russian bombs. We seized one. The Russians are in a pickle, because the bomb we seized was one of theirs. President Carpenter holds the upper hand. How he plays it will be very interesting."

"Sounds like you had a rough time in Tehran. Where you going from here?"

"A safe house in Scotland," Jarrett replied.

"Sounds like a good place to unwind. You promised to tell me about yourself. I think I know who you are."

"Really?"

"Well, not who you are. Your tag. You're Paladin. A rock star in the black ops world. A master assassin, who never uses a weapon. No one knows your identity. A SEAL buddy of mine sanitized a hit site of yours in Somalia. He told me all about Paladin."

Jarrett gazed at Nikas and smiled. "My name is Clint Jarrett. I live on a cattle ranch in South Dakota. I do special projects for the Oval Office three or four times a year, high-value targets. A guy named Dodge Sedgewick is my contact in the CIA. Someone tagged me Paladin when I was in the JSOC. In the Muslim world I'm called Jenni."

"I know what paladin means—a knight renowned for heroism. What does Jenni mean?"

"Shape-shifting demon is the short of it," Jarrett replied.

"I thought I was good with my hands, but I've never seen anything like what you can do. Karate?"

"No. Jujitsu. But like you, I had to learn how to strike. Comes in handy sometimes."

They laughed.

"So I was right," Nikas crowed. "You *are* Paladin. I've heard of Sedgewick. He's a fast burner at Langley."

"For sure. Already near the top. We were best friends in college. Played hockey and partied a lot. I joined the JSOC after graduation; Sedgewick went to law school. He took a job with the Company and hired me. He's a real character. One of a kind. You need to meet him. I could write a book about all we've done together. Probably several."

"From what I've heard about you, it would be an action-packed thriller."

"I've always worked alone, even when I was with the JSOC. You're the only one I've ever shared the front line with. I enjoyed it, Nick," Jarrett mused. "I suppose coming from someone like me, that's the highest compliment imaginable."

"Well, thanks. I'm honored. The feeling is mutual."

"It goes without saying, that what you've heard must never be repeated. If I didn't trust you, I wouldn't share it with you."

"Understood," Nikas said.

"I have a throbbing headache. Beer and adrenalin don't mix."

"Maybe it's the tzatziki sauce."

Jarrett laughed. "Maybe. I expect a call from Sedgewick any minute. We can move out then . . . hopefully. For now, I'm going to lie down for a few minutes."

CHAPTER 88

With a full stomach and sagging after the adrenalin rush, Jarrett was asleep in seconds with his phone at his ear.

As he sank deeper and deeper into darkness, four walls began to close around him. He was in the gloom of the foyer in the ramshackle building in south Beirut. The dirty-fingered girl and the shooter on the stairway with the Kalashnikov appeared.

"Come to me. Come to me," she pleaded holding out her arms.

The Kalashnikov's chamber ratcheted back and forth, echoing in Jarrett's head.

Then the evil-eyed Abu limped from the shadows into the foyer, dressed in a black shirt and blue jeans. His right shoulder was missing and he had a whip in his hand. The whip lashed out and snapped around Jarrett's waist.

Suddenly the four walls melded into undulating blue water and the overhead light swelled into the morning sun in a cloudless sky. Jarrett was straddling a gentle wave like a gymnast on a balance beam. Abu was gliding toward the sun astride a giant suitcase with a frothy wake behind him just out of Jarrett's reach.

When Abu disappeared over the horizon the water turned crimson, and a pack of dogs sprang at Jarrett's feet. But they weren't growling. Instead a rhythmic beeping rose from their throats.

As Jarrett awakened, the bedroom took form—a fan whirling overhead, spires of sunlight at the edges of blackout curtains, and a television monitor with a blank screen.

And a *beep, beep, beep* next to his ear.

Jarrett shot upright and looked at the clock.

They'd left the marina almost four hours ago.

Oh shit! It wasn't the go-fast, he thought.

He opened the call.

"You fucked up, Jarrett!" Sedgewick growled.

"I know I did."

"The boys in blue intercepted the boat from Greece. Searched it from stem to stern. No bomb. Just three old duffers with gold Rolexes and big bellies, three big-boobed bimbos, some drugs, and lots of food and booze."

"We missed the delivery at the marina by a few minutes," Jarrett told him. "The go-fast was idling out the channel when we got there. I thought the bomb was on board. I was wrong. It's on a boat that was moored next to it."

"How do you know?"

"There was a guy on the bow. He had a funny-looking shoulder like he had a shattered collar bone or something. I didn't see his face. If I had, I would have remembered him. He was the guy who whipped me. Name's Abu. It all came clear in a dream I was having when you called."

"POTUS is pissed."

"It's an older fishing boat with a white hull and gray house. It'll travel a lot slower than the go-fast. There was no name on the transom. Where is the navy vessel?"

"I don't know. It's an amphibious assault ship that happened to be nearby. Take me a minute to find out."

"I figure the fishing boat cruises at twenty knots tops. Maybe less. That means it's no more than eighty miles out now, fifty miles or so from the Lebanon coast. I need a chopper and a fast tender."

"We should let the boys in blue deal with this, Jarrett."

"No! I want the bastard who whipped me."

"I'll have to clear it with the big guy and his gang of five. I'm just outside the situation room. I didn't want to have this conversation in front of them."

"I'll head back to the Larnaca Marina, get info on the boat. Call me when you have the ship's location."

CHAPTER 89

The fishing boat was gone.

They found George eating lunch under an orange tree.

He told Nikas the boat had passengers going to Beirut. He knew nothing about the crate. He said the boat was old but ran well and cruised at eighteen knots tops. It was called *Fishin' Frenzy* and was registered in Cyprus. His nephew was the first mate. The captain was the boat's owner. The fuel tanks had been topped off yesterday.

"Ask him when it left."

"Right after we left the marina," Nikas said.

Jarrett's mind raced. How could they track it?

With the coast of Lebanon busy with afternoon boat traffic, the navy ship's radar would be a scattergram.

"Tell him the passengers are terrorists going to Beirut. We're American agents. We have to stop them. Ask if his nephew or the captain have cell phones."

As Nikas spoke to George, a look of fright came over him. He jumped to attention and recited his nephew's number from memory, then read the captain's from his cell contacts.

Jarrett checked his chronograph and called Sedgewick.

"Just about to call you," Sedgewick said. "The navy ship is sixty miles from the Lebanon coast. Seventy miles from you. It was supposed to pick you up. They have an inflatable that does fifty knots."

"The boat is called *Fishin' Frenzy*. Registered in Cyprus. It's been gone four hours and cruises at eighteen knots. Dispatch a chopper to the

Larnaca Marina. Send the inflatable to Beirut. We'll rendezvous with it there on the beach, then we'll go after the *Fishin' Frenzy.*"

"How'll you know where it is? I imagine there'll be lots of boat traffic along the coast."

"The captain and first mate have cells. They'll come into service fifteen to twenty miles out from the towers in Beirut. You order the boys at NSA to track the boat using the phones. We'll intercept it using the GPS coordinates they give us."

"Oh boy. That's a fucking tall order on short notice."

"Listen Sedgewick, you have the president of the United States there. He can make anything happen. The inflatable will be on the sand in a little over an hour if it leaves now. The chopper at top speed will take thirty minutes or so to get here and an hour to get us to the coast. We'll hook up with the inflatable on the beach. By then *Fishin' Frenzy* will be in cell range. NSA'll give us its location. We'll motor out and seize the damn bomb."

"That's a helluva plan. Why not meet at sea? It would be easier and a lot quicker."

Jarrett laughed. "I can't jump out of a bird into water. You know I can't swim very well."

"You're not allowing much time," Sedgewick said.

"Well, get on it then, damn it. There's a lot riding on this. And it's all we have."

Jarrett gave him the cell numbers of the captain and George's nephew and closed the call.

CHAPTER 90

Forty minutes later Jarrett and Nikas were harnessed in a SH-60 Seahawk with flotation vests over their Kevlars.

The coast of Lebanon came into view forty-nine minutes later. They set down on a sandy beach three miles north of Beirut.

The inflatable was waiting. It had three four-hundred-horsepower outboards with advanced electronics and a fifty-caliber machine gun. Its crew—Lieutenant Colburn and his first mate Ensign Malesky—was green-faced.

Nikas introduced himself as Nick and Jarrett as his boss.

The mother ship had sent two important messages. The first said the target craft was fourteen miles from the coast moving at fifteen knots southeast. But the second message, just minutes later, said the signal from the craft had become stationary.

The target's current coordinates were in the inflatable's GPS.

With a brisk southwest wind the seas were four to five feet. At fifty knots the ride was one bounce after the next. The lightweight craft skimmed across the tops of the waves, crashed down into the trough, and shot upward to the next wave . . . over and over.

Jarrett became queasy and hung on to the radar arch for dear life. Nikas and the crew shared stories, joking and laughing, oblivious to the rough ride.

Twenty minutes after launch Nikas sighted a gray house on a white hull. The *Fishin' Frenzy* was rocking in the chop and had drifted northeast in the four-knot current. They stopped a hundred yards off its bow.

"What now?" Nikas asked.

"Hail them," Jarrett replied.

Nikas used the inflatable's bullhorn. "*Fishin' Frenzy*. This is the United States Navy. Respond on channel sixty."

After a minute, Colburn shook his head.

Nikas repeated the hailing and added that it was an emergency. Still no response.

"Maybe they don't have a radio. Try something else," Jarrett said

"*Fishin' Frenzy* crew, show yourself. Now!"

The boat continued to bob up and down, the current turning its bow away from the inflatable.

Nikas repeated the message, but no one appeared.

"I don't like this. The vessel's abandoned," Jarrett said.

"Maybe it's a trap. They're luring us on board," Nikas added.

It's not a trap, Jarrett thought. *According to NSA the boat was adrift before they intercepted it.*

"We have to board," Jarrett said. "I'll take the radiation counter." Something was horribly wrong. He could feel it.

"I don't like this either. We need to cover our asses," Nikas said. He told Colburn to radio for backup.

"Good idea. But I don't want to wait. I have a bad feeling about this. Let's get on with it."

Closing on the boat with the inflatable's props at idle speed took four long minutes.

Nikas tied the inflatable to the gunnel cleats on the *Fishin' Frenzy*. Jarrett boarded. Nikas followed, while Malesky had their backs. Colburn stayed at the inflatable helm with an open channel to the mother ship. Two choppers were already in the air.

The boat made a rhythmic smacking sound on the water. The air in the cockpit was stifling and heavy with diesel fumes.

"Motors idling and screws out of gear," Nikas said as he climbed to the bridge to survey the surrounding seas with binoculars.

The boat was far enough out that the beaches of Lebanon were lost behind the earth's curvature. The nearest vessel was a container ship at least a mile away. To the south two sailboats and a cruise ship were barely visible. On the eastern horizon a small powerboat sped toward the coast.

When Nikas climbed down from the bridge, Jarrett pointed to the salon. "I'll go in first."

"Most likely there's a salon and galley with a small stateroom forward. If the crate is on board it'll be in the salon," Nikas said.

It won't be, Jarrett thought. *It's gone.*

With the afternoon sun reflecting off the tinted windows, the salon was pitch-dark.

As Jarrett opened the door, Nikas stood at his flank with an H&K MP5 up and ready. If there was a firefight, Jarrett couldn't imagine anyone better to have his back.

With the door open, the sun cast a teardrop of light onto the salon floor. The air inside had a telltale metallic odor. Just beyond the threshold the soles of two dirty feet stared up at Jarrett.

He moved inside cautiously.

Two men lay facedown on the salon floor with pools of blood spreading beneath them.

One was in a white T-shirt and cut-off jeans. He was older, with tufts of gray hair over his neck, narrow shoulders, and scrawny legs. His big belly mushroomed under him like a blob of gelatin. *The captain.*

The second was young and muscular with long black hair drawn into a ponytail. *George's nephew.*

Both had gaping wounds at their throats, their heads askew at grotesque angles.

Jarrett figured they'd been made to kneel for the ceremonial slashing.

"Nick. Come on in. We're too late."

Nikas circled the bodies to avoid the puddles of blood. "Shit. They're nearly beheaded." He pointed to the older man. "He must be the captain. The younger guy is George's nephew."

Jarrett touched the older man's leg. "He's still warm. The Hezbollah bad guys aren't long gone."

The layout of the boat was exactly as Nikas had described.

While Jarrett went forward to check the stateroom, Nikas lifted the hatch and looked into the engine room.

They found nothing.

The radiation counter registered only background noise throughout the boat.

After Nikas secured the engine-room hatch, he joined Jarrett in the salon.

A thought suddenly flashed in Jarrett's head. "Nick, why didn't they just throw the bodies overboard and scuttle the boat?"

Nikas's eyesbrows rose. "Let's get the hell out of here."

Both men ran from the salon. Nikas tossed the tie lines into the inflatable, and they both jumped, Nikas shouting, "Balls to the wall!"

Colburn crashed the throttles forward, the inflatable's engines roared, and a rooster tail of water shot up behind it. As the boat accelerated, the bow rose out of the water. Jarrett breathed a sigh of relief, bracing himself for a rough ride and a sick stomach.

When they were fifty yards from the *Fishin' Frenzy*, Jarrett heard a deafening noise. It sounded like a bolt of lightening striking in their wake.

A wave of intense heat with eight G's of concussive force swept across the inflatable.

The sky turned burnt orange, and the inflatable's bow shot underwater.

Jarrett was catapulted into the air like a missile launched from a submarine.

Then everything went black.

CHAPTER 91

"**F**inally, you're awake," Nikas said with a look of concern.

Jarrett imagined he was swimming into consciousness as the lights on the gray ceiling came into focus.

When Jarrett turned to Nikas's voice, he felt as if a steel ball with sharp spikes was bouncing inside his head.

Nikas stood next to him in navy fatigues with a nasty bruise under his left eye.

Jarrett coughed and cleared his throat. "You all right, Nick?"

Nikas touched Jarrett's arm. "I'm fine. Just a little headache. I'm glad you're okay. You've been out for several hours. Thank God your head scan is okay."

Jarrett pushed up on his elbows and looked around. He was in a small room in a bed with railing guards. A crisp blue sheet was folded across his chest. He had on a hospital gown that matched the sheets. A cardiac monitor beeped behind him, an intravenous infusion led to the back of his hand, and an oxygen monitor was on his index finger.

"Where are we?"

"USS *Tomahawk*, the inflatable's mother ship."

"What happened?"

"The *Fishin' Frenzy* blew up as we sped away. Not a damn thing left of it. The shock wave threw us out of the boat. I came to before the birds arrived. SARs pulled us out of the water. Very efficient dust-off I must say. The two young SEALS had helmets. They're fine. If you hadn't had the premonition about a bomb, we'd be dead."

Jarrett shook his head. "I thought it was strange the bad guys didn't throw the captain and the mate over board. Let the sharks have at them and scuttle the boat."

"With terrorists it's all about making a statement. Shock and awe. The explosion will hit the newswires like a Midwest tornado. An old fishing boat sinking in the Mediterranean with two crew would be local news at best," Nikas said.

"Glad I had a life preserver. I'm not the best in the water."

"Your Kevlar did its job. You were hit by something that took out one cell of your flotation device."

"The Hezbollah terrorists must have rendezvoused with another boat. The bomb is in Beirut now," Jarrett said.

"I saw a small boat speeding toward the coast," Nikas added.

"It's a damn good thing you had the rescue choppers dispatched before we went aboard. I would have drowned."

"All in a day's work for an ex-SEAL. Dodge Sedgewick called."

"My phone is at the bottom of the Mediterranean."

"Here, you can use this one," Nikas said handing Jarrett a phone. "Should I leave?"

"No. There's nothing you shouldn't hear."

Jarrett dialed Sedgewick's cell number. His friend should be at home sleeping.

"I've been waiting for your call, Clint. Couldn't sleep. You okay?"

"I'm okay."

He recapped what had happened.

Sedgewick sighed. "I'm glad you weren't hurt. It's over then, damn it. The device is in Beirut, in Hezbollah's deep, dark underbelly. We'll never find it. The world better brace for trouble."

"Maybe not. They moved it from the boat to a black site. It'll be the most secure place they have. Maybe the one where I was tortured. One corner of the room was set up for making videos. If we can locate the site, we might find the bomb."

"Tell me what to do, Jarrett. This is a big fucking deal for us. It's bad enough the Russians gave the Iranians nuclear devices, but now Hezbollah has one. We let it slip right through our hands. The balance of power in the Middle East has changed . . . for the worse." Sedgewick's voice was flat and plaintive.

"I don't have a clue where the black site is. But Monsour, the Mossad spy in Hezbollah, knows. He has to. He was there. All he has to do is give us the location. I'll go get the damn bomb and take care of the bastard who whipped me."

"The Israelis are worried about him. He's on thin ice now."

Jarrett thought for a second. "If he's been fingered already there's two scenarios. Either he's been exfiltrated by the Israelis or executed by Hezbollah. One or the other."

"Alfour's no dummy. Either way he'll assume Monsour gave the location of the black site to his handler in Mossad. It's an important piece of intel. My bet is it's closed for good."

"Perhaps," Jarrett said with a note of exasperation in his voice. "Time is critical if Monsour is still in Beirut and hasn't been fingered. The clock's ticking."

"With all that's happened, Mandazi must know by now you're a plant. That means Monsour's been fingered."

"I'll bet they questioned Kutnetsov's girlfriend. With a little pain she'll lay it all out for them. After that, Mandazi will tell Alfour that Safin was planted to steal the bomb. During that conversation Alfour might confess that one of his own, Rami Monsour, referred Safin and he's the Mossad spy they've been worried about. The conversation between Mandazi and Alfour is Monsour's death sentence. But we might get lucky. If Alfour hasn't heard from Mandazi yet for whatever reason, Monsour might still be in Beirut. The black site will still be active."

Sedgewick interrupted. "What would delay Mandazi getting the news about Sahin to Alfour?"

"The Russian girl. She might be lost in the system for a few days. You never know. She could spend a day or two in a city jail in Tehran, questioned by low-level detectives. You better than anyone know about bureaucratic inertia, particularly in a police state like Iran," he told Sedgewick. "It could take a few days to get her in the right hands."

"You mean Mogadan?"

"Exactly. And if Mir Abassi is the first to get the intel from Mogadan, I'm sure he'll delay passing it on to Mandazi. Mir knows what I'm up to."

"And the news about your mischief in Cyprus hasn't gotten back to Tehran yet. It was just this morning."

"Right. But it will soon. So if Monsour is still in Beirut, I need to meet with him right away. Then the Israelis can get him the hell out of there."

"I would be surprised if Mossad hasn't pulled him already," Sedgewick added. "They're very protective of their own. At the first sign of trouble they'll bring him home."

"Find out if he's alive. If he is, set up a meeting, wherever the hell he is—Beirut or Tel Aviv."

"Lots of ifs, my friend. I'll brief the president. This'll require a call to the Israeli prime minister. Sit tight. Enjoy the navy's hospitality. I'll get back to you ASAP."

CHAPTER 92

Things played out in Tehran almost the way Jarrett had figured they would. It took several days to get Kuznetsov's girlfriend into Mogadan's hands. She knew everything. When she confessed, Mogadan went directly to Mandazi. The wily head of Quds connected the dots—Yusuf Sahin was planted to steal the bomb, maybe by Mossad, but more likely by the Americans.

Mandazi's call to Alfour confirmed Hezbollah's lingering suspicions. They had a spy in their midst—Rami Monsour.

Alfour wasted no time.

While Jarrett slept in the infirmary on the USS *Tomahawk*, Ari Katz, aka Rami Monsour, was finalizing an exfiltration plan with two Mossad agents in his apartment in south Beirut. A team of terrorists surrounded the building and four of their best stormed the apartment. The Mossad agents killed the first wave of attackers. As the Israelis ran from the building, a sniper shot Katz in the chest and killed one of the agents. A Mossad SUV took Katz to a hospital in the Christian sector of Beirut.

Fearing the terrorists would finish the job with a suicide bomber, Mossad executed a brazen rescue. A helicopter outfitted as a mini-ICU and staffed by a surgeon, an anesthesiologist, and a nurse was dispatched. Accompanied by two Israeli gunships it flew under Lebanese radar with four F-16s circling over the Mediterranean just outside Lebanese airspace.

The helicopter landed in the hospital parking lot. Katz was whisked from the emergency room and flown to Rambam Medical Center in Haifa. With a flying distance of only eighty miles each way, the whole operation took an hour.

Katz underwent emergency surgery and was in critical condition.

With the rescue of one of their own from a foreign country, the Israelis had followed the American meme "No man left behind." The Lebanese were incensed while Washington stood by once again admiring the cunning and chutzpah of the Israelis.

* * *

After Jarrett's phone call to Sedgewick, things moved ahead at warp speed.

When the Israelis learned that the nuclear device they desperately wanted was in the hands of Hezbollah, they became very cooperative. Alas the tables were turned. The U.S. was enlisting Israel's help in a daring mission in the Middle East. Historically, Mossad had used deceit and disinformation to engage its American counterparts in a razzle-dazzle operation that often led to significant collateral damage.

President Carpenter convinced the Israelis to allow CIA operatives to meet with Katz. The critically injured Mossad agent was intermittently conscious but unable to talk because of a breathing tube in his airway.

Dodge Sedgewick was in a CIA jet over the Atlantic, sent to interface with the Mossad agents babysitting Katz at the hospital. The feeling in the Oval Office was simple: the less the Israelis knew about Jarrett the better.

Jarrett and Nikas flew from the USS *Tomahawk* to the Haifa airport by helicopter. Jarrett was Marwan Elias again. Nikas was back to being Albert Ross, a clerk in the American embassy in Athens. Sedgewick would bring the bona fides for their legends.

Accorded full diplomatic privileges, the two were treated like royalty the moment they set foot in Israel. They were put up in a plush hotel with an ocean view and given carte blanche—in ala carte Haifa. Their rooms were stocked with an array of fruits and munchies and a full bar. The only caveat: no guns.

CHAPTER 93

"This is an incredible view of the bay," Jarrett said, sitting with Nikas on the terrace of his hotel room.

"It sure is," Nikas agreed. "A nice cool breeze, too"

Jarrett glanced at his chronograph.

"Sedgewick's plane should have landed. He'll be here any minute."

As the words left Jarrett's lips, he heard Sedgewick.

"How the hell are you, Jarrett?" Sedgewick shouted, as the room door crashed open.

Jarrett jumped up and went into the room. Nikas followed.

For a moment the two stood gazing at each other like long lost brothers.

Sedgewick was a skosh under six feet tall with a short neck, sagging shoulders, and the beginning of a paunch. Although his hair was thinning and prematurely gray, he had a baby face with mischievious hazel eyes and a flirty smile. His brow was drizzled with perspiration.

"How'd you get in here?" Jarrett asked as they embraced.

"A friendly maid. Wanted to surprise you. This must be Nikas, the pirate killer."

"Nice to meet you, Mr. Sedgewick," he said as they shook hands.

"Call me Dodge. I've heard marvelous things about you from Jarrett and others at Langley."

"Thank you." Nikas gestured to Jarrett. "I'm honored to be working with this guy."

"He's always worked alone. You're his first ever sidekick."

"He's a legend in our business," Nikas added.

"That he is, and in his own mind." Sedgewick winked, while Jarrett shook his head and held back laughing. "Here's your stuff guys. Hand delivered from Washington." Sedgewick gave each of them a soft-sided attaché case. "Both passports have been updated. Just so you know, Elias left Tehran two days ago. Flew to Beirut then on to Haifa on business. Ross left Athens yesterday. Flew to Haifa to meet friends for a holiday. Usual litter is in the wallets and there's a wad of cash. And Jarrett, a special phone is in your bag as well."

"When do we meet with Mossad?" Jarrett asked

Sedgewick glanced at his watch. "We need to get going soon. They have a team at the hospital. The plan is to hook up with the guy in charge. He'll accompany us to the bedside. The doctors gave us five minutes. No more. The spy can't talk, but he's writing short messages."

"Nick, you'll wait here then. I'll get the location of the black site, and we'll be out of here tonight."

"I've booked both of you on an evening flight to Beirut and into a hotel. It'll take all of twelve minutes in the air. But you're wasting your time going there," Sedgewick said.

"Why? Nikas asked.

"If we get the location from the spy, we're going," Jarrett interjected.

"I hear you, Jarrett." Sedgewick held up his hands. "I know you're focused on the black site. But you both know what happened to Rami Monsour in Beirut, and how he wound up here. His real name is Ari Katz. If he knows the location of the black site where Jarrett was tortured, which he must, Hezbollah will have closed it. If it's closed, the device won't be there. We've had this conversation already, Jarrett."

Sedgwick began to chuckle. "Can you imagine Clint Jarrett, aka Paladin, aka Jenni, the vaunted Oval Office assassin with the deadliest hands in the world, whipped by some fucking terrorist with a bad shoulder and a limp?"

Jarrett thrust his shirt up and growled, "Look. The damn welts are just starting to heal."

"I'm only teasing. I wouldn't want to be that guy if you get your paws on him."

"I wouldn't either," Nikas agreed, glancing at Sedgewick. "I saw firsthand what he can do when he's mad."

"You were mad, Jarrett? I've never seen you mad. Well, maybe, once," Sedgewick mused. "When you were bloodied from a high stick."

"That Dartmouth asshole knocked my helmut off and hit me with his stick above my eye trying to defend my shot. But the puck went in at the buzzer."

"And we won. How could ever I forget?" Sedgewick glanced at Nikas. "It was our senior year. We were playing in a tournament over Christmas in the Garden. Which we won, I might add. There was blood all over the damn ice. Jarrett's girlfriend, Miss Julie Crichton, fainted in the stands right behind me. And believe it or not, that was the night of their engagement party. Jarrett showed up at the fancy restaurant in a suit with a black eye and a big bandage on his forehead. Nine stitches. He was the talk of the party. A wounded Ivy League warrior."

"Sedgewick was our goalie," Jarrett told Nikas, grinning. "All-American senior year. Drafted by the Rangers."

"Wow! I'm speechless," Nikas said.

"My exploits on the ice were nothing compared to Jarrett's. He was . . ."

"Enough, Sedgewick. Nick was talking about a Quds thug I dealt with in Cyprus. He elbowed me in the same spot the Russian brute kicked me in Tehran. It hurt like hell, even with a vest. I was pissed. Not mad."

"Speaking of Tehran, how's the Persian gal? I suppose since you lost your phone, you don't have a pic of her to share with us."

Nikas turned to Jarrett with a quizzical look as if to ask, "What the hell is this all about?"

Jarrett said, "It's the same bullshit every mission. Innuendos about women. He thinks all I do is play."

"Wait a minute, Jarrett. You've played plenty. All over the damn world. This Persian broad, Ziba Vijany, has hopped on the same love boat that a bevy of other women have cruised on over the years."

"Let's get going, Sedgewick," Jarrett said. "I want to crash the black site ASAP. Maybe we'll get lucky."

"I doubt it, but POTUS made it clear that you can do whatever the hell you want to get the device. You have max support. Anything you need," Sedgewick said.

CHAPTER 94

With the sparkling blue Mediterranean as its backdrop, the Rambam Medical Campus was an eyeful.

A picture-postcard cluster of shiny, new towers—a cancer center, a cardiovascular center, a medical school, and a patient tower with a helioport—stretched over several blocks in the Bat Galim section of Haifa. The medical campus was a badge of prosperity, one of many, that Israel wore with pride.

Sedgewick's driver double-parked in front of the administrative building, the original hospital structure built in 1938. The U-shaped, two-story stone building with its orange tile roof and manicured lawns dotted with palms looked like a transplant from the campus of Stanford University.

A dour hospital administrator met them at the door. "Follow me," he muttered, after Sedgewick introduced himself. Jarrett instantly disliked the guy.

As they followed the man down a long corridor with marble floors and soft lighting, Sedgewick whispered, "I've dealt with the Mossad guy in charge. Name's David. Their first name is all you ever get. He's a real hard-ass, extremely competent and secretive like everybody in their organization. I'm told security here is handled by uniforms, but there'll be undercover Mossad guys lurking around I'm sure."

"I don't like hospitals," Jarrett said.

"You just did a job for us in one."

"That's one of the reasons I don't like them. But I must say this is a little different."

They stopped at the end of the corridor, where two soldiers in desert fatigues armed with Uzis stood at attention at a double door. After the administrator spoke to them in Hebrew, one of them opened the door.

Sedgewick stepped into the room with Jarrett behind him.

The administrator disappeared and the door closed.

The room was appointed in the government's preferred décor—dark wood paneling, tall windows opposite the door, and plush blue carpet. Leather-backed chairs were perfectly spaced around a polished conference table with flat-screen monitors on two walls. The room smelled aromatic.

An elderly man sat at the table tamping tobacco in a pipe. A second man gazed out the window. When he heard the door close, he turned and walked toward Sedgewick. He was short and wiry with a somber look on his face. His eyes were red and puffy as if he'd just had an allergy attack. With a slow, measured gait he looked like a cat stalking its prey.

Something was wrong.

"Good to see you again, David," Sedgewick said, extending his hand.

They shook hands and David said, "We just got tragic news. Ari had a cardiac arrest and died."

Sedgewick hesitated for an instant searching for words, then said, "I'm so sorry. This is terrible."

Jarrett felt as if he'd been punched in the gut. He was responsible for Ari's death, and Ari had saved his life.

He drew a breath and said, "I'm sorry as well. He was a good man. He saved my life."

"I know. We heard about it from the agent who survived the shooting. It was risky for Ari to infiltrate Hezbollah. He had volunteered and saved many lives. But that doesn't make it any easier now."

Jarrett glanced at the man sitting at the table. He was a study in gray—gray hair, a neatly trimmed gray goatee, and gray-hued skin—and looked like he had a terminal disease. His face was wreathed in pain and there were dark shadows under his eyes. Yet there was an unmistakable softness about him. He lit his pipe and began to puff on it.

The gray man was the spitting image of Jarrett's high school biology teacher, a man named Edward McMurtry. Affectionately called Mack the Knife because of dissection skills in the laboratory, he was like a second father to Jarrett.

Who was he? Jarrett wondered. *A relative of Ari Katz, maybe even his father?*

"We came to meet with Ari. My colleague's been tracking the important package from Tehran now in the hands of Hezbollah." Sedgewick gestured to Jarrett. "We hoped Ari might help us locate it."

"I'm sorry. That won't be possible now."

Sedgewick sighed. "We know this is a difficult time. Please extend our government's condolences to his family."

David shook his head and frowned. "There is no family. His parents and sister were killed by rockets in 2006."

"I'm sorry to hear that. We ought to run along now," Sedgewick said.

They shook hands with David and excused themselves.

When the conference room door closed behind them, Jarrett paused. "Who do you think the gray man is?"

"A friend maybe. A Mossad coworker. Who knows. Ari must have had it bad for Hezbollah after his family was killed by the terrorist bastards."

"The gray man is distraught. I thought it might be Ari's father. Obviously not. Maybe his handler in Mossad. Let's talk with him."

CHAPTER 95

The gray man's name was Moshe. He *was* Ari's handler, or as David put it, his letter box—a conduit for information between Ari and Tel Aviv.

After David introduced Sedgewick as a U.S. intelligence official and Jarrett as an unnamed associate, they sat across from Moshe. David resumed staring out the window, but stayed within earshot.

"We're sorry about Ari. We'd like to ask you some questions," Sedgewick began.

"Yes, of course," Moshe said in a near whisper. "Ari and I were very close. Losing him is . . . like losing a son."

"Moshe, I feel bad about Ari," Jarrett said. "I was tortured by Hezbollah at a black site in Beirut. Ari saved my life."

"You're the undercover American agent involved in the deal for the nuclear device. We've heard about your exploits in Tehran, and elsewhere. You've quite the reputation in our part of the world. Our field agents whisper about a mysterious American assassin named Paladin. Is that you?"

Jarrett's half-smile answered the question.

"The bomb is in the hands of terrorists in Beirut."

"We know. You followed it to Cyprus. They took it from there to Beirut by boat. It's terrible. I fear we're headed for war."

"The bomb may be at the black site where I was tortured. I was unconscious when they took me there, and hooded when they drove me back to my hotel. I don't know where it is. Ari did. He was there that night. Did he give you the location?"

Moshe shook his head. "Ari didn't know the location."

"He didn't? Why?"

"They hooded him."

"He must have been taken there by someone."

"He was. Three times."

Jarrett glanced at Sedgewick. "The site might still be active."

Sedgewick nodded.

"Why only three times?" Sedgewick asked.

"Because its location was kept a secret," Moshe replied. "Why, I don't know. I suppose it was a special place for some reason. Ari wasn't high enough yet in their damn organization. He was what we call a *mista'aravim*, a Jew who looks like an Arab and speaks their language. Perfect to spy on them. But over the last months they became suspicious. He was worried. They're evil bastards, clever and wily."

"Did he tell you why he went there?"

"Yes, of course. Ari told me everything. The first two times he got a text message. There was a special meeting. He was told to go to a mosque at a certain time." Moshe paused to think and put down his pipe. "I'm pretty sure it's called the Mohammed Al-Attar Mosque. I'll have to check my notes at the office to be sure. I'm upset now, and my memory isn't what it used to be. Anyway, he was driven to the black site from there. Hooded, like I said. At the first meeting they discussed the deal with Iran. Ari told us about Meyer, and we turned him. Money talks." Moshe tried to smile. "When Meyer died in Tehran, there was a second meeting. I was told to instruct Ari to recommend you."

"Ari had a black cloth in his hands and his hair was tousled. At the time I didn't understand why. Now I do. It was the hood. How about the third time."

"Hezbollah was on edge after Meyer died. They blamed the CIA and us."

They were wrong, Jarrett thought. *It was the Chechens.*

Moshe continued. "They wanted the bomb. Iran insisted on an intermediary. Ari figured they'd interrogate you to be sure you weren't a spy. He found out you were taken to the black site from a young woman he was friendly with, very friendly with I might add, if you know what I mean. He went to your hotel with her and broke into your room."

The Muslim girl with the dirty fingernails.

"And he ultimately used my passport to save me," Jarrett added.

"Like I said, Ari didn't know the black site's location. The girl didn't either. But he had the driver's cell number, the guy who drove him the first two times. He called him, told him he needed to go to the black site right away. It was an emergency. Ari called me from a taxi on his way to the mosque to meet the driver. That was the last time we talked. Ari was scared of being caught. When I told him he was in danger, he used a code word. His mother's name. He said, 'Esther will watch over me.' He was telling me he wanted to come home as soon as possible."

"So you don't know what happened after the call from Ari that night?" Jarrett asked.

"We learned from the agent who survived that Ari rescued you at the black site. Ari told him the whole story."

Sedgewick looked at Jarrett. "That conversation between Mandazi and Alfour must have happened. Hezbollah learned you were a plant, and that Ari was responsible. So they tried to kill him."

"And just before that Mandazi decided to stop screwing around and send the bomb to Beirut," Jarrett said. "Via Cyprus."

"And here you are," Moshe mumbled.

"Did you recover Ari's cell phone?"

"That's a good question," David blurted, obviously eavesdropping. "I'll have to check."

"Was it the same driver all three times?" Jarrett asked.

"I don't know who drove him the third time. Like I said, he called the man who drove him before. So I would imagine he drove him again."

"Do you know the driver's name?" Jarrett asked.

"No."

"Anything special about him?"

"Oh yes. He's mute. Doesn't speak a word."

"Anything else?"

"He's called Red Beard. I suppose because he has a red beard."

Jarrett stood and shook Moshe's hand. "Thank you. You've been very helpful."

"Ari's death must be avenged," Moshe said, a new forcefulness in his voice. "It's our way. He won't rest until Hezbollah suffers. Nor will his parents. And I won't either, damn it. If you are who I think you are, maybe . . ."

Jarrett interrupted. "I'll fly to Beirut tonight. Track down Red Beard and find the black site. I'll get the bomb. When I'm done with the bastards, Ari will rest in peace. I owe it to him. You have my word."

"God be with you, my son."

CHAPTER 96

Jarrett left the meeting racked with guilt, the weight of Ari's death and the deaths of the Cypriot boatmen weighing heavily. His guilt festered for hours, finally fostering an appetite for revenge.

He tried to temper his disquietude by remembering what Churchill had once said: "Revenge is of all satisfactions the most costly and long drawn out." It didn't work.

You're right as always Sir Winston, Jarrett thought, *but I'll kill the bastards anyway and it won't be costly and drawn out.*

Jarrett and Nikas flew to Beirut that night and checked into a hotel with their legends. They hadn't heard from David about Ari's cell phone. A mission kit was delivered to Nikas's room.

Later that night they met with the CIA station chief and his deputy at the U.S. embassy. They learned that the Mohammed Al-Attar Mosque was controlled by Hezbollah. The clerics preached Islamist ideology, and it was a hot bed for radicalization and a major recruiting site for terrorists.

The mosque occupied one side of Al-Attar Square in the Dahieh suburbs of south Beirut—Hezbollah-held territory. The square was a beehive of activity with a carnival-like atmosphere. At its center stood a once-beautiful fountain—a Beirut historical landmark—that hadn't bubbled since the bombing of 2006. Although many of the storefronts were boarded up, a few small shops, a rooming house, and several cafés were open. But most of the business was conducted by street vendors, hawking just about everything—breads, fruits, cooked foods, and sundries.

Four streets intersected the square at each corner. Vehicles approaching the *saha* as it was called found the swell of humanity impassable.

291

Jarrett and Nikas spent an hour going through files of Hezbollah terrorists looking for Red Beard. They found no one with a red beard or with the tag Red Beard.

Jarrett hit the jackpot, though, when he stumbled across the evil-eyed man with the limp and saggy shoulder. His photograph had been taken outside a Sunni mosque that had been destroyed by a suicide bomber a week later. A half dozen aliases were listed for him, most recently Abu Mohammed Amed. He was described as a dangerous Hezbollah enforcer.

Before the meeting ended Jarrett had formulated a plan that centered around the Hezbollah driver. He asked for a linguist who spoke and wrote Arabic fluently and for use of a safe house. He was told his other needs were in a warehouse inside the embassy compound.

* * *

On the ride back to the hotel, Nikas said, "When you came across Amed you got quiet. Your eyes flashed with that crazy look, like you had when you beat the shit out of the Quds agent in Cyprus."

"I can't wait to get my hands on Amed."

"I hope I get to watch."

"I'm convinced the black site where they took me is still active. It's Hezbollah's secret place. The bomb's there. The guy with the red beard is key."

"How many terrorists in Beirut have red beards?"

"I imagine damn few. He drove Ari there at least twice. He knows its location."

"We just have to find him."

"We will."

"How?"

"He's part of Hezbollah. He prays at the Mohammed Al-Attar Mosque. We'll find him there."

CHAPTER 97

*A*dhan. *Adhan. Adhan.*

As the call to midday prayer boomed across Al-Attar Square, Jarrett squeezed between two street vendors.

The CIA had a pushcart filled with cheap sunglasses set up for a previous surveillance operation. Jarrett had dressed the part, in a white kufi and a light gray jellabiya with cheap leather sandals. His hair covered an earbud; a microphone was tucked under his collar.

A rack of freshly baked bread was on his right and a smoldering hibachi roasting split chestnuts was on his left. The vendors were annoyed when Jarrett claimed the narrow cranny between them. But after he bought a loaf of bread and a bag of chestnuts, they welcomed him. After all he was a *tajir alshsharia*, a street vendor—one of them.

Although the smoke from the hibachi burned his eyes, Jarrett was perfectly positioned across from the mosque with a view of the square and the four streets leading into it. Despite towering over everyone, he worried he might miss Red Beard in the afternoon shadows.

But Jarrett's worries were for naught.

As he made change for his third sale, he heard a high-pitched voice shout, "*Ahmar lahia! Ahmar lahia!*" over the thrum of the crowd. Jarrett instantly translated the words—red beard.

Red Beard stood twenty feet away in the center of a small group of men. Fair-skinned with a shaved head, he looked nothing like an Arab. His nose seemed to have outgrown his face and a gentle spray of freckles across his cheeks belied dark, manipulative eyes. He wore a white collarless shirt, baggy black pants, and scuffed work shoes. A brownish, red beard draped his mid-chest and looked like a wooly clew. In the U.K. he would have been called a ginger.

As the men jabbered on, Red Beard listened intently with a closed smile like a politician huddling with his constituency. When the call to mid-afternoon prayer boomed again, he bowed and flipped his beard up with the back of his hand. Jarrett figured it was his way of saying good-bye.

As Red Beard weaved through the crowd toward the mosque he was embraced like a visiting dignitary. He shook outstretched hands, hugged shoulders, and cheek-bumped a few children. And after each stop he flipped up his beard.

Jarrett radioed Nikas.

"Got him. He's on his way into the mosque. He's the shiekh of Al-Attar Square. Knows everybody."

"Good. What now?" Nikas asked.

"I'll close up and meet you. Stay where you are."

Jarrett wheeled the cart two blocks at a near run, dodging pedestrians and cars.

Nikas waited in a CIA beater van appropriately dinged on the outside but mechanically perfect under the hood and outfitted with state-of-the-art electronics. With his olive skin and costumed like Jarrett, he looked like the vendor's street-wise business partner.

Jarrett loaded the cart into the van and hustled back to the square.

The crowd had thinned and the vendors were packing up their wares. Although the air had cooled, a nasty fug of overcooked meat, grease, and tobacco hung over the square. The bread rack stood empty and the last tiny curl of smoke rose from the hibachi. The two vendors were huddled with friends sharing a bottle in a paper sack. Jarrett skulked behind them and disappeared in an abandoned storefront, nearly overcome by the odor of fetid urine.

Luckily, his suffering was short-lived.

Soon the faithful streamed from the mosque, some lingering near the entrance in small groups. Red Beard came out last, arm in arm with the cleric. Nervously looking over his shoulder, he acknowledged the imam's animated ramblings with hand gestures. It was obvious he was anxious to be on his way. After a few minutes they embraced. Red Beard flipped up his beard and disappeared down one of the side streets.

Jarrett stepped into the square and followed him.

Red Beard was on a mission, walking surprisingly fast—almost trotting—as if he were late for an important meeting. Jarrett stayed at a comfortable distance.

After two blocks Red Beard veered down a narrow alley. He stopped at a nondescript door, bowed to the doorman, and disappeared. As Jarrett walked past, he caught a fleeting glimpse of a gaggle of shabbily dressed men drinking beer under a cloud of smoke. He heard someone shout, "*Ahmar lahia!*" over Jimmy Page's guitar booming in the background. He continued to the next cross street and called Nikas.

"I followed him down an alley to a hole-in-the-wall bar. If I'm not mistaken Led Zepplin's 'Kashmir' was playing in the background. Amazing, right here in the heart of Shia country."

"I love that song," Nikas said.

"Me too, almost as much as 'Stairway'," Jarrett replied. "I'll bet he stays there until he's feeling no pain. Don't know which way he'll go when he leaves, though. We've got to watch both ends of the alley. Where are you?"

"Still parked."

Jarrett gave him the street name and Nikas set up in a coffee shop near the alley. Jarrett did the same at the other cross street.

The alley turned out to be a busy thoroughfare. The bar was a popular watering hole.

Jarrett was on his second cup of coffee when Red Beard appeared with another man who was taller and broader across the shoulders.

Jarrett checked in with Nikas and followed them.

They walked leisurely, the man chattering and Red Beard responding with hand gestures, some form of crude sign language. Occasionally they slapped each other on the back during a particularly vibrant exchange. At an open-air market they bought a chunk of bread and two oranges. Red Beard paid.

Jarrett watched them disappear into a three-story walk-up next to the market.

He radioed Nikas. "They went into a run-down building in a bad neighborhood. I'm standing nearby lighting a cigar."

"A cigar? Didn't know you smoked," Nikas said.

"I don't. But I bought it when they stopped in a market. Had to buy something. In this neighborhood it gives me an excuse to stand in the street."

Nikas laughed. "Your Muslim old lady won't let you smoke in the house?"

The words "Muslim old lady" sent a warm feeling through Jarrett.

He imagined Ziba Vijany cuddled next to him with her sweet breath warming his neck.

"Whoops. A light just went on. Top floor."

"Will they see you?"

"Blinds are closed. Where are you?" Jarrett asked.

"Two blocks away. I can see you."

"Get the van."

"What's the plan?" Nikas asked.

"When you're on your way, I'll go in and bring Red Beard out."

"Simple as that?"

"Simple as that."

"You don't have a weapon. Wait until I get there."

"I won't need one for this," Jarrett muttered.

CHAPTER 98

"I'm on my way," Nikas barked.

"Double-park in front of the building. This won't take long. When I come out, we'll high-tail it out of here."

"What if you don't come out?"

Jarrett chuckled. "I will."

"Good luck," Nikas said.

Jarrett hurtled up the narrow stairwell two treads at a time dodging cans, empty food containers, and a few dirty syringes. The building stank of cooking grease and kamouneh, a blend of Lebanese spices his mother sometimes used to flavor meat.

The hallway along the front of the building had three doors.

Three windows outside, three doors inside. The light came on in the middle one.

He tried the middle door. Locked. He rapped on it.

"Who's there?" a raspy voice growled.

"*Mataween!*" Jarrett shouted. "Open the door! Now!"

Jarrett's mother had talked about the infamous *mataween*, the voluntary religious police in Lebanon, feared by Muslims, particularly women, who challenged Sharia law.

"All right," the voice relented.

When the door cracked open, Jarrett shouldered it, knocking down the man behind it.

Red Beard sat at a small table peeling an orange. When he looked up his bleary eyes widened in surprise, and he threw the orange at the hulk lunging at him. The orange missed its mark, but Jarrett didn't. He hit Red Beard square in the mouth.

Lights out. Instantly. Red Beard fell to the floor unconscious.

The one-room efficiency was a disgusting hovel. Jarrett had never seen anything like it.

In a split second Red Beard's roommate was on his feet, a jambiya in his hand. Angry-faced, he lunged at Jarrett shouting, "Infidel bastard!"

Jarrett parried, and the man crashed into the table. It collapsed under his weight and he landed facedown on it.

The man quickly rolled on his side and swung the knife in a scything motion. Jarrett sprang backward. The blade barely missed his face.

The man righted himself to a sitting positon, slashing wildly at Jarrett.

Jarrett hit the knife-wielding arm as it came at him with a perfectly timed kick. The force broke the man's forearm, pinwheeling the knife across the room.

The man spewed a barrage of four-letter words as he fell on his back.

Jarrett was on him in an instant raining down hammer fists one after the next. The man tried to block the blows with his good arm, but it quickly fell limp. Jarrett locked his arm around the man's neck and snapped it.

Red Beard was still out.

Jarrett hefted him on his shoulder and ran from the apartment.

In the stairwell he squeezed by an elderly man and muttered, "Drunk. Taking him home."

* * *

As Nikas pulled away, Red Beard lay motionless in the back of the van with Jarrett hovering over him.

"What was it like in there?" Nikas asked.

"Disgusting. Filthy dirty. Smelled like rotten garbage. I need to shower."

"That bad?"

"Worse," Jarrett replied.

"Red Beard smells a little ripe back there. What happened?"

"I popped him in the snout. Held back a little. He should wake up soon. His roommate didn't fare so well."

"What'd you mean?"

"He attacked me with a knife. I sent him to terrorist heaven."

"Sorry I missed the show."

CHAPTER 99

The CIA safe house was a two-bedroom apartment in a high-rise in north Beirut. Red Beard was fully awake by the time they took him up the service elevator.

The unit was squeaky clean, furnished functionally, and looked like no one had been there in months. Although used primarily to house agents in transit, it had sophisticated electronics in every room.

Jarrett disconnected the equipment from its main power source. There was no reason to chance a congressional subpoena to explain enhanced interrogation to a committee of self-righteous politicians.

Red Beard's name on his driver's license was Sadeq Amir. Luckily his wallet and cell phone were in his pants pockets. Jarrett had forgotten to look for them in his haste to get out of the wretched flat.

Red Beard was surprisingly calm and cooperative. When asked, he indicated that he was right-handed. Nikas secured his legs and left arm to a chair in the dining room. Because he was mute, he would have to write answers to their questions. With Jarrett unable to read Arabic well and the answers critically important, likely involving an address and directions, they needed the CIA linguist.

Nikas had called her on the way to the safe house. When she offered to meet them there, Jarrett told her no. Other than Nikas there would be no witnesses to this interrogation. They would take photos of Red Beard's written responses and text them to her. She would text back her translation.

When Nikas appeared with a pail of water and a folded towel, the Hezbollah driver's eyes widened. Jarrett wanted to put the fear of Allah in him before they started.

For the first time Red Beard tried to speak, but all he could muster was a grunting sound like the mating call of a frenzied chimpanzee.

He sensed that these two brutes meant business and wouldn't hesitate to hurt him or even kill him if he didn't cooperate.

Jarrett held up a notepad and pen.

"I'll ask questions. You'll write answers. If I don't like them, we'll pour water on your face. Do you understand?"

Red Beard nodded.

"Let me show you what will happen if you don't cooperate," Jarrett added.

While Nikas held Red Beard's right hand, Jarrett pulled his head back, draped the towel over his face, and drizzled a little water onto it.

Red Beard shook as if he were having a seizure.

When Jarrett took the towel away, Red Beard hastily scrawled on the notepad.

Nikas texted a photo of it to the linguist. Jarrett wondered if she would be able to decipher the scratchings.

In a matter of seconds Nikas's phone beeped. The text read, "No more water. Tell everything." Beneath it was a footnote. "Writing nearly illegible. Try to get him to calm down. Thanks."

Jarrett said, "Relax, *Ahmar Lahia*. We won't hurt you. Just answer the questions. We'll be done in a few minutes."

Red Beard nodded and tried to smile. He was missing most of his front teeth and his breath was fetid.

"What's your name?"

Written response: "Mohammed Katar."

"Your driver's license says Sadeq Amir."

Written response: "Forged." The linguist noted that the literal translation was "a lie."

Jarrett glared at Nikas. "Damn it. Tell her I want exactly what he says. No editorials."

"Do you work for Hezbollah?"

Written response: "Pay me."

"What do they pay you to do?"

Written response: "Drive."

"Who do you drive?"

Written response: "Big ones."

"Give me their names."
Written response: "Don't know."
"Did you ever drive Rami Monsour?"
Written response: "No."
Red Beard's eyes fluttered.
He was lying, Jarrett thought.
Jarrett snapped Red Beard's head back and dropped a towel on his face.
"You're lying. You lie, you get water." He trickled a stream of water on the towel, then asked, "You drove Monsour to a special place from the mosque."
Red Beard began to struggle against the restraints, and his head jerked forward as if he were trying to nod. When Jarrett took the towel away and released his head, Red Beard was in a state of panic. After coughing for a few seconds, he scribbled on the pad.
Written response: "Three times."
"Where?"
Written response: "Big house in country."
"Give me the address."
Written response: "No address."
"Why no address?"
Written response: "In country. Will show. No water."
"Do you know Abu Mohammed Amed."
Red Beard nodded yes.
"Where does he live?"
Written response: "Don't know. Very bad."
Jarrett looked at Nikas. "We're done here. Let's have him direct us to the country house. It must be the black site."

CHAPTER 100

Nikas drove.

Red Beard sat in the passenger seat. Jarrett sat behind him with a Glock trained on the Hezbollah driver's head.

Jarrett had the linguist remain on call. They brought a notepad and pen . . . just in case.

Although it was dark, Red Beard knew the way. They traveled south from the mosque on surface streets, then onto a four-lane highway. Red Beard was told to raise two fingers when they neared the site.

After exiting the highway, they followed a paved road that meandered through fields pocked with bomb craters. A few houses had been rebuilt, but most were bombed-out shells. This had once been a lush farming area of grain fields, orchards, and grassy meadows.

They traveled farther into the countryside and the road narrowed between steep hills marred by basalt outcroppings screened with brush. It was dark, the moon but a tiny sliver, and there were no road signs. Jarrett wondered how Red Beard remembered his way.

As they approached an old stone barn, Red Beard sat forward and pointed to a gravel lane winding up the hill. After the first curve, he held up two fingers.

Nikas slowed. "What now?"

"When we come to the black site just drive on like we're passing through," Jarrett replied. "Remember, Red Beard said it's a big country house."

And it was.

A magnificent Mediterranean-style manor aglow with lights sat on a flat bench at the crest of the slope. It was breathtaking, apart from the eight-foot wall topped with concertina wire.

In daylight the view would be magnificent, Jarrett thought.

Built of cut stone the two-story structure had a blue tile roof and tall casement windows with light blue trim. From an ornate wrought-iron gate a teardrop-shaped driveway passed under a portico and looped back to the entry. A black Mercedes Maybach with deep tints sat under the portico.

A sentry with a scoped rifle huddled behind a parapet on the portico roof. A guard with an AK-47 stood at the entry gate smoking. A beat-up Toyota pickup was parked near a small barn across the road from the compound.

Jarrett figured this was Alfour's country estate. But was it the black site? He closed his eyes and jettisoned back to the torture room.

On the verge of blacking out, he'd sensed he was underground with a massive structure looming over him. Overhead fluorescent lights had flickered; the air had been cool and musty.

During the walk to Alfour's office he'd smelled earth and fresh concrete. The drive to his hotel from the black site had been a series of turns meant to disorient him. He was sure they were in city traffic the whole time.

The manor house was new and remote with only one way to get to it.

"Nick, continue down the road. Pull over when the house is out of sight."

As they passed the gate, the guard's eyes followed them while he blew columns of smoke through his nose. Nikas waved and smiled, and the guard thrust the AK-47 over his head.

Beyond the compound, the road sloped downward and was nearly impassable. When the house fell from view, Nikas stopped.

"This isn't the black site," Jarrett said.

"It has to be. This is where Red Beard took Ari."

Jarrett described the torture room, the tunnel to the office, and the elevator ride. "When I was strung up I had the sensation I was underground, with a big structure looming over me, like I was under the Empire State Building."

"There might be a room under the house with an elevator. Maybe the tunnel goes under the road from the house to the barn."

"Everything about the torture room was old," Jarrett remembered. "I mean really old. Ancient. This house is new and not high enough even with a room underneath. After I met with Alfour I was hooded and driven to my hotel. We were in traffic the whole time. Never left the city."

"So, if this isn't the black site, where is it?"

Jarrett thought for a moment. "Hook up with the linguist again." He pressed the Glock against Red Beard's head. "More questions my friend. If I don't like the answers, a bullet this time. No water."

Red Beard shook his head, indicating he'd write the answers again.

"When you brought Monsour here the first two times, what did you do at the gate?"

Written response: "Told guard his name."

"Were they expecting him?"

Red Beard nodded.

"What happened then?"

Written response: "Guard opened gate."

"What did you do?"

Written response: "Drove back to city."

"Were they expecting him the last time?"

Red Beard shook his head no.

"What happened?"

Written response: "Guard called house. Man came out."

"What did the man look like?"

Written response: "Young. Tall. Long hair. Ponytail."

Jarrett nudged Nikas. "That wasn't Alfour."

Turning to Red Beard, he asked, "What happened then?"

Written response: "Drove back."

"What did Monsour do?"

Written response: "In driveway talking."

"Was the black car that's under the portico now, there the first two times?"

He nodded.

"The last time?"

Red Beard shook his head no.

"Were there any other cars in the driveway?"

He shook his head no again.

"Nick, close with her."

"I know what happened," Jarrett began excitedly. "I'm certain this is Alfour's house. He's the head of Hezbollah. Called Sheikh Nassim.

That expensive car under the portico is his. The first two times, Ari was contacted about a meeting. He met Red Beard at the mosque and was driven here to talk about the bomb deal. Alfour was here for those meetings. Red Beard said his car was in the driveway. But the third time was different. Like Moshe said, Ari contacted Red Beard. He had his cell number from the first two trips. He told him there was an emergency, that he had to go to the black site. Red Beard drove him here. They weren't expecting Ari."

"Ari thought this was where they were holding you," Nikas added.

"Exactly. He thought this was the black site, because the first two times he was brought here. He had no reason to think differently."

"Which means he'd never been to the real black site," Nikas said.

"Right. Until that night. So when Ari told Ponytail he had important information for Alfour, Ponytail drove him to the black site. Alfour was there. Ari came and saved my ass."

"If you're right, we have to question Alfour or Ponytail to find out where the black site is."

"The sheikh is in the house. His car's here. Maybe Ponytail too."

"Let's hope so," Nikas said.

"What do you have in the duffel back there?" Jarrett asked.

"Our kit. You name it. Long guns, 9-mil handguns, fully auto MP5s, pineapples, C4 with all the fixings, Kevlars, binocs, and plenty of ammo."

"That's all?" Jarrett asked sarcastically.

"That's all. What's the plan, Clint?"

"We go in hot and wet. I'll drive. When I stop at the gate, you take out the sentry on the portico. Should be a chip shot for you. I'll deal with the smoker."

"We can use the van's winch to pull the gate down. Rules of engagement?" Nikas asked.

"None. But we've got to take Alfour or Ponytail alive."

"Gotcha. How about Red Beard?"

"He stays in the van," Jarrett said, as he cuffed Red Beard to a steel ring.

CHAPTER 101

Jarrett handed Nikas a Kevlar vest and goggles and they put in earbuds with microphones on their collars.

When Jarrett turned into the driveway the guard was lighting a cigarette. He signaled for the van to stop and walked toward it, shadowing the headlights with his hand.

Jarrett stopped ten feet from the gate. The silenced Glock was between his legs with his trigger finger set.

When the guard asked, "What do you want?" Jarrett shot him between the eyes. Simultaneously, Nikas was out of the van. An instant later the sentry on the roof was dead.

Nikas attached the winch cable to the gate. It came off its hinges with a loud crash, and they hurtled over it and ran to the main entrance.

The door was locked.

Jarrett glanced at the ornate brass knocker and thought, *not tonight.*

After Nikas shot out the lock, Jarrett kicked in the door. Cool air streamed across his face. When an alarm sounded inside, they stepped to either side of the opening.

Almost immediately a volley of bullets began pockmarking the Mercedes and ricocheting off the driveway. Nikas inched along the portico, kicked in a window, and sprayed the inside of the house. The gunfire inside stopped abruptly.

"Shooter down," Nikas said.

They darted through the door into a high-ceilinged atrium with a spectacular crystal chandelier and a central staircase leading to a loft. Beyond the atrium was the living room with ornate furniture and beyond that the dining room. Both were dark. A set of double doors was at the back of the loft and a catwalk with a brass railing leading to bedrooms wrapped two sides of the atrium.

The dead shooter was short and squat and sprawled across the top of the staircase. He wasn't Ponytail. No one else was in sight.

Alfour's in the master bedroom beyond the double doors in the loft, Jarrett thought and gestured to the stairway.

Nikas nodded and went first with Jarrett covering him.

He was on the third step when a bedroom door crashed open. A wild-eyed man with a long, thin face and a ponytail appeared on the catwalk brandishing an automatic weapon. Screaming *"Allahu akbar!"*, he began wildly spraying the atrium. Bullets hit the walls, the ceiling, and the staircase—everywhere—and shattered the chandelier. Fragments of glass rained down like sparkling confetti.

Nikas hurtled over the bannister and took cover under the loft.

Jarrett sprinted across the atrium, bullets whizzing all around him. When he reached the catwalk overhang he took cover under the crazed gunman.

The barrage of gunfire suddenly stopped.

Ponytail's reloading, Jarrett thought.

Nikas looked at Jarrett. His eyebrows rose and he mouthed, "What now?"

With his fingers mimicking a gun, Jarrett pointed upward. Nikas grinned and gestured for Jarrett to move a few feet to his left.

Ponytail screamed, *"Allahu akbar!"* again and the shooting resumed.

When Nikas gave thumbs-up, Jarrett emptied a fifty-round magazine from his MP5 into the overhang. Ponytail was directly above him.

At close range the nine-millimeter armor-piercing rounds cut through the overhang as if it were butter. The volley shredded Ponytail's legs and ripped him apart. Blood sprayed on the walls and ceiling, leaving behind a gory tangle of tissue and bone.

Chunks of plaster covered Jarrett. He brushed them off, cleared his goggles, and joined Nikas at the base of the stairway. "Ponytail won't be able to answer any questions."

"He went nuts. We had no choice." Nikas shrugged.

"The master should be behind the doors at the back of the loft. Sheikh Nassim will be there. We have to take him alive."

"Why hasn't he shown?"

"I don't know," Jarrett answered. "Let's find out."

CHAPTER 102

Jarrett followed Nikas up the stairs. The door to the master suite was locked. Nikas leaned into it as if it were a blocking dummy, but it didn't budge.

Jarrett stepped back and pointed to the lock.

Nikas opened fire. *Ping, ping, ping.*

After a short volley he stopped.

"It's a steel door. Let me try this," he said, as he retrieved a block of C4 from his backpack.

After kneading the explosive into a long bead the thickness of a pencil, he attached it to the doorframe and placed an electronic fuse. They crouched behind a sofa on the far side of the loft, cushioning themselves with pillows.

The explosion was ear-shattering.

The house shook as if it were at the epicenter of a Richter 10 earthquake. The steel doors blew in and the masonry walls on either side crumbled. Flying debris knocked down the catwalk railings and the windows in the atrium exploded. What was left of the glass chandelier was pulverized.

The first shooter's body flew down the stairway like a rag doll. Ponytail's body parts were strewn all over the atrium. The concussive force pushed the sofa against Jarrett and Nikas, but the pillows softened the impact

Jarrett coughed as they stood off to the side of the blown-out door. His ears rang and he could barely hear. "That was one helluva of a bang."

Nikas grimaced. "Might have used a little too much."

"Let's wait until it's clear. We won't be able to see. If Alfour is in there, he might open fire."

When they finally could see into the room, all was quiet. Nothing moved. No sign of life. Or death. With Nikas covering, Jarrett picked his way through the twisted steel doors and debris into the room.

It *was* the master suite, or what was left of it.

A film of dust covered everything. The remains of a canopy bed were on Jarrett's left with twin walk-in closets across from it. Straight ahead a wide archway led to a bathroom. Furniture, bedding, chunks of mattress, and pieces of a flat-screen monitor and electronics were strewn about the room. Between the closets the monitor's electrical connection sparked. The empty brass frame of a giant mirror hung over the head of the bed.

Jarrett quickly checked the bathroom and the closets.

No one home.

Where are you Alfour? I know you were here.

"All clear, Nick," Jarrett said.

Nikas made his way into the room. As he walked toward the bed he said, "Well, look here." A curl of smoke rose from a smoldering cigarette on the floor. He reached down and touched a plastic bottle near it. "Hmm. A cigarette still burning and a cold bottle of water. Someone was here when the action started."

"This was a safe room in case the house came under ground assault," Jarrett said, "but a bad place to be in an aerial attack. A tile roof wouldn't do much against Israeli bombs and rockets. There has to be a stairway to an underground bunker."

He found it in the man's closet.

The hanging clothes were blown off their racks exposing a wall panel ajar from the explosion. Behind it, Jarrett discovered a narrow stairway that lead downward into darkness. Cool air streamed up the stairway.

Nikas handed Jarrett a flashlight from his backpack.

After a dozen steps, Jarrett was stopped by a heavy metal plate blocking the stairway. He stepped on it and bounced up and down. It was rock solid and recessed into the first-floor concrete slab. A blast door. He scanned it with the flashlight and discovered a locking lever. He stepped upward onto the stairway and pulled the lever. The panel released, and he rolled it away.

Below the panel, the stairway was concrete—the steps, the walls, and the ceiling, an eerie tunnel leading into darkness. He descended cautiously, step-by-step, sweeping the light beam in front of him, the Glock in his other hand up and ready. The air was cool and musty with a hint of perfume that became stronger as he got deeper. He felt like Indiana Jones entering an ancient tomb. The stairway ended in a small space, barely big enough to turn around, with another steel door directly ahead of him

The door was locked. He rapped on it with his Glock and said, "Open up or we'll blow it. Same as upstairs." He repeated the warning, but there was no response.

Shit. Another round of C4.

"Nick, I'm coming up," Jarrett whispered into the radio. When he neared the top of the stairway, lights flashed.

"I found a light switch," Nikas said.

"There's another steel door at the bottom," Jarrett told him. "Locked. It must lead to a bunker. Alfour's in there. We need to blow it."

"If it's a blast door, we might not be able to," Nikas said.

"It's not. The blast door is a heavy steel plate straddling the stairs at the first floor. I rolled it out of the way. Concrete steps below it. Use less of the damn C4 this time. We don't want to kill the bastard."

"You got it. Just enough, but not too much." Nikas winked.

When Nikas returned, Jarrett was going through an armoire. He found a travel brochure addressed to Nassim Alfour but no cell phone or wallet.

"You're right," Nikas said. "The door's not a blast door, but I couldn't shoulder it. I went light on the C4 this time and closed the blast panel on the way up. Let's go out to the loft. I'll detonate it."

The C4 exploded with a low rumble like a thunder clap in the distance. The house groaned and the windows shook but nothing like the first explosion.

The blast door had done its job, but the concrete steps below it had cracked.

When the dust cleared, Jarrett stood in the doorway looking into the bunker. Nikas was wedged behind him.

The room was about twenty feet square. The furnishings were piled against the back wall—a table, four chairs, a sofa, and an end table—as if thrust by a tidal surge. A small refrigerator was on its side with broken bottles scattered around the room. No one was in sight.

Jarrett stepped into the room. Amazingly the ceiling lights were on and cool air streamed through wall vents. He smelled perfume again, stronger now. His eyes panned around the room. To his right a door stood ajar. He gestured to it and said, "Over here, Nick."

With Nikas next to him, Jarrett opened the door.

CHAPTER 103

It was a small bathroom.

Alfour and a woman in a fancy robe and slippers were huddled under a blanket between the sink and toilet.

When Jarrett pulled off the blanket, Alfour looked up. "It's you," he sneered. "I knew you were a fucking spy." Although stunned from the explosion, the sheikh was angry-faced and defiant.

"Yes, it's me." Jarrett sighed.

"You're an infidel pig. We should have fed you to the filthy animals."

Jarrett and Nikas pulled the two from the bathroom and sat them in chairs.

The woman was young and hard-looking with her hair pulled back in a tight bun and heavy makeup. Behind a look of smoldering indignation, her raccoon eyes bored into Alfour like gun barrels.

Jarrett was curious. Was she angry with Alfour? Because the compound had been breached and she faced death? Or something else? Alfour seemed oblivious to her.

Nikas searched Alfour and found his cell phone, wallet, cigarettes, and lighter, but no weapon.

"Where's the bomb?" Jarrett asked.

"It's being moved," Alfour snarled. "When you attacked, I called my warriors."

"Where?"

"To a safe place. You'll never find it."

"Where, damn it. Tell me or I'll shoot her."

"Go ahead. She's just a fucking whore. She means nothing to me."

311

The woman's jaw muscles tensed and she bared her teeth.

"Where's the bomb going?"

"Fuck you."

Jarrett shot Alfour in the knee.

As he shrieked in pain, the woman jumped to her feet. A gun appeared in her hand. She screamed, "Motherfucker!" and discharged the weapon.

Nikas blinked. A split-second later the woman's head exploded and she crumpled to the floor.

"She shot him," Nikas cried.

The shot had shattered Alfour's left shoulder.

Jarrett glared at Alfour. "The bomb. Where's it going?"

"Fuck you, asshole." Two bullets in a matter of seconds had stoked Alfour's furor and aroused his Islamist martyr complex.

Jarrett grimaced, took two steps backward, and shot him in the forehead.

"*Allahu akbar* and fuck you too," he muttered.

"A scorned mistress," Nikas said pointing to the dead woman.

"No woman likes to be called a whore, even if she is one. She was supposed to shoot us," Jarrett said.

"She was pissed at him. You could see it in her eyes. It had to be building for a long time."

While Nikas spoke, Jarrett thought back to Ari's third visit to the country estate.

Red Beard left Ari with Ponytail and drove back to the mosque. Alfour's car was gone. That meant Ponytail or someone else drove Ari to the black site in another vehicle.

"Clint, you okay?"

"Fine. Just thinking. Alfour wasn't going to tell us anything."

"I know. What now?"

"Let's check the barn across the way."

* * *

"The Toyota pickup belongs to the guards," Jarrett said, as Nikas shot the lock off the barn door.

A small tractor and a black Volvo sedan were inside.

A corner of the barn had a dropped ceiling, dark paneling, and a round table with six chairs. Jarrett figured this was where Ari had met with Alfour the first two times.

Nikas went right to the Volvo. He found the keys above the sun visor and started the engine.

"What was the date you were at the black site?" he asked, as he played with the display on the dash.

Jarrett counted backward and gave it to him.

"Let's see," Nikas murmured. "These are the GPS coordinates on that date. On the map. Here it is."

CHAPTER 104

"Al-Attar Square!" Nikas cried. "It's the mosque!"

The GPS in the Volvo SUV had a thirty-day memory with the coordinates of every destination stored by date and time.

On the night the terrorists had tortured Jarrett, Ponytail had driven Ari to Al-Attar Square in the Volvo . . . to the mosque. It was the Hezbollah black site.

How stupid of me, Jarrett thought. *The cavernous basement is under the mosque. The underground tunnel must lead to Hezbollah's offices.*

But were they too late?

Had Alfour's minions already moved the bomb?

They left Red Beard cuffed to the gate.

During the ride to the city they decided to explore the back of the mosque for an entry point. Going in through the main entrance on the square would attract undue attention.

It was late and there was very little traffic.

Nikas parked on the street behind the mosque across from a new four-story building. The building's lobby was bathed in shadows with just a pair of elevators behind an empty reception desk. A yellow Hezbollah flag with its green logo hung across one wall.

"This is Hezbollah's building. They took me here. To Alfour's office. Through a damn tunnel under the street. We would have saved ourselves a lot of trouble if I'd . . ."

Nikas interrupted. "Look at it this way, Clint. We took care of Alfour, four of his guys, and his unhappy girlfriend. What's done is done. Let's get on with it."

"You're right. I just hope they haven't moved the bomb yet."

The back of the mosque had two emergency exits. Security lights above them were burned out. Jarrett picked one of the locks. The door opened to a narrow hallway that ran along the back of the building.

They split up—Jarrett went left and Nikas right.

Jarrett followed the hallway to its end and peered around the corner. A wide corridor stretched to the foyer. Archways led to the prayer hall. No one was in sight.

The radio cracked and Nikas whispered, "Armed guard."

Jarrett turned. Nikas waved and pointed around the corner.

"In the corridor leading to the foyer?" Jarrett asked.

"About halfway down."

"Did he see you?"

"He's asleep in a chair. Snoring. There's a door next to him."

"Maybe the access to the basement. Wait there."

Jarrett found a push broom in a utility closet and joined Nikas.

"What the hell are you doing?"

Jarrett sneaked a look around the corner and said, "What do you think? Sweeping the floors. There's an AK-47 on his lap. No suppressor. We don't want to announce our arrival with a shootout. Wait here."

"You don't look like a janitor," Nikas said.

"Believe me I know how to use a broom. I've swept out our barn thousands of times."

"I can take him out."

"What if you miss?"

"I won't. Trust me."

"I know you won't. But if he get's off just one shot, we're in trouble. This'll be quiet. Besides I haven't played baseball in a long time."

Jarrett walked down the hall pushing the broom in front of him. When the guard looked up, the broom handle broke across his head. His eyes rolled back and he fell to the floor.

Home run, Jarrett thought.

But they had another steel door to contend with, and this one had a new police lock.

Nikas joined him. "Can you pick it?"

"These new ones are tricky."

"I can blow it. It's hinged to open inward."

"No. Too much noise. He's here to guard the door and to open it. Alfour's a big shot. He wouldn't carry keys for a basement door."

Jarrett checked the guard's pockets, his shoes, and under the chair. Everywhere. No key. Then he stood back and looked down at him. There was a heavy gold chain around his neck, and he didn't look like the gold-chain type. Jarrett pulled it off.

"Well I'll be damned. There's a pendant. A miniature AK-47."

"Isn't that part of the Hezbollah emblem?" Nikas asked.

Jarrett nodded. "But this one has no sight and there's a ridge and teeth along the barrel."

He slipped it into the lock and turned. When the door swung open, cool, musty air streamed over Jarrett's face, stirring memories of the quirt. He gritted his teeth and stepped onto the landing. "We're in. Come on Nick, this'll take us down."

Nikas muttered, "Enemy combatant," and shot the guard in the forehead. *Ping.*

He pulled the body inside and closed the door.

"Don't lock it," Jarrett said.

CHAPTER 105

At the bottom of the stairway, a wide passage led to the torture room. A stool sat outside the door with a tin can on the floor filled with cigarette butts. The odor of stale smoke gave Jarrett a bad feeling. If this guard was gone, the bomb was too.

The torture room seemed smaller than Jarrett remembered. The rings welded to the overhead steel beam still had pulleys with ropes attached. Dark stains discolored the concrete floor beneath the ropes. A corner was outfitted with light blue wall covering and umbrella lights. Nearby sat a large wooden crate. The top was on the floor with chunks of blue foam scattered about.

While Jarrett gazed around the room, reliving his nightmare, Nikas ran to the crate.

"Damn it! The bomb's gone. There's just padding inside."

Jarrett figured they weren't far behind it.

"Nick, go back up to the street, behind the mosque. Watch the office building. They took the bomb there. They'll move it to another location. You might catch them bringing it out. I'll take the tunnel to the building. Keep in touch by radio."

He reached for Nikas's backpack. "Let me take a couple of those bad boys."

"The black ones are fragmenters and the little guys are special mini-flashers."

Jarrett put one of each grenade in his vest pocket.

While Nikas backtracked to the stairs, Jarrett followed the passage to the tunnel. He hurtled down four steps imagining he heard traffic overhead.

Even though he'd been hooded the first time, the smell of fresh concrete and earth was unmistakable.

At the end of the tunnel six steps led to a landing with a heavy door. On the wall was a button that looked like a doorbell. He pressed it and heard a lock click.

He pushed the door forward and stepped into a large utility room. There were electrical panels covering the walls and a generator the size of a small car.

The radio beeped, followed by a burst of static. Jarrett said, "Go ahead, Nick." The radio beeped again. Static. Then a third time. Static.

No reception, he thought.

As Jarrett turned to close the door, a man sprang from behind the generator, thrusting the butt of his rifle stock at Jarrett like a spear. Jarrett twisted, and the stock missed.

The attacker's momentum threw him into the door.

Jarrett spun and hit him in the ribs with an elbow. The man grunted in pain, cursed, and swung the rifle like a baseball bat. Jarrett lunged backward and parried, but the stock hit his elbow. An electric shock pulsed up his arm and across the base of his skull. The attacker swung again and the stock grazed Jarrett's chest, but didn't hurt him.

As the attacker reset to swing again, Jarrett bounced on his toes and launched an axe kick. His leg—locked at the knee—shot up like a spring-loaded pendulum and hit the attacker in the side of the head. Stunned, the man fell to his knees and dropped the rifle. Jarrett followed with another kick. This one found its mark. Under full power, it snapped the attacker's head back, and he crashed to the floor with his mouth agape.

Jarrett wondered why the attacker hadn't shot him. One bullet and it would have been over. Maybe he feared damaging the electrical circuitry in the utility room. A shot in the wrong place would disable the building. Or maybe the terrorists wanted Jarrett alive.

Jarrett checked his radio. Dead. The attacker's rifle had damaged it.

A pair of elevators was outside the utility room, one on the first floor and the other on the fourth—the top floor. Jarrett was on the ground level.

A stairwell next to the elevators had a steel door with a small glass window.

He pressed the up button.

As the elevator on the first floor began to descend, he stepped into the stairwell. When the elevator opened, he cracked the door and peered around the corner. No one in sight.

Was there a shooter in the elevator?

He waited a few seconds, exited the stairwell, inched along the wall, then sprang forward in a shooting stance in front of the elevator door.

Empty.

The second elevator was still on the fourth floor.

He took the first elevator out of service and pressed the up button again.

But the second elevator had already begun descending.

Here we go, he thought.

CHAPTER 106

The elevator stopped at the first floor, one level above Jarrett.

He quickly stepped back into the stairwell. He heard a *screech*. A door had opened above him.

He looked up to the landing where the stairs reversed direction. Nothing. Then he heard the elevator door opening on the ground level.

"Throw out your weapons. Step out of the stairwell," a voice echoed over a loudspeaker near the elevators.

Shit.

A wave of fear shot through Jarrett. Fear as in, *fuck everything and run.* But there was nowhere to go.

He was trapped. One Hezbollah guard was in the stairwell above him, a second outside the elevator on the ground floor. Both were armed to the teeth.

How did the bad guys know where he was? *Hidden cameras*, he thought. He looked up, but saw none in the stairwell.

Jarrett quickly weighed his options.

If he stepped out of the stairwell, it would be an O.K.-Corral-type shootout. When the guard saw the door swing open he'd spray the stairwell. Jarrett's chances of surviving were bad . . . very bad.

If he climbed the stairway, the guard above him would cut him down before Jarrett registered a target. And the minute the guard outside the elevators heard shooting, he'd be through the stairwell door.

If either shooter went down in the firefight so be it. Killing Jarrett was all that mattered. They were Islamist terrorists. Dying for the cause meant rejoicing in the bounty of Allah. Seventy virgins. Not bad.

"Throw your weapons out now. Come out. Hands up," the voice repeated.

Jarrett retrieved the fragmentation grenade from his pocket, reminding himself that once he pulled the pin, he had four seconds.

The damn door better hold.

He pulled the pin and began counting. At one thousand three, he opened the door and tossed the grenade toward the elevators.

As the guard opened fire, Jarrett pulled the door closed, dropped to his knees, and covered his head with his arms.

Boom.

The shooting stopped. The door shook as if hit by a battering ram, but held. The window shattered, spewing glass up the stairway. Jarrett was unscathed.

He looked up the stairwell. Nothing but a trail of glass.

Where was the second shooter?

The door was jammed; he leaned into it, pushed, then pushed harder. It scraped across the concrete floor and opened.

When he stepped through the door, smoke clouded the hall in front of the elevators. His eyes burned and a familiar chemical taste filled his nose and mouth.

As the smoke cleared, a shape took form on the floor. The guard. On his back, faceless, his chest blown open, both arms missing. His rifle was ten feet away in two pieces, the stock shattered. The grenade had hit him the instant it exploded. It was a gory scene, blood and tissue splayed onto the floor and walls.

Jarrett shouldered the stairwell door until it closed.

The second elevator opposite the guard was damaged. The door was ajar and the lights flickered, but the first elevator appeared intact. He put it back in service and rode it to the second floor. After the door opened, he took the elevator out of service and jumped out, crouching with his MP5 up and ready. A long hall with doors extended in both directions. No one was in sight.

He stepped into the stairwell, quietly closing the door behind him. After tiptoeing down the stairs to the landing between floors, he peered down. The guard was gone.

Jarrett moved quickly down the stairs to the first-floor landing. He opened the door ready to engage. The lobby was draped in shadows and empty. He saw the outline of the van parked across the street. No Nikas.

He backed into the stairwell and heard the ground-floor door screeching. After quickly descending to the landing, he peered around the corner. The target—a black silhouette leaning into the door—registered instantly.

He sprayed it with the MP5.

CHAPTER 107

*D*ead.

Both of them. Now what?

The shooters had come from the fourth floor. The action was there.

Jarrett ejected the spent magazine from his MP5 and popped in a fresh one—his last—and sprinted up the stairs two steps at a time.

He stopped on the fourth-floor landing.

The stairwell was an emergency exit. The door swung inward. He opened it slowly, held it in place with his foot, and waited. Nothing moved. Silence.

Where were the bad guys?

The elevator shaft was next to the stairwell. An alcove with a set of double doors was across the hall from the elevators. Alfour's office?

Jarrett thought back to the night he'd been tortured. When the elevator had opened, Amed had grasped his arm and said, "Straight across the hall, Sahin." They'd stopped while Alfour had unlocked a door. After the hood had been removed, Alfour said, "This is my office. We'll talk here."

Jarrett's MP5 hung from a sling around his neck. The Glock was under his belt. He took the mini-stun grenade from his pocket. It was walnut-sized, small enough to conceal in his left hand while holding the spoon in place. Four seconds after he released the spoon, the metal oxidant mixture would explode.

He pulled the pin, held the spoon in place, withdrew the Glock, and darted across the hallway to the alcove. The door was locked.

He glanced in both directions. The hallway was steeped in shadows, but at the far end an open door cast a halo of light.

"Welcome, Mr. Sahin, or whoever you are. I've been waiting for you. Come down the hall," the voice said over the loudspeaker.

A *trap . . . to be sure*, he thought. *What should I do?*

He could take the stairway to the lobby and be out of the building in seconds, but not today. Not from these bastards. He hoped it was Amed egging him on. And maybe the bomb was with him.

"Be nice now, Mr. Sahin. I'm unarmed. I just want to talk."

The hallway was a perfect shooting corridor. In stride he would be an easy target for a shooter popping out of the door. So he moved with his back against the wall, sliding step-by-step, his Glock ready and the stunner in his left hand.

He stopped across from the open doorway.

CHAPTER 108

*A*bu Amed.
The sinister-eyed quirt wielder.
Alone.

Amed sat at a table facing the door with an I-have-the-upper-hand-and-you're-fucked smirk on his face. Tonight he was dressed for the occasion in a dark gray suit with a black collarless shirt. No kiffieyh or jellabiya. And no weapons in sight.

The room was small and well-lighted with no furnishings or wall hangings, just a panel of monitors—floor-to-ceiling—behind Amed. The windows were six feet behind them and blacked-out. A tangle of wires ran to the baseboard under the windows.

A jerry-rigged security center. Nothing fancy. Maybe an afterthought. The screens had live feeds from everywhere Jarrett had been except the stairwell.

"You've killed two of my men," Amed said.

As Amed spoke, Jarrett stepped across the threshold. He looked left, then right. No one. And no bomb. Images on the monitors of two dead guards stared at him.

"Four, actually. One in the utility room and one in the stairwell, not on your monitors. You'll be number five."

"I knew you were a fucking spy. Who are you? Mossad? CIA?"

"It doesn't matter who I am. I want the bomb," Jarrett said as he advanced toward Amed.

"The bomb," Amed sneered. "We have big plans for it. It's been moved to a safe place. You'll never find it."

"Alfour and his mistress are dead," Jarrett said.

"I figured you'd kill him after he called me. That's not so bad. I'll take over."

Two guards stepped from behind the monitors with AK-47s trained on Jarrett, one on his left and one on his right.

Jarrett glanced at them.

Their rifle stocks were tucked under their arms, barrels in hand. That meant full-auto—600 rounds per minute. Ten per second. Thirty-round magazines. Three seconds to empty.

Jarrett was caught in a crossfire. Dead center. Not a chance in hell. He could take out Amed and maybe one of the shooters, if he was lucky . . . or they were a skosh slow, but the second one would cut him to pieces. He adjusted his grasp on the stun grenade and dropped the Glock to his side.

"Which one of these bastards shot Monsour?"

"You mean Katz, the fucking Mossad spy?"

"Yes, Ari Katz," Jarrett replied.

Amed pointed right. The guard thrust his rifle out in front of him and a grin spread across his face.

"Toss that fancy piece on the table. And what do you have in your hand?"

Jarrett released the spoon. The timing had to be perfect.

When the Glock clattered on the table, he said, "You mean this?" and tossed the grenade at Amed.

As the stunner left Jarrett's hand, he dove under the table at Amed's feet, his ears covered with his hands and his eyes tightly closed.

The grenade exploded. A blinding flash and ear-piercing bang filled the room.

Instinctively the shooters covered their faces.

Amed was thrown backward onto the floor.

From his prone position under the table, Jarrett shot both guards. The one on his left first—a quick burst—*pop, pop, pop*—for Ari. Then the one on the right, both in a split second. When the MP5 sputtered empty, the monitor panel was wedged against the wall, the dead guards sprawled on top of it.

Amed struggled to his feet. He tried to cry out, but only guttural sounds rose from his throat. He stumbled past the guards and plodded aimlessly, his arms outstretched.

The terrorist's face and neck were ashen, his eyes molten craters, and his hair seared to his scalp. The stunner had exploded in his face.

Jarrett's eyes burned from the magnesium vapor, and the smell of burned flesh filled his nose. As he looked at Amed in horror, a wave of nausea swept over him.

Amed crashed into the wall next to the door and fell to his knees.

"The bomb. Where is it?" Jarrett yelled.

Nothing.

He shook Amed. "Where's the goddamned bomb, Amed?"

Amed was blind and deaf.

Jarrett stepped back. He found an AK-47.

As Amed began to smash his face against the wall, his lips flopping up and down like a marionette, Jarrett pressed the AK-47 muzzle against Amed's skull.

"For George's nephew, for the captain, and for me," he muttered and squeezed the trigger.

CHAPTER 109

Jarrett ran down the hallway to Alfour's office.

Maybe, just maybe.

He shot out the lock with the AK-47, kicked in the door, and turned on the lights. It was as he remembered it. He searched the office and adjoining bathroom. No bomb. And no place to hide it either.

He left the office and hurtled down the stairs to the first floor. In the lobby he pulled down the Hezbollah flag and shot out the glass entry.

When he stepped onto the sidewalk, Nikas was nowhere in sight.

The van was still parked across the street. It hadn't been moved.

"Shit!" Jarrett screamed, pumping the AK-47 up and down like a crazed jihadist.

A maroon Peugeot slowed and the driver gave Jarrett thumbs-up.

Jarrett thrust out his middle finger and shouted, "Fuck you, asshole."

A few seconds later, a white Toyota Hilux with deep tints turned the corner and stopped.

As the front passenger window went down, Jarrett braced himself.

"Need a lift, pilgrim?" Nikas asked with a winsome smile on his face.

Jarrett was dumfounded. Nick looked like he'd been at a picnic. Where had he gotten the truck?

Jarrett boomeranged the AK-47 into the Hezbollah lobby and got in the truck.

"Looks like you had a rough go of it, partner," Nikas said as he pulled away.

"You could say that. The bomb's gone. I'm fucking tired of killing people. This goddamned mission is over. I've had it. Let's get the hell out of here."

327

Nikas bit his lower lip to hold back laughing and gestured to the back seat.

Jarrett turned.

His eyes widened.

A smile swept across his face.

"Yes!" he cried.

The suitcase nuclear bomb was on the seat.

CHAPTER 110

Jarrett and Nikas delivered the bomb to a waiting CIA Gulfstream G650 at the Beirut airport. The device was gone over by two nuclear engineers who declared it safe for transport.

On the tarmac Jarrett embraced Nikas and said, "Come visit me in South Dakota. You'll meet Ziba. She's quite a gal. We'll have a lot of fun."

"You're going to your ranch after Scotland?"

Jarrett nodded. "She'll fly to Edinburgh and then we're on to the ranch. Sedgewick will get her a new identity."

"I'm going to take you up on your invitation. I've really enjoyed working with you, Clint. If you ever need help again, I'll be there."

"You going back to Athens?"

"In a few days. I'll have to meet with the station chief here first. There'll be lots of questions. I hope none about you. But when we met with him the night we got here, you were careful not to identify yourself."

"And if you remember, he never asked me who I was." Jarrett laughed. "I'm sure Sedgewick will see it stays that way. It's been a pleasure to work with you, Nick. You're the best of the best. I would never have gotten the bomb without you. This mission was different from any I've ever done. If I'd been working alone like always, I'd probably be dead. Be well, my friend."

After they shook hands, Jarrett walked up the jet stairway. When he reached the cabin door he turned.

Nikas hadn't moved and was gazing at him. When their eyes met, Nikas snapped to attention and saluted. Jarrett paused for a second, waved, then stepped on board.

Nikas is a special guy, he thought as he found his seat.

Jarrett felt a little empty leaving Nikas. The ex-SEAL had brought an element of security to the mission, something Jarrett had never before experienced. He'd had Jarrett's back the whole time. It was a good feeling, but now Jarrett was anxious to be on his way. Hezbollah would be hell-bent on revenge after the bomb was seized and their leader and a handful of his key operatives killed. He wondered what they'd do. Whatever it was, he'd be thousands of miles away.

After two double bourbons over ice served by a spunky young lady with a .40 S&W holstered at her waist, Jarrett took a short nap. Then he got down to tidying up loose ends. And loose ends there were.

First things first—a call to his mother in South Dakota. Long overdue. Choked with tears Miriam Jarrett told her son how much she missed him. Then she brought him up to date on things at the ranch. The livestock were doing well, and the hired man and some neighbors had just finished branding. She knew not to ask where he'd been the last two months.

Jarrett e-mailed Ziba that the Beirut mission had been successfully completed. He reminded her to fly on a charter to Scotland.

By return e-mail she congratulated him. She wrote that she'd purchased a ticket on Iran Air with her U.K. passport, and two bodyguards would accompany her. Jarrett wasn't happy about it, but what could he do? She'd call him from the airport in Edinburgh.

Mir Abassi received a text from an unidentifiable source. It read simply: "Mission complete." Almost instantly Jarrett received a response. "Wonderful. Congratulations."

Jarrett admired Abassi. God willing, their paths would cross again, hopefully under more favorable circumstances.

At the conclusion of their meeting in Haifa, Moshe had given Jarrett his personal e-mail address. Jarrett wrote that Ari's killer and Hezbollah's leader were dead. He said nothing about the bomb. Moshe answered simply, "God bless you."

CHAPTER 111

The Gulfstream was over Rome when he reached Sedgewick. The conversation had the flavor of a convoluted CIA debriefing. Questions were asked again and again. Answers were analyzed and reanalyzed, in no logical order. It drove Jarrett absolutely bonkers.

Jarrett relived the whole Beirut adventure—literally—step-by-step, blow-by-blow, bullet-by-bullet with a couple of C4 explosions thrown in for good measure. Sedgewick said that neither Alfour's death nor the shoot-out at Hezbollah headquarters had hit the internet. But they would, and it would rock the Muslim world.

"The Jews will be blamed for the mischief in Beirut," Sedgewick said.

"How do you know?"

"Because the Oval Office is already planting the seeds of blame in the fertile minds of the White House press corp."

"What will President Carpenter do with the bomb?" Jarrett asked.

"I imagine nothing right now. It'll stay a closely guarded secret until he decides to come down on the Russians and Iranians. It's all about timing and cashing in on political capital. But you haven't told me how you seized the device."

"I didn't seize it. Nick did."

"You're kidding. How?" Sedgewick asked.

"While I was in the Hezbollah office fussing with the terrorists, Nick was on watch outside. A suspicious-looking truck drove by, you know one of those little white Toyotas with deep tints. He followed it to the back of the building. He let the two bad guys load the bomb in the truck then dispatched them. *Ping. Ping.* Two head shots. Simple as that. Nick is an incredible shot.

I've never seen anything like it. When I finished in the building, I ran to the street. He picked me up in the truck. The bomb was on the back seat. We delivered it to the plane. It's on board now with two engineers. End of story."

"Nikas is something else."

"That he is. And humble. Not like most of you guys at Langley. I'd work with him anytime."

"I was told to patch POTUS into this call. Hold on a sec."

"Clint, Carpenter here. Let me thank you for what you've done. I knew you'd get the damn nuclear device for us."

The president's voice sounded different . . . a little more stressed or hurried than it should have. With the Russian bomb in Washington, his ship had come in.

"No thanks necessary, sir. I had a great partner in this one. Nick Nikas."

"I've heard about him from Dodge. I'm in an important security meeting right now and have to cut this call short. I'm sorry. We might need you again, Clint. Soon. I'll be in touch. Thanks."

"Thank you, sir," Jarrett said as the president left the call.

"You're a hero. Again," Sedgewick said. "Don't you get tired of it?"

"I'm no hero. Nick is. What's going on? Sounds serious."

"Another problem over there. There's always some bad shit going on in the Middle East. So tell me, what's your plan with the Persian gal after Scotland?"

"I'll ask you guys to put her in WITSEC."

"On the Capistran Ranch? In South Dakota?"

"That's the plan. I promised Mir Abassi I'd deal with Jago. He might be in Paris. I'd like to take care of him as soon as I get her settled. Can you start looking for him?"

"Name again."

"Javid Gil. He's in MEK."

"Get everything you can on him," Sedgewick said. "Relatives, friends, likes, dislikes. All the crap we need to track him down. And a photo if possible. It's not easy to find one of these Muslim bad boys in Paris."

"Ziba will bring Mir's file on him. It should have all you need. I'll e-mail it to you from Edinburgh."

"Sounds like a plan. Have a good flight. Call me when you get to Scotland. And it goes without saying . . . thanks."

"You're welcome."

Jarrett hung up, wondering what was brewing in Washington. Sedgewick had been coy, as he usually was, in the run-up to an Oval Office request for his services.

But Jarrett had no interest. Not now or for the foreseeable future.

He was a wreck. His muscles ached, his joints were stiff, and he had lost the bounce in his step. The shiner under his eye had morphed from purple to violet and at least two ribs were cracked. The welts on his abdomen still hurt. He needed time to heal.

And to make things worse he was mentally fatigued.

More than fatigued, he thought, *spent*.

The drive to finish the missions in Tehran and Beirut and to protect Ziba had drained him. He was tired of staring down the barrel of an AK-47 and fearing the concussive effects of an explosion. He was tired of being trapped in a time box that gave him mere seconds to plan his next move. He was tired of killing. He was just plain tired. Executing Mohsen would wear on him forever. The sight of Amed, horribly disfigured, would linger.

EPILOGUE

Jarrett sprinkled salt on a lump of butter floating in his Scottish oatmeal.
Breakfast was one of the things he loved about Scotland. After the oatmeal, he'd have two eggs over easy, a double rasher, and a grilled tomato. And to top it off, a tattie scone with a second cup of Artisan roast. *Yummie.*

He looked out from the breakfast nook to the moor stretching like a lush carpet to the foothills of a jagged peak called Arthur's Seat. The morning mist was beginning to lift, showing yellow and purple heath flowers hugging patches of greenish-brown peat.

Like the Scottish moors, a low-lying section of his ranch stayed green throughout the dry South Dakota summers. Year-round surface water from underground springs kept the grasses and clover lush and the wildflowers blooming until the first frost.

Jarrett was homesick.

He couldn't stop thinking about his ranch. He missed the simple things—a steaming cup of coffee after morning chores, a ride across the hills in late afternoon, and the smell of fresh-cut hay in the summer. His life in the Black Hills was just right. And he was miles from the political madness in Washington. He longed to be Clint Jarrett again. The hell with Paladin. At least for now.

Demus was dead, and the Iranians had lifted the contract on Jarrett's head thanks to Mir Abassi. The spy in the Guard had escaped. The theft of the suitcase bomb by the Chechen rebels and its transfer to Hezbollah had been stopped. The device was secure somewhere in the United States. The leader of Hezbollah and a handful of his minions were dead. With that, Ari Katz was finally at peace. At least Jarrett hoped he was.

With the mission complete a seven-figure deposit had been wired to Jarrett's account in the Cayman Islands. President Carpenter was generous with the taxpayers' money. Very generous indeed. Half of it would find its way to Nick Nikas.

Jarrett swallowed a mouthful of coffee and glanced at his watch. Ziba's plane would land in less than an hour.

His sat phone began to beep.

Ziba's early, he thought at first. *But she doesn't have this number. It had to be Sedgewick.*

"Jarrett here." Using his real name felt good.

"Clint."

Something was wrong. He could hear it in his friend's voice.

"What is it?"

There was a pause. Sedgewick sighed. "Clint, I'm sorry. It's Ziba Vijany."

"What about her?"

"She's dead.

Jarrett's mind went blank. *What did he say?*

"What did you just say?" he asked.

"Ziba's dead," Sedgewick repeated. "I'm sorry."

Jarrett suddenly felt breathless. A fist began to squeeze in his chest, a crushing pain, as if an elephant was sitting on him. The walls of the room were closing in around him. "Oh no," he murmured under his breath.

His nightmare had come true. Jago had killed her. He rubbed his face with his hands, took a few deep breaths, and slumped back in the chair.

"You still there?" Sedgewick asked.

"I'm here," he sighed. "Tell me how it happened."

"A car bombing in Tehran. Last night. A guy on a motorcycle attached a bomb to a car in traffic. Like the Israelis did to those nuclear scientists. The car was destroyed. Three dead. A woman and two men. We just found out moments ago that Mir Abassi's daughter was the woman."

"She was supposed to arrive in Edinburgh today."

"I feel awful, Clint. I know she meant a lot to you."

"I loved her, Dodge. I was going to spend the rest of my life with her."

"Is there anything I can do?"

"Yes. There is something you can do," Jarrett said, barely able to speak. He cleared his throat and continued. "Jago had her killed. Javid Gil. I told you about him. Put your cyber-wolves on him. Find out where he is."

"We're already on it. But we need the file you mentioned."

"I'll get it for you. Then make finding him priority one. Talk to the president if you have to. But find him. Damn it. Please. For me."

"I know this isn't the time, but . . ."

"But what?" Jarrett blurted, as his jaw muscles tightened and his head pounded unmercifully.

"POTUS has a job for you. An important one. Not with the same horrific downside as the bomb gig, but critical nonetheless."

Jarrett was seething. His soul was on fire, a raging inferno burning inside of him, his head about to explode.

Killing Jago would be revenge—pure and simple—for Ziba and Mir Abassi . . . and for him.

"You find Jago, and I'll do whatever you want."